FOR HOME
AND Country

❦ BOOK FOUR ❧

NAOMI FINLEY

Cover designer: Victoria Cooper Art
Website: www.facebook.com/VictoriaCooperArt

Editor: Scripta Word Services
Website: scripta-word-services.com

READING ORDER FOR SERIES

Novels:

A Slave of the Shadows: Book One
A Guardian of Slaves: Book Two

Novellas:

The Black Knight's Tune: Novella One
The Master of Ships: Novella Two
The Promise Between Us: Novella Three
The Fair Magnolia: Novella Four

Novels:
Whispers of War: Book Three
For Home and Country: Book Four

Novels can be read alone or with the novella series.
The author's shorter works are best read in the suggested order.

Other works

The British Home Children Series:
The Forsaken Children: Book One
Miss Winter's Rapscallions: Book Two

For those who faced oppression at the hands of others.
And for Marg; your support and guidance helped me
weave this series.

CHAPTER One

Charleston, April 12, 1861

CANNON-FIRE WHISTLED AND CRACKED, AND WITH EACH EXPLOSION, I jumped, my nerves spun tight since the onset of the battle taking place in the harbor. The roar and thunder of shells unleashed on Major Anderson of the US Army and his garrison at Fort Sumter had been going on for hours. The South Carolina militia, led by General Beauregard, controlled the beach and the surrounding forts. Citizens remained on rooftops and balconies, and gathered at the Battery and in the streets to witness the bombardment. Older men and boys too young to fight patrolled the streets, intent on protecting the city and keeping the Negroes under control.

I paced the foyer of our townhouse, awaiting Bowden and Captain Gillies's return with news on the damage to our warehouse and ships. The muscles in my neck and shoulders ached from the tension, aggravated by the relentless thundering of cannons.

Jane, the butler's wife and our housekeeper, walked down the hallway with a silver tray rattling in her hands. She and her husband—freed blacks—had managed the townhouse for as long as I could remember. "Missus Willow, you must rest. I've fixed you some coffee and breakfast."

I eyed the lanky woman of sixty or so. "I can't possibly eat at a time like this."

She strode into the parlor and set the tray down on the sofa table. "You look ready to drop where you stand. Running to the window in hopes Mr. Armstrong and the captain have returned won't make their arrival come any faster."

"The wait is unbearable." I chewed on the corner of my mouth, now raw from gnawing.

Another crack ripped through the morning, and I ducked as though expecting the shell to land in the room. Jane gripped the doorframe, her wide eyes flitting to the window.

"I must return to Livingston at once." I straightened and eyed the small retinue of house staff hovering in doorways and at the top of the stairs. "Folks would have heard the ruckus and concerns will be high."

Jane released her hold on the doorframe. "What do we do if the army takes the city?"

The hissing of cannon-fire was loud in the silence as I thought. "Although Major Anderson seems to be at a disadvantage, circumstances could change. When Bowden and Captain Gillies return, we'll know more of what is to be done—" The rapid-fire boom of shells lodged my heart in my throat, and Jane and I clung to each other.

"Fort Sumter returns fire," shouted an informant, a boy of nine or ten clad in a long gray coat, as he raced along the street.

"Anderson has finally shown up," a man shouted in his wake.

I gawked at Jane, and we rushed to the parlor window and drew back the dark blue velvet drape.

Atop his mount, Josephine's husband, Theodore Carlton, garbed in a similar homespun coat, addressed the citizens. "This war will be over before you know it. General Beauregard has the advantage."

In the North, men had joined the US Army, while in the South, capable men formed militias and aided in the Confederate cause. Like Mr. Carlton, those too old took up policing, accompanied by boys not yet old enough to fight.

"The South will persevere, and our menfolk will return." He thrust out his chest. "Lincoln and his ambitions will fail to take

hold. Let the North be reminded that the South won't be defeated."
He struck at the heavens with a fist, and the citizens erupted in
cheers.

"There is no certainty in what you say." Bowden's voice rose,
and I pressed my cheek against the windowpane to find him in the
crowd. Locating him standing some feet from the front steps of
our townhouse, I released the drape and raced for the door.

Stepping outside, I descended the stairs to join him. He looped
an arm around my waist without looking sideways. Soot and grime
covered his face and hands, and the odor of smoke wafted from
his clothing.

"Providing hope for the people is one thing, but offering false
hope is a pitfall." He gazed at Theodore and the two young boys
on either side of him. "If you intend to man the city and countryside, ensure your efforts will benefit those needing it. Our womenfolk need men they can count on."

Carlton turned his intense blue eyes on Bowden, and the men
engaged in a standoff of glares until Theodore broke focus and
turned to scrutinize me with open fascination. My legs trembled
under a predatory gaze that defined me as the prey. He had earned
a reputation for pressing himself upon women and quarter slaves.
His attention unsettled me. With our men away, men like him
would seek to rise in power.

"And what the South needs is decent menfolk who are willing
to defend our cause. Yet you're still here, while the good men have
already left. Why is that?" He leaned forward, resting an elbow on
his thigh.

Bowden tensed. "I will be gone soon enough."

Carlton smirked. "And, in your absence, I will see that your
lovely wife is well cared for."

At that, Bowden gripped my elbow and turned to climb the
steps. He hurried me inside and shut the door.

"Jane."

"Yes, Mr. Armstrong?" She came forward.

"Pack our things. We leave at once for Livingston."

She bowed and hurried away.

"Uriah?"

"Right here, Mr. Armstrong." The butler held out a glass of whiskey, which Bowden took without hesitation and drained.

The windowpanes vibrated with reverberations from the cannons.

"In my absence, I hope that I can keep you employed to care for the place. Of course, until the threat to your safety makes that impossible."

Years had hunched Uriah's towering frame; no longer did he have to duck to walk through doorways. "We stay as long as needed. Don't have no place to go anyhow. We talked 'bout staying with our boy in Georgia, but don't reckon any place is going to be safe after this." Concern pulled at his face.

"I fear you are right. I will leave a stable boy to tend the animals." Bowden glanced around at the staff on the upstairs landing and the main floor, all waiting for answers. "All other employees are to return to your homes and family until we can bring you back. If there is a place to come back to."

Murmurs lifted.

"Come, come." Bowden made a brushing gesture with his hand. "We mustn't delay."

The staff scurried to do his bidding.

"Bowden?" I gripped his arm. "What is the situation at the docks?"

He turned, and the look in his eyes hollowed my stomach. "Not good. The *Olivia I* has capsized, and all but one of our fleet is engulfed in flames. The warehouse remains, but the damage is severe. Our goods are ruined and unsellable."

I gulped, afraid to ask the question that had been governing my thoughts. "Is it as Captain Gillies said?"

"You refer to Northern militia?"

I nodded.

He shrugged. "If so, they are long gone."

"And with what is unfolding in the harbor and your leaving, there is nothing we can do about it," I said.

"I'm afraid not. Now I must leave, and all of the madness is left in your hands." He rested hands on my upper arms and held my gaze.

"We will manage." I offered reassurance while my insides roiled with uncertainty and fear. Reuben McCoy was out there, scheming, and with Ben and Bowden away, it would be up to Jones and me to manage and protect Livingston.

"I will have the carriage readied, and we will return home," he said before brushing my lips with his.

As our carriage rolled toward Livingston, I sat closer to Bowden, enjoying his warmth as the battle in the harbor faded behind us. My ears continued to ring from the hours of explosions. The uncertainty of what was to come had captured our thoughts, and we sat in silence. The scent of smoke never faded, and when we were a few miles from home, Bowden's body tensed. "Do you see that?"

I looked to where he pointed. Smoke was rising above the trees. My heart thudded. "Livingston!"

He lifted the reins to urge the team to greater speed, but paused at the sound of approaching horses. In one swift movement, Bowden grabbed the rifle under the seat.

Two riders came around the bend, and I quickly recognized Mr. Sterling and a neighboring farmer.

"Sterling, where does that smoke come from?" Bowden asked as the men reined in their horses.

The look in Mr. Sterling's eyes confirmed our fears. "Your place. Northern militia attacked about the same time as the sky lit up in the direction of Charleston."

"No!" I wailed.

Bowden didn't wait to hear more. "Out of the way!" He lashed the reins, and the team charged forward, forcing the men to touch heels to their horses to clear out of our path.

Please, God, no. The team's manes and tails snapped in the wind of our passage.

"Dammit!" Bowden cursed.

I clutched the side of the carriage to avoid being launched overboard as we charged toward Livingston at a bone-jarring speed. An invisible weight compressed the air from my lungs. We should never have left. Never. I eyed Bowden askance, and the panic clear on his face made my heart beat harder. Images of what we would find upon our arrival swarmed my mind. The next few miles seemed to move at a painstaking crawl. Whisking away blinding tears, I forced down the bile burning my throat. *Please, God, I'll do anything you ask of me.*

When we reached the main gates, I fought to clear the relentless tears obscuring my vision. As our buggy charged up the lane, I glanced over my shoulder to find Mr. Sterling and the farmer on our heels.

"Good God!" Bowden leaned forward and whipped the reins harder.

A wail escaped me as I beheld the smoldering main house—still standing, but its windows shattered and the exterior scorched. Our chamber and the nursery located on the left side of the house sat exposed to the heavens.

Bowden slowed the team as we went around the house to the work yard.

"No!" My agonized wail echoed off the ruined buildings as I viewed the rows of bodies covered by blankets.

"Willow," someone called, and hands reached for me.

I sat numbly in my seat but turned my head to stare at the speaker, too dazed to make out their face or voice.

"Come," they said.

My body moved, but I wasn't sure if I'd been lifted from the carriage or advanced of my own accord.

Somewhere Bowden conversed with someone, but I couldn't make out his words.

"Willow." Hands shook me.

I turned my head, frantically trying to concentrate on the person's face. "Magnus?" My vision cleared as I came to my senses. "What happened?"

Dried blood, soot, and grime marred his face. "They came out of nowhere."

"Mary Grace and the children. Are they—" Fear snatched my words.

"We are fine." Mary Grace rushed toward us and crushed me in her arms.

My legs buckled, and I clutched her for support. "Why? Who?" I muffled into her shoulder.

"It was as we feared. The McCoys advanced just before dawn."

I stiffened at the reference before withdrawing from her arms. "McCoys?"

She bit down on her lip. "You need to see for yourself, or you will never believe me." She took my hand and pulled me toward the lines of corpses.

Jones stood next to Bowden, who crouched next to a body and peeled back the blanket. I frowned at the familiarity of the deformed face. It couldn't be. I glanced at Mary Grace, and she swallowed hard and bobbed her head. But how?

"It appears the bastard never died after all," Bowden said.

I gawked from him to the face and the distinguishing markings on the forehead. My hand rose to my throat. Rufus McCoy.

"Angel gal?"

I turned, and a sob lodged in my throat as I saw Mammy grip the sides of her skirt and bound down the back steps. I rushed toward her, not stopping until we clutched each other in an embrace.

"Mammy. Oh, Mammy." The strength of her embrace kept me from crumpling to my knees. "You're alive."

"Yes, gal. I all right." She pulled me back and cupped my cheek. There was a profound sadness in her eyes. "Can't say de same for others."

My breath caught as I thought of who may lie under the blankets. "Where is Ben?"

"At de hospital, taking care of de wounded."

I glanced around at the weary folks sorting through the wreckage and ashes of outbuildings and cabins for survivors. My heart struck harder, and without looking at her, I said, "Sailor?"

"He fine. De chillum and de womenfolkses dat made et to de river are all fine."

"And Jimmy?"

"He at de sick hospital." Her voice hitched, and I turned to look at her.

"Providing my uncle aid?"

She gripped my arm, tears welling in her eyes. "No, angel gal. He hurt real bad."

Pulling my arm free, I stumbled back, shaking my head. "No."

The concerned faces before me vanished in a river of tears, and without another word, I turned and fled. Pulse roaring in my ears, I pumped my legs faster. Pain radiated in my chest by the time the sick hospital came into view. Wounded quarter folk and Jones's men lay on makeshift beds constructed of blankets spread out on the ground. Kimie looked up at me as I slowed my pace. Blood stained her apron, and she lifted bloodied fingers to smooth back her blond locks. Tears of devastation glittered in her blue eyes. Whitney knelt beside an injured woman offering her water, and our eyes met as I grasped the magnitude of the destruction that had befallen Livingston in my absence.

"Willow," Ben said, and I followed the sound of his voice to find him standing on the hospital stoop. Face tense, he waved me forward. As I met him on the stoop, he put his arm around my waist, and I leaned on him for support.

"Is he…" Fear captured my voice.

"He is alive, but barely. If he makes it through the night—"

"No." I shook my head. "It can't be." I collapsed against his shoulder, sobbing, my fingers grabbing at his shirt. "This is all my fault."

"You are not to blame," he consoled me. "The McCoys are."

"He warned me," Bowden said, his voice grave and vacant.

Lifting my head, I located him through my tears. Face ashen, he stood observing the sea of injured people. "Who?" I said, my voice rasping.

"Gray. The dreams. The visions. All warnings." Gripping the sides of his head, he dropped to his knees and released a guttural wail.

I rushed to his side and tenderly cradled his head against my waist. Turning, he buried his face into the fabric of my dress and wept like I'd never seen him do before.

CHAPTER Two

ENTERING THE SICK HOSPITAL, I LOOKED TO THE COT BY THE WINDOW and recognized the face of Gray's pa, who had chosen to remain at Livingston after Bowden had sold his plantation. Nausea roiled in my gut. He lay unconscious, his breathing shallow. As I turned my gaze to the other cot in the room, my body shook, and I fought back a cry as I saw Jimmy's bloody form. My feet rooted to the planks, but the gentle urging of Bowden's hand on the small of my back pushed me forward.

The warmth of his hand faded as he left me and went to kneel beside Gray's pa. "Hello, old friend," he said, his voice thick as he took the man's hand.

A sob caught in my chest, and I turned back to Jimmy. He lay shirtless, a bloodstained bandage wrapped around his torso. Elsewhere, flesh wounds had been left by a blade. His breathing was ragged, and I knew that he held on to but a glimmer of life.

I knelt beside him and slipped my fingers under his hand, lying at his side. "Jimmy, it's me, Willow." My voice was tattered. "You will be just fine. I'll see to it." I stroked his hair. Tears streamed down my cheeks and tickled my neck before soaking into my bodice. "You're too stubborn to die," I said with a laugh, blinking off tears. His eyes fluttered open, and my breath caught, but they quickly closed, as though his subconscious had reacted to me. "I need you. More than you will ever know." I closed my eyes and laid my cheek on his chest, finding comfort in the beat of his heart. "Ruby, Saul, Mercy—we all need you," I whispered.

A shadow fell over me, and I opened my eyes to find Ben

standing at the foot of the bed. I pushed to my feet and walked a few feet away, and he followed.

"He can't die," I said in a low voice, my lips quivering. "He mustn't. He is like a father to me in all the ways that matter. He loved me and taught me things my own could not." Misery and fear wrenched at my heart, and thoughts of hurting him didn't enter my mind until too late. Catching myself, I gasped, "I'm sorry. I don't mean to—"

"Do not apologize for speaking the truth." I saw compassion and understanding in his eyes. "His love for you radiates, as does yours for him. Regardless of your parentage, Miss Rita and James raised you and stood in when we could not. My brother's and my failures will always haunt me, but there is no time for regrets of the past. I've done all I can for him. The rest lies in God's hands. Both men need a miracle." He looked wearily from one cot to the other.

As Bowden joined us, I said, "You all are supposed to leave today. I can't possibly manage—"

"We have no choice but to leave. We will send word of what occurred here, and hope they will grant us a few days." Bowden strode to the door and called out to Kimie. When she entered, he gripped her shoulder. "Are you capable of caring for the wounded in our absence?"

"I-I…" She looked from Ben to him.

"The next best person to a trained doctor," Ben said.

Her expression uncertain, she gulped, then squared her shoulders. "I'll see to them."

"Good." He released her. "Willow will ensure that any capable womenfolk are made available to help you."

I had yet to realize the number of lives lost at Livingston. My pulse quickened. When I did, could I face the knowing? What of the bodies scattered across the work yard requiring burials? My gaze turned to the window, and the injured spread across the lawn. So many hurt and needing attention.

"But what am I to do?" I gawked at Bowden, dumbfounded.

As I thought of the impossible task ahead, my panic mounted. Recalling the damage I'd observed upon our arrival, I pointed at the window. "Destruction is everywhere: our ships, the warehouse; the main house is partly destroyed; the kitchen house and smokehouse are gone. How can I possibly make Livingston functional again with no menfolk around? I can't do this. It's too much." Concealing my face in my hands, I let sobs rack my body.

"Come." Bowden took my hand and led me outside.

We left the quarters and strolled along the path leading to the family cemetery and the ponds.

"I know it is a lot to ask of you," he said. "Too much, really. But you will have Jones, and after we assess our losses we will know exactly what we are up against. Unfortunately, in these uncertain times, many are forced to do things we don't want to. Not only the men who have enlisted, but the women left behind to manage the land."

I took a deep breath to relieve the tightness in my chest. Although my heart remained heavy, the numbness I felt over what had occurred was slowly evaporating with the determination to put everything in order. Bowden needed me to be strong. The people of Livingston needed me. I couldn't possibly crumble now. "I know," I said as we stepped from the tree line and the graveyard came into view.

I froze. "No, no, no!"

"What is it…" Bowden's words faded as he too beheld the sight. "My God!" Bowden raced forward, hauling me behind him.

At the edge of the cemetery, I dropped to my knees and gawked in horror. The fence had been demolished, gravestones uprooted, and the graves of my son, mother, father, and grandparents trampled. The McCoys had sought to desecrate their very memory.

A part of my soul fractured, and with a forlorn wail I fell forward, pulling at the grass and dirt. Why? Had we not suffered enough?

Bowden knelt and wrapped me in his arms, and I lifted my head and looked at him. Silent tears stained his cheeks. Had I cursed my husband in our union? Why was God bent on unleashing pain on my family? Had I brought misery and suffering to Livingston? I collapsed against Bowden, sensing the galloping of his heart, and his trembling body.

"H-how do we go on?" I sobbed into his shoulder.

"We must." His hard voice made me look at his face. There was a cold glint in his eyes.

I gulped. "Please don't leave. I can't bear it. I can't."

"I have no choice." He hauled me to my feet and turned me in the direction of the house.

All of me wanted to curl up and die and leave the cruelty of a world I wasn't designed for. I wanted to rewind the past days—we would never have gone to Charleston, and perhaps we could have prevented the devastation that had befallen Livingston. In that scenario, the slaves hidden in the warehouse would have perished in the fire.

Wait. I stopped in my tracks and turned to him. "The men that set fire to our ships and the warehouse—do you think it was the McCoys?"

"I believe it's impossible that it was anyone else." He clasped my hand and continued toward the house.

"But how can you be certain?"

"Because amongst the bodies are men clad in states' militia uniforms," he said.

"Missus Willow, Masa Bowden." Mammy's voice drew our attention. She was hurrying toward us. Big John, supporting his weight with a makeshift cane, hobbled behind her. As they got near, I noticed the bandages covering his hands and the way he wheezed.

"You all right?" I asked.

"Nothing time won't heal," he said with a bow of his head.

"He tried to save de house, and 'bout killed himself in de

process." Mammy scowled up at him and he grinned, finding amusement in her feistiness.

"Miss Rita, I need you to take my wife up to the house and give her something to calm her nerves."

"No." I pulled away from him. "I will not be set aside as though I'm too weak to handle what needs doing. I—"

He pulled me to him and placed a finger to my lips, stilling my words. "Look at me," he said gruffly. I looked at him. "Do you think I don't know what you're capable of? You're capable of more than even you realize. I'm counting on you while I'm away. The people need you more than ever before. I fear the trials will be many, but together we must stand united and see this to an end."

"But what if you don't come back?" My voice trembled at the thought. "What if none of you do? Am I to have a graveyard of loved ones?"

"Missus Willow, you mustn't think lak dat. None of de misfortunes and losses dat befell dis place or your family got anything to do wid you." Mammy touched my shoulder. I pulled from Bowden to face her. "Life ain't fair. Why, et downright unjust at times, but we got to keep moving anyhow. Now come along and do as Masa says. You won't do anyone any good if you don't keep a sound mind." She took my arm and escorted me across the work yard. I glanced over my shoulder at my husband, who stood staring blankly after me.

Turning back, I considered what lay ahead, and worry gnawed into my fear. Would we survive what was to come?

CHAPTER
Three

Drifter

MY EYELIDS OPENED, AND I GRITTED MY TEETH AT THE PAIN ricocheting through my skull. Touching the damp bandage compressing my head, I frowned as the recollection of how I'd received the injury deserted me. Parched, my tongue thick, I licked my lips to relieve the burn of cracked skin. My hollow stomach gurgled, demanding food. Blankets soaked in sweat clung to me like a second skin, and my nostrils rebelled at the smell of my body.

Senses tuning to the musky, woodsy scent enveloping me, my gaze went to the animal pelts hanging from the plank walls of what appeared to be a one-room cabin. The door was ajar. A table sat next to an open fire where an iron skillet sizzled.

Where am I? Struggling to sit up, I grimaced at the ache of bruised ribs. I sensed my lack of clothing, but before I could locate any the doorway darkened. I regarded the mountainous man with silver plaits and an unruly beard who lingered on the front stoop, with a blade in one hand and a slab of meat in the other. It appeared freshly carved from an animal's carcass; blood dripped over his fingers onto the dirt floor.

My heart beat harder. The weakness in my limbs and the awareness of my nakedness made me feel vulnerable. In a panic, I glanced around for my trousers or something resembling clothing.

"You return to the land of the living." His voice was gruff, but not unfriendly. He strode into the cabin and tossed the meat into the skillet before wiping his hands on buckskin trousers.

"How did I get here?" Thirst made my voice a rasp.

"Weeks back, I found you belly-up by the river about ten miles from here." He turned to face me, and his brown eyes held a keen glint. "It appears you took a shot to the head. You're one lucky son-of-a-gun. Someone must be watching out for you, 'cause you should be dead. Fixed you up the best I could. I couldn't find an exit wound, so I reckon the bullet is still in there. If my woman was still around, she would have fixed you up good. Sickness took her about five years ago. She was one of the last of her tribe," he said matter-of-factly.

The only good woman is one that doesn't draw breath, a voice chimed in.

I examined the cabin's shadows for the speaker, but we were alone. Turning my gaze to the open door, I detected no one outside. I heard only the chatter of the forest critters, and the neighing of a horse.

The grizzly fellow strode to my bed and held out a tin cup. "My name's Samson. What do they call you?"

I opened my mouth to speak, but memory failed me. What was my name? Frowning, I regarded the man as he waited for an answer.

Say nothing, the newcomer said.

Sweat beaded on my brow as I found no recollection of anything before the opening of my eyes. Panic surged, and my heart galloped faster. Who was I?

"Well, do you got a name, or what?" His eyes narrowed, and the deeply etched channels in his jowls and pocked and weathered flesh gave him an intimidating appearance.

He asks too many questions. End him before he has a chance to tell.

Tell? Tell what? I hid my hands in the blankets to conceal their trembling. My attention slid to the blade he'd set on the table. I studied it before directing my eyes to the outstretched hand holding the cup. A vision of his lifeless body, gutted and splayed out on the cabin floor, flashed through my mind, and I shook my head to dispel it. I swallowed hard. This must be damage from the gunshot wound. It was concerning.

I gawked at Samson. His penetrating eyes scoured my face in a quest for answers. "Name's Preston Lawson," I said. The name rattled from my head as naturally as a next breath. *Preston Lawson.* I rotated the name in my mind. Why did the name sound so foreign?

Yes, that will do. Glad to see you haven't lost all sense, the voice jeered.

"Drink." Samson gestured at me with the cup.

My pulse slowed to a calmer pace. Reaching for the cup, I noticed the steadiness of my hand.

"You get a look at the one who shot you? Ain't messed up with the law, are ya?"

I took the cup and drained the contents before handing it back to him. "In the wrong place at the wrong time. Rode into a meadow just as a hunter lifted his rifle to shoot; next thing I know, I'm waking up here." The story rolled off my tongue with no sense of recognition.

An uncanny chuckle made me eye Samson, but he stood with lips pressed together. I trembled at the mounting awareness that the voice may occur only in my head.

"Got ten lives, I reckon." Shaking his head, he returned to the skillet as the odor of scorched meat drifted.

As I observed him, the image of an auburn-haired woman with voluptuous curves and rouge-stained lips surfaced, and my jaw tensed at the vision. Who was she? And why did I get a feeling of bad blood between us?

Exhausted, I slumped back and allowed sleep to take me.

CHAPTER *Four*

Willow

THE DEATH TOLL AMOUNTED TO HEARTBREAKING NUMBERS. Knox, Mr. Barlow, Magnus, and some of the surviving quarter folk took on the task of burying the bodies.

Destruction touched every corner of the plantation. Bowden oversaw the construction of makeshift living quarters to replace the cabins reduced to rubble in the attack. By dusk, newly constructed tents sat with the few remaining cabins on the quarters' scorched earth. We assessed the damage to the main house and the outbuildings. The lumber that hadn't been set aflame would be used to fix the main house and build a new kitchen house, barn, and smokehouse. I feared we wouldn't have enough supplies to make the repairs, and if the chaos unleashed in the harbor continued, would it even be worth the effort?

As darkness fell over the Lowcountry, Bowden and I sat in the rockers on the back veranda. We discussed what I would do when he, Ben, and Knox took leave the following morning.

The shuffle of someone's approaching footsteps drew our attention to the work yard. "Evening, Mr. and Mrs. Armstrong." Jones stepped into the light from the lanterns hanging on the veranda posts. He removed his dark hat, sullied with dust and soot, before ascending the steps.

"Have you finished the head count?" Weariness lined Bowden's face as he regarded the overseer.

"That I have." Discouragement shone in Jones's eyes. "There are twenty-seven quarter folks left. Most of the ones who took up arms now lie in graves. Some who fled to the river at the outbreak of the attack haven't returned."

"One can hardly blame them." A shiver shot through me as I thought of the panic they had to have experienced to flee to the deadly swamps. "All folks' emotions will be high, with what has happened…is happening." I glanced at the horizon, where the siege of Fort Sumter continued. "I fear for our people's safety, with the country at war."

Bowden cursed under his breath before standing to pace the veranda. "The McCoys had their revenge—the unnecessary end of so many lives." He threw his hands in the air. I rose and, like Jones, stood staring at my husband. Bowden regarded us as though expecting an answer. "And the battle in the harbor…" He gestured in the direction of Charleston, where the cannons rumbled, and the sky gleamed crimson and orange. "How many of our countrymen will die? And for what? Because the South fear they can't run their lands without slaves, and the North's desires for tariffs. Both are generated by fear of each other's influence. Are we not brothers?" Tears of frustration dampened his eyes as he came to stand in front of us.

Jones grunted. "I stand by your belief," he said, "but we've been left with no choice but to face what is to come."

Bowden gave his head a shake to clear his thoughts and took a deep breath before clasping Jones's shoulder. "You are right. Forgive a man's weakness. Charles trusted you, as do I." He glanced at me. "I trust that you will care for my wife and the folks here in my absence."

"Livingston has been my home since your wife was waist high." Fondness reflected in the overseer's eyes as he directed a look at me. It swiftly dissolved, and he returned his attention to Bowden. "I'll defend this plantation and all who live here with my life. You both will continue to have my loyalty." Jones's voice was emotionless, but his statement revealed his devotion.

"Gratitude." Bowden's voice broke with sentiment, and he coughed to clear his throat before continuing. "The north field's crop is gone. The transporting of goods will become more constricted than before. We need to plant as many food crops as possible to feed the people, as supplies and monies will be limited. I suggest you set those not assigned to repairs to prepare the east field for that."

"I will see to it." Jones tipped his hat and dismissed himself.

Bowden held out his hand and I gripped it. He spun me into his arms, and I settled there, absorbing the abundance of his love, for tomorrow, he'd be gone.

"Willow. Bowden." Magnus's voice rose from below us, and I parted from my husband's arms to look down at him and Mary Grace, standing in the work yard.

"Yes?" I strolled forward and rested my hands on the railing. Bowden joined me and placed a hand on the small of my back.

Mary Grace and Magnus exchanged a look, and she took the lead. "We wish to marry tonight."

"Tonight?" I said, dumbfounded. "How do you suppose we do that? We can't possibly send for a preacher at this hour, let alone amidst the battle happening in Charleston. And if we could, you know the South's views on such a union. It is illegal."

"We are well aware," Magnus said. "But we do not need the permission of the courts. And there is no need to send for a preacher." He stepped aside and gestured at someone behind him. "Come on, now."

A man of seventy or so shuffled forward with the assistance of Mary Grace. I recognized him: Abe, the preacher from the quarters. His eyesight had left him some years back.

"Abe has agreed to marry us," she said.

Someone cleared their throat behind them. Ben stepped into the light of the veranda with Pippa clasping his elbow. "You are right. We are at war. Therefore there is no need for legalities." He wrapped Pippa's shoulders with an arm and pulled her in to his side. "I thought if Mary Grace and Magnus don't mind, we could make it a double union."

"Of course not," Magnus said with a grin.

"But the marriage wouldn't be legal," I said. "The war could be over within the week, and you could marry then."

"And if not?" Ben raised a brow.

I stood silent, unsure of how to respond.

"Besides, a union before God is what matters. Isn't that right, Miss Rita?" Ben looked past us.

"Reckon so," Mammy said with a toothy grin.

I spun as she and Big John stepped out onto the veranda. I gawked from one person to the next. Had all those that remained shown up for the conversation?

"Many slaves have married in de eyes of de Lard 'cause de whites don't allow dem to marry." She smiled up at her man, and he returned a look of loving devotion.

I shared a glance with Bowden, and for a moment, the horror that'd transpired at Livingston and the uncertainty still unfolding evaporated. I smirked, and lifting my chin with pure satisfaction, I jostled his side with my shoulder. "I guess my matchmaking paid off."

He threw back his head and erupted with laughter before smacking his leg with a hand. "Alrighty, it appears we have ourselves a double wedding."

I ushered Mary Grace and Pippa inside, with Mammy panting close behind.

"Ain't got time to make special brooms," Mammy said anxiously.

"We could forgo the brooms and create something new for such a special occasion. How about—"

"Angel gal, we ain't got no time for your wanting to break tradition. Jumping de broom bin a custom amongst our people for as long as I can 'member. Big John say et come all de way from South Africa."

"And the English claim they originated the tradition," Pippa said with a smile.

"I sho' dey do," Mammy said with a snort.

Mary Grace patted her mother's arm. "How about we leave the squabbles over who introduced what for another day? Best not to keep the menfolk waiting."

"She is right. I moved my clothing that survived the fire to the guest chamber. Mammy, why don't you go with Mary Grace and Pippa and help them pick gowns for the ceremony. The fit may be slightly off, but it will have to do."

After the women left to change, I wandered to the closet under the stairs to get a broom. I peered at the sharp slant of the broomcorn from Mammy's left-handed sweeping. "Hardly fit for the union," I said.

"Suppose et have to do."

I whirled to look at Tillie, who'd entered the house undetected.

"It feels like an insult to bless their marriage with this." I held the broom out for her to see. "But Mammy insists on tradition."

She eyed the broom. "I wid you. Seal deir union wid a curse 'fore dey even start deir lives together, wid dat old broom."

"Perhaps doing something different would suffice."

"What you got in mind?" She studied me.

I pondered on it for a minute or two before an idea came to me. "I've got it. Gather a lantern and collect what flowers in bloom you can find. I will look for fabric and ribbons. We will create a rope that they can jump together."

Tillie's eyes brightened with enthusiasm. "Dat a right fine idea, Missus." She spun and raced down the corridor.

Later, those who remained at Livingston gathered under

the stars in the work yard. The couples to marry stood before the quarter preacher and recited their vows.

"You may both kiss your brides," Abe said with a smile.

A cry of happiness erupted from our small gathering as the men turned to their blushing brides and sealed their marriage and love with a kiss. My heart felt like it would burst with joy.

The couples broke their embrace and turned to face us. Mammy and I strode forward with the rope Tillie and I had hurriedly fashioned and laid it on the ground.

"You did good, angel gal," Mammy whispered as we stepped back.

I beamed with delight at her approval. Ben and Magnus took their brides' hands, and together the newlyweds jumped the rope.

Soon after, Ben and Pippa left to take a stroll by the river. Magnus lifted his new bride into the front of his buggy. Noah and Evie sat in the back, their eyes gleaming with happiness. My heart broke a little for what I had lost, but the delight on the family's faces smudged out all selfishness. Mary Grace deserved the new start life had granted her, and I wouldn't stand in her way.

I walked to her side and reached up and clasped her hands. "I'm afraid I have no gift to offer you." I recalled the beautiful nightgown I'd gifted her on the eve of her and Gray's union.

"That is quite all right," she said with a smile. Magnus climbed into the buggy and settled on the seat next to her. "I have all I need."

Mr. Barlow, atop his mount, said, "We need to get home. Your mum and Callie will be waiting up."

"I suppose they are in for a surprise." Magnus looked back at the children, and love and pride radiated from his face.

Mammy strode forward and gripped Mary Grace's knee. "You take care of yourself, gal. I sho' gwine to miss ya." Tears thickened her voice.

"Oh, Mama," Mary Grace said, and leaned forward to embrace her. "I will miss you too. But I won't be far and will come to visit."

"Et ain't safe, wid de militia running 'bout burning down plantations, and de country at war. No, sah. Et bes' you stay close to de house."

Mary Grace didn't bother to argue, and Mammy, seemingly satisfied, stepped back and rejoined Big John. I followed her and went to stand with my husband.

"Good night." Magnus flicked the reins, and the buggy jerked forward.

"Bye, Evie, I'm gonna miss you." Sailor raced after them. The girl twisted in her seat and waved with enthusiasm.

As the buggy disappeared into the dark, Sailor stood with his shoulders drooping, and Bowden and I exchanged a look and walked to stand beside him.

"There, there, son. She won't be far." Bowden placed a hand on his shoulder.

"But I wanted her to stay here," he said, "where we can play together."

My heart broke for the boy. I, too, would miss Mary Grace and the children, but I supposed eventually we would learn how to go on. "Come, let's see if Miss Rita has a spiced butter cookie or two to heal a broken heart." I steered him back toward the house.

"Missus Willow?" His voice was filled with concern.

"Yes?"

"Who is going to care for me now? Where will I sleep?"

I looked at Bowden as we walked. "What if I fix you a pallet on the floor in our chamber for tonight?"

He halted and craned his neck back to stare up at me. "Your chamber?"

I smiled and nodded. "Would you like that?"

He grinned. "Yessum."

We approached the back veranda. "Now go inside and find Miss Rita and inquire about that cookie."

He let out a whoop and raced up steps.

"You spoil the boy," Bowden said. "Allowing him to sleep in the house is one thing, but our chamber is another. It's dangerous."

"I know, but he has been through a lot today. We all have. Tomorrow I will talk to Tillie about permitting him to stay with her."

"Tonight and only tonight. You need to be extra careful, especially now."

"I will, I promise." I clasped his hand, and we strode inside.

CHAPTER
Five

THE MORNING AFTER MAJOR ROBERT ANDERSON HAD SURRENDERED Fort Sumter to the Confederates, Bowden and Ben prepared to leave Livingston.

Knox waited on his horse as Bowden and Ben adjusted their saddles in the front yard. The men would soon ride out and report to General Beauregard and the South Carolina militia, leaving the plantation in the hands of womenfolk and slaves. Whitney and Pippa stood next to Mammy and Big John, all of them looking concerned about what was to come. True to her nature, Whitney stood stiff and guarded, but a slight quiver in her jaw revealed that her heart ached like mine. The exhaustion in her face revealed a restless night.

I stood to the left of Bowden and fixed every detail of him into my memory for the nights and days I feared would be long and worrisome. He hadn't slept much the night before, as mental turmoil had him tossing and turning until eventually he'd risen to pace the floors. I never asked him what disconcerted him; his struggle mirrored mine. Were we standing on the right side of the war?

Eyes blurring with tears I regarded my husband, already yearning for his safe return. My heart mourned for all of the families whose menfolk would journey into the unknown with the belief they were doing what was right. My gut tightened with knowledge of the price we would pay for a war there was no turning back from.

Lost in my feelings and reflections, I had forgotten about Sailor standing next to me until a soft sniffle pulled my attention to the warmth of the hand clasped in mine. I squeezed his hand gently, and he peered up at me through tear-filled eyes.

Bowden turned and looked at us and gave me a tender smile before turning his attention to Sailor. He bent to be eye level with the boy and nudged his chin with a knuckle. "Surely you aren't weeping for me?" he said with a grin.

Sailor leaned in to my side and bobbed his head. I wrapped an arm around his shoulders.

Love gleamed in Bowden's eyes for the son we secretly loved as our own—a gift granted us. His face twitched with building emotion, and he reached for Sailor and embraced him. After a moment, he pulled back and held the boy by the shoulders. "I reckon I need to ask you a favor."

"From me?" Sailor's brow puckered.

"That's right. I can't think of a gentleman more suitable."

Sailor tilted his chin with pride at the reference. "What is it?"

"I need you to take care of Missus Willow until I get back." He looked earnestly at Sailor, as though the task he assigned him was a hefty one. "Can you do that for me?"

"Yes, Masa. You ain't got to worry about her." Sailor gripped my hand and gave me an adoring look, appearing to take his new task very seriously.

Bowden patted his shoulder and smiled at him. "How about you go see Kimie at the sick hospital and check in on how James is faring?"

"Yes, Masa." He turned and raced off.

Bowden stood and faced me. I looked up into my husband's eyes, so blue, yet so green. I rested there a moment, enveloped in the love and tenderness they held for me. I wanted to beg him to stay, to hold me and never let go, but to voice the longing in my heart would only cause him more anguish. I had to be the pillar he required.

"I shall miss you," I said.

"And I, you." He searched my face, and I sensed the battle within him.

"You needn't worry about things here. Pippa and I will manage just fine."

He nodded and tenderly stroked my upper arms with his thumbs. "I don't know what we are up against, but I will try my best to get letters through to you whenever I can."

"I'll wait for them," I said.

"We need to get going," Knox said from his saddle.

Bowden glanced at him and inclined his head in acknowledgment before returning his attention to me. He gathered me in his arms and pressed a passionate kiss on my mouth. His body trembled.

When our lips parted, I clutched him closer and whispered in his ear, "May God protect you and return you safely to my arms."

He swallowed hard and pushed himself back. Tears dampened his eyes, and he cupped my cheek. Before dropping his hand, he removed the blue ribbon tied around the end of my plait. He pressed it to his lips, then turned to his saddlebag and removed his journal, and tucked the ribbon inside.

"We take care of Missus Willow and Missus Hendricks. Don't you worry none," Mammy said.

"We are counting on it." Ben bestowed on Mammy an endearing smile. He stood holding Pippa's hand, and the gold band on her finger glimmered in the sunlight. So little time had passed since they'd wed. My sympathy for the newlyweds swelled.

I walked to Ben, and he released Pippa's hand, and I stepped into his embrace.

"We will return. Try not to fret," he said.

I laid my cheek against his chest. "I will await the day."

He gave me a gentle squeeze before releasing me to grip my hand. He reached for Pippa's and exchanged a smile with us both. "I'm counting on my women to take care of each other."

Pippa regarded me with affection. "We will spend our time getting to know each other better."

He released us and joined Bowden and Knox. I took a position between Whitney and Mammy.

Mounted, the men looked down at us, and no matter how each tried to hide his concern, it reflected in their eyes.

Bowden pressed his lips together to hold back his emotions and turned his mount. After one last look at me, he kicked his heels against his horse's flanks and raced down the lane. Ben offered a small wave and followed after him. Knox started to pursue them but halted when Whitney called out.

"Wait." She darted forward and stopped beside his horse. Gripping his hand, she tugged it urgently. "Now don't go getting yourself killed, you fool. You have a wife at home, and responsibilities."

Knox grinned. "If I didn't know any better, I would say you've come to your senses and finally see the man before you."

She swatted at his leg, and a small smile touched her lips. "You could say that. Now go on and get out of here. Don't keep the others waiting."

She started to step back, but he quickly gripped her shoulder. "Shouldn't a soldier secure a kiss to warm his heart?"

Whitney's lips parted, and she sent an awkward look at her observers.

"Come, let us go," I said to the others, and we turned to leave and allow the Tuckers the privacy Whitney required.

∾ CHAPTER ∾
Six

WEEKS AFTER THE MEN HAD LEFT, JIMMY SHOWED SIGNS OF recovery, but Gray's pa now rested in the graveyard with the others who had lost their lives during the McCoys' attack.

I smiled with delight the day Jones helped Jimmy down the sick hospital's front steps.

"You be careful, now. I don't want that wound opening again." Kimie exited behind them and stood on the small stoop, eyeing Jimmy with concern.

"I fine, Miss Kimie. You did real well." Jimmy waved in dismissal as Jones led him away.

"You are impossible!" Kimie stormed back inside.

I smirked, recalling how she had dropped into a rocker one evening, her face exhibiting frustration and defeat. "He is simply the most dreadful patient. You would think he would enjoy some time where he doesn't have to work. But no, all he wants to do is get back to the forge."

I had tried my best to hide my amusement, because as long as he was making matters difficult that meant he had the fighting spirit that would see him to wellness.

Jones and Jimmy walked past me. "Good day, Missus Willie." Jimmy shot me a cheery grin as I fell into step with the men.

"I'm glad to see you're up and moving."

Scowl returning, he said in a low voice, "I glad to be leaving dat place. Miss Kimie hovers over me lak I a child in need of constant nursing."

I chuckled and gave him a sideways glance. "You'd think you'd enjoy a pretty girl tending to your every need."

Hammers pounded as menfolk from the quarters continued repairs to the main house and the construction of the kitchen house and the smokehouse.

He snorted. "I bes' at tending to de horses. Bin itching to git back to de forge. A person ain't meant to be lying 'round. Don't rightfully know how white folkses sit 'round in de big house all day, or bask in de sun on deir verandas, sipping on lemonade."

"Is that what you think of us?" My amusement deepened. "Lazy, are we?"

"I ain't saying dat. Just saying I would go stir crazy widout somepin' of importance to do each day."

"Yes, well, with the war, there is no time to be idle. Our men need us. The ladies in town have organized gatherings to make bandages and uniforms. We can't fight alongside our men, but everyone has a part to play until this is over."

"Have you heard from Masa Bowden?"

An ache centered in my chest, and I inclined my head. "No, but I'm sure a letter will come eventually."

"I'm sho' you right. Masa will write as soon as he can." The faith in his tone buoyed the optimism I'd had no choice but to hold onto since Bowden's departure.

We paused at the pasture, and Jimmy inhaled deeply. A grin parted his lips as he held out a hand to a mare, and she trotted closer to greet him. "How ya doing, Honey gal?" he said as if speaking to an old friend as she nuzzled his hand.

"Missus Willow?" Tillie's voice carried.

Turning, I located her on the back veranda. She waved urgently. My gaze shifted to Moses and his small family. They stood next to the back steps with their eyes pinned on me. The man turned his gaze to Tillie and appeared to be speaking to her, but I couldn't hear over the activity happening outside the main house, where men from the quarters balanced on ladders to replace scorched boards on the lower level. The broken windows on the upper had been replaced, but the main floor's windows had been boarded up, as the glass supply was limited.

I waved at Tillie to signal I heard her before taking a quick look around the grounds. "Do you suppose the repairs will be done soon?" I directed my question to Jones.

"We are doing what we can, but there aren't enough hands for the tasks," he said.

I heaved a sigh. "I'd best go and see what Tillie wants. Now, you take it easy." I placed a hand on Jimmy's arm.

"Yessum," he said. "I ain't gwine back to dat sick hospital, not today or any day. You go on up to de house and don't worry none 'bout me. Wid dem Home Guards patrolling de roads lak a bunch of Northern spies, you can't chance dem seeing you catering to a nigger. You de missus, and you need to git on up to dat house and act lak et."

"James is right," Jones said. "The last thing we need is Carlton getting any suspicions and giving us more to worry about than Union soldiers showing up."

I knew they were right. "Very well." I narrowed my eyes at Jimmy. "You take it easy, and that is an order."

He saluted me. "Yes, Missus Willie."

I smiled before turning to walk toward the house. "Cantankerous as they come," I said under my breath.

As I approached the back veranda, Moses's woman, Helene, pulled in closer to her man while eyeing me uncertainly. Moses had been at Livingston since he was a young boy, and Helene had come from Bowden's plantation. The couple had a child, who straddled his mother's hip and peered at me from the shelter of her neck.

Moses shuffled his feet and looked from his woman to me, but before he could speak, Tillie approached the edge of the landing. "Miss Willow."

"Yes." I looked up at her.

She edged closer while wiping her palms on her dress and

casting a glance at the family. "Helene and Moses come luking to speak to ya."

"Have they now?" I swung back to look at the family. "What can I help you with?"

"We…" Moses kept his eyes on the ground, where he used the toe of his boot to draw small circles in the dirt. "I knowed you and the masa bin good to us, and I reckon you could use all de help you could get right now, wid de masa away and all. But me and Helene bin thinking et bes' ef we strike out on our own."

I swallowed my growing concern. "B-but it's more unsafe than ever out there. Not only do we have the Home Guards roaming the roads—"

"And we knowed dat," Helene said. I arched a brow at the determination in her tone. I had come to know the woman as meek. "But we willing to risk et." She adjusted the child on her hip.

"And where do you plan on going?" I asked.

Moses took a step forward. "We fixing to head north. Masa Bowden's grandpa sold off Helene's sister to a masa from New Orleans."

"You intend to go searching in the middle of a war?" I gawked at the couple in disbelief. Had they lost all their senses?

"Wid all respect, Missus, ef we don't go now, den when?" he said.

I pressed my fingers to my temple and paced. I didn't want to stand in their way, but the country had been turned upside down. Now, more than ever, hostility could meet them at every corner. I paused and looked at their son as Helene bent and placed him on the ground. "But what of Jasper? He is so young for such a journey."

"When he too tired to walk, we will carry him." Moses squared his shoulders. "We made up our minds. We gwine."

I braced at the resolution in his tone. "I will not stand in your way, but you will not go without food and water."

"We have some." Helene patted the makeshift sack tied to her waist. "When we need more, we find et. God be watching over us."

I nodded, tears dampening my eyes. "Stick to the river, and travel at night."

"Yessum." Moses tried to smile, but worry oozed from his every pore.

Josephine had visited last week and reported that several of their slaves had run off. With Mr. Carlton too busy with policing Charleston and the surrounding countryside, he couldn't track them down, and they were long gone. I supposed like those and many others who would follow suit, Moses and Helene figured it was safer to take their chances off the plantation than to wait for the war to come to our front step.

Our numbers had dwindled to a scarce few. Those closest to me had yet to make the decision to venture out. With Mary Grace and the children at the Barlow plantation, we had hardly seen them enough to appease Mammy or I. On Mary Grace and Magnus's most recent visit, he had informed us he sought to take her and the children north until they could return to England.

"Very well. I will pray that you reach safety and you can find your sister."

"When Big John found Miss Rita, I knowed et warn't impossible," Helene said with hope shining in her eyes.

I tamped down the nerves congregating in my stomach and smiled. "I wish for you a similar union."

"Thank you, Missus," she said.

"We won't forgit your kindness." Moses inclined his head. "We wait till dark and den we go."

When the family turned and walked off, I spun to look up at Tillie.

"I don't lak et one bit," she said. "My stomach a mess of nerves."

"Mine too." I climbed the steps to stand beside her. She continued to observe Moses and his family as they stopped to embrace each other. I gave her a sideways glance, grappling with the question I wanted to ask because I feared the answer. I stood quietly beside her for a moment before wandering inside to ponder how long it would be before Tillie and Pete also sought to leave.

I halted when Pippa exited the library. "The house is much too quiet today, don't you think?"

She frowned and regarded me as though I had lost my mind. "I was trying to read, but the noise from the repairs makes it impossible to concentrate, so I thought I'd go for a stroll. Care to join me?"

"I'm afraid I would be terrible company," I said with a small smile. "Perhaps another time?"

"Of course." Her face softened.

She sauntered down the corridor, fetched a shawl hanging on a peg, and went through the front door. I stood staring into the empty space of her retreat, lost in the chasm expanding inside me.

"I suppose one would get used to aloneness," I said to the empty corridor, and my words echoed. I wrapped my arms around myself and sighed.

"You all right, Missus Willow?" Mammy said.

I swerved to find her standing behind me, scrutinizing me with the same look Pippa had given me moments prior. Where had she come from? I hadn't heard her approach. "I'm fine. A bit lonely, I guess." I heaved another sigh and looked about the place.

"De place ain't so lively as et once was. I use to hearing footsteps everywhere. Slave folkses listening in corners and de yard filled wid folkses and chillum running 'bout in play. De spirit of song drifting from de yard and fields. Et lak de place done lost all life."

"Moses and Helene are leaving tonight."

She shook her head. "Ain't gwine to be nobody left soon. Just you and de masa, ol' James, and my John and me."

"And what 'bout us?" a voice asked, hardly audible.

We turned to find Tillie watching us. She looked from Mammy to me. "We here too," she said meekly.

"You don't intend to leave?" My heart leaped at the news.

"Pete ain't leaving his pappy, and my mama is buried here. I want to be free as much as de next person, but dis is my home."

Before I could catch myself, I launched myself at her. She gasped as I snatched her into a hug and kissed her repeatedly. "Oh, I'm delighted to hear that." I lingered, lost in my happiness before I became aware of what I was doing, and released her. "Please forgive me."

"Dat's quite all right, Missus." She flashed an awkward grin. "You took me by surprise, is all."

"When you said you didn't intend to leave, I was overcome with gratitude. It's wrong of me, I know, but the thoughts of..." I lowered my gaze as shame stole my words.

"We care 'bout you too, Missus Willow. You lak family, whether you white or not," she said with more assertiveness than I'd ever recalled seeing in her.

My head whipped up at her statement, and my heart soared. "Oh, Tillie, I'm so happy, I could squeeze you."

"You already done dat," she said with a cheeky grin.

I laughed and clasped my hands under my chin, hope humming in my heart.

For the rest of the day, I daydreamed that, if matters shifted in favor of abolishing slavery—and I prayed it would be so—perhaps Tillie and Pete could have their own piece of land where they could raise a family right here at Livingston.

↶ CHAPTER ↷
Seven

Drifter

WARM BLOOD SPLATTERED MY FACE, AND I HOWLED IN exhilaration as excitement coursed through my veins. The scrape of my blade as I withdrew it left me feeling reborn. The ever-present residents inside my head championed and praised me for a job well done. I straightened to stare down at the lifeless body of Samson, splayed in a pool of crimson on the cabin floor. The man had given me refuge and nursed my wounds, but the pressing urge, the *need* to end his life had nagged at me for weeks.

A similar vision of a woman splayed in a puddle of blood on a cabin floor flashed before me, but emotions that were quite different erupted in my gut. I felt grief—an emotion that seemed foreign—and also a sense of love for her. I realized that the woman was, in fact, my mother. Had I been responsible for her death? No, surely the madness inside my head hadn't led me to kill my own mother.

No, but you should have, the voices chimed.

"Enough!" My voice reverberated off the cabin walls, and agony ripped through my chest. The voices muttered and faded, and I gulped back the tears swelling in my throat.

I stretched my hands out to behold the blood staining them and the blade. I held it up for inspection, then peered back at the body, and my jaw relaxed. I had gutted the man and taken great pleasure in the act. I lowered the blade and wiped it on my trousers before setting it on the table.

Striding to the crate under the cabin's window, I poured lukewarm water from a pitcher into the metal basin. I removed the dirtied trousers and shirt and washed the blood from my face, hands, and forearms, discovering satisfaction in how red muddied the water. I moved to Samson's bed, gathered his spare buckskin trousers and shirt, and slipped them on. The fit was off, but they would do until I could obtain more suitable clothing.

I packed a satchel with food and filled a waterskin before retrieving the money Samson kept in the wooden box on a shelf by the fireplace. At the table, I looked at the dirtied dishes from the morning meal. The smell of bacon still hung in the cabin. My attention turned to the small pile of kindling positioned to the right of the fireplace. Slinging the satchel over my shoulder, I reached for a piece of kindling and held it to the glowing flames. As the stick ignited, I eyed it with wonder, then another vision crackled to life: a scream-filled night; a mansion and surrounding buildings aflame. I frowned, unsure what I had seen, but the same sense of urgency I'd felt since I'd awakened kindled, like a niggling in the back of my mind of a mission left unfinished.

The flame came ferociously to life, and I pushed away all pondering and straightened. At the far end of the room, I torched the bedding, curtains, and all else that would ignite. As the flames went on a rampage through the cabin, I paused a moment to revel in the beauty. The voices in my head crowed with glee when I threw the kindling onto the bed. I strode to the cabin's open door, scooping up Samson's bedroll lying against the wall on the way by. Pausing on the threshold, I took a final glance around and rested my gaze on Samson's body as the flames raced toward him. Joy danced on my soul and parted my lips.

I closed the door and strode down the stairs, and made my way to the pasture where the chestnut bay grazed.

After saddling the mare and securing the bedroll and satchel,

I led the horse from the pasture. At the same time, the cabin windows shattered. Angry flames leaped through the windows and rose like hungry spirits in search of a victim.

I swung up onto the mare and took one last look at the cabin before I rode out. The same plaguing thought niggled at the back of my mind: who was I? Throughout my confusion since awakening in Samson's care, I had pondered the question, never coming up with an answer. The voices inside my head had given me a sense of power, but they never enlightened me with the answers I sought.

The horse picked up speed, and another image surfaced, one of a beautiful brunette woman. Who was she? A lover who had defied me? My fingers clutched the reins tighter as an understanding that the woman was anything but a lover resonated. But if not a lover, then why did she stir a profound hunger inside me to see her dead?

✌ CHAPTER ✌
Eight

Madame Amelie Laclaire

I RAN A JEWELED HAND OVER THE GREEN TAFFETA WITH ADMIRATION, relishing the exquisite feel of the fabric under my fingers. The chatter of gentlemen and the girls droned on in the background. Usually the purchasing of new material would fill me with delight, but not today. I gritted my teeth as the obnoxious braying of one girl's laughter carried. She was the ordinary sort, but with a voluptuous body that men couldn't resist. And, because of that asset, she was one of my best-paying girls.

"Luther!" I swung to look at the pianist lazing on a settee with a brunette on his lap.

His gray eyes widened, and he tossed the girl to the side and leaped to his feet. "Yes, Madame?" He ran a hand much too small for a man over his balding head.

The girl jumped to her feet, gave him a scowl, and stormed off.

"Play something to boost the spirits of the place."

He scurried to the piano and sat down, and I turned back to regard the black seamstress eyeing me tentatively. The sound of the piano drowned out the chatter and eased my nerves.

"Where were we?" I said.

She gestured at the fabric.

"Oh, yes, I will take it. Do you think you can have the garment finished within the month?"

"It shouldn't be a problem, Madame."

"Good," I said. "Thank you for coming by."

She nodded and glanced around the place before gathering the three bolts of fabric she had brought for my inspection and hurrying out the back.

I turned and leaned my hips against the bar and observed the captain trailing his fingers along the cleavage of a busty blond. The odd man had come in and out of my establishment for the last four days, never taking a girl upstairs but instead sitting in the parlor to fondle each one in the strangest way. I figured he liked to arouse himself with the mortal flesh of a woman while exerting his willpower. As bizarre as he was, I'd seen too much in my life to waste time pondering on his behavior.

I wrenched my attention from the gentleman as a nauseating scent that chilled my blood wafted my way. Before she spoke, I knew the past had presented itself.

"I never believed it could be true," a woman said from behind me.

It was her. My heart sprang into my throat, and I turned to face a gray-haired woman clad in a tattered, rust-colored gingham dress.

I gripped the bar to brace myself. "Mother…" My voice drifted. How could she still be alive? Had she come to make me pay for the murder of the congressman?

At my address, she stumbled back, and I moved to catch her, but she gripped the back of a chair to remain upright. I stopped and regarded her with horror and fear. She stood trembling, appearing ready to collapse. "I never believed it," she said again before looking back at me. "It's you."

I looked around to observe if anyone was paying attention to us before marching forward and gripping her arm with a fierceness foreign to me. Ignoring her frailness under my fingers, I hauled her toward the back, away from my patrons and staff. I didn't release her until I'd pulled her into a storage room, out of sight. I let go of her arm so violently that she sailed backward and hit her hip on a wooden crate. She let out a howl of pain, but I cared not. She could rot in hell, for all I cared. If there was a God, why had he let her exist this long? She didn't deserve to draw breath.

"What are you doing here?" The inner storm that had rumbled at the very thought of this abhorrent person who'd birthed me erupted.

Gathering herself, she rubbed her hip before opening her mouth to speak, revealing rotten and missing teeth. She appeared dreadfully thin. "I suppose I didn't expect a warm welcome."

I scoffed and planted my hands on my hips. "And why would I ever welcome a monster back into my life?" I took pleasure in the flicker of pain on her weathered face.

"I deserve that."

"Damn straight, you do!" My whole body vibrated.

Her shoulders slumped. "Esther, p-please—"

I sprang forward and pinned her by the throat to the wall. "Don't ever call me by that name. You have no right!" My fingers tightened. I wanted to end her life, to snuff out the pain and memories of the past.

Tears welled in her eyes. "Do it. I wouldn't blame you. No one would."

I squeezed tighter until she gasped, and her eyes filled with fear as she fought to breathe, as I had under the weight of the men she forced on top of me. *Die! Just die!* But, for some unconscious reason, my grip eased, and I stepped back. Her body slid down the wall, and she crumpled to the floor.

"I'm sorry. So very sorry," she said and began to weep.

I hated her, even the mere sight of her. Hadn't I envisioned her as she was in that moment—on the ground before me, begging for forgiveness? Every muscle in my body vibrated. I swiped a hand over my face and moved a safe distance away from her.

Numbed, I rested my weight on a crate and waited for her to gather herself, and soon her pathetic sobs of self-pity ceased. Eyes red-rimmed and puffy, she pulled to her feet before searching my face. "Why didn't you end both of our misery?"

The hatred I held for her twisted in my gut like a soured meal. "I will not have your death on my hands. You've tainted my life enough with your poison."

She nodded and dropped her gaze. "Yes, and for that, I am sorry."

I glared at her. "Too late for that. Do you think marching in here and stating you're remorseful makes everything better? Well, it doesn't. You robbed me of my innocence." All my pain and fear erupted as I struggled to smother the daunting memories of my childhood.

"I know. I don't seek your forgiveness. I know that's something someone like me can never get. But I'm dying, E-e..." My birth name faded from her lips.

I leaped to my feet. "Do you think I care? I thought you were in hell where you belonged for years. I haven't given you a thought since I left that day." The lie delivered the painful impact I wanted.

After briefly floundering, she braced herself and continued. "I deserve that. God knows I do. I had hoped you would have escaped and made a fresh start in life."

"I did."

"Yes, I can see that, but I hoped for something better."

"And just when did this motherly concern blossom? It sure wasn't when you forced your male callers on me. 'Two for the price of one.'" I mimicked her cheerful banter, which was seared into my head.

She gulped and lifted guilt-filled eyes, but remained silent.

"Don't look at me like that!" I said before turning away from her to pace the floor. How dare she show up here, acting as though she had been to a revival and found God. The buried despondency ripped through my chest, and it heaved with rising tears. "Get out!"

She started to protest, but I marched forward and shoved her out the door and into the hallway. "I don't ever want to see your face again. I loathe the day you birthed me. May you die a cruel and painful death." I slammed the door in her face and held my breath until my lungs felt like they would burst. Only when her footsteps moved down the hall did I release my breath and crumple to the floor.

"Why are you so cruel?" I looked at the heavens. "Why did you have to remind me of her? Why did you have to make me relive the pain?" Tears cascaded down my cheeks, and I pulled my knees up to my chest and cried as I had each time her callers defiled my body…and the time after I'd tried to save Big John from the jailor. As much as I despised her, I hated what I'd become—her protégé.

An hour later the door opened, and the ring of his spurs lifted my head from the corner where I'd settled. Compassion shone in his eyes as he strode forward and dropped to his knees before me. I launched myself at him, wrapped my arms around his neck, and held onto the one person who'd become a rock in my life.

"Where were you?" I said, my chest heaving, though no tears came.

"Getting the supplies you requested," he said before pulling me back to inspect my face. "What has caused you so much distress?"

"S-she was here." I rocked back on my knees.

"Who?" He stared at me in puzzlement.

I could never have imagined when I hired him for protection, the evening the Tucker woman and I'd visited the Rawlings, that our lives would become entangled. He'd become my constant companion, bodyguard, and something more. Emotions stirred in my stomach each time he stepped from the shadows or entered a room. Love was a foreign emotion for me, and I'd deceived myself into believing I was incapable of it. Zeke Montgomery had shown me that, in truth, I'd felt unworthy of love and held a distorted opinion that I was defective and had caused my mother to reject me and manage me in unthinkable ways.

"My mother."

His mouth unhinged, and then he snapped it shut. Once he recovered from his shock, he said, "Forgive me for my bluntness, but I thought you told me she was dead."

"I did because I thought she would be by now." I pushed to my feet. He stood and regarded me, bemused. "For years, I wished for her death—so much that I'd come to believe it was true. And then she shows up here, looking ready to drop at any moment."

"Where is she now?" He gripped my arms.

"Gone." I wiggled from his grip and walked to the doorway before turning back to face him. "I don't know where. But she is, and I'm glad for it."

I walked down the hallway toward the gaiety of lust and drunkenness drifting from the grand parlor. Pausing, I took a deep breath, squared my shoulders, and waltzed into the room.

"Arthur." I gestured to the new bartender as he walked behind the counter and set down a box of liquor.

"Madame?"

"Pour me a glass of whiskey."

He frowned at my request but took a glass, poured an inch into the bottom, and pushed it toward me. I lifted the glass and stared into the amber liquid before throwing it back. The inviting burn of the whiskey trailed down my throat and warmed my belly.

"Another." I pushed the glass at him.

He poured again, and when he stopped, I reached for his hand and gripped the bottle. "Leave it."

"Yes, ma'am." He released his hold, gave me another puzzled look, and moved to unpack the box.

I drained the glass and then another before swerving to peer at a patron who eyed me with admiration and lust gleaming in his eyes, which only fueled the self-loathing I felt. I looked around the establishment I'd created and despair anchored in my gut. I grabbed the bottle and headed for the staircase.

At the bottom step, someone gripped my wrist. "Amelie." I heard the concern in Zeke's voice, and turned to face him. His tender expression made my body tremble—not with desire, but a deeply rooted belief that I didn't deserve his kindness.

"I'll be fine. Please see that I'm not disturbed." I took the first step.

"Do you want me to sit with you?"

I paused and turned to cup his cheek. "No, my darling, I must face my demons alone." I let my hand drop, gathered the side of my skirt, and ascended the stairs.

CHAPTER
Nine

Willow
July, 1861

I SAT AT THE BREAKFAST TABLE WITH PIPPA. MAMMY HAD DRAWN THE heavy burgundy drapes closed to keep out the heat. Pippa's face grew distant as I half-listened to her usually intriguing chatter. The night before, as I'd lain in bed worrying and wide awake, an idea seeded itself in my head, and all morning it'd occupied my mind.

Yes, it could serve very nicely. I traced the edge of my plate as I worked out the plan. *It would take some convincing, but it definitely could work.*

Pippa's voice elevated. "Willow?"

I jerked and blinked to clear my mind and noted her puckered brow. "Yes?"

"You haven't heard a word I've said. Care to inform me of what has captured your mind?"

I smiled sheepishly. "That obvious, is it?"

She regarded me tenderly. "I've come to recognize that far-off stare, and when your gears are turning. Do you care to share what has you so preoccupied?"

I hesitated, and my gaze focused on the empty seat at the head of the table to my left. The sadness that filled me felt like an open hole in the center of my chest, forming each morning when I'd turn over and regard the empty place next to me in the bed. The daunting realization of the nightmare encompassing the country would return, and I'd come down to breakfast and be reminded again of Bowden and Ben's absence. Then there was Mary Grace and the children...

The ache of loneliness became too much. I stifled it and looked at Pippa. I'd come to care for her deeply; she'd added life to the place. "I can't stand sitting here while they are out there fighting. With Lincoln requesting enlistment for a Union Army, folks are saying the war will not be over anytime soon."

"It appears that way." Concern shadowed her face.

"I wish we could receive word from Bowden or Ben. The not knowing is unbearable."

"I feel your pain."

"I'm thinking that, if this war shows no signs of ending soon, we should spend our time by reinforcing this place for the greater good."

"How is that?"

"What happens in wars throughout history?"

"Death and brutality," she said before taking a bite of her eggs. Every gesture and movement she made exuded the grace of a lady, sometimes making me feel awkward and anything but a proper Southern belle.

"Yes, all of that." I gulped at her response and pushed away the vision of Bowden and Ben on the battlefield. "Also, the troops come to raid the nearby villages. We womenfolk must think ahead and seek to do what we can to protect our resources, and if we need to aid our soldiers, we can."

She'd lifted her napkin to pat her lips, and paused in mid motion to gawk warily at me. "What is turning in that lovely head of yours? I promised Ben I would see that you don't put yourself in unnecessary danger."

I smirked and shook my head at the revelation. "I assumed as much when he insisted you move into the main house with his leaving."

"It wasn't like that." Her blue eyes pleaded with me for understanding.

I waved a hand at her. "You needn't worry. I quite like having you here." I offered her a smile before continuing. "As I was saying. We must outmaneuver our enemies. The well-being of the folks on this plantation, and our men, has to be our first priority."

"I agree. What do you seek to do?"

Mammy walked into the room with a fresh carafe of coffee. I scraped back my chair and rose. "Come with me," I said to Pippa, who stood and laid her napkin on the table.

"Where you womanfolkses off to? Dis here food git cold, and I won't be happy 'bout et." Mammy balled a hand on her hip.

"I have an idea and wanted to show Pippa."

"Why I got an inkling I ain't gwine to lak et?"

"I haven't got time for your lectures," I said firmly. "But you'd best come so that you understand my plan. So you can apply grace to the folks trotting dirt all over your floors." She started to object, but I put up a hand to stop her. "Hear me out, and then you are free to inform me of your opinion. If you wouldn't mind, please follow me."

I marched out the door and down the hall to the supply closet under the stairs. I pulled the door open and stepped back. The women glanced past me into the narrow closet.

"What we luking at?" Still holding the coffee carafe, Mammy exchanged a look of confusion with Pippa.

"I've been thinking about how we need to hide food, medicine, and supplies. And if need be, soldiers."

"And how you reckon dat closet gwine to hold much? I can barely fit in dere." Mammy swiped a hand at the closet.

"We go up," I said.

"What you meaning?" She regarded me like I'd lost my mind.

"Oh," Pippa said in dawning understanding. "The attic."

"Yes," I said with a smile. "If soldiers come, they will look for an attic. Jimmy can fortify the space to appear as though it's simply a closet, but the shelving will pull out, and we will build stairs going up to the attic."

Pippa frowned. "If the attic is the first place they would look, then why—"

"Because a false wall in the current attic will discourage further questioning and searching. I will have Jimmy draw up plans, and I'll assign a few men to start the construction. Our menfolk are counting on us, and I, for one, will not let them down."

"I don't know how you do et," Mammy said, shaking her head.

"What do you mean?" I twisted to regard her.

"Dat head of yours. I reckoned when de good Lard made you, he made you wid de brain of a man."

"That is where you are wrong."

"Oh?"

"When the Lord made us, he made us with the brains and strength of women. Look at Joan of Arc and all the women throughout history who had courage as great as any man. Look at Harriet Tubman and the risks she continues to take for her people."

"And de Moses 'oman got a bounty on her head," Mammy said with a snort. "Now, listen: I admire her efforts as much as de next nigra, but she ain't you. For years I've paid heed to de history lessons you've given me, and I believe in you, but I ain't luking for you to go playing dis Joan of Arc or de Moses 'oman. No sah, I got me one gal off on her own where I can't luk out for her, and I ain't fixing to have any more worry den what you two already cause me."

"We must help. I won't stand by and do nothing. Who knows, perhaps we can make our own history, one that isn't so tainted by society and laws on women."

"Dat is crazy talk. Do you hear yourself? You've done lost your mind. 'Omen's place is in de home, taking care of deir menfolkses and chillum."

"Just like a black is a slave and nothing more?" Passion for the cause ignited in my gut. "No, Mammy, we must change. We must broaden our perspective and step out of the errors of the past."

"'Course I ain't saying blacks are to be slaves," she said with a huff and narrowed her eyes at me.

"Mark my words. One day, all slaves will be free. And maybe, one day, women will even earn the right to vote. Can you imagine?" I grinned at a fantasy Whitney and I had often talked about.

Mammy swatted at the air as though abolishing such an outlandish idea. "Hogwash. You've always bin a dreamer."

I shrugged. "Perhaps, but dreaming is good for the soul."

She lifted a brow and eyed me before cracking into a wide grin. "Reckon dat dreaming of yours gits to other souls too. Very well, ef you say we gwine to build, den we gwine to build, and deir ain't a Northerner or Southerner dat can stand in our way."

I cradled her shoulders with an arm and looked from her to Pippa. "What do you say, ladies?"

"I say it's a brilliant plan." Pippa clasped her hands together at her chin, her face radiating excitement.

CHAPTER
Ten

THE CONSTRUCTION OF THE HIDING PLACE IN THE ATTIC BEGAN that day. Still grieving his father's death, Parker jumped at the chance to become Jimmy's right-hand man on the job, and the two worked well into the night.

One afternoon I descended the newly constructed steps leading from the secret room, barely big enough to house a person as well as supplies. I hoped we would never need to hide anything but rations. Exiting the closet, I stepped into the corridor on the main floor when the pounding of running footsteps drew my attention to the open door leading to the front veranda.

"Missus Willow!" Big John darted through the open door.

"What is it?" I hurried toward him.

He paused to catch his breath. "Et de Home Guards, Missus, dey coming up de lane."

I glanced over his shoulder and observed the cloud of dust of their arrival. "God in heaven!" I raced back down the corridor. "We have company," I called up into the opening of the attic, and my voice echoed back.

The hammering ceased and there came muffled voices before someone dashed down the stairs. Parker came into view, and without our exchanging words, I stepped in to help replace the false wall.

"What is all the ruckus?" Pippa said from behind me.

I spun to find her clothed in a pale-blue silk day dress and peering down from the railing overhead. "The Home Guards are coming. Please help put everything back into place while I see to them."

She hurried down the stairs, and I passed her on my way back to the front of the house. Mammy now stood with Big John in the foyer. He clasped her hands to his chest and comforted her in hushed tones.

As I slowed my pace, I lifted a hand to smooth back my hair. "Mammy, you'd best gather yourself. Your fretting will make the men suspicious for sure." I looked at Big John. "You better make yourself scarce." Since his arrival, we had taken extreme precautions because his presence wasn't one someone could easily forget, and the risk was too great.

"Yessum." He raced from the house, dashed down the stairs, and disappeared.

I stepped out onto the veranda and shut the door behind me. Steadying my breathing, I walked down the steps to greet the men as they reined their horses to a stop at the end of the path. I gritted my teeth before feigning a smile at Josephine's husband. "Gentlemen." I looked from him to the rest of the group, composed of boys and elderly men. "To what do I owe the pleasure?"

When I spotted Mr. Barlow, Magnus's father, seated on a chestnut bay, the tension in my jaw eased. Callie had told me he had joined the Home Guards, but I hadn't been aware he rode with Theodore Carlton. Surely he hadn't forgotten how Theodore and several other men had sought to run him and his family off after their arrival.

Theodore tipped his hat and sat like a prized peacock upon his mount. "Mrs. Armstrong, I see you are faring well," he said with a smile that made my skin crawl.

"I'm as well as can be expected. How is Josephine?" I hoped to turn his thoughts to matters at his own home.

"She fares well. She longs for her life in Charleston. But, like many, we were forced to abandon our home and man the plantation. Every day the damn slaves run off, and with my work securing the roads and Charleston, it leaves my wife to manage the plantation and those that remain."

"I hope she will find time for a visit soon. I do enjoy her company."

"It's not safe for you womenfolk to be left to manage the homes alone. And all the more dangerous for you to travel the roads, with all these damn Union soldiers and slaves on the loose. Niggers are likely to take advantage of you in your vulnerable conditions."

"I carry no concern that the blacks will harm me or what is mine. It is our countrymen that give me cause to worry." I gestured at the still-scarred Livingston.

"Yes, we are all troubled by what happened here. It makes people question what enemies your husband has made, like your father before him." His piercing eyes regarded me as though he were hinting at something more.

My mocking laugh was loud and clear, while nerves congregated in my stomach. "This was no enemy, other than those that seek to hold the South in ruins. The men who attacked Livingston were nothing more than the vicious Northern militia. Ask Mr. Sterling or those who came to our aid. My husband is an honorable man, much like my father was."

"Do you attempt to convince me that the sinking of your ships was also the work of the Northern militia?" He sat poised and self-assured while I felt myself unraveling inside and scrambling with what to say next.

"A casualty of war. Has the battle in the harbor faded from your memory so fast?" I glared at him, losing all sense in the anger rising within me at this fool of a man.

He sat up taller, and he looked uneasy. "Of course not."

"We aren't here to interrogate Mrs. Armstrong but to assist her, if need be." Mr. Barlow nudged his mount forward and bestowed a kind smile on me. "You haven't faced any more trouble, have you?"

"No, we haven't. Thank you for asking." I relaxed, grateful

for his presence and his handling of Theodore, whose expression revealed his displeasure with Mr. Barlow's input.

Theodore inserting himself into the affairs of Livingston was the last thing I needed. I'd take my chances with the Union Army encroaching on my property before enduring another visit from him. "I do appreciate your concern. But we have managed so far." I peered up at him with all the sweetness I could muster.

"If you need anything at all, let me know." He rested his hand on his thigh. "You solitary womenfolk are an easy target for those with ill intentions." He looked past me, and his expression grew appreciative. I swerved to find Pippa striding toward us. "This must be the lovely English lady who has stolen your uncle's attention," he said as she came to stand beside me.

"How do you do?" She curtsied.

News had traveled of his visit to a small plantation not five miles from Livingston. The young woman's husband had left with the other men, and Theodore had made advancements toward her, but she had run him off with her husband's rifle. He had underestimated the strength of the women left to tend the home fronts. He ought to dangle from a rope for his attempts to take advantage of us. I would protect myself, my home, and all those who chose to remain at Livingston—so help me, God!

"You will find, Mr. Carlton, that Southern women are stronger than you may think. We are more capable of caring for ourselves than our men give us credit for. This isn't the first war that has forced women to care for the homesteads in men's absence." *And with men like you in positions of power, it won't be the last.*

"Very well," he said, none too pleased. "We have done our deed here. Good day, Mrs. Armstrong; Mrs. Hendricks." His gaze lingered on Pippa before he raised a gloved hand and ordered the others to ride out.

Mr. Barlow nodded farewell and shared a look of exasperation with us before following after them.

I turned to head back inside, and Pippa walked beside me. "That man is dangerous," I said.

"He does seem like the odd sort. You said he is the husband of the boy's mother?"

I sent her a sideways glance. "That's correct."

"He isn't the gentlemanly sort, is he?" Her dress's bottom swayed and bounced against mine.

"No, and I believe he could be very dangerous if he were to become your enemy."

"Yet you challenge him." She paused and regarded me with a furrowed brow.

"I don't seek to challenge, but to let him know I will not be intimidated."

She patted my arm. "Be careful, my love. That is a man who could be every bit as dangerous as the men who sought your demise before."

I eyed the wisps of gray in the blond hair escaping the silver combs I'd helped Ben purchase. "This I'm aware of, and the next time he comes I will do better at keeping calm—for the good of us all."

She smiled, and we continued toward the house.

My thoughts turned to Reuben and his whereabouts. He'd been wounded in the attack on Livingston, and may God forgive me, but I hoped his corpse lay decaying or picked clean by the scavengers of the Lowcountry.

CHAPTER
Eleven

I'D RISEN EARLY TO SPEND THE MORNING GOING OVER THE LEDGERS, and our profits compared to the previous year had plunged dreadfully low. Sitting back, I rubbed my temples before turning to look out the window. I'd come up with the best plan I could think of to stretch our food and money until peace once again embraced our country. But there was no certainty that the army wouldn't move in and take what we had left, or when the war would end.

"Missus Willie."

"Yes?" I pulled my gaze from the window and found Jimmy standing at the threshold, grasping a small wooden box.

"I found somepin' tucked in the wall in de attic."

Interest piqued, I summoned him forward. He placed the box on the desk in front of me, and I lifted the lid. Inside were pamphlets and newspaper clippings from the 1830s, about the Grimke sisters. I'd heard folks whisper about the female abolitionists who had fought for the women's rights movement. All documents referring to them had been destroyed because Charleston wanted to snuff out their existence. To my knowledge, the women were very much alive, and their mission to see slavery's end and the progressiveness of women's rights continued.

As I flipped through the clippings, I noticed my mother's handwriting. My heart pounded with exhilaration. I closed the lid and ran a hand affectionately over the top of the box. An image of her clutching the pamphlets and reading them with intensity brought a smile to my face. I'd grasped that the woman had a fiery spirit from hearing Ben's and Mammy's memories. My yearning to have known her never eased.

"Dere, dere, Missus Willie, don't you cry none." Jimmy crept closer.

I regarded him through blurred vision before lifting a hand to wipe my tears. "They are happy tears," I said before glancing around the study. "My mother may be gone, but her presence lingers. She truly was the heart of this place."

"I never knowed your mama." He took a moment to admire her portrait hanging on the wall. "From what I hear, you jus' lak her."

I followed his gaze and paused to reflect on the woman I had been told I resembled. If I could be a mere image of the woman she was in spirit, I would die content. Her passion to right the wrongs our family had done in enslaving people had been admirable but unattainable. The sins of Livingston were great, no matter how much my family had tried to change our legacy. We couldn't erase the past, but we could shape the future.

"Well, I bes' git back to work. Pete be wondering what I dallying for."

I smiled. "Thank you for this." I laid a hand on the box.

His eyes gleamed with delight before he turned and ambled out. I stared at the empty doorway, and my thoughts turned to Jimmy's daughter Ruby, her husband Saul, and their daughter Mercy. I'd written to her a few months ago, but no reply had come. When the war was over, I would send an invitation for them to visit Livingston. It had been far too long, and it would do Jimmy good to see them again.

I opened a desk drawer and tucked the box inside before leaving the study.

"Dey here!" Mammy clapped her hands together in glee as she exited the parlor.

I listened and heard the approach of a carriage.

Mammy waddled to the front door. "Dis is a blessed day." She had hummed all morning, moving from room to room, occupying herself with cleaning until the arrival of Mary Grace and the children.

I smiled and hurried after her.

On the veranda, I waited as Mammy went to greet them. Mary Grace disembarked, clad in a navy taffeta dress and a matching grand hat with feathers and exquisite embellishments. On her slender wrist dangled a drawstring handbag, and I placed a hand to my throat, appreciating her grandeur.

"Hello, Mama." She embraced her mother and planted a kiss on her cheek.

Mammy hugged her fiercely before stepping back and grasping her arms. "Let me git a luk at you. Turn 'round." Mary Grace obliged and twirled for her mother's inspection. "Well, ain't dat somepin'. You are a sight. You luk lak a fine English lady." Pride warmed Mammy's voice. "I see life at de Barlows' has bin good for you."

"It has." Mary Grace smiled and offered a cheerful wave to me.

I walked toward them as Evie and Noah leaped out of the open carriage and rushed to embrace their grandmother. She showered them with kisses, causing Noah to squirm in an attempt to get away. "Grannie, I'm too old for such carrying on," he said sheepishly.

She displayed a scowl. "Boy, you ain't too grown. Long as you be alive, you gwine to be my grandbaby. And I won't hear no fussing 'bout et."

"Yes, ma'am." He looked down at her.

"May I go and find Sailor?" Evie looked at me.

I smiled, gesturing for her to do as she pleased, and she bounced off.

"Where might I find James?" Noah asked.

"He is inside working on a project." I signaled to Big John, who had helped Isabella down from the driver's seat.

He released her hand and strode forward. "Yessum."

"I think today will be a day of rest."

"But it ain't Sunday." His eyes widened.

"Yes, well. Nothing is normal anymore, is it?"

"No, Missus. Et sho' ain't."

"I believe this day calls for a celebration. Please tell Parker and Jimmy to come out here."

"Yessum." Big John walked off to do my bidding, and Noah followed him to wait by the front steps.

I turned back to look at Isabella as she came to stand beside Mary Grace.

"Thank you for being kind to my gal," Mammy said. "Et helps me to know she is in good hands."

"It is easy. You've raised a fine daughter. I'm delighted I can now call her mine." Isabella encircled Mary Grace's waist with an arm and gave her an affectionate squeeze.

"They've been so kind." Mary Grace beamed.

"We love having her."

"Have you all forgotten about me?" Callie stepped from the shadows of Isabella and Mary Grace with a feigned pout on her face.

My heart expanded with love and excitement, and I embraced her and pressed a giggle from her.

"It's good to see you." She gripped my wrist and gave it a gentle tug when I released her.

"Willow," Isabella said with a smile. "How are you, my love?" She leaned in, and we exchanged a kiss on the cheek.

"I'm well. We've looked forward to your visit all week."

Callie let out a squeal. "Nothing could keep me away a moment longer. I simply missed you too much." She tried her best impression of a Southern accent and failed miserably.

"I've missed you all," I said. "Come; Mammy has prepared refreshments. What do you say we visit in the garden house?"

"You all go on ahead. I will help Mama," Mary Grace said with a smile that reflected pure joy.

Marriage and life off the plantation had done her well, and my heart swelled with happiness for her.

After Mary Grace and Mammy had wandered inside, I led the others to the garden house.

"How are you faring with Mr. Barlow away from home and Magnus off fighting?" I asked.

"The days are long." Isabella looked sad. "I worry for both of them. But I gather comfort from Callie, Mary Grace, and the children, which is more than some have."

"Our decision to move to America may have been a bad choice," Callie said with a huff of frustration. "Perhaps if we had known we would be launched into the middle of a war, we wouldn't have come."

A twinge of disappointment tightened my chest. "But, if you hadn't come, then we never would have had this time together." I failed to hide the emotion in my voice.

Callie's face paled. She leaned forward and gripped my hands in hers. "I'm glad we came, honestly. Some days it's hard; sometimes I miss my friends terribly. Now with Magnus at war and Dad off with the Home Guard from morning until night, it makes me long for England."

I nodded my understanding and pushed away the old feelings of abandonment.

"Have you heard from Bowden and Ben?" Isabella asked as Mary Grace and Mammy approached, balancing silver trays of refreshments.

"No, not at all." My shoulders slumped at the reminder.

"I'm sure he has written. The delays of the mail are painfully long." Isabella offered me a comforting smile.

Mary Grace perched beside me on the bench, and the scent

of jasmine wafted from her. I regarded her with admiration and wonderment, from her pearl earrings to the cameo clasping her high-collared ivory blouse. Her beauty radiated, and happiness twinkled in her eyes. She was truly regal.

"Have you heard from Magnus?" I asked her. She winced. I patted her hands where they rested in her lap and realized how much I had missed her. "I've missed you."

"Yes, as we have you. Evie has asked to visit Sailor every day. And Noah has wanted to get back to James. They miss this place." She looked around. "I can't say the same."

I gulped at the remark but knew she had every right to feel that way, and before I could speak, she continued.

"But I suppose, if I hadn't been here, I'd never have had your friendship, which is irreplaceable." Tears welled in my eyes. "Or met Magnus and the ones who would become my family." Her gaze ran over Isabella and Callie, and I sensed the tenderness between the women.

I looked to Mammy, who stood back observing, and saw the aching longing that swept across her visage before she pushed it away and strode forward. "Let me pour you ladies some tea."

"Won't you join us, Henrietta?" Isabella said.

"De help ain't suppose to be sitting wid de whites..." Her words trailed off as she caught herself. I reckoned her statement came from the same feeling of alienation I had felt. Callie, Isabella, and Mary Grace were united as a new family, and although admirable, where did that leave us? I chastised myself for my selfishness.

"Now, Mama, you know you are amongst like-minded folks," Mary Grace said. "Besides, you aren't a slave."

Mammy stood taller. "No, I ain't, but I don't need dem Home Guards riding up in here and causing dis here gal no trouble. She got 'nuf on her shoulders, wid de masa way and all."

"I appreciate your concern," I said with a smile of

reassurance. "We will hear their approach." I patted the seat on the other side of me. "Come, sit for a while. It's not every day your daughter comes to visit. I, for one, want to soak in each precious moment."

Mammy looked back in the direction of the house before settling her gaze on Mary Grace. "All right, but we got to keep our ears open."

Under the warmth of the afternoon sun, our gaiety carried us away. Relishing each other's company, we forgot for a while about the chaos of a country at war.

CHAPTER
Twelve

THE ATTIC SPACE WAS COMPLETED, AND THE NEWLY STRUCTURED kitchen house stood like a new fawn, bright and juvenile against the scorched outbuildings and grounds empty of life. As I'd stood back and beheld the new structure, hope had buoyed in my heart. We could never repair Livingston to its former beauty, but I endeavored to honor the ones who'd been the family I loved as much as my own; those who'd freely given their lives to defend a plantation and family who'd stolen their freedom. The ache of shame never eased. Their souls cried to me from the mass of graves in the slave cemetery. Determination to rewrite Livingston's legacy guided my days and intensified with the war. If the North won, would slavery be abolished? A part of me dared dream of such a day, but I had little faith in the men governing our country.

"Please, bring our men home safely," I prayed in a whisper, "and allow justice for the blacks."

I rose to my feet and stood back to admire my work on the old hearth in the kitchen house. I had scrubbed at the bricks all morning. "That will have to do." My voice echoed in the empty room. I wiped soot-smudged hands on the pinafore covering my tan gingham dress before resting them on my hips. As I looked around the place, nostalgia filled me. The old kitchen house was gone, but I would always hold near to my heart the memories Mammy, Mary Grace, and I had made. The old hearth would be the centerpiece of those memories.

The voices of approaching men drew me to the front stoop.

Jones and Pete carried a newly fashioned table Jimmy had built. I stepped out of the way so they could bring it inside, and my sadness deepened. Gone were the character marks etched into the old table. Countless times, I'd sat at the table and poured out my heart to Mammy and Mary Grace, but we'd also shared moments of merriment and bliss. I smiled at a particular memory of when I had hidden from Mammy—something I had done often as a young girl, and lain in wait for her to find me. The day I'd engraved Bowden's and my initials into the planks. The recollection conjured another, when I had stormed out the back door and down to the kitchen house to scramble under the table and scratch away any evidence of the feelings I'd carried for Bowden after he had humiliated me in the schoolyard.

"And to think I married the man," I said to myself.

Jones cast me a perplexed look as they shuffled past me.

Once the table sat in the center of the room, Jones said, "Pete here will build the shelving, and we will get Miss Rita back in here today."

"She will be happy. She has been dreadful while waiting for a functioning kitchen."

Pete smirked, but Jones remained...well, Jones.

"And what of the smokehouse?" I asked.

He removed his hat to scratch his head before flipping it back on. "Week's end, I expect."

"Good. I hope..." My words drifted as I heard the drumming of approaching hoofbeats.

Jones strode past me to the door and stuck his head out. "We have company. Can't get a look at them from here. Best we go see."

Pete hurried off, and Jones walked with me to the front yard, where we stood awaiting the rider's arrival. Jones shielded his eyes in the afternoon sun. "If my eyes aren't lying, it appears to be Sterling."

My heart leaped. "Maybe he brings news from Ben and Bowden."

Jones grunted and kept his eyes aimed at the lane. I scowled at him. Sometimes, I swear, the man had the personality of a bucksaw.

I squinted to get a better look. "Yes, it's Sterling." I fought the urge to run to him and demand to know if he brought letters. I stayed rooted, waiting until he reined his mount to a stop.

"Missus Armstrong," he said with a nod. "How are you today?"

He observed my condition, and I self-consciously smoothed back my hair and brushed at the smears on my pinafore. Becoming aware of my reddened knuckles and chapped hands, I hid them within the folds of the fabric of my dress. "I'm fine, Mr. Sterling. I trust your wife and family fare well." I offered pleasantries, but my gaze drifted to his saddlebag.

"We all are good, given the circumstances. We long for our son's return and do what we can to help the folks around here and our boys on the front lines."

"Yes, something we all must continue to do," I said, and hurriedly asked, "What brings you to Livingston?" I didn't give him time to answer. "Has any mail gotten through?"

He gave a soft chuckle. "Indeed there has, and I got some from your menfolk."

I glanced at Jones and let out a squeal. All modesty left me, and I rushed forward. "Please, let me see." I stood eagerly beside his horse while he dug through his saddlebag.

"Here you go." He held out a bundle of envelopes.

I grabbed the bundle and shuffled through to find an envelope addressed to Whitney from Knox, and another for me from Bowden. "There is no word from my uncle?" A knot formed in my chest.

"I'm afraid that is all I was given. I'm sorry."

I dropped my gaze to regard the envelopes through blurred vision and tore open Bowden's letter. I scanned his ghastly scrawl.

My dearest wife,

I hope this letter finds you all well. My heart longs to be in your company and to hold you in my arms again. To smell your sweet perfume and to feel your lips on mine. Until that day, I hold to the memory of our last night together.

Heat rushed over my body, and I angled away from the men as I hungrily read every word.

The days are long, and the death around us daunting. We all long to return home. As expected, Ben has been assigned to Medical for General Beauregard, and last I heard, they marched to Virginia along the Bull Run River. Knox and I have been stationed together under General Johnston's command in the newly formed Confederate army. Knox's humor has made the days livable. He misses Whitney, as I do you.

A post carrier is heading out tomorrow, and my letter will go with him. I pray it reaches you.

Sending you all my love,

your loving husband

I folded the letter and held it to my heart. He was well.

"Well, what does he say?" Mr. Sterling leaned forward on the neck of his horse.

"That my uncle serves in Medical under the command of General Beauregard. The last Bowden heard, they marched to Virginia along the Bull Run River."

Mr. Sterling straightened, and triumph shone on his weathered face. "Reckon he was a part of the attack on General McDowell. They defeated the Federal soldiers and sent them rushing back to Washington with their tails between their legs.

From what I heard, onlookers brought picnic baskets to relish the day's events."

I snorted with disgust. "As though the lives taken didn't matter. Some folks have no shame."

"We are at war, Mrs. Armstrong. Have you forgotten?" Mr. Sterling arched a brow.

"Of course not. How can I forget?" I held up the bundle of letters and shook them at the repairs still underway on the main house. I centered my attention on him. "But I can't help but grieve for all our countrymen and the loss we will face as a nation if this war continues much longer."

"It has already gone on longer than expected," Jones said. "One can only hope it is worth the fight."

"The South will never fall." Mr. Sterling straightened, pride alight in his eyes. "We will give the North a good licking and remind them that without the South and our cotton, their factories and goods wouldn't exist."

"Perhaps we can come together and form a new future, one that isn't built on the backs of slavery," I said.

Mr. Sterling snapped his attention back to me. "Be careful, Mrs. Armstrong. Talk like that will get you hung around these parts."

Jones shifted and gave me a grunt of warning.

"I'm just stating that perhaps there is a better way we can do things here in the South. I am a proud Southern woman with love for the South and my home. But I carry a vision of a better future—a more honorable one."

"I have been a friend of your family for years. Your parents and grandparents have a name for the good they have done around these parts. Your granddad and Charles, as well as your husband, are known as powerful slave owners. But I've always known you took after your mother, and her beliefs caused folks to alienate her, no matter the good deeds she accomplished. I'm not a rich man and never owned a slave of my own. My loyalty to your family remains, but so does my belief in the ways of the South. I caution you to tread lightly with what you say. Don't paint yourself in the same picture your mother did in the eyes of folks around here, or death will surely follow such talk."

My heart thumped faster, and I inclined my head in respect. "I heed your warning."

He eyed me with unease and concern, but instead of pressing the matter further, he tipped his hat. "I have other mail to deliver and folks yearning for letters from their menfolk. Good day, Mrs. Armstrong. Jones."

"Thank you," I said. "You bring us hope."

He waved and turned his mount to gallop back down the lane.

Jones and I stood without speaking until Mr. Sterling rode out the gate. Then I turned to look at him and found him eyeing me. "What?" I frowned.

He scratched at the gray scruff shadowing his face and shook his head as though exasperated. "You've become lax in your guard. War or not, this is not a time to let your defenses down." He pointed at the lane. "And a friend or not, we need to tread carefully because you heard the man—he is a proud Southern man who believes in owning slaves. And no matter the man your father was before he changed his ways, we can't allow others to find out what things were like here before the war and before the McCoys attacked. Or have you forgotten you still harbor a runaway?" He gestured to Big John, walking across the work yard toward the forge.

I knew Jones was right. Had I become debilitated in Bowden's absence and since the onset of the war?

"I've stood by your family because I believe in your cause," Jones continued.

I fumed inside. For a man of few words, he sure had a lot to say on the matter. "All right!" I threw my hands in the air. "I heed your warning."

"Good," he said. "Now, if you will excuse me, ma'am, I'll get back to the fields. The land won't work itself."

I pressed my lips together. "No, indeed."

I regarded his back as he walked away before heaving a sigh and looking back at the gate. "Let's hope I didn't add any suspicions," I said to the bird perched on a rosebush at the end of the stone path. The critter tilted its head at me as though trying to understand.

"Do I see Mr. Sterling riding off?" Pippa exited from the house dressed in a yellow day dress and apron.

I glanced down at the letters clutched at my side, and guilt washed over me. She longed to hear from Ben as much as I had, but it broke my heart to tell her no word had come. "Yes." I strode up the path and mounted the stairs.

"Did he bring word from Ben and Bowden?" Optimism gleamed in her blue eyes.

I gulped at the thickening in my throat. "He did."

"Well, come now. Let me see." She nodded at the letters I had instinctively tried to hide behind my back.

"There is no word from him."

Her hand dropped, and her brows dipped. "Oh…"

"Bowden says that he's stationed somewhere else. But don't lose heart, I'm sure his letters will arrive soon." Hollowness and uncertainty echoed in my voice.

"I see." Her voice trembled, and she avoided meeting my gaze. "I'm happy for you."

"Pippa…" I took a step forward, wanting to wipe away the pain on her face.

"I'm all right. If you will excuse me." She whirled and darted back into the house, and my heart dropped.

Tears caught in my throat, and I wandered to the porch swing and sat down with a heaviness that sent it swaying. I gripped the chain to steady myself and ease the movement.

I opened Bowden's letter and reread it through damp eyes.

Why did something I longed for, for so long, feel so wrong? The answer lay within my heart. I had grown to care deeply for Pippa and wanted nothing more than a letter from Ben to soothe her aching heart. I, too, wished to hear from him, but I had my husband's letter for encouragement.

The front door opened, and someone stepped out. I quickly folded the letter and wiped away my tears.

"Missus Willow, you all right?" Tillie said.

"I'm fine."

"Did somepin' bad happen?" She crept forward.

"No. I received a letter from Bowden. But no word came from my uncle."

"Is dat why Missus Hendricks gone up to her room and asked not to be disturbed?"

My shoulders slumped. "I reckon so."

"So I'm guessing dat is why you crying and luking lak someone done gone and died?"

I nodded and bit my lip to quell the trembling.

"You count your blessings, Missus. Ain't no need for you to feel sad. I knowed Missus Hendricks wouldn't want you feeling bad either." She offered a kind smile. Although nobody could fill the void left in my life by Mary Grace, Tillie had come close. She was as brilliant as my dearest friend and had given me so much comfort in the years since she had become my handmaiden.

"Thank you, Tillie. You truly are an angel." I stood with the desire to embrace her, but Jones's warning ran through my head.

She grinned and dipped her head. "I don't know 'bout dat, but I jus' happy I could ease some of your sadness. We got 'nuf of dat 'round here."

"You are a good soul, and regardless of the situation that casts me as your mistress, I think of you with fondness. Perhaps one day, when this is all over, and if the North is victorious, you will consider me a friend. I hope you can forgive me for my family's wrongs against you and those you love." I eyed her earnestly.

"Ef a day come when I a slave no more, I give thanks as much as de next slave. But I won't become my own jailor, imprisoned by hate of de wrongs done to me. No, sah. I ain't fixing to remain a prisoner of de past either. And et bes' you don't become one shaped by your own guilt."

The power and passion in her words hit me straight in the heart, and I gasped. She regarded me with compassion before she turned and returned inside.

I strode to the railing and looked out over the front grounds, captivated by the wisdom in her words. Folks were fools to think Tillie and her people were any less intelligent than us. Perhaps it was time we learned from them. Had I been a slave, would I have extended the same decency and empathy Tillie had to me? I hoped so, but self-doubt swelled.

I whispered a prayer to the heavens. "Make me a vessel of light in the darkness that encompasses this world. Show me a way to help others. Help me right the wrongs of my family." Like an embrace from the angels, a warmth cloaked my shoulders, renewing my spirit and profound devotion to erasing the prejudices inflicted on the Negroes.

"Parker," I said as he rounded the corner of the house.

"Yessum?"

"Can you have Jimmy prepare a buggy? I have to pay the Tuckers' farm a visit."

His eyes widened with hopefulness. "Yessum, straightaway." He turned to shuffle off.

"Parker," I called out.

He braced and turned back, his dark eyes searching my face.

"I will require a driver. It isn't safe for a lady to be out on the roads alone." His yearning pulled at the corners of my mouth. "I know a certain young lady who would be delighted if you accompanied me."

He let out a yelp. "I dying to see Kimie."

I laughed merrily. "Very well, then, make it swift. We will leave as soon as the buggy is prepared."

"Yes, Missus Armstrong." He whirled to hobble off but spun back, and while walking backward, said, "Thank you, Missus. Thank you kindly."

I nodded and waited until he disappeared around the house before going inside.

CHAPTER Thirteen

PARKER BOUNCED ON THE BUGGY SEAT NEXT TO ME AS WE VENTURED along the road to the Tuckers' homestead. I studied the passing countryside while securely gripping the letter from Knox between gloved hands. *May the letter bring Whitney comfort,* I thought before my stomach knotted with the recollection of Pippa's disheartenment. Before my guilt could take me on a journey, Parker's voice brought me back to the present.

"Wagon coming."

I swung my attention back to the road and squinted to get a better view. "It appears to be a lone woman."

Parker's grip on the reins eased, and he steered the buggy to one side. "Don't luk lak she in any hurry."

I noted the slumped shoulders of the woman, whose floppy straw bonnet sheltered her features. As she drew near, I recognized Mrs. Davenport. I had met the woman at social events in Charleston. Her husband had died last year, leaving her with five boys. The oldest, who was barely eighteen, had joined the Southern Militia at the start of the war.

"Stop the buggy." I touched Parker's arm. "Good day, Mrs. Davenport." I offered her a cheerful smile before noticing her puffy eyes and the evident misery in her face.

She reined her team to a halt. "Hardly a day of any good," she said with a voice empty of all emotion.

"Has something happened? How are you and the children getting on?"

She swallowed hard, and tears welled in her dark eyes before she nudged her head at the back of the wagon. "My Jacob is in the back."

My hand went to my throat. "Oh, dear." I strained to peer into the bed of the wagon. "Is he injured?"

"Dead," she said dryly.

I bit back a gasp and snapped my gaze back to her face. "No..." My words ended with a groan.

"He was severely wounded, they told me. But by the time the doc got to him, he was gone. There isn't enough help to go around. Our menfolk win battles only to die in the street outside wayward hospitals. It doesn't seem just." The agony in her eyes shattered my heart.

"My condolences to you. If there is anything I can do..." I let my words drift as I struggled with the right thing to say.

"There isn't anything we womenfolk can do but sit and wait for news. And when the information comes we breathe a little easier, or we do what needs doing and collect the bodies of our boys." Her voice trembled. "My Robert has been stomping ground, seeking to join his brother in the war. He turned sixteen last month, and I'm afraid I won't be able to hold him back for much longer."

Lost for words and tears gathering, I nodded my understanding.

"Well, I best get him on home and lay him to rest next to his pa."

"Go with God," I said.

Her hands moved to slap the reins, but she paused and leveled an austere look on me. "I will not bury another member of my family in my time." Determination registered in her eyes. "If you want to do something, aid our army in whatever means possible." She directed her gaze back to the road and urged the team forward.

Parker continued on, and I lowered my gaze to the letter I held with trembling hands. I blinked off tears and remained silent for the rest of the journey.

The Tucker place sat in the embrace of a meadow. The quaint, two-story white house had a partial wrap-around piazza and black shutters woven with climbing Carolina jessamine. The charm of the home stopped there. Whitney had never been one for gardening, and with no one to work the land but Kimie and her, the grass and weeds had grown to encompass the front steps and overtake the walkway. A small barn sat to the right of the house next to the kitchen house. Chickens scurried around the front yard. A horse in the pasture stood eyeing us, and in a nearby field cows lifted their heads from grazing.

Parker reined the buggy to a halt, hopped down, and came to assist me. "Et luks a bit unkempt, don't et?" he said as I placed my hand in his.

"It does." I stepped out.

"Ef et all right wid you, Missus, maybe I can give Missus Tucker a hand and cut de grass and weeds."

"That is very kind of you. I'm sure the Tuckers would be grateful."

"Parker. Willow," Kimie cried, and we turned to survey the grounds in search of her.

"There she be." Parker pointed toward the barn as Kimie turned to secure the door before racing toward us.

Face pearled with sweat, yet radiating delight at our arrival, she wiped bloodied hands on her apron as she came to stand before us. "What a lovely surprise." She looked at me before favoring Parker with a shy smile.

"I bring word from Knox," I said. "Where is your sister?"

Her face grew serious. "She fell ill a few days ago and only today left her room to sit in the parlor for a spell while I tended to Daisy. She has been laboring all night. Gave birth to a healthy calf this morning."

"Is there anything you can't do," I said with a smile. I admired the bright young lady for her many talents and her eagerness to take on any task without fear.

She blushed, and I patted her on the shoulder. "I'll let the two of you catch up while I see to Whitney." I left them and headed inside, where I removed my bonnet and shawl before walking down the hallway to the parlor.

From the threshold, I regarded Whitney. Dressed in a night-gown and night-robe, she sat in an armchair, looking paler than usual. "Whitney?" I entered the room.

She turned her gaze from the window to me. "I thought I heard someone ride up. It's good to see you." She tried to smile.

"Kimie says you've been unwell."

"Yes. Quite a sight, aren't I? I got a glimpse of myself in the looking glass when she helped me come downstairs. I look like I'm at death's door. If Lucille could see me now, she'd never let me forget it."

"Since when do you care what Lucille thinks?" I said with a huff and took a seat to her right. "I have something that will wash that melancholy right out of you."

"Oh? What's that?"

I retrieved the letter from my velvet drawstring handbag. "A letter from Knox."

"Really?" Tears welled in her eyes, and she tried to sit up straighter.

"Indeed," I said with a grin and held out the letter.

She took it with trembling hands, and the painstakingly slow way she opened the envelope spoke to her weakness.

I sat quietly as she read the letter, noting she read it a second time before lowering it to her lap. "Nothing came from Jack?" she asked, yearning filling her face.

"No, and nothing from Ben."

"Pippa must be disheartened." Sympathy shone in her green eyes.

"Very." I thought of what Tillie had said about Pippa retiring to her room and requesting not to be disturbed.

"My husband isn't much for words. Has more a gift of the gab, but I'm thankful he wrote." She looked peaceful. "I knew I would miss him, but I never guessed to what extent."

"Look at you—the dedicated and doting wife. Who would ever have thought?" I said with a chuckle.

Her pale lips parted in a soft smile. "And the fact I find contentment in it is even more bizarre."

"At least we know that he and Bowden have each other."

"Yes, that does bring me comfort. Kimie is talking about going in to Charleston to help at the hospital. They require volunteers. I suppose it's about to get more desolate around here. We can't keep up the house, the land, and the animals together, and it will be almost impossible with her gone, but I don't want to discourage her. And with the length of time this war is carrying on, they need all able bodies." She looked to the window.

I followed her gaze to where Parker balanced on his cane while swinging a scythe at the grass.

Sadness reflected in her eyes. "When she goes, I won't be the only one who misses her."

"He jumped at the chance to come. He is a good man. I hope one day he and Kimie can have the future they desire," I said.

"Such a future would be hard and not easily obtained in the South." Whitney had come to accept the love between the pair, and I dared believe she had grown fond of Parker.

"In the South or another part of the country, I don't believe their union will be welcomed. But I believe in their love for each other and know they will overcome whatever comes their way."

"Yes, well. Time will tell," she said, sounding weary.

"If Kimie goes to Charleston, you could come and stay at Livingston until the war is over. It would be like old times." I grasped at the chance to have her near and safe under the same roof.

She chuckled. "Only this time I'm married, with a farm to run."

"We could bring the animals to Livingston. It's not like your stock is plentiful."

"True, and I'm glad Knox didn't make the purchase of twenty

cattle he intended to make before the attack on Fort Sumter, or I'd find myself in a fine mess."

"Perhaps you could hire a farmhand."

She rubbed an ache in her neck. "I can't afford to hire anyone."

"With the scarcity of our numbers, I have no one to lend."

She eyed me with a defeated expression. "We awake to a different world, don't we?"

"Yes," I said.

Her shoulders slumped, and she leaned back in the chair. "I wish I could offer you refreshments, but I'm afraid I would collapse with the effort."

"I am fine. What can I do to help you?"

"Would you be so kind as to help me bathe and wash my hair?"

"Of course." I stood.

Once bathed and dressed in fresh nightclothes, Whitney sat at her vanity while I combed her hair. "Do you think our men will return home?" She looked at me in the mirror.

I stopped in mid stroke. "What do you mean?"

"I worry that the war will make us widows."

"You mustn't talk like that," I said, more sternly than I'd intended.

"You've always been a dreamer," she said with a roll of her eyes.

"A practical one, I might add."

She shook her head in disapproval. "Always choosing to tread this life with your head in the clouds. If one can plan for the worst outcome, then life doesn't seem so frightening."

"Maybe, but if I think of the what-ifs, I may lose my mind. Although the responsibilities at Livingston have lessened, the burden seems more significant. I believe the war will change the South as we know it, but I hope to have a home and land for my family to come home to. If not, what did they fight for?"

"All we have is this land right here. And all thanks to you." The tautness in her face faded, replaced by a softer expression.

"This war just goes to prove that life holds no certainty. You can forge the best-laid plans and still come up with nothing."

"There is truth in that." She patted my hand as I set the comb on the vanity. "Now, if you don't mind, would you help me to bed."

After she lay back against the pillows, she smiled at me. "Thank you, Willow. You indeed are my dearest friend."

"That's because no others would put up with your sass."

Her eyes smiled as weariness took over. "Perhaps, but I care not for a bushel of friends. Other women grate on my nerves."

And you theirs, I thought with amusement. "Perhaps I'm the fool who puts up with you," I said lightly as I adjusted the covers over her. "You rest, and I will go downstairs and tidy up. Then I'll see how I can assist Kimie while Parker finishes up."

CHAPTER
Fourteen

Amelie

WINTER HAD COME TO NEW YORK, AND I SHIVERED UNDER the heavy blankets draped across my lap. I observed the congested streets from the carriage window while Zeke sat next to me, reading the newspaper.

"In President Lincoln's inaugural address, he proclaimed his desire to keep the Union intact but not to end slavery. He bans the blacks from enlisting and declares the fugitives as contrabands of war..."

He continued, but my attention shifted to a feeble woman weaving down the boardwalk, flailing her bare arms and gripping passersby. I tensed before leaning forward in my seat to pull back the velvet drape. Unkempt gray hair hung down her back, and she wore the same clothes she had on the day she visited the brothel.

Mother? I pressed my face against the glass to get a better look as a man gave her a shove, and she went down hard. I winced, and my stomach knotted.

"Stop the carriage." I struck the roof.

The carriage drew to a stop.

"What is it?" Zeke lowered the newspaper, concern gleaming in his eyes.

I ignored him and threw open the door.

"Amelie?" Zeke folded the newspaper.

Without answering him, I disembarked. My gaze pinned on

the man and his fancy lady friend as they hovered over the fallen woman. I crossed the street to the boardwalk.

Zeke called after me, but I didn't stop.

"Go back to the slums where you belong," the man said before kicking at the form on the ground.

Another passerby spat on her, and a fierceness charged through me. I hurried my steps as the man drew back his boot to strike again.

"Enough!" My voice reverberated.

The couple looked in my direction. Once I stood in front of them, I looked to my mother, where she lay curled into a fetal position, her arms shielding her face from the next blow. I gawked from her to the man and took a second look. I recognized him. He visited my establishment on the weekends.

He gulped and looked from me to the petite blond woman holding his arm.

"Is this your husband?" I directed my attention to her. She was stunning and appeared to have all a man would desire in a woman, but unfortunately, that wasn't enough for some. I had seen my fair share of men like her husband.

She jutted her chin. "Yes; what of it?"

Zeke came to a stop beside me and clutched my arm.

I gritted my teeth. "Get her up and into the carriage."

Zeke hurried to help my mother up while I turned my attention back to the couple. "Where does your husband tell you he goes on the weekends?"

Confusion shone in her eyes, and her tone was sharp. "What business is it of yours?"

I waved a hand in annoyance. "Let me introduce myself. I'm Madame Amelie, owner of a brothel that your husband frequents every weekend."

She lifted a delicate hand to her throat. I looked her husband directly in the eyes and delivered, with much satisfaction, my own kick to his ribs. "His favorite girl is Beth—a lovely little creature.

I'd guess her to be ten years your junior." I returned my gaze to his wife, who stood with her mouth agape and her flesh ashen.

The man gripped his wife's arm and started blabbering a defense. I spun and marched back to the carriage, where Zeke stood observing me.

"Am I to believe you know this woman?"

"Yes, she is my mother. Instruct the driver to take us home." I boarded the carriage and took a seat across from her. I coughed and removed my handkerchief from the cuff of my sleeve to cover my nose. The smell of her took my breath away. She sat gawking at me, but her eyes had changed since I had seen her last. They appeared glazed and empty, as though the spirit inside her body had fled. Ugly sores spotted her face and exposed flesh.

"What is wrong with her?" Zeke had seated himself beside me. He gagged at her odor.

"I don't know." Tears caught in my throat.

"Food?" Mother held out a trembling hand. "Please, ma'am. Just a small bite to eat."

I nodded.

"Bless you," she said as though she understood, but her next words alerted me to what I already knew in my heart. "Food? Please, ma'am. Just a small bite to eat."

I turned and buried my face into Zeke's shoulder. He cupped my head with a hand and held me while I wept. How could a woman who had been so influential in my youth have become pathetic and vulnerable?

When we returned to the brothel, Zeke helped me from the carriage before assisting my mother.

"Here, hold her upright while I pay the driver," he said.

I shook my head and shrank back. I didn't want to touch her, let alone help her.

"Do you expect me to let her lie in the street?" The firmness in his tone snapped me from the panic rising within me, but still, I couldn't move closer. "Amelie! For the love of God."

"All right." My jaw tensed. I stepped in and placed an arm around her thin waist. The smell of her was no less potent in the fresh air. She stood shivering, teeth chattering.

Zeke paid the driver and moved in to assist me. "Let's get her around the building and up the back stairs."

Inside, my mother slumped in to Zeke, and he was forced to gather her up and carry her. To my relief, we met no one in the corridors as we made our way to my suite. I hurried ahead to open the door. My living quarters consisted of a small parlor and bedchamber.

"Where do you want me to put her?" Zeke asked as he stepped inside.

"On the settee, I suppose." But as he strode forward, I said, "Wait."

He spun to look at me with annoyance.

I dashed into my chamber and grabbed some linens before returning to the parlor. I spread the linens over the settee, and he laid her down.

"What now?" He stood back to observe her.

"I don't know." I rubbed my hands on the sides of my day gown. "I suppose we will need to bathe her and send for a doctor."

"Why are you doing this?" he said. "After everything she has done to you."

I shrugged. An emptiness settled in my chest as I turned and left the suite. Why was I tending her? The last thing she deserved was my help.

"Luther." I entered the empty grand parlor to find him fluffing the pillows on a gold velvet settee.

He stood and turned to regard me. "Madame?"

"Send for a doctor.

"You." I gestured at one of my girls. "Get hot water, and have my tub brought to my suite."

She frowned but hurried off to do as requested.

"Beth," I said to another. "Ask the cook to prepare a tray of food and see it's delivered. And someone air this place out. It smells dreadful in here." The scent of my mother lingered in my nose and most likely had seeped into my clothing. "And see that you are ready to entertain by ten today," I finished.

"But we don't usually open until noon," a girl protested.

"Yes, well, the new group of soldiers seem to require more attention than usual patrons do," I said over my shoulder before walking from the room.

❦ CHAPTER ❦
Fifteen

Willow
December, 1861

AFTER TAKING PORT ROYAL SOUND, THOUSANDS OF UNION
soldiers disembarked onto South Carolina soil and moved
on to Beaufort. The Federal soldiers reveled in their
victory, and the North praised Lincoln for his political win.

In the days that followed, Whitney decided to move to
Livingston until the war ended, for which we prayed each day,
and for the safe return of the menfolk. We aided the Women's
Societies that had formed across the country to assist in the war
efforts. At Livingston, we did our part to cook and sew for the
soldiers and delivered blankets, uniforms, food, and letters to lift
their spirits. My heart called for me to leave Livingston and take
my position on the front.

It was late evening, and the fire crackled and snapped in the
hearth in the parlor. I lowered the uniform I had been darning
and regarded Pippa and Whitney, who sat across from me. The
encounter with Mrs. Davenport on the road some time back had
never left my mind; "If you want to do something, aid our army
in whatever means possible," she'd said.

I heaved a sigh. "I've been thinking…"

Whitney glanced up and pursed her lips.

"What is it?" Pippa lowered the garment she was mending
and offered her full attention.

"Why does my stomach clench when you get to thinking?"

Whitney adjusted herself in her chair before gesturing for me to continue.

"Makeshift hospitals are being erected all over the country, and with Kimie gone to help at the wayside hospital in Charleston, it has inspired me to do our part to help too."

"What do you call this?" Whitney held up a Confederate coat before lowering it and holding out her pierced fingers for my inspection.

"This is hardly good enough. We must do more. Sitting here waiting for word will send me to an early grave. Besides, I can't get poor Mrs. Davenport out of my mind. What if it was Jack, or one of our husbands in the back of that wagon?" I said. "To think of our loved ones waiting for a doctor's care that may never come… What do you say about us turning Livingston into our own wayward hospital?"

Whitney thrust her hands at the heavens. "Oh, how the tides have turned."

I frowned at her, uncertain of what she referenced.

"Your family has spent decades seeking to protect Livingston and their cause from outsiders. Now you want to invite Confederate soldiers to lodge here."

"That's exactly what I intend to do." I squared my shoulders. "Our endeavors in the cause have come to a halt for the time being. There are too few of us to move folks along the road to freedom, due to the war. And, with their masters away, slaves just leave, and little attempt is made to retrieve them. This means that, at the moment, we've nothing to hide and have no cause for concern. Livingston has plenty of room to care for the wounded. We can't sit idly by." I pushed to my feet. "Livingston will become a wayside hospital to *all* in need. Tomorrow I will set things in motion. I hope I can count on support from both of you."

"You can count on me." Pippa offered me a tender smile. "I'm sure Isabella and Callie will also offer their assistance."

I exited the parlor and walked to the foyer with Whitney following on my heels.

"I don't know the first thing about nursing. That's Kimie's forte," she whined.

I turned to face her and gripped her forearms. "We will figure this out together."

"I hope you're right, and we are making the right decision."

"Can one ever be certain?" I studied her.

"I suppose not." She rubbed a hand over the nape of her neck. "All hopes of this war ending swiftly have vanished. I fear the months will turn into years. It has been nine months since we've seen our men, and who knows how much longer we will endure."

"Your concern is also my own." I gave her hand a gentle squeeze before fetching my shawl. I wrapped the garment around my shoulders and stepped out onto the front veranda.

The scent of smoke hung heavy in the air; in the direction of Charleston, gray billows of smoke rippled across the sky. My heart struck faster.

"That can't be good," Whitney said.

I turned to look at her grave face. "What do you suppose is happening?" I returned my gaze to the horizon.

She shivered and drew her shawl closer. "I'm afraid to find out."

That night Whitney and I never retired to our beds but drifted off in the rockers in front of the fireplace, in case word came of what destruction had overtaken Charleston.

Two days later, Jones returned from delivering uniforms and food to General Robert E. Lee and his troops in Charleston. I noticed him coming down the lane as I entered the front yard carrying two water pails from the well. He wasn't alone. He rode alongside a buggy, and my gaze turned to the driver, then the passenger seated beside him—a willowy black lady wearing a red head rag. Uriah and Jane? What were they doing here?

A horse tied to the back trotted behind the carriage. Chickens clucked from their cage on the back seat, next to the goat that bleated its distress.

I lowered the pails and darted forward. "Jane? Uriah? What has happened?"

"The townhouse is gone." Exhaustion and soot besmirched her face.

"A fire engulfed the city," Jones said. "The Cathedral of Saint John and the South Carolina Institute Hall are no more. Hundreds of other buildings in its path are all gone."

"Good God." I gripped the side of the buggy to steady myself.

After the initial shock dissipated, I glanced up at Jane. "Where will you go?"

She cast a nervous glance at Jones. "Mr. Jones…well, he—"

"I told them that you may put them up here," Jones said.

"Oh," I said. "Yes, of course." I patted Jane's knee and swiftly pushed away my apprehension at the thought of two more mouths to feed. "Welcome to Livingston." I wielded cheerfulness when I felt anything but.

"Bless you, Mrs. Armstrong," she said as I stepped back.

Uriah drove the buggy to the carriage stone, and Jane gathered the sides of her dove-gray cotton dress and stepped down.

"Uriah, if you will follow me, we will unhitch the buggy and tend to the horse."

"Yes, sir, Mr. Jones."

After the buggy had pulled away, I looped my arm in Jane's and led her toward the front veranda.

She gawked at the house with a mixture of awe and disbelief. "I always wondered why you loved this place so much. I can see why." She twisted to gaze at the pond and the swans, then at the ancient oak trees and house. "A palace fit for royalty. Are you a princess, and we didn't know it?" She chuckled softly.

My face heated, and I dipped my head. "I assure you I'm not, or I would have had guards to defend the grounds in my absence," I said soberly.

She noted the boarded windows and the reminders of the McCoys' attack that marred the grounds and home. Her footsteps stilled, and she turned to eye me with concerned, dark eyes. "How are you faring, with Mr. Armstrong away?"

"We are doing the best we can. Have you heard from your son?"

"I have." Her face turned grim. "He has moved his family north and hopes one day to enlist with the Union," she said, her tone critical.

I had known her for as long as I could recall, but I'd never formed a relationship with her like I had with the folks at Livingston. "Do I sense disapproval at your son's decisions?"

"Yes," she said with more sharpness than I'd ever heard in her voice. "The boy is a Southerner. His loyalty should be to the South. He has no more sense than a slave."

My mouth unhinged, but I quickly snapped it shut. Perhaps Jane and Uriah residing at Livingston was a bad idea. Her opinion of her son's desire to enlist with the Federals left me perplexed. What side of the war had she moored her loyalty on? My nerves thrummed.

I'd spent all my years running Livingston with an eye to protecting the cause my parents and I had fought for. I'd assumed, on Jane and Uriah's arrival, that I embraced allies, but now I wasn't so sure. I suppose I had assumed that, because she was black, she would hold the same values as me. That we would share the same belief that no human deserved to be owned by another. That we were all equal and one in the eyes of God.

Maybe I was reading too much into it. Maybe her words were kindled by a mother's disappointment, was all.

"Are you all right, Mrs. Armstrong? You look pale." She touched my shoulder.

"Yes." I fell back on pleasantries. "I will ask Miss Rita to fix us some refreshments. You must meet Pippa. My uncle and her married, you know."

"Did they really? Well, what splendid news." Her delighted smile gleamed. "I would love to lay eyes on the lovely creature that finally secured the heart of the handsome Mr. Hendricks."

I laughed as we ascended the steps and strode into the house to find Whitney and Pippa. But I was concerned over what Jane and Uriah's staying at Livingston would mean to us all.

∽ CHAPTER ∽
Sixteen

WORRY HAD PINCHED MAMMY'S BROW WHEN I INFORMED HER of my decision to turn Livingston into a wayside hospital. She hadn't protested but quickly excused herself, and in the days that followed, kept herself occupied.

The morning the army wagon transporting injured soldiers turned up the lane, heated voices erupted in the corridor.

"I'll be right back," I said. Leaving Whitney and Pippa to finish preparing the cots lining the emptied parlor, I went to see what all the fuss was about.

In the foyer, I found Big John comforting a fretful Mammy. His eyes met mine over the top of her head, where she stood with her face buried in his chest.

"Mammy, what in heaven's name is the problem?" Concern pulled at my heart, and I hurried down the corridor. I placed a hand on her shoulder but was taken back when she shook her head and angled her body away from me. Perplexed by her brush-off, I regarded Big John with wide eyes.

I retraced the previous day and the morning in my head, contemplating every conversation, wanting earnestly to understand. I recalled how she had roamed the hallways, mumbling to herself and whispering prayers of protection. I felt a twinge of guilt as I realized, too busy with preparing for the soldiers' arrival, I had pushed away her discomfort over the situation. How could I have been so insensitive to her needs? My decision to shift the house into a hospital had disrupted the sanctuary she had forged around herself. But what choice had I had?

"Mammy." I touched her elbow. "Please look at me." My voice quivered with my need for her to hear me out. "Please."

She shifted, revealing puffy eyes welling with fresh tears, and lifted her chin.

"I'm sorry my decision has made you uncomfortable." I gripped her shoulders. "You're safe here. I will never let anyone harm you. You must believe me."

She lifted the corner of her apron and dabbed at her eyes. "Sometimes things are out of our control. No matter de intent you set. Ef a man gits an aching, he takes what he wants."

I considered the aging woman before me and the gray halo that captured more of her dark tresses with each passing year. Although the beautiful woman of her youth had faded, the memories of her abuse at her master's hands had not.

"That time has passed," I said with the utmost tenderness. "Mary Grace is no longer here and requiring your protection. You must release the obligation to protect you both. There's no need to look over your shoulder anymore."

"Missus Armstrong is right." Big John gave me a look of appreciation. "Masa Adams dead, and he and no man ever gwine to hurt you in dat way again. Ain't got no reason to hold on to dat fear no more."

Dawning realization softened Mammy's face, though she frowned before her tension eased. It was as though the anxiety and fear she had carried all her life had dissipated with this new understanding. "Suppose you right," she said with a sniffle.

I smiled and stroked her arm. "Together we will manage this new situation. Remember, the gentlemen are Southerners, and we are offering them help. They have no cause to harm us. We are in this together." I looked from her to Big John. "We will provide them with the care they need and then send them on their way."

Mammy nodded and took a deep breath before rolling back her shoulders. "We do dis your way, angel gal."

"Good." I gave her a reassuring smile. "Big John, I know you are our biggest asset with your skills in medicine, but due to your status elsewhere, you must stay away from the house."

"I know, Missus. I mighty grateful, what you have done for me, and I ain't luking to cause you no harm." The sincerity in his dark eyes provided me with much-needed comfort.

"Of course. Having you here has put a smile on Mammy's face. And made her almost...sweet."

He chuckled, and to my delight, Mammy did too. He wrapped her shoulders with an arm, and my heart swelled. God had been smiling on us the day He guided Big John to us, and I would take every precaution to see the two were never separated again.

"Here they come," Whitney said.

I gripped Mammy's wrist for support as Pippa and Whitney dashed from the parlor to join us. I strode to the doors, paused for a moment to adjust the white pinafore covering my navy cotton dress, then, squeezing my eyes tightly shut, I whispered a prayer before seizing the doorknobs.

"Everyone ready?" I cast a glance over my shoulder.

"Ready as we ever be," Mammy said.

Whitney and Pippa returned nervous nods.

"Come then, let us greet our guests." I opened the doors, and my entourage and I stepped out onto the veranda. I descended the stairs and walked to the end of the path to await the wagon.

A glance at the flowerbeds in desperate need of care filled me with dismay at the grounds' condition. Then I admonished myself guiltily. Men were risking their lives every day, and I concerned myself with the lackluster appearance of my home. Taking a deep breath, I cracked my neck side to side and prepared myself for the task at hand.

A soldier of perhaps thirty pulled the team to a stop. Another man seated next to him jumped down to assist the others in the wagon bed. The driver tipped his hat. "Afternoon, ma'am." He climbed down and strode toward me. "The Southern army and the South are grateful for your willingness to open your home to help." His gaze rolled over the house and the grounds. "It appears this war hasn't been easy for you."

"Northern militia attacked us at the outset of the attack on Fort Sumter. Because of the war and our menfolk's absence, it's been hard to keep the fields tilled and planted. The maintenance of the grounds has become less of a concern."

"As with most across the country, I would expect." He pressed his lips together, and his pale-blue eyes reflected sympathy. "Let me introduce myself. I'm Lieutenant Williams, and this is Private Cooper."

I glanced at the soldier standing at the back of the wagon, awaiting orders.

Lieutenant Williams looked past me. "You." He gestured at Pete as he rounded the corner of the house. "Come give Private Cooper a hand with the men."

"Yes, sah." Pete hurried to oblige.

The lieutenant looked at me. "Do you mind showing me where the men will stay?"

"Certainly." I graced him with a smile while, inside, my heart pounded faster. I swerved and walked toward the house.

The lieutenant's boots clicked on the stone path behind me. As we strode past Whitney and Pippa, he paused. I came to a halt. "Ladies, how do you do?" He bowed his head.

"We are well, Lieutenant," Whitney said, her tone lacking all warmth.

I gulped and openly gawked at her.

His brow dipped at her standoffishness. "Do I detect a Northern accent?"

"Yes." Whitney lifted her chin and stood with unbending pride. "I was born and raised in the North. I lived there until my father purchased a plantation here."

"I see." He took a long look at her. "I hope we have no reason for concern about your loyalties to the South."

"This is not my war, sir."

I braced as her expression grew determined. Whitney would back down to no one when it came to her convictions, but we had no time for her pride or honor.

"No?" He removed his hat and arched a brow.

"If it were up to the women of this country, we would have figured out another way to balance the need for power."

My fingernails bit into my palms. *For the love of God, be quiet! Has she lost her mind?*

"Is that so?" He bristled before shifting his gaze to Pippa. "What about you, ma'am? Do you share the same beliefs as Miss…" He sent a quick look at Whitney.

"Tucker. Mrs. Tucker. My husband fights for the South."

His consternation grew. "You don't say. Well, I hope his fight isn't for nothing. A traitor within his own household would be too much for most men to bear." He returned his attention to Pippa and awaited her reply.

Pippa gave him a warm smile. "I am here to serve your soldiers in whatever way I can."

He tensed when she spoke. "Another foreigner." He swung to face Pete and Private Cooper, who advanced up the path with an injured soldier between them. "Halt!" He lifted a hand to stop them.

Pete froze, and the young, wide-eyed private looked from his superior to each of us womenfolk. The lieutenant spun on his heel to face me. My insides trembled, but I kept my hands lightly clasped before me while every part of me wanted to rebuke Whitney for her foolishness.

"I'm astonished, Mrs. Armstrong," he said, his voice laced with contempt. "When I was told a well-esteemed Southern woman had opened her home to aid the Confederate army, I had no idea we would be concerned about leaving our men in the hands of a Northerner and a Brit."

I inclined my head and replied with a docility that churned my stomach. "We are only women committed to helping our menfolk. Does it matter where we originate? My uncle is a doctor serving Confederate soldiers on the front lines. He is married to Mrs. Hendricks." I gestured at Pippa, who curtsied with the grace of a proper Southern belle, or in her case, an English lady, regardless of her loss of station. "And Mrs. Tucker has been my dearest friend for years. I assure you our intentions are pure of heart. No man in our care will go without. They will receive the care I hope others would offer our menfolk." The sadness that washed over me caught in my throat, and I lifted teary eyes to him.

His Adam's apple bobbed as he swallowed hard. His next words came gentler. "Yes, well. Please forgive me. I don't mean to bring distress. One cannot be too certain, with the spies planted amongst us."

"We understand. Don't we?" I looked past him to Whitney and Pippa.

"Most certainly." Pippa inclined her head.

I arched a brow at Whitney as Lieutenant Williams turned to give her a hard stare.

Whitney curtsied and offered him a fetching smile, like the one she'd presented to Reuben the day he'd ridden in to Livingston seeking slaves to help with the Widow Jensen's homestead. The smile was better served on the officer and left him flustered. I quietly congratulated Whitney's performance and redemption.

The lieutenant lifted a gloved hand and gestured for the private and Pete to continue.

"Now, Mrs. Armstrong, if you will please show me where the men will be staying."

"Of course. Follow me."

As we walked past Mammy, she braced and looked straight ahead. I noted the tension in her jaw. The officer strode past her, never pausing to acknowledge her presence. He opened the door, and I hurried after him.

"This way." I motioned toward the parlor.

He stopped on the threshold and looked at the two rows of cots lining the walls.

"As you can see, we are equipped to house five men in this room," I said. "And if you will follow me—"

I turned and hurried down the corridor to the library. "In here, we can take another six."

He strode along the aisle between the cots without speaking, eyeing every detail of the room. He regarded everything from the boarded window to the scorched walls and ceiling, the aftermath of the torch that had been thrown through the window. He gestured at the walls. "Am I to assume this fire also happened in the attack?"

"Yes. As you can see, we suffered immense devastation here. The cowards advanced while my husband and I were in Charleston."

"The Northern militia would be fools to advance so far south." He eyed me and lifted an eyebrow. "You mystify me, Mrs. Armstrong."

I tensed. "Why is that?"

"Not only by the company you keep, but also your claim that the Northern militia invaded your plantation."

"I don't know what you want me to say. The men wore Northern militia uniforms. My uncle and the slaves did their best to defend Livingston, but we suffered a great loss that night. Many of our slaves were killed." The anger I felt toward Reuben McCoy kindled in my chest.

"Your slaves defended the place?"

"Yes."

His brow furrowed. "An odd loyalty for niggers, and slaves at that."

"Livingston has enslaved many since my grandparents built it. My husband and I handle the ones in our care differently than most. We have the firm conviction that if we treat them fairly, they will do right by us. And their aid in defending this place confirmed our belief."

He gawked at me, skeptical.

"You see, if we hadn't given them reason to help us, this place wouldn't be standing to offer shelter for your men."

"Am I to believe that I'm not only leaving my men in the care of a Northerner and a Brit, but also a nigger-lover?" He eyed me intensely, as though studying a traitor.

"On the contrary. Rest assured that you're leaving your men in the capable hands of folks looking to see war's end, to again know peace and welcome the return of our loved ones. I might add that the battle of Fort Sumter took my merchant ships. We have sustained a significant blow to our finances. We have lost much in this war, and if Negroes and whites have to come together to see it end, so be it." Passion fueled my words.

He stood as though pondering what I'd said. "Where are all these slaves now? A plantation this size would require many to help it run."

"Dead or run off." I bowed my head.

He released a breath, and I heard satisfaction in his next words. "So it appears you were wrong to put your faith in these slaves. Where are they now? You could use their help to tend the fields and grounds."

I lifted my gaze to meet his and shrugged.

I saw pity in his eyes. "We agree on one thing, Mrs. Armstrong."

"What is that?"

"That this war must end, so menfolk can return to running the plantations. Left in the hands of women, I fear what the men will return to."

My hands balled, but I kept them hidden at my sides. "I suppose you are right." I feigned meekness while fire sparked in my chest.

"Well, it appears everything is in order. But I warn you, Mrs. Armstrong, I will be keeping an eye on you," he said with all sincerity. He strode to the shelving featuring Father's and my collection of books. He stopped to admire the titles and said, without turning, "Your husband has a remarkable collection."

"Those were my father's books."

"Am I to assume your father is no longer with us?"

"You assume correctly," I said to his back. "He was murdered some years ago, and the men are still at large…" My words faded at the information I hadn't intended to share. In the time leading up to the soldiers' arrival, I had run over a script in my head of what I would say when questioned on the condition of the grounds and home. I hadn't expected to divulge my father's murder. My heart and mind raced as I scrambled to come up with an explanation.

The lieutenant spun around with his mouth agape. "And the plot thickens." His brows drew together.

My nerves thrummed. "I offer you transparency in hopes of squashing any mistrust you may have. I seek only to prove to you that when we are beaten down, we get back up. Yes, our men are gone, but we won't be so easily dismissed. We seek to do our part in this war, and that is all."

What had I gotten us into? Had I been wrong in offering Livingston as a wayside hospital?

Pete and Private Cooper halted at the doorway with a soldier slumped between them.

"Over here," I said, and strode to pull back the blanket on a cot.

They lay the soldier down. He wasn't but eighteen, and he looked up at me with feverish eyes as I bent over to tuck the covers around him.

"Mama, is that you?" He lifted warm fingers and touched my face.

I smiled at him, thinking of Whitney's brother, Jack. "Rest now." I removed his hand and gently laid it on the bed.

He closed his eyes, and I brushed back a sweaty blond curl from his forehead before turning tear-filled eyes on the lieutenant.

He nudged his chin at the soldier. "That is my sister's boy."

"I'm sorry to hear that. I will see that he and all who enter my home receive the best of care."

He inclined his head. "Thank you." His gaze grew determined. "We will end the North's interference once and for all. They will fall under our swords." He crossed the room to stand before me. "Thank you for offering your services. You can understand my leeriness."

"Of course," I said.

"This war has put everyone on edge, I reckon. The Federal Army's taking of Port Royal is of great concern. They aid the Negroes and have constructed a hospital—here, on our own soil." He pressed two fingers to his temple and rubbed the flesh there.

"You must be a very busy man," I said. "You need not worry about the men here. They will receive the care of trained hands. Rita here—" I gestured at Mammy, who stood in the corridor, awaiting instruction "—hasn't failed me yet. She has skillful hands. Her husband was a medicine man in his country, and he taught her many things before he was sold by her last master." We walked from the room and into the corridor. "My parents purchased her before my birth, and regardless of being willed her freedom, she has remained at Livingston."

"Is that so?" He took a good look at Mammy. "And why did you choose to stay?"

"Missus paid me well," Mammy said, keeping her eyes trained on the tips of his boots.

"But now, surely Mrs. Armstrong can't afford to pay such a fine wage when food and wealth aren't as available."

"No, sah, she can't. But dis family have my loyalty 'til de Lard take me home."

"Such dedication is rare and unheard of for a nigger." He gave her a keen look of admiration, but as one would admire a racehorse.

Mammy pressed her lips together and spoke no further. The lieutenant gave her one last glance before exiting the house.

After the last soldier had been assigned a cot, the lieutenant and private took their leave. Whitney and Pippa stood on either side of me on the veranda, watching until the wagon disappeared out the gate. I released the first full breath since the soldiers arrived.

Whitney tilted her head toward me and said in a low tone, "We aren't in the clear yet."

"You are right, and from here on out, can you save me the gray hair and control your need to have the last say? Please, for the sake of us all," I pleaded while avoiding revealing my own blunder in the library.

Stubbornness flashed across her face, but it dissipated, replaced by regret. "My apologies."

"Well, we have patients to tend. What do you say we get to work?" Pippa said, and strode inside.

"Is it too late to turn back?" I said to Whitney.

"I'm afraid so." She linked arms with me, and we followed after Pippa.

CHAPTER
Seventeen

Amelie

MOTHER'S CONDITION WORSENED IN THE WEEK THAT FOLLOWED. The evening her breathing had grown shallow, the elderly woman I'd hired to sit with her came to fetch me in the grand parlor.

"Ma'am." A gentle tap on my shoulder drew my attention. I glanced over my shoulder and tensed when I saw her. She stood wringing her hands.

"Will you excuse me?" I turned back to the silver-haired major I'd sat with for the last agonizing hour while he'd droned on and on about the war.

He sat with his ankle crossed over his knee, and an arm slung over the back of the settee. "Certainly, Madame, but please don't keep me waiting too long. I think you will find how we chased off those Confederate bastards quite amusing."

I feigned a smile. "Of course," I said. "In the meantime, why don't you enjoy the company of one of my girls. I know how lonely it can be for a man out there."

He waved a hand. "I'm a happily married man. I don't require the comfort of a woman in my bed."

"But surely it's been too long since you've enjoyed the companionship of your wife."

"It has." Sadness reflected in his gray eyes as he glanced around the parlor. "One can only endure the callousness and stench of these soldiers for so long before longing for the tenderness and companionship of a woman."

"I admire your devotion to your wife. She is a fortunate lady." I stood.

He rose, seized my hand, and placed it to his cool lips. "You're the most exquisite creature my old eyes have ever beheld."

No stranger to the swooning of men, I inclined my head in appreciation. "You are too kind. Now, if you will excuse me."

He released me, and I turned and hurried after my mother's caregiver.

Upstairs in my suite, I strode to the cot I'd set up in the parlor for my mother. I noted her shallow breathing and the raspy echo of death's approach. My heart raced, and panic erupted. "How long has she been like this?" I asked the woman.

"For some hours."

I shifted back to stare at my mother, my awareness shifting to the grayish condition of her flesh. "Why don't you go home. I will sit with her tonight."

"Are you certain?"

I nodded, and she mumbled a goodbye, but as she walked to the door, fear beat in my chest and snatched at my breathing. I couldn't bear to be alone with my mother, but before I could speak, the door closed. All strength abandoned me, and I dropped into the chair by the cot.

My body felt numb. Emotions relating to my mother rose unchecked, and I trembled under their assault. I had wasted my life striving not to become her while seeking to pluck her existence from my mind. Yet she had infected me like a disease. The looking glass taunted me with reminders of our resemblance: how I held my mouth, the shape of my eyes, and my curves. Despite striving to forget where I'd come from, I couldn't escape the fact that I was the daughter of a whore.

Tears blotted out the figure before me, and a deep ache hollowed my chest. Oh, how I'd yearned for her to love me, to nurture and protect me, and in the end, it was I who sat by her bed as she clung to the last minutes or hours of life. *Why are you doing this?* I'd asked myself in the days after I'd given her refuge. Each time, I came up answerless. She hadn't deserved my compassion, but for some unknown reason, I had offered her grace.

A question burned in my heart. "Why couldn't you love me?" Years of relentless pain echoed in my words and clotted my throat. "Was it too much to ask?"

All my life, I had felt undeserving of love. If my own mother couldn't love me, how could anyone else? My shoulders slumped as sorrow washed over me. "Now here you lie, dying, and it is I who comes to your rescue, to save you from a death not even you deserve. No one should die alone," I said as though to convince myself.

I looked at her hand, lying beside her, and the small child within me yearned to find comfort in a mother. Nerves knotted my belly as I touched the top of her hand with a single finger. Her skin felt warm and almost waxy in consistency. At first I sat regarding the fragility of her slender hand and the tiny blue lines beneath her flesh. I traced each one with my fingertip while permitting my mind to draw me into memories of the past.

My mother had withheld the nurturing and protection a child needed. I had never understood why. Was she incapable of love, or had she lacked the understanding of how? I supposed I'd never understand. My chest tightened, and a tear slid over my cheek as I lifted her hand and cocooned it in mine.

Mother passed that night, and her death expanded the void inside of me. Months before, if someone had told me I would give her shelter, sit holding her hand as she took her last breath, or shed a tear at her passing, I would've called them delusional.

As the gravediggers lowered the casket into the earth, I thought of her end. No one would miss her. She had done nothing worth remembering in life. And in the weeks following her death,

I contemplated my own life. Would I, too, become a washed-up whore, forgotten by the world, and buried in a pine box?

Weeks later, dressed in a burgundy wool traveling suit, I stood on the street and craned my neck back to look up at the brothel. Drunken laughter and the sound of Luther pounding on the keys drifted from the establishment. Business had been better than ever with the soldier boys' comings and goings, and prosperity had been mine for the taking, but my soul cried for something more. The place had become a suffocating tie to the past and my mother, and even to Oliver...Reuben McCoy.

Since the day in Five Points when I'd knelt over the bodies of Burrell and Rose Rawlings splayed on the floor of their home, I'd studied every darkened corner, omnibus, and street for Reuben to step out and end my life. But he had never come, and with the country at war I wondered into what crevice he'd crawled and what poor soul had lost their life so he could assume their identity.

A warm hand touched my arm. "Are you ready?" Zeke's husky voice banished the emptiness in my heart.

A smile touched my lips, and I turned to look into earnest brown eyes, grateful for his companionship. "Yes, darling."

He gestured at the waiting carriage, and when I took his hand he helped me inside. Once I was seated, he climbed in beside me, and the carriage lurched forward.

Through the small back window, I took one last look at the place that had seen my rise to wealth and status, and I felt as if cords were being severed.

"You aren't having qualms about selling, are you?"

"No regrets." I lifted a gloved hand and cupped his cheek.

Unlike Reuben, Zeke wasn't a beautiful man, but the tenderness in his eyes held more significant meaning. I used my index finger to trace the scars lining his strong jawline before stroking the blemish that had left sparse hairs at the corner of his right brow. His nose had been broken in a brawl or two—he was the very image of a fighter. At a towering six feet, with broad shoulders and a permanently unsmiling countenance, he intimidated people. I had come to know him as anything but a fighter. Like me, he was a survivor with chancy origins, born into an imperfect world.

Later, at the train station, I stood on the boardwalk and glanced around, trying to quell the nerves as I thought of what we were about to do.

"You sure you want to do this?"

"Where you go, I go," I said, jutting out my chin. "And yes, I'm more sure than I've ever been."

"There is no turning back, once we do this."

"I know." I clasped my satchel and tucked my hand in the curve of his arm.

Our paths had crossed for a reason, and perhaps we were destined to die together. I couldn't comprehend what the future held, but I knew but one thing: I didn't want to go out as the madam of a cathouse. I wanted my existence to have meant something. The journey ahead felt like the only way to tip the scale of justice and right past wrongs. And perhaps bring me the peace I desired.

My legs trembled as we strode toward the ticket office, and I clung to my determination to do something right in my life or die trying.

⌒ CHAPTER ⌒
Eighteen

Ruby

"THE INJUSTICE!" SAUL'S DEEP VOICE RUMBLED THROUGH THE main floor of our home.

"Darling, please," I said, closing the door behind me.

My husband rarely got riled, but after his third inquiry with the US Army about joining to fight, he had fallen into the foulest mood for the entire ride home.

Aisling, the young Irish woman I'd found near death in the slums of Five Points, entered the foyer with Mercy, our daughter, on her heels.

"Please take her upstairs." I removed my hat and coat.

"Yes, Mrs. Sparrow." She placed a hand on Mercy's shoulders and guided her toward the stairs.

"Why is Papa so angry?" Her brow furrowed as she looked up at Aisling.

"You needn't worry, lass. What do you say we have a little tea party with that new dolly your papa brought you last week?"

"All right," Mercy said in a chipper voice. She was growing fast; it seemed like only yesterday that she had crawled around the floors, pulling down everything she could get her little hands on.

I followed Saul into the parlor, where he dropped into his favorite armchair and steepled his long fingers under his chin. His dark eyes glittered with anger, as they had since the war started. He sat tapping his feet repetitively on the floor.

"Saul, darling, you mustn't let it bother you so. All you can do is keep trying." I crossed the room to stand in front of him.

"Lincoln binds our hands. Free or enslaved, we are turned away from joining the Union cause. They let immigrants take up arms beside them, but keep the doors closed to their own countrymen because—why? We are black." He thrust out his hands for emphasis before lowering them to rest on the arms of the chair. "His fear of pushing bordering states into joining the Confederacy prevents him from accepting the assistance he needs to help end this war before our nation lies in ruins. He is a fool!" His nostrils flared.

"Come, come. You must calm yourself." I knelt before him and took his hands in mine.

Like my husband, I yearned to join the war. I thought of the times Kipling and I had entered dangerous territories to help fugitives. I was as skilled as most men, and the Northern army required scouts, spies, and soldiers. But the discrimination that held America in thrall had thwarted all blacks' attempts to assist. Still, regardless of my heart's desire, I had my daughter to consider, and if a time came when we were allowed to fight alongside the whites, I wouldn't risk her growing up parentless.

"We will get through this. Maybe soon, President Lincoln and the whites will see that they need us." I attempted optimism while, internally, I grappled with despair.

"I pray for the day. America must adapt. We are citizens of this country whether they like it or not." The passion in his voice revealed how much he wished for change.

But I feared, if allowed to enlist, my people would continue to get low-paying jobs and face prejudice and injustices. Would the deaths and the heartache brought by the war have been for nothing? I lifted my head and looked into his face. "All we can do is our part to see the war end and to take a stand for our people."

"Yes, at least we can do that." He stood. "If you don't mind, my dear, I think I will rest for a while." He leaned down and pecked my cheek.

"Of course," I said with a smile.

After he left, I moved to the mahogany veneer desk in the far corner of the room and sat. I opened a drawer, pulled out a piece of stationery, and dipped the quill. Then I began to write.

My dearest Willow,
I hope this letter finds you well...

CHAPTER
Nineteen

Willow

LIEUTENANT WILLIAMS HAD LEFT EIGHT MEN IN OUR CARE, AND THEY were a welcome distraction. My days became so busy that loneliness and yearning for Bowden's and Ben's return only arose at night when I fell into bed, exhausted. For the briefest of moments, their images drifted in, then out, before my lids grew heavy.

"Missus Willow?" Sailor said one morning as we boiled dressings in the oversized cast-iron kettle in the work yard.

"What is it?" I brushed a hand over my forehead to swipe back the sweaty tendrils that had escaped my hair combs.

"Can't we buy us some more slaves to help around here?" He regarded me innocently, but I was taken aback by his request.

"No," I said a bit too sharply.

He flinched.

"We don't need more slaves," I said in a gentler tone.

"Why not?" He stared into the simmering pot. "With Masa Bowden gone, things are real hard around here. Miss Rita said we don't have supplies to waste on making peach cobbler." His face fell. The boy had a sweet tooth like no other. "And earlier I tried to sneak me a bit of cornbread, and she struck my hand. Made it sting like it was on fire. Said that we needed to keep the cornbread for the soldiers."

I imagined Mammy with her hands planted on her hips, delivering to Sailor "the look" that made everyone quiver in their shoes.

"Don't fret none. Miss Rita didn't mean any harm; she is trying to ration our supplies, is all."

"I wish those soldiers hadn't come here."

"Why do you say that?" I removed the steaming bandages from the boiling water and dropped them into a basket.

"Because Miss Rita is grumpier than usual. And you're always busy in the big house caring for the soldiers and ain't got time to visit me in the quarters. All we do is work, and I don't reckon I like it much. If we bought a slave or two, it would help us."

I'd bent to gather the basket but froze at his words. Gulping back the tightening in my throat, I lifted the basket and turned to look at him. The same innocence from moments ago shone in his eyes. Had I spoiled the boy so much that he had formed a belief or understanding that Negroes were here to serve us? Guilt tightened my gut. "Those times are gone," I said.

He tilted his head to eye me. "You mean it's always gonna be this hard?"

My eyes welled. "No, I think in time it will get better." I wondered how I could explain to him in a way he'd understand. "My wish is that all of this won't be for nothing. That when Mr. Armstrong and Mr. Hendricks return, there will be no more slaves."

"But I heard Parker say that the…Con-fed-er-ates fight to keep slaves."

"That is true."

His brow pleated. "So that's what Masa's fighting for."

"No."

His brow dipped lower. "Then what is he fighting for?"

I waved a hand around at the grounds and the main house. "For our land and home."

"Oh." He looked around the plantation in dawning understanding. "I like being a slave. I wish Evie still lived here—then we could be slaves together." He lowered his head and kicked at a stone. "I miss her real bad."

"I know you do. Now come, let's get these bandages hung."

He walked beside me, and I noted his slouched young shoulders. Love gripped my heart, and I wanted to gather him in my arms and protect him from the world. Gone were the days when I could pull him onto my lap and soothe away his pain. He had become more independent and sought an understanding of the world. He had declared in recent months that he no longer wanted to be treated like a baby. It had broken my heart, but I recalled a similar incident when I was younger: the evening I'd informed Mammy I no longer wanted her to tuck me in at night. The pain in her expression had mirrored the pang I felt at Sailor's request.

"Missus Willow?"

"Yes."

"Evie told me that Masa Bowden or Masa Ben be my pappy."

His response snatched my breath and caught me off guard. I ached to tell him that he wasn't born a slave and that no paperwork of ownership existed. He deserved to know the truth about his parentage, and that he had the blood of a prominent Charleston family in his veins. I wanted to share his parents' love story with him, to let him know he was conceived from love, not a masa's lust, but I knew that would mean danger for everyone involved.

"You…" The words stuck in my throat. Too afraid to speak them, I halted and turned. He paused and looked up at me. "You are special to me, and I love you very much. Do you understand that?"

"Evie said 'cause of your love for the masa, you love me too."

"That simply isn't true." My heartache echoed in my tone, combined with annoyance at Mary Grace's daughter for planting seeds of doubt and confusion in the boy's head. I brushed that away. The girl had the same cleverness as her mother, and of course her mind would shuffle through possible explanations for the affection I held for Sailor.

I busied myself with pinning the bandages on the line.

"Do you know which one is my pappy?" Sailor said.

I braced, and my heart thumped harder as I grappled with

the right words to say. "I can't say. But you must know we all love you." I shifted to look at him before looking toward the house to survey for prying eyes. Finding no one, I turned back and cradled his cheek with a hand. "Mr. Armstrong and I love you as though you were our son."

"But why? White folk don't like us blacks."

"Not all white folks see it the same. In fact, a lot of white people don't own slaves at all."

"Why do you?"

I shifted with unease at the question. "Because my family owned slaves long before I was born. When my father died I became the owner of all he owned, and that included the slaves."

"But ya hardly got any slaves now."

"Yes, and that is for the better. We aren't meant to own people, nor should we seek to have power over another. One day I hope that all slaves are free. But we can't tell anyone that, or it would endanger us all."

"Does Masa Bowden think like you?"

"Yes," I said.

"What if slaves are freed? Where would I go?" His lip quivered. "I don't want to leave you."

I bent to look him in the eye and gripped his chin. "You never have to leave here. This is your home and we're your family, regardless of what the looking glass reveals. You are my son!" Passion erupted in my chest.

He threw himself at me and squeezed me around the neck. I rocked backward from the impact but caught myself and wrapped my arms around him.

"There is nothing for you to worry about." I held his trembling body. "I will never leave you." The truth in my claim resonated to the very depths of my soul. I would die for the boy before I let harm come to him. Although I hadn't carried him in my womb like I had my son, I loved him just the same.

After a moment or two, I pulled back and regarded Jimmy in

the pasture, tending the horses. "Why don't you go help Jimmy."
I pointed in his direction.

Sailor followed my finger and quickly shifted back to look at
me. His face brightened.

"I can finish up here," I said with a smile of encouragement.

He let out a cheer, and I stood to watch him sprint across the
yard. Jimmy greeted him with a tender pat on the head. My soul
ached. One day I would tell Sailor the truth about his parentage,
and I hoped he would forgive me for keeping it from him.

Balancing the empty basket on my hip, I strode back to the
house and inside.

I collided with a soldier exiting the library and dropped the
basket. I clutched his arm to keep him from falling. "My apologies," I said.

He shuffled and rebalanced his weight on the crutches Jimmy
had fashioned. "It ain't no trouble," he said with a pleasant smile.

My shoulders relaxed. When he glanced at my hands still
clutching him, heat washed over me and I laughed. Releasing him,
I mumbled another apology. He grinned, appearing amused, before inclining his head respectfully and continuing down the corridor to the front door.

Tillie exited the warming kitchen without a look in my direction, appearing flustered and on edge. Balancing a rattling silver
salver holding wooden bowls of steaming stew, she hurried across
the hall to the library and disappeared inside.

"Girl, get on over here." Impatience echoed in a soldier's voice
that I recognized as belonging to Corporal Jacobson. Whitney
had identified him as a problem, and I couldn't have agreed more.
Darkness burned in his eyes, revealing his anger at life itself. "Get
me on the chair. What took you so long to return? I've needed to
relieve myself for the past twenty minutes."

"Yes, sah," Tillie replied softly.

I retrieved the basket from the floor before walking into the
library. "Good afternoon, gentlemen. What do you say we get you

situated to have your afternoon meal?" I strode to each window and drew back the drapes to allow the sun's rays to embrace the room. "It's a beautiful afternoon. A bit chilly, but I say those who are up to it can join Private Tanner on the front veranda."

Someone entered the room behind me, and I turned to find Whitney. "Mrs. Tucker." Relief washed over me. "I was just telling our guests that those who want to sit outside for a while can enjoy their meal on the front veranda. Corporal Jacobson needs to visit the privy. Do you mind assisting him?" I glanced at the corporal and reveled in the crimson creeping over his cheeks and ears. If anyone could handle his demands, it was Whitney.

She marched forward. "Now, I'm not about to put up with any of your sass today. I'll leave you in the privy with your drawers down."

He glared at her. "You watch yourself, ma'am. Don't forget who I am."

"And don't you forget we're here to help, not to be abused because you're angry at the world," she said before looking at me. "Willow, do you mind helping me?"

"Be right there." I turned to Tillie. "Go to the parlor and see which of the men want to go outside."

"Yessum." Tillie curtsied and dashed from the room.

I hurried to help Whitney. We got the corporal into the wheelchair, and despite his sour disposition my heart went out to him. A canon had taken his legs, and now, unable to fight, he'd soon return home a mere shadow of his former self. Three others in our care would return to the front lines. Following their departure new soldiers would come, and the long nights of sitting with the men who darkened death's door would continue.

CHAPTER
Twenty

CHRISTMAS APPROACHED, AND LIKE MANY FESTIVITIES ACROSS THE nation the yearly banquet at Livingston was canceled. The melancholy of the war had overshadowed the joyfulness of the season. Still, Pippa, Whitney, and I tried to bring life and gaiety to the parlor and library to lift the men's spirits.

Humming a Christmas carol, I draped holly on the mantel before stepping back to admire my work.

"It looks right fine, Mrs. Armstrong," a pleasant voice said, and I turned to smile at our newest arrival.

Bobby Jo was a messenger boy of ten, with bright copper hair that gleamed in the sun pouring through the window. The mass of freckles on his face reminded me of an army of ants that left little ground unoccupied. I had become quite fond of the boy and enjoyed time in his company.

"We will make this season what we can…" My words drifted as I noted the crimson stain on the bandage around his middle. I strode to his bed and knelt beside him to inspect his dressing. "It appears you have opened your wound again."

"I reckon I moved around too much last night." His cheerfulness faded, replaced by a solemn expression.

I eyed him. "Something troubling you?"

"It's, well…my ma." He looked at the other soldiers to ensure no one was eavesdropping before continuing in a low voice. "You see, she died the eve before the war broke out, and we were already losing the farm. The neighboring plantation owner had tried to buy my ma out for years, but she refused. I reckon he is the proud owner now." His shoulders slumped. "A man from the bank was set to come the following day. With my ma gone and the farm—I didn't have anywhere to go, so I enlisted. When this is over, I don't know where I'll end up."

"Surely you have relatives or someone who'd take you in?" I removed his dressing.

"No, ma'am. I'm afraid it's just me." His jaw trembled ever so slightly as he struggled to suppress his worry.

I gulped at the fear in his gray-blue eyes. He was too young to face the world alone. "I don't know what the future holds. I suppose no one does. But, when this is over, perhaps you could find your way back here."

His brow furrowed. "Here?"

"That's right. Maybe we will have work. The grounds are vast and require many hands. Depending on the situation in the South, if we can't offer you a wage, at least you'd have a home and food."

"You'd do that for me?" His eyes welled with tears.

I nodded. "I know what it's like to feel alone in the world."

"You?" He gawked. "But, how is that possible?" He swept a hand around the parlor. "You have all of this, and slaves to wait on you."

"Possessions do not fill the void in one's heart. My mother died when I was a little girl, and I don't remember her. My father was always away on business, and he wasn't the easy sort. I had no extended relatives I knew of, and my father left me in the care of overseers and the quarter folks." I glanced at Mammy as she entered the room with a vessel of water. After a quick glance at the other soldiers, who sat playing cards at a nearby table, I turned back to him. "You see that woman over there?"

He bobbed his head.

"She was the only mother I knew."

"A black?" His jaw unhinged.

"Yes, and if it wasn't for her and the blacks of Livingston, I would have felt more abandoned and alone than I did. They embraced me as their own. I played with the slave children, and Miss Rita tucked me in at night and comforted me when I fell down. She held me and wiped my tears when I cried for the love of a parent." I applied fresh bandages to his wound.

"But why would she do that? People say the blacks are incapable of love."

"Is that how you honestly think, or is that what others have told you to believe?"

"Well, I reckon I don't rightfully know. Folks never treated my ma and me any better than the blacks. Ma said because we were poor, they looked down on us." He rested his head back against the pillows, weariness sweeping over his visage. "There was this slave boy about my age—his master's plantation bordered our farm. I watched him work the fields from dawn to dusk. Our eyes would meet across the property line—him with his cotton bag and me driving the plow and mule. Sometimes he would wave, but I was too afraid to wave back. Ma said if you get too close to a black, they will suck out your soul because they're heathens. She said, in their country, they feed on humans. The day I decided to cross the property line and speak to him, ma took a horsewhip to me. I couldn't sit or lie down for weeks." He winced at the memory.

My jaw tightened at such ignorance and the fallacies people created about the blacks—no wonder uneducated prejudices continued for generations. Folks had schooled hatred and mistrust about the blacks into their children. "In all due respect, your ma was misguided." I spoke tenderly for the boy's sake while inside I seethed at such idiocy. I adjusted the blanket around his naked torso.

"Maybe so," he said.

"Did you ever speak to this boy?"

"No. The last I saw of him was when he sat in the back of a wagon headed to market." He took another gander at the other soldiers and said in a low voice, "After he left, I daydreamed about him and me running through the woods and fishing in the stream.

I suppose he was my imaginary friend. It made the days on the farm seem less long and lonely."

I smiled. "I'm glad you allowed yourself that friendship."

His face softened as though I had given him permission to embrace the memories.

I stood and looked down at him. "You rest now."

"Mrs. Armstrong," he whispered as I turned to leave.

I shifted to regard him. "Yes?"

"I wish I had gotten his name." Sadness played on his young face.

"How about you give him a name of your own."

His eyes widened and then, as though delighted at the idea, he nodded.

I squeezed his hand where it lay beside him. "You're the master of your own thoughts. Our parents and the adults in our lives influence us with their belief systems. But there comes a pivotal time in our lives when we must make our own choices and shape our own beliefs. We can see others as different, or we can view each other as God intended. We can choose light and love, or hate and darkness."

He lay staring at me as though pondering my words. I left him and walked down the hall to the library.

"Afternoon, Mrs. Armstrong." A private lifted his hand in greeting.

"How do you fare today?" I strove to appear happy while my mind remained on Bobby Jo.

"Oh, I'm good enough. Missing my girl, is all."

I recognized the homesick look I'd witnessed in others. "Maybe I can ease your heart by providing a listening ear." I strode to his bedside and helped him sit up.

Pippa sat next to a gravely ill soldier and spooned broth into his mouth. We hadn't expected him to pull through another night, but when the morning had come, he still breathed, and I'd offered a prayer of gratitude.

I propped the private's pillow, and he leaned back. "Are you going to tell me about this girl or not?" I said with a smile.

Red tinging his ears, his eyes met mine, then he ducked his head. "It's just, I miss her something terrible. And I'm afraid she will move on while I'm gone. When I signed up, I didn't think the war would carry on so long."

"I don't think anyone did. But we must believe in its end."

"Reckon so. I figured maybe if I signed up, Betty Sue would see me as a war hero or something," he said with a sheepish grin. "Sounds rather foolish, don't it?"

"Not at all," I said. "You needn't worry about another gentleman swooping in and stealing the heart of the lucky Betty Sue."

"How can you be so certain?" Hope and yearning reflected in his green eyes.

"We women like our men brave," I said lightly. "Besides, with our country at war, who is left behind to win her heart? There isn't anyone but old men, children, and women."

A grin broke across his face, and his shoulders relaxed. "You make a good point."

I laughed and patted his shoulder. "You will be back in her arms before you know it."

His eyes took on a far-off look as I pushed to my feet, and I left him to his daydreams of Betty Sue.

"Willow, do you mind giving me a hand?" Whitney balanced on a ladder, holding a garland. I dashed forward to assist her. "I thought we could drape this above the window to conceal the remnants of the fire."

"A splendid idea." I gathered the other end of the garland. The fresh scent of pine delighted my senses, and for the briefest of moments, joy danced in my soul. Until I locked gazes with Sergeant Absher, who sat on the edge of his cot, his full head of silver hair glistening like threads of gleaming silk. "How are you today, Sergeant?" I asked him.

Ignoring me, he reached for his cane and struggled to get to his feet.

When he'd arrived, I felt uneasy when his piercing eyes had met mine. He hadn't given any reason to heighten the feeling in his time with us, but still, it hadn't diminished. I'd brought my concern to Whitney, and she'd reminded me that we'd stopped aiding runaways at the commencement of the war, so I needn't worry. However, my apprehension continued because, in the secret room in the attic, we'd hidden all articles about Harriet Tubman, Douglas Fredricks, and other abolitionists; records of slaves passing through Livingston; and books, papers, and slates we'd used to teach the quarter folks. Not to mention the grain, food, and miscellaneous supplies we'd stored.

"I am as well as one can expect," the sergeant said in an emotionless tone. "As soon as I'm healed, I will return to my regiment."

"Yes, and we hope that Livingston will bring you the peace you need to recover." I doubted he'd return to the battlefield anytime soon, but hopefully, the army would find a use for him. The sooner he left, the better for us all.

"I'm sure you'll be delighted to see the last of me." He stood eyeing me with a direct gaze.

Inside I squirmed under his imposing regard, but I fought to stay composed on the surface. "Why do you say that?"

"Because I see the way you look at me. As though I'm the enemy."

I swallowed hard. Had I been that transparent? I scrambled to come up with something that would dismiss that idea. "You misread my tension. I worry about the length of this war and if we'll have enough supplies and food to provide for ourselves and the soldiers we take in."

"The army will see that you have all you need while you care for our men," he said gruffly.

But at what expense? At the hardship of other plantations and farmers. People talked about the army showing up and leaving them with only the basics to get by. What if the military no longer required Livingston to house their men? Would we, too, suffer the fate of other South Carolinians?

He walked from the room, and I stood staring after him until Whitney gave the garland a tug.

As we finished decorating the library, I regarded the sergeant as he stood on the back veranda, smoking the pipe protruding below his precisely trimmed mustache. I wanted to see him gone from Livingston as soon as possible.

❧ CHAPTER ❧
Twenty-One

LATE ONE DECEMBER EVENING, AFTER WHITNEY AND PIPPA HAD retired to their chambers, I gathered my shawl and exited through the back door. The harmony of the night critters melded with the fluid sound of the river current. I strolled across the work yard and past a small group of quarter folks sitting around a small open fire. Our numbers grew fewer, but the burden of providing for those who remained never eased.

"Evening, Missus." Parker eyed me across the fire. Other folks nodded and offered greetings.

"Evening," I said with a smile.

I'd ascended the knoll between the house and the river when I heard shuffling footsteps behind me. I swung around and held the lantern high. "Who goes there?"

"Et's jus' me, Missus," a male voice replied.

"Parker!" I exclaimed in disapproval. I placed a hand to my chest to quell my pounding heart. "You scared me half to death. These are trying times, and one can never be too certain of who lurks in the woods."

"I'm sorry, but I bin hoping to talk to you on a matter."

I sensed the reason he had sought me out. Since Kimie had left for Charleston to help at the wayside hospital, he had fallen into a state of wistfulness. His elongated face and slumped shoulders had gathered Whitney's attention.

One day as he strolled by us in the work yard, she'd leaned in and whispered, "Poor soul can't think straight with the condition of his heart." She'd shaken her head and favored him with a sad smile. "And to think some time back, I would have mocked such a display of lovestruck weakness."

I'd smiled with amusement at the reformed woman who openly declared her love and pining for Knox. If Whitney Tucker could change her outlook on life, it gave me hope for our nation.

I waited until Parker caught up. He leaned his weight on his walking stick before lifting agony-filled eyes to me.

"Well, don't hesitate, tell me what has you chasing after me."

"I was wondering ef de next time Jones or you head in to Charleston, ef I can go wid you."

"You're hoping to talk to Kimie?"

"Yessum."

"You know the dangers involved. Especially now."

"I knowed et. But I reckon ef I can git one look at her, dis here ache in my soul would go away."

For the time being, I thought. Compassion pulled at me. I considered the measures I'd take to have a mere moment with Bowden. "You know we rarely venture into Charleston anymore. What supplies we can gather that the army hasn't already claimed, Jones gets from Secessionville."

"Please, Missus. I must see her." His eyes pleaded for my reconsideration.

He had claimed a place in my heart since my father had brought him and his father, Owen, to Livingston. "I'm sorry, Parker. I wish I could help, but I can't."

"Yessum." His shoulders slumped as though I had knocked hope right out of him.

Desiring to be far removed from all responsibility, I continued walking. To my surprise, he fell into step beside me. I welcomed his company, and for a while, we walked in silence along the river's edge, relishing the calm and peacefulness of the night. I contemplated his request and wrestled with how I could make it possible before brushing off the reckless idea. I gave him a sideways glance.

"You must believe me, if I could risk going in to Charleston, I would take you with me."

"I know," he said.

"Perhaps Kimie will come for a visit…" My words faded when I heard a moan. I froze. "What was that?"

He swung to face me with confusion in his eyes. "What?"

"I thought I heard something." I strained to hear above the rushing of the river's current. Hearing nothing, I shrugged. "Perhaps it was an animal."

I took another step, and the moan came again, louder and more pronounced. "There, did you hear that?"

Parker gawked at me and nodded. "Sho' did. Et sound lak et coming from over dere." He pointed at some underbrush on the riverbank.

"Let's take a look." I stepped by him to go and investigate but he gripped my arm.

"You got to be careful, Missus," he whispered. "You don't know who or what be out dere."

"You're right, but I have your protection." I motioned for him to follow.

He snorted and knocked his leg with the walking stick. "Wid dis busted leg?"

"Come." I moved toward the location of the moan. Holding the lantern high, I squinted into the darkness. Grateful for the aid of the full moon, I advanced. When the moan came again I halted, causing Parker to run into me.

He clutched me around the middle to keep us from going down, then swiftly released me, a look of alarm on his face. "Sorry, Missus."

I dismissed him with a wave. "Don't be silly. You rescued the both of us."

As the noise pierced the night again, I clutched his arm, and we crept forward. My heart pounded in my ears, yet every sound around me seemed magnified. Each terrifying outcome I could think of rushed through my head. What if it was a rabid animal? Or Reuben lying in wait? Everything in me screamed to turn and run, but my feet pressed on.

As we drew closer, I recognized the noise as human. Seeing movement, I craned my neck and saw a man in uniform sprawled on the ground.

Parker inhaled sharply. "Lard help us all. Dat dere a soldier."

I noted the Federal uniform and moved in to get a better look.

"Careful, Missus." Panic strummed in Parker's voice.

The soldier lay with his face turned away. He never stirred at the sound of our voices. I stuck out my foot and jostled him, but he remained motionless. Careful not to get too close, I passed the lantern over him to inspect for injuries, pausing at his chest, where a dark stain and a bullet hole marred his coat.

"I wonder what he is doing out this far." I knelt beside the man.

"Willow…" the man moaned.

Startled at the sound of my name, I held the lantern to his face and pulled back the shadowing branch. "God in heaven. It's Kip." I set the lantern on the ground and bent forward. "Kip, can you hear me?"

No response came. I brushed his cheeks and forehead. "He's delirious with fever. We have to get him to the house."

"But, you can't!" Parker exclaimed before he caught himself and lowered his voice. "Have you forgotten 'bout dem Confederates you keeping up at de big house? Ef you walk up dere wid Mister Kip, dey will kill him for sho'."

I rocked back on my heels and brushed a hand over my forehead. "You're right. Let me think." After a moment, I said, "Go fetch Jones, and then ask Mrs. Tucker to bring a change of clothing." I held out the lantern for him to take.

"Straightaway." Without delay, he wobbled off.

After he left, I sat on the ground and fumbled for Kip's hand. "Everything will be all right. I will see to it." Tears sprang to my eyes as concern over Kip's condition took hold.

I envisioned Bowden and Ben wounded and needing aid. If a Northerner found them, would they show them kindness, or would— "No, you mustn't think that way. You'll only drive yourself mad." I shook my head to dislodge the worry and considered what I would do with Kipling.

After what seemed like hours had passed, I braced at racing footsteps.

"Jones, that you?" I pulled closer to Kipling, seeking to shield him from whoever approached.

The lantern shone on the ground in front of me, and I released the breath I'd been holding when Jones came into view. He ran the lantern over Kip. "It's him, all right," he said. "Kind of skinny compared to what I recollect."

I regarded Kip's gaunt face. "There's no telling how long he's been like this, or how he ended up here."

"Maybe he fought at the battle at Point Royal."

"But that was weeks ago."

"I reckon so." Jones holstered a hand on his narrow hip.

"We need to get him where we can assess his injuries."

"I don't like this. You're asking for trouble." His eyes narrowed.

"What do you expect me to do, just leave him here?" I snapped.

He never answered, just stood scratching at the days-old gray scuff shadowing his chin. After years of observing this complex man, I figured he was running through scenarios.

"I'm going to need your help." He moved to stand at Kip's head. I scrambled to help. "Put his arm around your shoulder, and we'll haul him up."

I did as instructed, and Jones looked across at me. "You got him?"

"Yes."

"All right, up!" he said, and grunted as he bore the bulk of Kip's weight.

Kip let out a wail, never opening his eyes, and again muttered my name.

"It's a mighty good thing we found him and not someone else," Jones said between heaving breaths as we half dragged Kip back toward the plantation. "Him going around calling your name is the last thing we need. People around here would nail you to the cross, labeling you as a traitor as sure as nothing."

I recognized the truth in his words.

We had only made it a short distance before Whitney and Parker came over the knoll and dashed down to the river bank. Whitney raced ahead, with Parker struggling to keep up.

"How bad is he?" Whitney's brow pleated as she tried to assess him in the dark.

"We won't be able to tell until we get him inside," I said. "Let's lay him down. Jones, you and Parker get him into the fresh change of clothes."

Released of the burden of Kip's weight, I stepped away to allow the men to do their work.

Whitney and I stood with our backs turned and looked out over the river. "I don't like this," she said. I glanced at her, but she kept her eyes on the river. "Not only do we have to worry about being prey to any Federal armies passing through, but if they show up here, the men inside will surely die. Federals seizing control of Port Royal Sound is too close for my liking."

I tried to still the trembling overtaking my body.

"And now, with Kipling here, the risk becomes that much greater."

"Would you have me leave him to die?" I turned to her.

"Of course not. Don't make me out as the villain. He's my friend too."

"I don't like harboring a Federal any more than you. But, at the start of this, we all agreed we wouldn't turn anyone in need away. And it's Kip, for God's sake." I thrust a hand in the air.

"Calm yourself," she said. "I'm just worried, is all." She glanced over her shoulder before stiffening and quickly turning back.

"We'll hide him in the barn for the night, and in the morning we will figure out what to do."

"What if someone reports us?" she said.

"Are you referring to the quarter folks?" I thought of Jane and her views on blacks, which had seemed hypocritical and disingenuous.

"This war has proven to displace loyalty."

I squeezed her hand tighter and gave it a gentle tug. "Together, we have proven to be an unstoppable team. We will get through this."

"All right, let's hurry," Jones grumbled.

Whitney stepped up to help. "No." I grabbed her arm. "My dress is already stained with his blood. Go fetch Big John and tell him to meet us in the barn."

She nodded and dashed off into the shadows of the night.

"Parker." I swerved to face him. "Gather his bloodied clothes and wash them in the river."

Jones's unruly brows narrowed. "You should burn them."

"They may come in handy," I said.

"Yes, Missus, I do as you ask," Parker said.

My nerves thrummed as I looked at Jones. "Let's get him out of sight."

Big John's large frame darkened the threshold, and his gaze fell on Kipling lying on the fresh straw, dressed in Bowden's clothing. He dashed past me, and behind him, Mammy waddled in wearing a deep scowl, her brow glistening with beads of sweat. She looked over her shoulder for prying eyes before placing me in her crosshairs.

"Angel gal," she said in a hushed tone, "what ya done gone and got yourself into now? Have you forgotten 'bout dem soldier boys up in de big house?" She marched forward, and Jones hurried to shut the door behind her.

"What are you doing here?" I said. "Who's watching over things at the house?"

"Missus Hendricks and now Missus Tucker." She looked past me. "Lard sakes, et is Mr. Kipling." She looked down at Big John as he and Jones removed Kipling's shirt.

"The bullet is still in him," Jones said. "Just missed his heart."

Kip stirred, and his hand thrashed at the ground.

"He ain't safe here." Mammy glanced at the door. "Probably in more danger dan he was out dere on his own."

"Do you think you can get the bullet out?" I wrung my hands.

"I do my bes', Missus," Big John said. "Rita, you hold dat lantern over here."

Mammy did as instructed.

I chewed the inside of my lip raw as I stood helplessly by.

"I sho' glad you here, Big John," Mammy said. "Wid Masa Bowden and Masa Ben away, we would've had no choice but to call on Crazy Eyed Henry…" Her words drifted as she recalled Henry was no longer with us. "May God rest his soul."

Henry had lost his life in the attack on Livingston. An image flashed of his lifeless body, pitchfork in hand, lying amongst the dead, and a knot formed in my gut. Such images awoke me at night, and I would sit upright, my heart hammering. I wished for it all to be a nightmare, but I'd lay back and stare at the ceiling, knowing it was reality. I questioned what purpose God had in allowing them to die. Why did He let the pain and horrors happening around the world occur? When He had the power to stop wars, why didn't He? The struggle to understand never ceased.

Mammy prattled on. "Henry and me never did git on dat well."

I recalled the incident with Mammy's tooth some years back and how Mary Grace and I had enlisted Henry to help us. The memory of Mammy circling her chamber, causing a fuss and swatting at him, brought a smile.

Big John worked on retrieving the bullet, and after what seemed like forever he let out a grunt and held up the bloodied ball.

"Lard be praised." Mammy's eyes gleamed, and she looked from Big John to me.

My heart soared, and I drew her into an embrace.

She patted my back before pushing away. "'Nuf of dat. What ef dem soldiers seed you acting lak dat?"

"Well, they aren't here." I squeezed her tighter before releasing her and sinking to my knees beside Kipling. "I will stay with him tonight." I whisked back the lock of sweat-drenched hair shielding Kip's left eye.

"But what 'bout de sergeant? He sho' to know you missing. I don't lak dat man one bit. De sooner he gone, de better," Mammy said.

"I believe we all will be happy to see the last of him, but until then we must endure." I studied Big John's skilled hand as he applied the last stitch to Kipling's wound. "Do you think he will make it?"

"Only time will tell, Missus. He lost a lot of blood. He in Orisha's hands now." Big John pulled to his feet.

He held fast to his home country and the Yoruba people's beliefs, while Mammy, born and raised in the South, upheld the Christian faith. A matter that sometimes caused disputes between the two, but now she remained silent.

"Ef he pulls through, we feed him real good. Ain't nothing but flesh and bones." Mammy handed me the lantern before covering Kip with a blanket.

"He will survive," I said with determination, regarding his gauntness and his pale flesh.

"De good Lard be de decider of dat," Mammy said matter-of-factly. She turned her inspection on me. "You need to git out of dem clothes. I git Mrs. Tucker to bring you a blanket and clothes."

Jones had them slip out the side door before returning to

extinguish the lanterns, except for the one he hung on a hook over the stall. "It will get a bit chilly in here tonight," he said.

"I'll make do."

"Best you seat yourself next to him on that clean straw. Body heat will do you both some good." He patted his hand on the stall door, took one last look at Kip, then turned and exited through the side door.

Whitney arrived with blankets and fresh clothing. I changed, and she gathered my clothes and left.

I positioned myself next to Kipling, my back against the wall. Drawing my knees to my chest, I pulled the blankets over us and rested my head back. Through a gap in the rafters, I peered at the night sky and whispered a prayer: "Please, let him live…and return my husband home safely."

CHAPTER
Twenty-Two

THE NEXT MORNING I WOKE TO THE WARMTH OF A HAND ON MY wrist, the pungent scent of horse dung, and straw poking through the fabric of my dress. I opened my eyes, recalling the previous night, and turned to look at Kip's hand resting against my flesh.

During the night I had laid down but didn't recall doing so. Upon stirring to the warmth of Kip's hand, I'd expected to find him looking back at me, but he remained unmoving, his eyes closed. Colorless lips melded with his pale flesh, and his chest rose and fell in shallow breaths. He would recover. I set my jaw, refusing to believe any different. I wouldn't lose another person I cared about. Until he recovered, I would give him shelter.

I thought of the room in the attic. "What good will it do me now?" I regarded the horse that hung his head over the stall to observe us. "We'd have to get him into the house and upstairs without the soldiers knowing."

The horse nickered his evaluation.

"I agree," I grumbled.

Hauling myself to my feet, I brushed and picked the straw from my clothing and hair. I considered the time as I listened to the pesky rooster's crow. Through the barn planks, I spotted him perched on the fence post. I abhorred the bird. He was the nastiest critter I'd ever encountered, and now he stood between me and the house.

I exited the barn through the side door, scanning the perimeter before slipping outside. Closing the door behind me, I checked over my shoulder before turning and racing around the corner of the barn. I collided with someone. We grabbed onto each other to keep from reeling backward.

"For heaven's sake, watch where you're going," a woman said, her tone heavy with displeasure.

I gasped, "Jane?"

She stepped back and gulped as she recognized me. "Mrs. Armstrong, my apologies." But she had no sooner mumbled the apology before her brow narrowed, and she gave me a lengthy inspection. "Where are you headed in such a hurry? And looking such a mess. You look as though you slept in your clothes."

"I did," I said quickly. "I couldn't sleep and read far into the night." Inside, I winced at the lame explanation.

She eyed the dust marring my cornflower-blue dress and my hair. After a moment, she shook her head and said, "Well, you'd best go get cleaned up. Rita has sent me to fetch some eggs from the hen house. With Mrs. Hendricks taken to her bed, I will be helping with the soldiers until she is on her feet again."

"Pippa is ill?"

"From what I understand, she hasn't felt good for the last day or two."

"But she didn't mention feeling ill."

"Most likely didn't want to put any more pressure on your shoulders." Her smile never moved beyond her lips as she swerved past me and continued on to the hen house.

I stood observing her until I was sure she wasn't heading to the barn. I had no reason not to trust her. She had been a dedicated employee for years. But her stance on the war and her displeasure at her son's choices gave me pause.

"You look a mess," Whitney whispered in my ear, and I whirled to face her.

"So I've been told. How are things at the house?"

"They could be better. I think the last group of soldiers

brought sickness with them. Pippa appears to be fighting an ailment along with three of the men."

"Splendid. This is exactly what we need," I said with exasperation. I sent one last look toward the hen house and tensed when I saw Jane watching us.

"Why are you so suspicious of her? You've always spoken fondly of her before."

I turned back to Whitney. "Yes, but it appears this war is revealing people's true colors."

Sergeant Absher stepped out onto the back veranda, lit a cigar, then stood eyeing us.

"I need to make myself presentable and see to matters at the house. Can you see that Jones takes care of our little issue in the barn?"

Worry shone in her green eyes, but she nodded and headed toward the kitchen house. I figured it was a decoy move to keep the sergeant from becoming suspicious. Grateful, I walked across the work yard to the back steps.

"Good morning, Mrs. Armstrong." The sergeant rested his elbows on the railing and peered down at me.

"How are you this morning?" I ascended the back steps.

"Better than some of the men." He nudged his head toward the library window.

"Mrs. Tucker informed me that some have fallen ill."

He eyed me in the same way Jane and Whitney had. "You look a bit weary yourself."

"As I told Mrs. Tucker, I couldn't sleep. I worry about my husband and uncle. Each time a new group of soldiers shows up here, I wonder where they are and if they're safe. Concern over their safety keeps me up at night."

"Understandably so. But surely your bed must provide better sleep than bedding with the animals."

"Pardon?" My blood chilled, but I tried to stifle my surprise.

He leaned forward and pulled a piece of straw from my hair, and held it out for me to examine.

My nerves thrummed, but I presented him with a light chuckle. "You caught me." I held out my arms in surrender. "You see, when I was a young girl, I would often go missing, and my father would find me asleep with the animals." The explanation sounded hollow.

He arched a brow. "You don't say?"

"Indeed. I used to give my mammy and him quite a scare. Last night I retreated to the quiet of the barn and the solace of the animals. Imagine my surprise to awaken this morning." I shook my head in feigned amusement.

A stern look shadowed his countenance. "Very well. Don't let me keep you."

"Thank you, Sergeant." I favored him with a smile before dashing inside.

I took the servant staircase, hurried to my chamber, and closed the door behind me. Heart striking in my throat, I leaned against the door and slid down to the floor. Glancing around the room, my eyes paused at the chair under the window where the shirt Bowden had worn the day before he'd left remained undisturbed. I had refused to let anyone wash it. Having it there gave me comfort and enabled me to daydream of his return. Almost a year after the commencement of the war, my husband's scent had long faded from the room.

CHAPTER
Twenty-Three

I COULDN'T RISK ATTRACTING ANY MORE SUSPICION, SO I KEPT TO THE work yard and house, sending word to Jones to update me on Kipling's condition. By the end of the week, whatever illness had befallen the soldiers and Pippa had dissipated, and no one else fell ill.

Kipling had yet to return to the land of the living, and I feared he never would.

Overhead the sky rumbled with a storm approaching from the north, and I closed the door to the kitchen house to ward off the wind.

"Sho' luks lak et's gwine to come down hard." Mammy stood by the hearth, holding a ladle, her gaze fastened on the single window.

The scent of braising beef filled the room, and I glanced from her to the evening meal simmering in a cast-iron kettle. Lately my appetite had diminished, with the increased worry plaguing my days.

"The storm is the least of my worries." I walked to the table and added a measure of cold butter to the pie crust.

"Mind you mix dat jus' right, so et flakey." Mammy crossed the room to oversee my work. "Dat woman Jane can't cook a lick. Dat meat pie she baked last week had a crust as tough as boards."

"Trust that you taught me well and let me make the pie." I scowled at her. Tension had knotted the muscles in my neck and shoulders, and I'd awoken with a headache that never ceased.

"You bin in a mood all morning." She returned my scowl.

I stopped mixing the pastry and took a deep breath. "I'm sorry. It's just some days I want to run and keep running."

"Says a white gal," Mammy said with a snort before marching to a nearby shelf and pulling down a jar of dried herbs.

I was in no mood for her sass and pivoted to level a glare at her. "You know what I mean."

"And what, leave us?" She eyed the window and said, in a hushed tone, "You fixing to sign Mister Kip's death warrant yourself? Or have you forgotten 'bout dem soldiers crawling from evvy corner of dis place? You ain't a quitter, angel gal, so don't start now."

I turned back to the dough and molded it into a ball while tears of frustration rose in my eyes. My despondency left me when the door flew open, sending a gust of wind through the room. I braced when Sailor dashed inside in a fit of tears and slammed the door behind him.

"Whatever is the matter?" I regarded him with concern.

He paced a moment or two before halting to regard me with pain-filled eyes.

I walked to him and squatted down. "Tell me what has you so upset."

Using the back of his hand, he wiped the tears before flicking his tongue to catch the drippings from his nose. "Ain't nothing." He tried to square his shoulders.

"It doesn't appear that way." I took his hand in mine, and he looked at the dough coating my fingers. "You know you can always tell me what is troubling you."

"One of them soldiers called me a n-nigger. Said that I was worse than a nigger. That I was a half-breed." His small chest heaved with silent sobs. "Said, 'Nigger, get over here and hand me my cane.'" When I didn't do as he said because I didn't know who he was talking to, he shouted, 'Are you deaf, nigger?'" Sailor's body shook, and again he broke into uncontrollable tears.

I gritted my teeth and thought of wringing the soldier's neck for his treatment of the boy. How dare he! I wrapped an arm around

Sailor's shoulders and drew him close. "Shh, my love. Don't pay any mind to the soldier. He must be an angry and frightened man."

I had tried to shelter Sailor from the discrimination and enmity toward blacks in the world outside of Livingston, but he had endured prejudice amongst the quarter folks. "Who are my people?" he'd asked the week before, when I found him in a similar state over mistreatment from the other children. "If they don't want me, where do I belong?"

Sailor's body trembled, and he mumbled into the collar of my blouse, "He don't seem frightened."

I pulled him back to look at him. "Forget about the soldier. What do I always tell you?"

"That we all the same. And that God created us in his image."

"Meaning?"

"That each of us is just as he planned."

"That's right. The soldier has poor manners, but you, my love, are a proper Southern gentleman who shows kindness, respect, and love to all of God's creations." I adjusted his shirt before using a finger to tilt his chin. "You take pride in who you are. You hear me?" He bobbed his head. "Good boy. And let no one tell you you are anything but that perfect creation." I kissed his cheek before standing to regard him. "What were you doing inside the house, anyway? I told you, with the soldiers there, you need to stay away."

"I was looking for her." He nudged his head at Mammy. "Miss Rita told me she had something special for me and to come and find her today." A hint of anger, mixed with confusion, crossed his sweet face, as though he blamed Mammy for his troubles.

"Land sakes, boy. I warn't 'pecting you to go marching into de big house." She shook her head in disbelief. "Come on over here and sit down. I got dat somepin' special right here." She waddled to the counter and removed a hidden piece of sugar cane.

Sailor dashed forward and dropped onto a chair at the table, eyeing her eagerly. "Where did you get that from?"

"Asked Mister Jones to git me a piece at de market on his

recent trip to town. He paid a hefty price to purchase dis treat to satisfy your sweet tooth."

I smiled at the exchange between the two. "If you can finish up here, I will head up to the house to make sure everything is running smoothly."

"We be jus' fine," Mammy said without looking up. "Dis young man can sit wid me for a spell."

I left them and walked toward the house. The wind slapped the fabric of my skirt and pulled wisps of hair from my pins. Movement on the back veranda drew my attention, and I spotted the sergeant seated with his boots resting on the railing. My hands knotted at my sides, and the desire to give him and the other soldiers a good tongue-lashing surged.

"Mrs. Armstrong?" Jones's voice lifted over the wind's whine.

I halted and turned to observe him striding across the work yard toward me. My gaze drifted back to the sergeant before I turned my back and waited for Jones's approach.

He glanced over my shoulder at the house and grimaced. "He is always watching. Suspicious by nature, I assume."

I fought the urge to share in his observation of the sergeant. "What is it you need?"

His gaze pulled to my face. "Big John sent me to inform you that Kipling is awake."

My heart leaped at the news, but I restrained my happiness. "Please tell him when I think it's safe, I will come. It may not be for some time."

"Yes, ma'am." He tipped his hat and left me.

I took a deep breath and summoned the courage to head back to the house. To my relief, the sergeant had disappeared. I looked around the grounds and didn't spot him. I would not allow the man to intimidate me in my own home. The sooner he returned to his regiment, the better. I prayed for his swift recovery and set my mind to aiding God's hands in making it so.

CHAPTER
Twenty-Four

S EVERAL DAYS PASSED BEFORE I COULD SEIZE AN OPPORTUNITY TO SLIP to the barn unnoticed. Christmas day had drawn to a close, and twilight stretched across the plantation.

Pippa had insisted on serving the soldiers a proper Christmas feast. Fattened and mirthful from the Christmas goose, with stuffing made of apples, chestnuts, onions, and plum pudding, they retreated with us womenfolk to the parlor. Pippa, looking ever beautiful, in a rose-colored silk gown, seated herself at the piano, and the nostalgic sound of "Silent Night" filled the room. The men's chatter ceased, and Whitney positioned herself at Pippa's right and began to sing. I leaned into the doorframe and let the tranquility flow over me. The men, with whiskey snifters in hand, gathered around the piano and joined Whitney in song. As our voices melded, so did our hearts in the pining for our loved ones. That day we never spoke of the war and the hardship our nation endured.

When the song ended, Pippa took on requests from the men, and soon they shuffled the cots out of the way and asked Whitney and I to dance, to which we obliged.

Pippa looked on with a grander smile as Whitney and I whirled around the room from one soldier's arms to another. Determined to enjoy the evening and not let my thoughts carry me to troublesome worries, I doted my attention upon each soldier.

Over my dance partner's shoulder I regarded Whitney as she belted out laughter, seemingly amused by the young private who stood chin height to her.

"You don't say." She whirled around the room, a vision in a pale green gown.

Soldiers stood to the side of the room, chatting and looking on with merriment. I smiled, discovering joy in their happiness.

The soldier dancing with me paused, and I almost lost my footing when he released me and turned to face Sergeant Absher.

"May I?" Sergeant Absher said.

"Of course." He bowed, but before stepping away he looked at me with gleaming blue eyes. "Thank you, ma'am. The dance was most enjoyable."

I curtsied. "The pleasure is all mine."

His eyes glimmered with appreciation as he took a broad sweep, observing from the hem of the ruby gown Bowden had purchased for the last Christmas banquet to the ruby-clustered necklace resting between my breasts. "You are a sight, Mrs. Armstrong."

"Thank you, Sergeant." I inclined my head.

He swept a hand over his gleaming silver mane and handed his cane to the soldier before taking my hand. A wince came from him, and I noted the struggle in his face as he tried to support his weight. Determination set his jaw, and he moved me around the room at an awkward and stiff pace.

I fixed a smile. "Have you enjoyed yourself this evening?"

"Indeed," he said with a grunt, as a bead of sweat trickled down his brow.

"Tell me, sergeant, is there a wife who waits at home?"

He tensed, and the briefest glint of pain shone in his eyes before he pushed it away. "No, ma'am. My wife died twelve years ago."

"Oh," I said, wishing I could retrieve my question. "I'm sorry to hear that."

"It's quite all right." A sadness reflected in his visage, and he regarded me with intensity. "My Clara was a woman you couldn't forget. She had a way of getting under your skin."

I sensed his need to talk about her and offered a light laugh before saying, "Us women do that from time to time."

The reserve in his demeanor shifted, and he said, with more pleasantry than I had ever witnessed in the man, "She was a little thing with more spirit than one man could handle. When she set her mind there was no stopping her. She would stand up to anyone that tried to cross her." The pleasantness of his light chuckle and the tenderness alight in his eyes waltzed on my heart.

"You don't say." My smile deepened. "A woman after my own heart, I might add."

A trace of a smile touched his lips. "Yes, you remind me of her in ways. I didn't know how to deal with it at first; I was so taken back. It was like I was thrown into the past, and all the memories and loneliness vented."

"I'm sorry to have caused you distress."

"On the contrary," he said, coming to a sudden stop. "Clara always said I had an unapproachable manner and that I was lucky she didn't discourage easily with the number of times I rejected her attention. The woman showed her determination to win my heart, and after five years I finally saw what was before me all the time." His gaze contained a far-off look. "We spent eight wonderful years together, and she made me a better man." His vulnerability retreated, and gruffness took front and center as he regarded me. "I thank you for the dance; for a few moments, I could imagine what it would be like to hold my Clara once more." No longer fighting to hide the pain, he leaned heavily on me.

A soldier stepped in to help, and we led him to a nearby chair. He dropped into the chair with a thump before removing a handkerchief to wipe the sweat from his brow.

"It was a pleasure, Mrs. Armstrong." Tears gleamed in his eyes.

"Yes, it was." I curtsied and dismissed myself.

"May I have the next dance?" A soldier approached on my right.

"Do you mind if I sit this one out?" I said, on the verge of tears. "I need some fresh air."

"Of course." He bowed and stepped back.

Not seeking to draw attention I kept my pace light, and only when I stepped into the corridor did I look back to observe for onlookers. Sighting no one, I hurried my steps, and at the back door, retrieved Mammy's shawl and wrapped it around my shoulders before exiting the house.

On the back veranda, I observed the work yard for movement and found no sign. After one last look at the house, I descended the stairs and raced across the yard to the barn. At the side door, I surveyed the perimeter before darting inside.

The dim light of a lantern shone from the loft. I fumbled my way through the darkness to the ladder.

"Big John?" I placed a hand on a rung.

"Dat you, Missus?"

"It is. Shine the lantern over here so I can come up."

Shuffling occurred overhead, and Big John's shadow elongated over me as he came into view. I climbed the ladder, and when I reached the top he held out a hand and helped me up.

Kipling sat with his back against the wall, regarding me. "We meet again, my friend," he said with a feeble wave.

"I'm glad you decided to join us." I noticed the tray of food, barely touched, beside him. I placed a hand on Big John's arm. "Why don't you go eat, and let me sit with him for a while."

"But don't you got a celebration happening up at de big house?"

"Yes, but if you make it quick, I can be back before anyone misses me."

"Yessum," he said.

I took the lantern and held it while he climbed down before turning back to Kipling. I strode to his side and seated myself on the straw next to him, smoothing out the flounces of my gown.

"I'm glad to see the war hasn't claimed all the pleasures of life," Kipling said.

I waved a hand of dismissal at him as heat touched my cheeks. "Your flattery will do no good on me."

He smiled, but weariness tugged at his face. "A vision nonetheless."

"What happened to you? How did you end up here?"

"Soon after we took Port Royal, the army sent out a small patrol to gather supplies. We met a group of men and boys on the road, and they didn't hesitate to open fire. I pulled my gun as one advanced toward me, but realizing he was but a boy, I hesitated, and he didn't." He shrugged. "Pain erupted in my chest, and my horse took off. I recall gripping its mane to stay upright in my saddle. I must have lost consciousness because the next thing I knew, I was lying face down on the riverbank, and the heavens were pouring down on me. I followed the river for days before infection set in." He regarded the hole in his chest, which appeared to be healing. "How I ended up here, I'm uncertain. I somehow recognized your husband's old plantation between periods of delusion, and I headed in this direction. I don't recall anything after that night. From what Miss Rita and Big John have told me, you not only harbor a fugitive but a house full of Confederate soldiers." He shook his head. "Leave it to you to place yourself in jeopardy by taking on the injustices of the world and the enemy."

"They are hardly the enemy. They are Southerners like you and I. Has your time in the North caused you to forget your origins?"

"Of course not," he said. "Never thought I would see the day when you and I stood on opposite sides."

I lowered my gaze. "Nor I, but as you can expect, my heart is torn."

"Yes, well, war doesn't show mercy now, does it?" His eyes were blank.

I was afraid to ask him the question that had troubled me

since I'd found him by the river, but I couldn't contain myself any longer. "Bowden...did you see him?"

"Nah, and thank God for that," he said. "That's a choice I pray I never have to make."

I swallowed hard. "You wouldn't harm him, would you?"

"And make you hate me forever?" His eyes flashed before he lowered his gaze. "Not intentionally."

"But what if you were forced to?" I pressed.

"What do you want me to say, Willow? It's war. When you're on a battlefield, you don't have time to think. The stench of death is everywhere. Brothers killing brothers. It's a sight I never thought I'd see."

Heart fracturing, I covered my face with my hands as sobs racked my body. Last week my letter and care package to Bowden had been returned; days later, Whitney and Pippa's had too.

"Please don't cry." The warmth of Kipling's hand on my arm only made me weep that much harder.

He shuffled around, and his arms encompassed me. For the briefest of moments, I contemplated the inappropriateness of our embrace, but loneliness and yearning stopped me from pulling away.

"Not only do the Union blockades limit our supplies, but they have cut off mail service." I rested my cheek on his naked chest, taking solace in the beating of his heart. "The letters we write are returned. I have written to Ben and Bowden numerous times, and only one letter has gotten through from him."

"Lincoln has appointed Montgomery Blair as Postmaster General. He's responsible for cutting off the mail service to all Southern states that seceded from the Union."

I pulled back, indignation thumping in my chest. "And in doing so, he carves out the heart of the Confederate soldiers and their families."

"Again, this is war. What did you expect to happen?" Kipling said bluntly.

I grimaced and swallowed the pain from his words.

"I don't mean to cause you affliction, but you must know what is happening out there, and until this war is over, it's going to get a lot harder."

I picked at a piece of straw. "I've prided myself in being a strong person, but I don't know how much more I can take."

"Well, in true Willow form, you've taken on too much." Tenderness softened his assessment.

"We all must do our part," I said. "I did what I thought was right."

"And to keep yourself busy so your mind doesn't dwell on what is happening out there. Am I right?"

"Yes, I'm no stranger to the pressure of running this place, but with our supplies limited—"

"Does the army not provide rations for the men?"

"They do, but the allotments are inadequate. I fear that our next crop will not get in the ground. And if it does, I worry how much we can get planted."

"Surely your slaves and Jones can get the fields planted." His brow furrowed.

"We don't have the help we once did." I briefly informed him of what had happened to our ships, and at Livingston the night Fort Sumter was attacked.

"My God," he said when I had finished.

"All one can do is go about each day believing the next will provide some glimmer of hope," I said before giving him a warm smile. "Like learning death wouldn't claim you this time."

"If it had, I would have haunted you from the other side," he said with a wide grin.

"Once you are strong enough to move, we need to get you out of here."

"The army has probably deemed me a deserter or prey to the Lowcountry predators."

"Well, if one of those soldiers at the house finds out I'm hiding a Union soldier, they will execute us both."

"I'm sorry for the trouble I brought to your door."

"You are my friend, regardless of the uniform you wear. Your safety is worth the risk." I pulled to my feet, and he grabbed my hand. I flinched as his finger stroked my flesh.

"My hallucinations were filled with your image. It was your face that pulled me through this. I had the craziest vision of you lying next to me and the warmth of your body as it sheltered my own." His eyes revealed the love he held for me.

"The mind is a crazy thing." I recollected the first night, when I'd stayed by his side. I evaded telling him that what he thought was a hallucination was, in fact, reality. "I will rest tonight after seeing for myself that you're on the road to recovery."

He released my hand, and we exchanged a few words before I returned to the house and the gaiety of the men.

CHAPTER
Twenty-Five

THE DAY THE SERGEANT AND HIS MEN DEPARTED A SENSE OF liberation enveloped the plantation. No news had arrived of a new shipment of soldiers, and we welcomed the leisure time that followed.

I gathered the last of the linens from the cots, and arms overflowing, I walked outside. Tillie jabbed a poker at the embers under the large steaming wash kettle.

"This is the last of them." I placed the linens in a basket on the ground. "Where is Jane?" I glanced at Uriah, who was sweeping debris from the back veranda. "I asked her this morning to help you get these linens washed and hung."

"Not sho'. Haven't seen her since 'fore de soldiers left."

I frowned and scoured the grounds. Jane hadn't proven to be the helpful sort, and I wondered why she had remained employed by my family for so long. "We must all pull our weight around here. If you see her, please send her up to the house."

"Yessum," Tillie said.

I leaned in and lowered my voice. "I'm going to check on our little matter in the barn."

So far, we'd kept Kipling out of sight, and only Big John and Tillie had been permitted to visit the barn. The fewer people in and out, the better, Jones had insisted.

"De li'l matter took a walk."

"You can't be serious!" I bristled.

She dropped a load of linens into the boiling water. "Took off toward de river soon after de soldiers rode outta here."

"It's good to see he is feeling better," I grumbled under my breath. "Can you manage here while I go and tend to the matter?"

"Yessum," she said with a hesitant nod. "But…"

"But what?"

"I reckon Mister Kip got tired of being cooped up in de barn. Et's bin weeks…" Her voice drifted with the narrowing of my eyes.

"We will see about that." Indignant, I spun on my heel and marched across the work yard in the direction of the river. Although I appreciated Tillie's attempt to defend Kip's risk of exposing himself and us, he'd receive a good tongue-lashing when I found him.

The usually invigorating sounds of Carolina chickadees singing and the river's warbling current grated on my nerves as I approached the riverbank. From above, I regarded Kipling standing on the rocky bank below with his arms extended and his face tilted to the sky, letting the morning sun wash over him.

Rocks skidded and fell as I climbed down the bank, alerting him to my presence. He spun around with his hands positioned and ready to take on an attacker.

"It's just me," I said. "And you're lucky it is. What were you thinking, exposing yourself?" I stormed toward him.

His eyes widened. "Your guests have left. I needed fresh air and to feel the sun on my flesh. One can only handle the dreariness of the barn and the smell of horses for so long."

"I understand that, but it isn't safe." I surveyed our surroundings. "You never know who is watching. The Home Guards come out of nowhere."

"I am aware of that. Have you forgotten they're the ones that attacked my patrol on the road?"

I folded my arms across my chest. "How do you expect Southerners to act? Our plantations are looted by Federal troops. Beaufort citizens were forced to abandon their homes and the town. Now both Beaufort and Port Royal have been seized by the US Army. Not only do I have to worry about the Federals coming here, but also new Confederate soldiers or folks from neighboring plantations who could ride in here at any time. We must take all precautions. We've kept you hidden from most folks here on this plantation, and I intend to keep it that way until you've recovered enough to get you out."

"I'm leaving today," he said.

"Today?" I dropped my arms. "You're hardly fit to return to the battlefield."

"I'll manage. I'll head out under the cover of night." He took my hands in his. "I can't thank you enough for what you've done for me, and I won't put you in anymore danger." His eyes roved over my face. "Thank you, Willow. Not only for your help but for your friendship."

"You will always have my friendship," I said. "If you're to leave, you won't do it on foot. I will see you get back to Point Royal."

I turned to leave, and he held onto my hand. "No." The intensity in his voice carried, and he lowered his tone. "I won't allow you—"

"You don't really have a choice. I will deliver you to Point Royal. And that's that." I pulled free of his grip and strode to the foot of the knoll before looking back. "We leave when darkness falls and the plantation settles. Until then, can you please make yourself scarce?"

He closed the distance between us in three strides. "Fine. We will do this your way." He grinned down at me. "Maybe I'm the fortunate one, and Bowden is the unlucky bastard."

I scowled at him. "What are you referring to?"

"You're a lot of woman to manage, and imperious as they come."

I balled my hands on my hips. "Well, I'll have you know—"

He chuckled, and I sensed I'd played right into his hands.

"Oh, you." I waved a hand in dismissal before turning to scale the bank. "I have little patience for your teasing."

His merriment continued as he darted ahead to offer me a

hand up. I dug in my heels and swatted his hand away. "You're impossible."

I reached the top and, without waiting, swerved to walk back to the plantation.

A rustling noise snatched my attention, and I froze.

"What is it?" he said.

With an eerie sensation that we were being watched, I scoured the trees lining the pathway. At a flash of movement, Kipling sprinted forward. Someone let out a squeal, and I homed in on a person as they took off running. My heart clenched as I recognized the red-flowered head rag. *Jane.* Had she been spying on us? If so, why? I charged after Kipling as he bounded through the trees.

He caught up and seized her by the back of the collar, pulling her to a halt.

"Get off of me." She swatted at him, her eyes alight with terror.

He spun her around and eyed me as I reached them. "She from around here?"

"Unhand me this instant." Defiance shone in her eyes. "I'm not one of the slaves to be handled in such a manner."

He glanced to me for instruction.

"Jane and her husband are staying with us. They managed our townhouse in Charleston until the fire took it."

He released her and stepped back. "Sorry, ma'am," he said with sincerity. "Wasn't sure who was spying on us."

She glowered at him before turning her displeasure on me. "You welcome the enemy into your home and offer him protection?"

I gawked at her, my heart thudding with mounting panic.

Jane gestured at Kipling but kept her gaze trained on me. "The day I caught you coming from the barn, disheveled and looking like you had bedded with the animals, I had my suspicions you were hiding something. Tried to follow you the night you left the celebration up at the house to sneak down to the barn, but Uriah interfered, and I never got to see for myself what lured you there. Then just this morning, I caught Tillie entering the barn with a satchel and leaving empty-handed soon after. Imagine my surprise when I slipped in and hid in the shadows to overhear Mr. Jones having a conversation with him." She nudged her head at Kipling without so much as a sideways glance. "Didn't take overhearing but a few words to know that this here man is a Federal soldier."

"He is my friend." My defense sounded futile to my own ears.

"That may have well been before war broke out. And Union soldiers encroached on South Carolina soil," she said with an up-turn of her chin.

"Jane, please…what if this was your son?"

"Leave my boy out of this."

I ignored her and pressed forward with my plea. "What if the war persists and Lincoln is forced to allow blacks to enlist? Your son could very well be him." I motioned at Kipling, who stood gawking from me to Jane.

She crossed her arms and looked away, but I sensed her mind was scrambling.

"You've been employed by my family—"

"It does not matter. I can't condone your actions. Keeping your secret to hide a Union soldier is something I can't turn a blind eye to."

"Am I missing something here?" Kipling said. Jane turned to look at him, and he directed his words to her. "The Union fights to free you from slavery."

She squared her shoulders. "As I stated, I'm not one of Mrs. Armstrong's slaves. I am a free woman. Born free."

His brow furrowed. "Am I to believe that because you have never felt the chains of bondage, you've chosen to disregard the injustices the blacks suffer by turning a blind eye?" He tossed the idiocy of her claim back in her face, and she winced.

"I care about the conservation of the South. My granddaddy was a freed man and overseer to one of the most prestigious families of South Carolina, as was Father. He taught me to see myself as removed from the Africans brought to work our lands."

"Unbelievable." Kipling's face reddened. "How can you in good conscience dismiss what is happening in this country to your own kind?"

"I am free…" she stammered.

"You may be free, but that ensures nothing. You are as black as any slave. You are denied rights and regarded as the minority by the whites," he said with exasperation. "Surely such injustice doesn't sit well with you?"

"I'm aware of the inequity to slaves, but free blacks can live in peace and prosperity amongst the whites."

Awareness of Jane's privileged mentality elicited by her upbringing left me lost for words.

"Can you believe this?" Kipling rocked on his heels. Passion and rage gleamed in his eyes as he peered at me. "This woman's principles are as defiled as those of any slave owner."

I touched his arm. "Let me handle this."

"Very well." He threw his hands in the air, and veered past Jane to march back toward the plantation.

She observed him before shifting to face me. "I'm disappointed in you, Mrs. Armstrong. I've carried the utmost respect for your father and you, but I can't uphold the knavery of what I witnessed here. Mr. Armstrong and Mr. Hendricks and good men like them risk their lives to preserve the ways of the South while you trifle with the enemy."

I gasped at her brashness. "How dare you?" I seethed. "I've given you shelter when you didn't have a home to go to. Maybe the real enemy here is you!"

She gasped, and her hand slipped to her throat.

Tears of frustration swelled in my eyes, and I closed my eyes to squeeze them off. "Please, Jane." I regarded her. "If you have any measure of mercy in you, I beg you not to cause any trouble. I will see he leaves here today."

"I suggest you do," she said.

I fought the urge to tell her to remove herself from my property within the hour, fearing that approach would cause more harm than good. I avoided meeting her gaze as I swerved by her and strode back toward the house.

"Mrs. Armstrong, everything all right?" Uriah's brow wrinkled as I stormed up the back steps.

"Yes," I said in a daze and whirled to discover Jane headed our way. I couldn't stand to be in her company for a moment longer and circled the veranda to the front.

Whitney lazed on the porch swing with a book. She looked up as I marched toward her and straightened. "What has you all stirred up?" She lowered the book and peered behind me as though expecting someone on my heels.

I didn't answer until she was within arm's length. "Jane knows about Kipling and has threatened to expose us."

"Threatened you?" Whitney's hackles rose, and her green eyes flashed.

"Keep your voice down," I said through clenched teeth. I planted my hands on my waist and paced in front of her. "Tonight, we will get Kipling out. You and I will take the old wagon we used for transporting fugitives. We will take him to Point Royal."

"Are you insane?" She caught my wrist and yanked me to a halt. "If you thought transporting runaways was dangerous, this is like laying your head in the mouth of a lion. The roads are policed by the Home Guards, not to mention Confederate and Federal soldiers prowling all over this state."

"Do you think I don't know that? We have no choice. Our hand is forced," I whispered back.

"All right." She wrung her hands. "Say we get him out, and by some chance, we get back here undiscovered; what are you going to do about the traitor in our midst?"

"I don't know," I said helplessly.

"Surely you aren't considering letting her remain at Livingston—"

The pounding of horses' hooves distracted us from our conversation and we spun to peer at the lane. My heart skipped, and I clutched Whitney's arm. "It's the Home Guards. I have to hide Kipling." I raced across the veranda. "You see to them," I said over my shoulder.

"Me?" Whitney cried. "But—"

Her voice faded as I charged around the side of the house and collided with someone.

"Take it easy, ma'am," Uriah said, gripping my arms to steady me. "What is the trouble?"

I gulped, panic stealing my words. I spotted Jane observing us from below, but as she heard the horses approaching, her gaze shifted to the front yard. A look of relief spread across her face.

I tore myself from Uriah's grip and raced down the back steps and across the work yard to the barn. I threw open the door and charged inside.

"Kipling," I shouted. "Kip…" I spun around.

"I thought you insisted I lie low, but here you are bellowing for all to hear." He stepped from the shadows.

"The Home Guards are coming up the lane. We need to get you inside and out of sight."

I grabbed his hand, and we raced back the way I'd come.

"Get Jane," I said to Jones as he exited the kitchen house with a slab of ham in hand. "She knows."

Jones's gaze drifted by me to the front of the house. He cursed, dropped the ham, and bolted off.

Kipling and I raced toward the back steps and rushed inside the house.

"In here." I halted at the closet under the stairs.

"Willow, is everything all right?" Pippa descended the stairs.

"Pippa, thank God. Get him hidden." I released Kipling and raced to the door. Pausing to catch my breath, I gripped the doorknob and looked back. Pippa opened the closet, and she and Kip ducked inside. I whispered a prayer before stepping outside to meet whatever fate awaited us.

My heart hammered against my ribcage, and a stitch formed in my side.

"Good morning, Mr. Carlton." Whitney stood at the end of the path as Josephine's husband and his posse reined their horses to a stop. "How do you all fare today?"

"Good, good," he said before studying Jones where he stood clutching Jane's arm.

I guessed Jones had been too late to remove her without causing suspicion. Uriah stood at the corner of the veranda, eyeing Jones and his wife, appearing confused.

"We are doing our rounds in this area," Theodore Carlton said. "What's the trouble there?" He nudged his head at Jane.

"Nothing I can't handle," Jones grunted. "Caught this one trying to run off. Hauled her back to administer the whipping she's had coming for a while. The rebellious sort."

Uriah gasped and, eyes widening, he looked to me. I lightly shook my head, my eyes pleading for him to remain silent.

"Run off, ya say," Theodore said with a snort of disgust. "Soon as our backs are turned, these damn niggers take to running. In fact, I just captured this one along the road." He pointed the butt of his whip behind him, and I leaned to see past him before fighting back a sob at the lifeless, bloodied form of a slave boy slumped over the rump of a young guard's mount. Theodore grinned. "His master told me he'd run off, and I told him if I ran across him, I'd haul him back. Didn't expect the dog to put up such a fight."

I descended the stairs, and all reasoning left me as I went to the side of the horse holding the dead boy. "He isn't but ten," I said, wrestling back the tears. "I'm sure when his master asked you to keep an eye out for him, he didn't expect you to bring him back dead." I kept my eyes lowered, afraid they'd reveal the profound ache in my soul and my mounting rage.

"They're hiding a Federal soldier," Jane blurted.

I froze.

Theodore stiffened and twisted in his saddle. "What did you say?"

I moved away from the dead boy and circled the horses to stand in front of the Home Guards.

"As I'm sure you're aware, Livingston has become a wayside hospital for the Confederate soldiers," I said.

Theodore shifted his piercing gaze to me. "I've heard. But what of the nigger's claim of you sheltering a Union soldier?"

My shoulders slumped, and I lowered my gaze, pressing weary fingers to my temples. "Our days are long and exhausting, with caring for the soldiers the army brings here. We are weary. One's mind becomes consumed with the horrors of war. Long after I lay in bed, I hear the soldiers' cries. My nights are filled with nightmares of the Federal Army invading our lands and overtaking us." I lifted my gaze and glanced at Jane as Uriah positioned himself at her side and whispered something to her. "The blacks are delicate creatures, so I reckon it's been too much for her to handle. She has suffered from night terrors and dashes through the house claiming a Union soldier is on her heels. As you can imagine, it gives everyone quite a fright."

"She is lying. I saw him for myself," Jane interrupted.

Uriah looked at his wife, dumbfounded, and gripped her arm. "Woman, be silent."

Jane shook him off and hurled a glare in my direction. Fear and determination glistened in her dark eyes. "I'm not crazy. I speak the truth."

Theodore looked from her back to me.

I shook my head and extended my arms. "If it would ease your mind, you can examine the grounds yourself."

Theodore nodded at an elderly man and a boy. "Bedford and Singleton, check the house."

"The barn. He is hiding in the barn," Jane said, struggling to get free from Jones.

"Jones, release her. And show these gentlemen to the barn," I said. "Let's settle this matter once and for all. I'm sure Mr. Carlton and his men have more pressing matters."

The muscles in Jones's neck corded, and he shoved Jane at her husband. "See to your woman."

After the men and Jones stalked off toward the barn, I looked up at Theodore to find him regarding me with curiosity. "Is there something wrong?" I said.

He swung off his horse and stood looking at the house. "If you don't mind, me and the boys will take a look inside."

I swallowed the nerves churning my stomach. "Of course. Follow me." I feigned cheerfulness and spun to walk inside. Whitney ducked her head to avoid my gaze and strode slowly and calmly ahead of us.

Inside, Theodore and the others tromped from room to room, tracking mud over the floors. Mammy stood at attention in the corridor with her head bowed and jaw set. I could only imagine the distress and annoyance rising inside her.

Legs leaden, I guided them up the stairs and through each chamber before returning to the main floor. "And that is all," I said. "I hope the tour of my home satisfies any suspicion she has caused."

Theodore looked around before his gaze halted, and he gestured to a boy. "Have you checked that door?"

I glanced in the direction he pointed, and my breath caught as he motioned at the closet under the stairs.

"No, sir," the boy squeaked.

"Then do it," Theodore said sharply.

The boy hurried down the corridor, and Theodore returned his gaze to me. I graced him with a smile while inside, I felt anything but calm.

"All clear, sir," the boy called.

"All right, let's saddle up." Theodore marched to the door and strode outside as Jones and the others returned. "Well, did you find anything?"

"All clear," they said in unison.

Theodore glowered at Jane, who gawked at him.

"He is here somewhere. I swear."

"Lying nigger," Theodore spat and descended the stairs. Before pulling himself up onto his horse, he eyed me. "It would do you good to teach her a lesson. If only I could stay around to witness it myself. I would find much pleasure in seeing her lying skin peeled from her body."

My hands tightened at my sides. "She will be dealt with, I assure you. My apologies for the trouble she has caused."

The Home Guards mounted and rode out.

"What have you done?" Uriah shouted, and I turned as he struck his wife across the face. "Have you forgotten who you are? Or that I too was born a slave?"

She stood cupping her cheek. "You must believe me, Uriah. I saw him with my own eyes," she pleaded. "Just this morning." She sent an accusing glare my way. "She is hiding him."

The channel of rage inside me erupted, and I stormed at her. "Have you witnessed nothing? Did you see that boy slung over their saddle, his feet raw from the chase? If I know Theodore, the boy didn't die easily. How can you stand for that?" I stomped my foot and kept my hands pinned at my sides. God help me, but I wanted to wring her slender neck between my hands. "You're no better than a slave master. Do you possess any compassion in you at all? You are a mother, for God's sake. And a black, at that."

Jane swallowed hard but tilted her head with unbending pride.

"Mrs. Armstrong," Uriah said. I looked from his wife to him. Regret etched his expression. "I'm deeply sorry for the inconvenience she has caused. Your father was my friend and never showed me anything but kindness and respect during my years under his employment. My wife has dishonored that friendship with her treachery. We will pack our things and be gone."

"Unfortunately, I think it's best," I said with a heavy heart. "I can't house someone who seeks to harm me and those I care about."

He bowed his head in acquiescence before clutching Jane's elbow and leading her away.

I waited on the veranda with Whitney and Pippa as Jane and Uriah walked down the lane not long after. Uriah's usual leisurely gait had been modified by determination, and he walked briskly to put distance between him and his wife, forcing her to half run to keep up. Despondent, I rubbed the chill from my arms. "I hope no harm befalls them."

"And what would it matter if it did?" Whitney's voice lacked all empathy. "After you gave them a home, she repays you like that?"

"The crime isn't Uriah's. Besides, I can't help but feel sorry for her."

"Sorry for her?" Whitney threw her hands in the air. "You can't be serious." She swung to face me. "The woman almost signed our death warrants."

I never let my gaze leave the couple. "She can't see past the privileges awarded to her as a free black. She is deceived by the disease of hostility that rules our world."

"Has chosen to be deceived, you mean," Whitney huffed.

"Perhaps we shouldn't come to a conclusion too quickly about her."

"And why not?"

"Because," Pippa said. I turned to lean against the railing as she continued. "Too often, we judge and attack each other instead of choosing to stop and truly listen to the reasoning behind another's actions. If we would but heed each other's pain and concerns, we could stop this war and any that might follow."

"Pippa is right. Fear has become our ruler. If we don't stand unified, it is all of humankind that will suffer."

"Well, thanks for the Sunday sermon, ladies, but I think I will need a day or two to process my annoyance with Jane." Whitney marched inside and the door shut on her retreat.

Jaw unhinged, I looked at Pippa. "Well, she took that well."

"She will come to her senses; we are all under a great deal of pressure." She encircled my shoulders with an arm and led me to the door.

"I hope so…"

CHAPTER
Twenty-Six

"WELL, AIN'T YOU TWO A SIGHT." MAMMY MARCHED INTO my chamber as Whitney stepped from behind the privacy screen, dressed in men's apparel.

"I don't lak et one bit. Not one bit, I tell ya." She balled her hands on her ample hips. "Dem soldiers git ahold of ya, dey gwine have demselves a grand ol' time wid two purty gals lak you."

"Oh, hush, Mammy. Don't talk like that. I won't be drowned in your fears today," I said with a scowl. Nerves had chased me all day, and her grievances wouldn't help.

"Et ain't fear but good sense. You two shouldn't be out dere on dem roads alone."

"It hasn't stopped us before." I fastened the last button on my husband's shirt before donning his coat.

"And you ain't bin in de middle of a war 'fore." The creases in her forehead deepened. "I knowed you put me in my grave 'fore my time. Done knowed et since I laid my eyes on ya."

"Would you prefer that Kipling stays? You saw what happened today. It's too dangerous."

"I know he got to go, but why can't Jones take him?"

"Because we need Jones here in case the Federals show up."

She huffed and grumbled under her breath.

Whitney pinned up her auburn locks before setting a floppy hat overtop and pulling it snuggly down. In an extravagant show, she twirled around for us to get a good look at her. "Well, how do I look?" Her grin spread from ear to ear.

"Like Ruby when she showed up here in disguise with Kipling some years back." The image of Ruby flashed in my mind's eye.

"Well, it's been a while since you and I have been on an adventure."

"Adventure?" Mammy's voice rose. "Is dat what we are calling et? Dis war has gone to evvyone's head. I'm sick of dem soldier boys lying all over de house, bleeding all over my floors. De sooner dis war is over, de better. You know I lak a clean—"

"Yes, Miss Rita, we know. You like a clean house," Whitney said brightly. "Just think, when this war is over, they will be gone, and you will continue to raise hell for years to come."

Mammy scoffed and narrowed her eyes. "Dat ain't no fitting way for a lady to talk. Ef I were your mama, I would have—"

"Put the fear of God in me?" Whitney's eyes glittered with sly merriment.

I held my breath as the bear before us exited her den and unhinged her jaw. "Now you listen here—"

"Oh, Mammy, I wish you wouldn't fuss so. We will be careful and return by week's end." I strode to the looking glass and regarded the young man gazing back at me. I imagined if I had a younger brother, he would resemble this reflection.

"Have et your way. I know you gwine to anyway." Mammy came to stand beside me and fully inspected my reflection.

"What?" I said when her brow puckered.

"Ef someone git a couple feet from you, dey gwine to know you ain't men. Ef you fixing to do dis—wait here; I'll be back." She marched to the door and disappeared.

Whitney sat on the edge of the bed, and I walked to a chair by the window and sat to wait for Mammy's return.

"What do you suppose she is up to?" Whitney sent me a nervous glance after several minutes had passed.

"I don't know. But she never ceases to surprise me." I drummed my fingers on the arm of the chair.

"That woman scares me." Whitney glanced at the doorway, and a part of me enjoyed seeing her squirm.

She jumped to her feet when weighted footsteps sounded in the corridor. Mammy walked into the room, pail in hand and huffing to catch her breath.

"What do you have there?" I stood and gestured at the pail.

"Mud," Mammy said.

"Mud?" I frowned. "What in heaven's name for?"

She strode across the room as though on a mission and halted in front of me. "You may be wearing dem dere clothes, but dat soft skin and rosy cheeks give yous away for sho'." She scooped her hand in the pail and withdrew a slimy clump of mud, and I braced when she slapped it on my face. I curled my nose at the earthy smell as she caked it across my cheeks, forehead, and lips before removing the excess.

"You next, Missus Tucker."

Whitney cringed and stood ramrod straight as Mammy masked her flawless pale flesh.

"Dere." Mammy stood back to admire her work. "Now you luk lak a pair of farmers." She leaned in to sniff me. "And you smell lak one too." She gave a hearty chuckle.

I gawked at her before shifting my gaze to Whitney, who stood mortified. I broke into laughter.

Whitney scowled at me. "I'm glad you're enjoying this." She marched to the looking glass to take a gander and gasped at her reflection before swinging back to look at us. "Well, I have to admit, I do agree with you, Miss Rita."

Mammy's shoulders rolled back. "We ain't in de clear yet. After what dat woman did today, I don't trust no nigra. We got to git you downstairs, outside, and out of sight widout anyone seeing you."

I slipped on a pair of gloves. "Let's go."

"Let me see ef et's clear." Mammy poked her head into the corridor. "Et's safe. I'll go ahead and check downstairs." She exited the chamber and descended the stairs.

Whitney and I stepped into the corridor and peered at her over the railing. At the bottom landing, Mammy looked up and down the hallway before signaling to us it was safe.

We joined her, and not a second later footsteps in the parlor warned us of someone's approach. Whitney and I ducked into the warming kitchen, and I grabbed the door to still its movement. I held my breath and stared at Whitney as we waited.

"I bin luking for de missus," a house girl said. "You know where she be?"

My heart hammered in my ears.

"She gone. Missus Tucker and her gone off to visit de Barlows. What you need her for?"

"Et can wait till she returns." Footsteps moved away.

Whitney and I exchanged a look of relief.

"Sweet Jesus," Mammy said.

I cracked the door to peek out, and Mammy gestured that it was safe.

"You gals put me in a real bind. Gwine to have to make up stories on where you be for days. You bes' hope de army don't arrive wid a new shipment."

"Jones will see to them if they do." I touched her shoulder and planted a kiss on her cheek.

Mammy swaddled me in the warmth of her embrace. "Lard, please don't let no harm come to angel gal and Missus Tucker," she whispered and released me.

Whitney and I stepped out and hurried down the corridor to the back door. We slipped into the night, our elongated shadows moving like racing puppets across the work yard. At the blacksmith shop, we darted inside and found Jimmy pacing the floor and talking to himself.

"Dere you are." He threw his hands in the air.

"Is everything prepared?"

"Yes, Missus Willie."

"Good," I said, and without further delay strode toward the side door that led to the field and the wagon trail.

"You two be safe. And keep your eyes open," he said.

"We will." I opened the door. My mind raced to the time I had waited until dark to help Georgia and her brother escape the old well at the Barry plantation. Upon arrival, Jimmy had climbed out of the back of the wagon and given me a fright.

We found the wagon where he said it would be, and Whitney clambered into the driver seat, and I scrambled up beside her. She kicked her heel at the secret compartment under the seat where we had hidden slaves over the years and helped them along their journey to freedom. "You good?" she asked.

"As good as one could expect," Kip's muffled reply came.

Whitney slapped the reins, and the team lurched forward. The lantern on the post swung side to side. "Can hardly see anything." Nerves hitched Whitney's voice.

"We will take it slow. You mind the road, and I'll keep a lookout."

We set a slow pace, and when dawn shone on the horizon, we stopped to stretch and water the horses. "How are ya doing?" I knocked on the false wall under the seat.

"My bones feel like they will break," Kip said.

"It isn't safe for you to get out." I climbed into the driver seat and untied the reins. Whitney looked at me from her position in the back of the empty wagon bed. "I need to rest my eyes for a spell."

I nodded and slapped the reins, and again we were off.

Throughout the day, we passed several plantations and farms, and with each one, I noted the quiet that had taken over the countryside. We met no carriages along the road, except a peddler who sold an assortment of goods and tried to sell us war propaganda and perfume for our wives. We declined and kept on, passing by a bounty hunter with a train of Negroes trudging behind him.

"Good afternoon." He tipped his hat.

"Afternoon," I said in a gruff voice. As we rode on, I looked into the despondent eyes of the men and women he held captive. My hands tightened on the reins as helplessness plagued me. I offered up a prayer and left the matter in the Almighty's capable hands.

For the next hours, I pondered on the future and the end of the war. What would become of us all? If freedom came to the enslaved, would Southern states give them jobs or sell them goods? I feared the end of slavery would not stop the hardships people would continue to inflict on the blacks.

Before dusk, we rounded a bend to see a blood-chilling sight. I gasped, and Whitney gripped my arm. "Dear Lord," she said.

The lifeless bodies of Confederate soldiers were splayed across the road and grass. Pins and needles coursed through my body, and the hair on the nape of my neck rose. I pulled the wagon to a stop and tied off the reins.

"What are you doing?" Whitney grabbed the back of my coat when I moved to jump down.

"Going to see if there are any survivors."

"Are you crazy?"

"Not the last time I checked." I pulled myself from her grasp and hopped down.

"Willow, what are you doing?" Kip said.

I ignored him and reached for the loaded '51 Colt under the seat.

"Get back up here." Whitney's eyes flitted around, looking for danger.

"We can't get through without moving some of the bodies," I said through clenched teeth. "I suggest you get down here and help me, so we can be on our way." Heart throbbing in my throat, I spun on my heel and marched toward the sea of bodies. A thud sounded behind me, and I glanced over my shoulder as Whitney hurried to join me.

"We stick together," she said through her teeth. "The things I let you talk me into. We should've let Kip find his own way back."

I tensed and shot her a look, but the panicked way her gaze scoured the roadsides silenced any rebuke for her lack of concern for what happened to Kip. She was scared, and so was I.

"The ones responsible are probably long gone," I said. "We look for survivors, move the dead out of the way, and carry on."

"And if we find a survivor, what do you suppose we do? Take him along and hand him over to the Federals?"

"We hide him," I whispered.

"You can't be serious."

"Dead serious. And on the way back, he'll take Kipling's place, and we'll take him to Livingston."

"And let's say we find more than one." She jabbed at a corpse with her boot.

"I hadn't considered that."

She looked at me with a raised brow.

"Listen, I'm no expert at this any more than you. We do what we can and figure out the rest."

"Fine. Let's make this quick." She crouched to check the pulse of a man whose flesh had turned pallid.

I threaded through the corpses until a rustling noise stopped me. Listening, I swept my eyes along the roadside, pausing at the trail of blood crossing the road and disappearing into a gap in the underbrush. I cocked back the hammer on my gun and kept my finger on the trigger as I moved in. My heart galloped with trepidation at what lay beyond the brush.

A gunshot rang out, and I jumped to the side as a bullet whizzed by.

Crouching low, I eyed Whitney, who had dropped to the ground and gaped back at me. I signaled for her to circle around, and she nodded mechanically. I waited for her to move into position. With her at the person's flanks and moving in, I crept forward.

"Don't shoot. We are here to help. It looks like you're injured," I called in a low voice.

"Who are you?" a man called back.

"Farmers," I said as Whitney came up behind him. "You a Federal or Confederate?"

"Confederate," Whitney said, and another shot rang out, followed by a scuffle. "Damn fool. Didn't you hear my friend? We are here to help."

"How can I be certain?" The soldier sounded young.

"I'm coming in. Don't shoot." I parted the thicket with the gun and discovered a soldier slumped against a tree trunk.

He swung his gaze from Whitney to me and feebly tried to point his gun at me. Whitney kicked it from his hand and swiftly retrieved it. "We are Southerners like you," she said.

"You don't sound like no Southerner to me." He glowered up at her.

She didn't bother explaining, but squatted before him and examined the injury on his leg. "You're lucky they didn't blow that knee clean off." She swatted at the flies hovering around the wound the soldier had managed to tie off.

Whitney stood and took my arm, leading me a safe distance away. "He needs help. And not the kind of help we can offer." She anchored her hands on her waistline and pressed her lips together. "He isn't but Jack's age."

"We can't take him with us, or the Federals will finish the job." I cast a worried glance at the soldier, who sat regarding us.

"The best thing we can do is hide him. And hope he is alive on our way back." Whitney shrugged, not in the insensitive way she sometimes did, but with a sense of helplessness.

We returned to the soldier. "Listen, we have something we have to take care of, and it can't wait," I said. "We can't take you with us. But if you can hold on until we get back, we will take you to the nearest hospital."

A gleam of hope shone in his blue eyes before fear replaced it. "I don't know how much longer I can hold on. The pain is so bad, I slip in and out of consciousness." Sweat beaded his brow.

"Well, it's the best we can do," Whitney said. "Stay alive, and we will return."

"Yes, sir. I'm mighty obliged."

Whitney dipped her head in acknowledgment. "We have to move you away from the road because the first Federal that comes through will look for survivors. And if they find you—"

I elbowed her.

When we moved him, he wailed so loud I was sure anyone within a mile would hear him. He lay on the ground, ghastly pale and clinging to what life he had left. Whitney brought food, water, and bullets she had scavenged from the corpses.

"We will be back. I promise," I said.

He closed his eyes and feebly nodded. We gathered branches and covered him before returning to the road.

"Here, help me." I gestured at a body of a fallen soldier. "There is no way we can hide that trail of blood, but if we place him in where we found the other, perhaps it will keep anyone that comes by from searching farther in."

We moved the soldier into position and returned to the road to clear a path for the wagon to get through.

"How are you making out?" I knocked on the false wall.

"Like I've been plowed into by a team of horses and trampled," Kipling said. "Don't know how much longer I can take this."

"By my calculation, I think we should be at Beaufort by nightfall. The Federals will take you from there." I climbed into the driver seat.

Beaufort came into view as the sun perched on the horizon. My nerves thrummed as I drove us closer to the blockade patrolled by Federal soldiers.

"It's not too late to turn back," Whitney said.

"Well—"

"Halt! Who goes there?" a soldier shouted.

"You were saying?" I said with a clenched jaw.

"I'm going to be sick." Whitney shifted in her seat. "I have a bad feeling about this."

"Who goes there?" the call came again.

I reined the horses to a stop. "Name's Willy."

"Willy?" Whitney chided under her breath.

"Yes, Willy and Fred," I said as the two soldiers strode forward with their rifles pointed at us. I kicked the plank under the seat. "Well, it's your time to shine, my friend."

The soldiers positioned themselves on either side of the wagon. "State your business." The soldier to my left jabbed my arm with the butt of his rifle.

"We came across one of yours some weeks back. He was in bad shape. My wife cared for him the best she could until he was fit to travel."

His brow furrowed, and he regarded me with suspicion. He signaled at another soldier who joined us. "Shine that lantern on the wagon bed."

"That won't be necessary," I said. "He is under the seat."

"They speak the truth," Kipling said.

The soldiers jumped, and looked frantically into the darkness for the owner of the voice.

"I told you, he is under the seat."

The soldier directed the other to hold the lantern closer to inspect my claim.

"If you don't mind, my friend, Fred, here, and I will climb down and show you."

He narrowed his eyes, and several nerve-racking moments passed before he motioned us down.

Feet on the ground, Whitney and I turned to face each other, and I noted my fear mirrored in her eyes. We pushed on the corners of the false wall with extra force, and the planks sprang open, and Kipling tumbled out.

He gasped with relief. But the sound of cocking rifles stilled my breathing, and my body went numb.

"State your name and rank."

"Name is Kipling Reed. I'm a recruit under Flag Officer Samuel F. Du Pont of the South Atlantic Blockading Squadron." Kipling shifted to a seated position and held up his hands. "These farmers found me a few days' ride from here. My patrol had been sent out to gather provisions, and some rebels attacked us on the road. If it wasn't for these men, I would be dead."

"Climb down, and we will check your claim," the soldier said.

Kipling did as instructed.

"Come with me." He shoved Kipling forward with the butt of his rifle. "You to stay here." He ordered the other soldiers to watch us until his return.

An hour or more passed while Whitney and I sat waiting for their return. When footsteps drew our attention, I squinted into the dark and breathed a sigh of relief as Kipling strode toward us. The soldier walked a pace or two behind him with his rifle lowered.

"Everything all right?" I said when Kipling joined Whitney and me.

Kipling waited until the soldiers wandered back to their post before speaking. "Listen, I can't thank you both enough for what you've done." He regarded Whitney with a reverent expression. "You both have more courage and honor than most soldiers I've fought alongside." His gaze turned to me and he smiled tenderly. "I've always carried respect for both of you, but my respect has deepened. Again, I can't thank you enough."

"You are safe. That's what matters."

"I asked that you be given shelter for the night, but regardless of what you have done for me, you're considered the enemy and possible spies."

"We understand," Whitney said. "We need to be on our way. There is a matter that needs tending."

"If his condition is as you stated, I fear you'll have no matter to attend to," Kipling said with a grimace.

"You may be right, but we still have to try to get back in time," I said. "Goodbye, my friend." I held out my hand.

Kipling looked in the direction of the soldiers who stood regarding us. He thrust out his hand and clasped mine.

"God speed," he said. "Stay alive. And, when this is all over, I hope we'll see each other again."

I swallowed back tears and nodded.

Kipling shook Whitney's hand. "I know she pulled you into this and persuaded you to help me. I want you to know I will never forget this."

"Yes, well, Willy here," she said with a smirk, "may willingly put our necks in a hangman's noose more often than I care to face, but he acts with heart, and for that reason, we are better people for having met each other. A friend of his is a friend of mine."

Kipling smiled and waited while we boarded the wagon. Whitney turned us around, and I lifted a gloved hand. "Until we meet again."

He inclined his head and stepped to the side. "Be careful."

The following day we arrived at the area where we had left the injured soldier to discover a burial party had returned to bury the bodies in shallow graves.

Whitney and I walked the short distance to where we had left the soldier and pulled the covering brush away. My heart sank when I saw his lifeless form.

"Dammit." Whitney thumped a fist on her thigh.

"Best we bury him," I said.

"And how do you suppose we do that?" She threw her hands in the air. "With our fingers? Or I know—a stick?"

"Listen, I don't have any patience for your sass. I'm as worried and tired as you. He deserves a proper burial, so I guess we have no choice but to take him with us."

"And risk being caught with his body." Her voice rose.

"I'm not leaving him here. We will put him in the compartment under the seat."

"And smell his decomposing body for the next day or so?"

I shrugged. "You will live."

We struggled to carry the body, and Whitney didn't help by grumbling the whole way back to the wagon.

The smell of the corpse was unbearable, and with handkerchiefs secured over our noses and mouths, we rode in to Livingston resembling thieves seeking to loot the place.

Jones sat on the front veranda steps, whittling, and at our approach, jumped to his feet, his hand flying to his holster.

"It's us, Jones," I called out.

His hand dropped, and he dashed down the steps as Mammy exited the house.

She squinted into the dark. "Dat you, angel gal?"

"Et dem, Miss Rita." Jimmy entered the yard.

Mammy gripped the skirt of her dress and winced as she descended the steps, alerting me that her arthritis had flared up.

Jimmy reached me before Jones and gagged. "What in tarnation is dat smell?"

"A dead Confederate," I said as he reached up to help me down.

Jones had circled the wagon to help Whitney, but she swatted his hand away and dropped to the ground.

"She insisted we bury him," Whitney said with annoyance.

"You git Mister Kipling safely back?" Jimmy regarded me hopefully.

"Yes." I patted his shoulder. "Will you help Jones tend to the dead man? I think Whitney and I could use a bath."

"No bath or time will remove that scent from my nose," Whitney tossed over her shoulder as she marched toward the house.

I rolled my eyes and followed her. "Lord grant me the patience to endure her for another moment," I said with as much hyperbole as Whitney.

Mammy chuckled. "Sleep will do both of you some good. I ain't about to hear you two at each other's throats for de next few days. I 'bout had all I can handle. Besides, we have guests."

"A new shipment?" I paused to look at her.

She nodded. "Came in earlier today."

I heaved a sigh and walked into the darkened house. Placing a hand on the banister, I looked at the sleeping forms on the cots in the parlor.

Seeking to put the last days behind me, and weary in body and mind, I ascended the stairs to my chamber.

∽ CHAPTER ∽
Twenty-Seven

Amelie
April, 1862; Pittsburg Landing, Tennessee

ENERAL ULYSSES S. GRANT AND BRIGADIER GENERAL WILLIAM
T. Sherman had led us into battle and drove back the
Confederates and General P.G.T. Beauregard, sending
them into retreat toward Corinth. The victory was ours, and while
my comrades had roared with exultation, I had stood examining
the carnage.

My ears rang from the cannons and gunfire that had domi-
nated the day. Crimson blurred my vision from a slash over my
eye. Soldiers wove through the bodies, searching for the wounded.

Where was Zeke? During the battle, I had observed him engaged in a duel with a Confederate officer who moved with skill
and mastery, but when a soldier had come at me from the right, I
had lost sight of him.

A triumphant thump on my back from a soldier rattled my
skull and broke my survey of the battlefront. "We live to fight another day," he said before racing off to assist the others.

"Soldier," the coarse voice of Lieutenant Jackson bellowed
behind me.

I spun to look up into his intense, unchanging face. The breath
of his horse tickled my flesh.

"We have no time for standing around. Get out there and
help." He waved his sword at the fallen.

I adjusted my kepi cap to shadow my features, saluted my

superior, and replied in a husky voice, "Straightaway, sir." I turned and dashed off to assist.

Movement under the butternut-trousered legs of a lifeless Confederate soldier drew my attention. I lifted gloved fingers and wiped away the trickle of blood clouding my eye, and strode forward. I dropped to my knees and grunted, struggling to roll the body off the individual trapped underneath. After I'd succeeded, I regarded the wide-eyed young brunette clothed in Union garb staring back at me with panic in his eyes.

"Please, I-I…" His voice trailed off as he realized that in his fright, he'd revealed his secret. He wasn't a he at all, but a woman. She looked around for a way to escape, but a gaping wound in her middle had rendered her helpless. A once-white leather-gloved hand, now stained with her blood, pressed against the injury.

I retrieved a cap lying nearby and pulled it down over her head, shadowing her delicate features. "Come, son, let's get you to Medical." Hooking my hands under her armpits, I hauled her to her feet before encircling her small waist with an arm.

She gawked at me with large brown eyes, and as they welled with tears, she quickly concealed them and nodded. Placing an arm around my neck, she aided me as best she could.

I stumbled under her weight, but regained my footing. "You," I said to a lanky soldier we passed. "Help me get him to Medical." He moved in and took most of her weight.

At the medical tent, injured soldiers lined the ground. Inside we found the doctor and two nurses, elbows deep in blood and surrounded by cots holding wounded men crying out in agony.

"Please help me." A soldier held out a hand to us, his eyes glazed and delirious. Blood gurgled from his lips.

"I don't want to die," another recruit of twenty or so sobbed. He slumped on the floor next to a pile of discarded limbs. A fattened raven perched on top, feasting.

My stomach roiled at the gore staining the tent walls and the crimson streams flowing over the ground. I stifled a gag.

The doctor, a red-haired Irishman, looked at us with weariness gripping his brow. "How many more? We are out of places to put them."

"Plenty more where this one came from, doc," the soldier aiding me said.

"Well, there is no more room in here. Find the lad a spot outside with the others. I will get to him when I can." He turned back to the soldier on the table and instructed the nurses to hold him down while he tied off an arm severed at the elbow.

Outside I found a dirty blanket infested with lice and shook it. I spread the blanket on the ground. After we got the woman situated, I regarded the soldier. "I will take care of him from here."

He nodded and dashed off to scour the battlefield for more wounded men.

The plaints and prayers of the dying filled the late afternoon, and the invisible hand gripping my throat tightened. For the most fleeting moment, I yearned for the sanctuary of the brothel.

"Why are you helping me?" the woman said in a hushed tone.

I returned my attention to her, and in a gruff voice said, "The reasons you're here are not my concern. Rest."

Her shoulders relaxed, and she laid her head back against the wool blanket and closed heavy lids. Her pale, thin lips moved. "Thank you."

I patted her shoulder, stood, and left.

Threading through the injured, I considered the mothers, fathers, siblings, children, and wives who had lost their loved ones to the war. At the massive pile of bodies, my stomach clenched, and I skidded to a halt at the sight of a familiar face. Atop the mass of corpses baking in the Tennessee heat lay the musician, a cheerful boy of eleven who had played the accordion at night and sung to lift the soldiers' spirits. "No, no, no." I gulped back tears. How had he ended up on the battlefield?

My stomach threatened to revolt, and I dashed behind a nearby tent and vomited into the blooming rhododendrons.

What was I thinking? I used the back of my hand to wipe my mouth. I wasn't cut out for this.

"Victory doesn't seem so victorious, does it?" a familiar husky voice said.

"Zeke." I launched myself at him and squeezed him with all my might. Tears blurred my vision. "You're alive."

He peeled me off of him and cast a glance around. "Do you seek to expose yourself?" Although his tone was scolding, tenderness gleamed in his eyes.

"Sorry. I was worried sick." I took a few steps back.

"Trust me when I say I want nothing more than to hold you in my arms and kiss you," he said in a low voice. "Are you badly injured?" He eyed a soldier as he cast us a look on his way by.

"Just some superficial wounds. And you?" I regarded the darkened spot on the leg of his trousers.

"Nothing I can't sew myself," he said.

"Good. I will find you tonight," I said, veering past him.

He gripped my arm on the way by. "Amelie…" The passion in his voice made my heart flutter. "Be careful."

"I will," I said, and smiled up at him before racing off to help the others.

CHAPTER
Twenty-Eight

Bowden

T HE CONFEDERATE LINE OF DEFENSE EXTENDED FROM RICHMOND, Virginia, along the railroad north of the city to the James River. We were holed up in our encampment, waiting on orders to strike the Union's General McClellan and his army before they lay siege to the capitol.

It was dusk, and outside the tent I shared with three other recruits, men sat around the fire, talking of home and family. Others wondered what would become of them the next day.

Sickness caused by the climate, the food, viruses, infections, malaria, and pneumonia continued to plague the troops. In the tent next to ours, a soldier suffering from tuberculosis coughed and groaned in pain. His feverish cries filled the evening and grated at one's sanity.

Seated at the small desk in the center of the tent, I wrote a letter to my wife. The arrival of her letter some weeks back had given me the strength to carry on. Each morning I had awakened weary but grateful I still drew breath, but the loneliness never eased.

I replaced the quill in the inkwell and picked up Willow's letter, placed it to my nose, and inhaled the fading scent of her perfume on the stationery. I folded the letter and put it to my lips before walking to my cot and gathering the leather journal next to the worn Bible I had read every night in hopes the Good Lord would grant me the courage to face another day. I opened the journal and tucked the letter inside with Willow's ribbon, stained and dirty from time and pining.

"Lord, I know I've not always done right by folks and have sinned against mankind, and that I've been prideful and stubborn, but I ask that you will guide the hearts of my brethren in the North and South and bring this war to an end. Return us to our families…"

The tent flap swung aside, and Knox's bulk filled the opening. He looked to the open journal in my hand. "Her words will fade from the pages with how you pine over it." Knox tried to sound cheerful, but he too had grown solemn with the continuation of the war.

I set the journal down before lowering myself onto the edge of my cot. "What I wouldn't give for a proper meal and the company of my wife. And a night of peace." I nudged my head at the tent wall as another wail rose from the soldier.

He stepped inside and let the flap close. "Poor bastard yearns for death, and one can't blame him. I long for the day when this damn war is over." The weariness in Knox's face mirrored my own.

"I suppose we could be worse off. At least we were stationed together and haven't succumbed to the battlefield or to illness," I said.

Knox sat on the edge of his cot, and it groaned under his weight. He removed his muck-covered boots and placed them beneath his bed before sprawling out, his head resting on his arm. "Never thought I'd fight alongside Italians, Germans, and Spaniards."

"A mixed bunch we are." I followed suit, lying back to peer at the tent ceiling. "Each time I step onto the battlefield, I wonder if it is the day my blade ends the life of my brother or my Northern friends."

"Makes you want to go back to the days when life seemed easier before we married."

"Hardly a more peaceful time," I said. "Although I relish those years, I examine the man I used to be and the wrongs I've done. I fear the man that would've joined this war with enthusiasm and a distorted belief system."

"A reminder that there is hope, and people can change. Better to look to the future than wallow in guilt over what you once were. What is that verse from the Bible you read to me about casting stones?"

I recited the verse in John 8:7 to the best of my recollection: "He that is without sin among you, let him first cast a stone."

"Yes, that one. It's about time you stop casting your own stones." His words struck me hard, and I swallowed back the surge of emotion clotting my throat. Several moments of silence passed before Knox spoke again. "It gives me comfort to know Whitney has moved to Livingston."

"With the Union traversing the length and breadth of South Carolina, I can only imagine the women's distress. And learning that Willow decided to turn our home into a wayside hospital has me concerned."

"Yes, well, Willow acts on passion. One can't blame her for that."

"I know, but sometimes her passion places her in unnecessary danger."

"Evening, fellows." A recruit by the name of Marco Rosetta ducked his head through the tent opening and stepped inside.

"Evening, Rosy." Knox sat up and swung his feet to the ground.

The young recruit hadn't been fond of the name Knox had given him, but in time the kid had stopped putting up a fuss. He had immigrated to America with his family as an infant, and they had taken up farming. Marco strode to his cot and sat down, eyeing us uncertainly before withdrawing a letter he had gotten that morning. The envelope appeared to be unopened.

"You going to open that there letter before the year is out?" Knox said. "Men are dying to hear from their families, and here you've waited all day to read yours."

"It's just that…" Marco bowed his head. "I-I can't read."

Dawning washed over Knox's face. "You don't say. Well, Bowden here will be obliged to read it for you."

I regarded my friend, aware of his own struggle to read.

"Do you mind?" Marco said, turning dark, hopeful eyes on me.

I shook my head and gestured for him to hand me the letter. After I related what his ma had to say, I folded the letter and returned it.

Tears glistened in his eyes. "Ain't nothing like the love of your ma, is there?" Calm and serenity softened his face.

"No, there isn't." The faded image of my mother had often brought me solace, and that night it hadn't failed.

Later, when the camp grew quiet and Knox and the others' snores rose and fell, I contemplated how we each, Union and Confederate alike, clung to images and memories of our families and encouraging words from home. Although we stood on opposite sides of the war, our human need unified us and provided the fortitude to endure what lay ahead.

CHAPTER
Twenty-Nine

Drifter

I HAD ENLISTED IN THE FEDERAL ARMY UNDER THE NAME PRESTON Lawson and served in the Union Army of the Potomac, commanded by Major General George B. McClellan. I didn't care which side of the war I stood on, and this insight had stumped me.

As time passed, I succumbed to the voices in my head, and I found a strange comfort there, like a sense of home and belonging, although I couldn't figure out where home was. Visions of the auburn-haired woman clad in lavish silks and jewels often melded with those of another, a brunette with distinctive, intense green eyes. I felt absolute loathing each time the images visited, and I came to assume the women had to have impacted my life. I had scoured the blankness of my memories for answers, but came up empty.

As our lines broke and merged with the Confederate scum, the deafening booms of gunfire and cannons, and the bellows of charging soldiers and cries of the fallen, filled the hot afternoon.

Exhilaration sang in my soul as I removed my blade from the gut of a blank-eyed soldier now lying lifeless on the ground before me. I glanced to the left as a horse carrying a Confederate officer reared up, and I sent my blade into its chest. The beast squealed and went down, pinning the officer beneath its massive bulk. He struggled to get free. Adrenaline stormed through my veins, and

I grinned, pulled my pistol, and placed a bullet between the soldier's eyes while mentally adding his life to the ledger in my head.

You were born for this! the voice in my head squealed, delighted.

Battle fever governed my body, and I plunged deeper into the melee. Each soldier I encountered heightened the need for blood, and as the warmth of their death splattered my flesh, my heart beat faster, and a familiar ecstasy erupted. In the sea of moving blue and gray I sliced my sword through the air, not caring who fell at my hand.

A Confederate in front of me removed his blade from a fallen man and paused for a brief moment to assess the blood staining his left shoulder. I charged forward, and as if sensing my approach, he swerved, and I halted my advance within arm's length as I looked into familiar, piercing eyes.

Armstrong? The name erupted in my memories. A vision flashed of the man clenching the reins of a wagon as it dragged him behind it, and he fought to keep from being trampled. Another memory surfaced of him strolling through a crowded town with the brunette who'd haunted me walking beside him, her hand tucked in the crook of his arm. I scowled at the vagueness, but yet felt a profound sense of recognition. She was mine, and he had taken her from me. No…I wanted her, but he'd claimed her heart. As quick as the revelations sprang, so did the flashes of my life in its entirety before I had acquired the alias Preston Lawson. I felt a profound hatred for the life that stood before me, and I launched my attack before he could blink, plunging my blade through Bowden Armstrong's abdomen.

"Die this time, you bastard," I said through gritted teeth.

My blade cut through his middle like slicing fine silk, and he gripped my sword as surprise and then annoyance widened his eyes before pain gripped his face. "McCoy?" His knees buckled, and he went down.

"Bowden!" a man bellowed above the clashing of swords and the wails of the fallen surrounding me.

I whirled as a brute of a man rushed at me like a raging bull. *Knox Tucker.* The man's name formed in my mind. I went in for the attack. In his concern for his friend, Tucker had let down his guard; he was defenseless against my first blow. His blood splattered like spray from a fountain and, more swiftly than Armstrong, he dropped to the ground like a ton of bricks. I struck him repeatedly before his body went slack, and his sword tumbled to the ground. He fell backward, his legs pinned beneath him.

I looked over my shoulder at Armstrong, lying unmoving, before I threw back my head and howled at the sky, savoring the rain of blood. I was Reuben McCoy, and I had been reborn.

CHAPTER
Thirty

Bowden

AS MY EYES FLUTTERED OPEN, MY HEART CLENCHED AT THE ILLUSION of the beautiful brunette leaning over me. "Willow?" I whispered through dry, cracked lips. Pain radiated through my left shoulder and gut.

The fogginess clogging my brain cleared, and I regarded the warm chestnut eyes of a girl not more than eighteen. She wore a nurse's uniform smeared with blood, and dark circles of exhaustion rimmed her eyes. "I'm glad you could join us. I figured you were a goner for sure," she said.

I frowned, trying to recall how I had ended up in this condition. Visions of the battle unfolded, and I recollected the shot that had struck my shoulder but hadn't taken me down. I sorted through the images and gasped as I recalled turning and standing face to face with a Union soldier I recognized. My own shock, united with the confusion in Reuben McCoy's eyes, had given me pause. After a brief hesitation, his lips had whispered my name. It'd all happened so fast, and before I could react he'd sent his sword through my gut. I'd lain on the ground, helpless and incapacitated, bleeding out as horses and men raced about. Then darkness had claimed me.

I focused on the moaning and movement around me, observing the tent and the injured soldiers lying in cots and any empty spots. I ached for the suffering of my countrymen.

"Here," a soft voice said. "Drink this." The nurse leaned down, hoisted my head, and placed a cool metal cup to my lips.

I drank with urgency.

"Slowly," she said as I broke into a coughing spell.

After the spasm had subsided, I relaxed back against the pillow, surprised at the exhaustion caused by the mere task of drinking. "What is your name?" I studied her freckled face and wheat-colored plaits.

"I go by Clem."

"Clementine?"

She set the cup on the stand by my cot and gave me a disapproving look, and I sensed her dislike for the name.

"You remind me of someone," I said.

"Willow?" She gave me a bold stare.

"No, that is my wife. We have a girl that works in the sick hospital on our plantation. Her name is Kimie. She has nursed plenty of us and our slaves back to health. Our doctor says she is a fine nurse."

"A sick hospital and your own doctor?" Her eyes widened in awe. "You and your family must be wealthy."

"We have done all right."

"Makes me wonder who has more to lose in this war, the rich or the poor. My pa died when I was small, and it has only been me and my ma. After Federal soldiers burned our farm to the ground, we went to live with my uncle in the city." I observed her while she talked. The lack of laugh lines and the rigid way she held her mouth informed me she was the solemn sort. "I've always wanted to be a nurse, but Ma forbade it. When I saw an advertisement calling all able bodies to help in the war, I asked for her permission to join, but she refused."

"But here you are..." I winced and clutched my abdomen.

"Easy now." She swatted my hand away, and I pulled it back like a scolded child. She peeled back my bandage to take a gander, and her serious expression deepened. She retrieved scissors from a tray of dressings and cut the binding free. "One day after Ma had left to do errands, I packed my satchel and hitched a ride in the back of an army supply wagon heading to the Confederate camps." She pulled the dirtied dressing out from under me, and I regarded the gnarly sutures on my torso. "Someone stuck you good. Their sword went clean through you. The doc removed the ball in your shoulder, but this wound gave him the most concern."

"How many days have I been in this bed?"

"Five days or so, I reckon. Your regiment has moved on, under the command of a general by the name of Robert E. Lee. They renew the fight to drive the Union out of Virginia."

"Robert E. Lee? What happened to General Johnston?"

"I overheard an officer say that General Johnston was severely wounded and had been replaced by a Robert E. Lee."

My thoughts turned to Knox. "Has anyone come to see me?"

"No. Did you expect someone?" Her eyes held mine as she pulled the blanket up to cover my naked chest.

"Another soldier. A friend." I took another quick survey of the room, scanning for Knox's bulk on the cots.

"No one has come that I know of."

I tried to sit up. A ripping sensation moved through my middle, and I let out a yelp.

"Serves you right." Clem pressed her hands against my chest. "Stay still, or your wound will reopen, and I can't say when the doc will be able to see you again. The wounded stretch as far as the eye can see."

I complied with her orders, seething in frustration at my frailty. "Can you inquire about the whereabouts of a recruit named Knox Tucker?"

"I'll do my best, but I don't get to go far. We are overworked and understaffed. The wounded are dying while waiting for our attention. You would have been lying out there still if I hadn't been drawn to your delirious calling for your wife."

"You brought me here?"

"No, someone brought you to lie outside with the others to wait for the doctor. During my rounds of checking for the severely injured, I discovered you."

I glanced at a man lying on a cot across from me, with bloodied compresses covering the stumps where his arms once were. "But surely my wounds are insignificant compared to others."

She followed my gaze. "We cauterize the ones with missing limbs, give them some morphine if it's available, and move to the next. You were bleeding to death. How you hadn't already bled out astonished the doc and me."

I glanced back at her. "I assumed my guardian angel would be more of a fellow of stature, not a pint of a girl like you," I said with a chuckle.

She shrugged. "Well, you got me."

"And I'm mighty obliged." I grew serious. "Now, about my friend."

"What about him?"

"Can you ask around for him?"

"I told you the wounded are many. It would take forever to locate him. For his sake, I hope he's well and has moved on with your regiment."

I gripped her small wrist as she started to move away. "Please."

"All right. If I get a break, I will look into the whereabouts of your friend."

"Much obliged," I said.

She turned to leave.

"Clementine?"

She tensed and turned back. A fire sparked in her eyes.

"…is a fine name."

Her testiness eased, and I saw a hint of a smile before she ducked her head and walked off.

After she departed, I stared at the peak of the tent and thought of Knox and why he hadn't come to inquire about me. Was he lying wounded somewhere, or worse…dead? I gulped at the burning in my throat.

The memory of the animosity in Reuben's eyes sent a chill over me. He had stood cloaked in the garb of the Federal Army, but that gave me no peace of mind. Reuben had ruthlessly assumed aliases, and for all I knew, he could be in our camp under a Confederate disguise. This thought left me gravely concerned, and I cursed the weakness confining me. "Stuck in this bed, I'm as helpless as a new foal." I pounded the cot with a fist.

I felt eyes on me and twisted my neck to find the armless soldier regarding me. I swallowed my self-pity and looked away.

Once Clementine found Knox, I would tell him what had happened out there on the battleground. My thoughts turned to Willow, and I decided against telling her of Reuben or his attempt to kill me. There was no need for her to worry. If he was enlisted, regardless of what side he was on, it meant he was far away from my wife and the folks of Livingston, posing no immediate threat. I found reassurance in that.

Another three days passed before Clementine delivered the news I had pestered her for each day she tended me.

"Did you find him?" I asked as soon as she stood over me.

"Yes." She set a basin of water and fresh clothes on the ground before kneeling beside me.

"Well, out with it. Is everything all right?" My heart hammered, and my agitation grew at her unreadable, solemn expression.

She lifted concerned eyes to meet mine. "I'm afraid your friend has been gravely wounded. The doc fought to save him and has done all he could. Your friend requires a miracle and barely clings to life."

I felt the color drain from my face. "I must go to him." I gripped the gray woolen blanket that covered me.

"You will do no such thing." Clementine pressed her small hands on my shoulders with more strength than I expected from a reedy girl like her.

"Move out of my way," I said through clenched teeth.

Equally determined, she warned, "You will do as I say, or I'll have you restrained. Give it a few more days for your injuries to heal, and then you can go see your friend."

"He may not be alive by then." I bit my tongue to keep myself from cursing the girl out.

Her eyes challenged me, and I knew better than to resist her in my state, so I stopped fighting for the time being. Sensing I'd relaxed, she released me, picked up a cloth, and dipped it in a basin. I studied her profile while wondering how to get the answers I sought.

"Where are they keeping him?"

Her hands paused their movement, and she tipped her head and raised a brow. "I may be a simple farm girl, but I ain't a fool. If I gave you that information, you would slip out of here as soon as my back is turned." She began to wash my chest.

The girl was too smart for my liking. I fumed at the physical weakness that kept me prisoner in the bed. I felt like a helpless baby relying on the care of its mother. Then my determination rallied, and I set my mind to getting on my feet.

"You aren't the easiest of patients, you know," she said.

I grunted at her and avoided responding, caring little for what she thought. My mind turned to a problematic patient I had dealt with at medical school. The young man had been determined to leave the hospital before he had fully recovered, and days later his father had returned with him in a worse state than when he had first arrived.

Clementine changed my bandages and left me to my misery. I closed my eyes and envisioned Willow standing on the front veranda clad in an emerald-green taffeta dress. Her smile pulled at her full lips as I strode up the path and gathered her into an embrace. I released a sigh, savoring the fantasy.

Another two days would pass before the doc required the bed, and Clementine and a soldier came to move me to another tent. I winced as they helped me to my feet, and Clementine froze.

"I don't like this. It's too soon." She grunted under the weight of my arm encircling her shoulders.

"I'll be damned if I let you put me back in that bed. I will see him today, or else…" Knox still clung to the realm of the living, and it's a good thing he did, or I would've cursed him for leaving me to endure the war without him. The fool had been the only light amidst the death and bloodshed.

"Or else what?" She peered up at me, delivering a look that said not to test her. She wasn't beyond defying the doc and dumping me back in the bed. I needed her, and the annoyance of knowing that had left me seething for days. I grumbled inside. Of all the nurses I could have, why her?

"Look, I'm sorry. I don't mean to sound ungrateful. You have taken right good care of me, and I thank you." I delivered my words with as much humbleness as I could muster, pushing away the irritation that she'd played warden with prisoner me.

"I'm glad you've come to your senses." Her upturned nose rose a little higher, and approval shone in her eyes.

To my relief, they took a step forward. Splendid—I would see outside of the tent at last. Hope buoyed in me as I took each painful step, trying my best to hide the agony. By the time we reached my new accommodations, I was sweating and fighting within myself to continue.

"Here we are," she said between heavy breaths.

"All right. Release me and let me manage on my own."

"I'll take it from here," Clementine said to the soldier, who gave me an uncertain look but left at her insistence.

I stood on trembling legs and lifted fingers to brush the sweat dripping into my left eye. "Now, out with it," I said. "Where is my friend?"

"He is in the last tent." She pointed in the direction we had come.

"You can't be serious." I fixed my jaw. "Why in tarnation didn't you take me there in the first place?"

"Because you need to rest." She reached for my arm, and I jerked it away.

"I will see him today." I turned from her and took a few steps before my head started spinning. I halted, squeezing my eyes closed. "Son-of-a…" Jaw twitching, and without turning to look at her, I asked, "Can you please assist me?"

"I see you aren't going to listen. I should've left you to die outside the tent. You're simply the worse patient ever." She slung her arm around my waist, and I put mine over her shoulder. The girl felt like she would break under my weight. She gritted her teeth, looking determined. "Let's go before I change my mind."

After retracing every agonizing step, we stood outside the medical tent. I shifted to bear my own weight and released her. "I'm good. You can return to your assignments," I said. "Thank you."

She pressed her lips together and shook her head.

"What?"

"I hope this friend of yours is worth your own health."

"He is. And more." I eyed the opening of the tent and swallowed hard. What would I find inside? I moved toward the entrance.

"I will send a soldier for you in ten minutes, so make it quick," she called after me.

I didn't reply, but gratitude for her resolve to see me well rose. I stepped inside the tent and regarded each of the men in the cots until I located Knox. One painful step at a time, I walked toward him, my nerves humming with anticipation.

When I reached him I paused at the foot of his cot, taking in his pale flesh and the gauntness of his jawline and thick neck. Someone came to stand beside me, and I never looked to see who until they spoke.

"They are keeping him heavily sedated, but the blockades limit the supply of medicine. So they won't be able to continue because there are many soldiers in need. I fear he will become another casualty of this damn war."

I snapped my head sideways to regard the speaker and almost toppled over, but he caught me.

"Jack…" I regarded the shoulder boards on his coat, marking his rank. "My apologies, Lieutenant Barry. What are you doing here?"

Dark skin rimmed his eyes, and days-old scruff shadowed his face. "I serve under General Lee's command. I read the ledger of patients, and you can imagine my dismay to learn that Knox had been gravely wounded and that his condition hadn't improved much. To see your name on the list only added to the concern."

"But I thought the general's army had moved on to protect the capitol."

"The general gave me leave to check on Knox. Whitney would have my hide if I didn't see to him. After seeing his condition for myself, I fear he will rot away in an army hospital or be abandoned because he's deemed beyond hope." He removed his slouch hat and regarded his brother-in-law, who had been more of a father to him. Unmasked worry pleated his brow.

I stood on quivering legs and kept my gaze pinned on my friend. A thought occurred to me, and I pondered on it before broaching the subject. "Perhaps I could take him home?"

He shifted to peer at me. "You? You can barely stand on your own two feet." He noted the sweat beading my forehead.

"Give me three days, and I will be good as new. You could put a word in with the general and ask for my leave to take him home to Livingston. In Kimie's care, he is sure to recover."

"I take it you haven't heard." He arched a brow.

"Heard what?"

"That my sister doesn't reside at Livingston but spends her time aiding the army hospital in Charleston."

"No, Willow never made any mention of that." My brow furrowed. Why had she withheld the information from me? "Regardless, Knox should recover at home. You said it yourself about the likelihood of him rotting in an army hospital. The doctor and nurses are too busy to care for him here. New soldiers arrive every day, and soon his cot will be needed, and he will be removed, where death will surely find him. What do we have to lose? The risk of the journey is worth trying to save him."

He lowered his head and pressed his thumb and index finger to the bridge of his nose before elevating his eyes to regard me. "Very well, I will ask General Lee to grant you leave to take him home."

"Thank you." Hope erupted in my heart.

Someone cleared their throat, and I turned to discover a young recruit standing nearby.

"I've been sent to help you back to your tent."

I resolved to take the next days to recover, because if Jack came through with my leave, I would take Knox home and hold my wife once more.

News arrived that General Lee had granted our request and given me two weeks' leave. The road between the medical camp and the railroad station would be dangerous, but Jack had assigned a patrol to take us.

The morning I was to leave, I pulled a shirt over my head and slipped my arms through the sleeves, and winced at the tearing and burning sensation in my gut. Dread filled me when I looked down and noticed my wound had reopened. I checked over my shoulder for Clementine, who stood some feet away with her back to me. I grabbed a clean dressing and doubled it before tying another around my middle to keep the blood from soaking through my clothing.

I sensed eyes on me and looked at the grinning soldier in the cot next to me.

"Don't worry, I won't be ratting on ya. I want out of here as bad as you, and Clem is worse than a doting mother."

"You can say that again." I wiggled into my coat and hurried to button it.

"If all my hard work and endless hours of caring for you were in vain, I won't be pleased," Clementine's disapproving voice called from behind me.

The soldier and I shared a look, and he chuckled before shaking his head. "Better you than me."

I fixed my jaw and swung to face Clementine.

"It's too soon for you to be bouncing around on a wagon seat."

I knew she was right, but the need to see Knox safely home and to relish a moment or two with my wife would see my mission through. I donned my hat before inclining my head. "I thank you for your service. May we never meet again, and if so, may we find each other in good health."

That drew a small smile from the girl. She tilted her nose up. "On that, we can agree."

I rested a hand on her thin shoulder. "Take care of yourself, Clementine," I said before swerving past her and marching toward the exit.

"It's Clem," she said after me.

I waved a hand in dismissal.

Outside, I found the wagon ready. Knox lay in the back, swaddled on a bed of furs, his eyes closed and appearing more haggard and paler in the sunlight than he'd looked in the dim light of the tent.

I straightened at Jack's approach and saluted him. "Lieutenant Barry."

"At ease, soldier," he said.

I eyed the four soldiers standing in his shadow. He stepped aside and gestured at the men. "Private Palmer and these men will accompany you to the station."

"Much obliged," I said.

Jack approached the wagon and stood regarding Knox. I studied his face and caught a glimpse of the young man I had peeled off Parker in the work yard after he had attacked him because of the affections he held for Kimie.

As quick as Jack's vulnerability surfaced, he shuffled it away, cleared his throat, and took a step back. "Thank you."

"Of course." I dipped my head in homage to my superior. "He is my friend."

He offered a light smile and capped my shoulder. "Please send my love to Whitney, and if you see Kimie…" His voice drifted.

"I will."

Pain radiated, and dizziness blurred my vision as I clambered into the wagon. I seated myself and gripped the reins as one of the soldiers climbed up next to me. I squeezed my eyes shut to stop the spinning. It would take more than a miracle to return home safely.

"You all right?" Jack said, looking up at me.

I looked down at him. "Never better. The faster we get to the station, the sooner I'll relax."

"God speed." He tipped his hat. "And thank you."

It was to him I owed the thanks, but I gave him one last nod and urged the team forward.

CHAPTER
Thirty-One

Willow
June 1862

THE EARLY MORNING CRACK OF DISTANT CANNONS AND GUNFIRE propelled my heart into my throat, and I sat upright in bed, dazed and heavy with sleep. My mind struggled to sort reality from the beautiful dream I had been dreaming of traversing Paris's streets with my husband and Callie. The veil between the dream world and the present faded as the next explosion of gunfire shot me back into the nightmare of the war. I kicked back the blankets and darted to the window; pressing my face against the pane, I strained to observe the horizon.

"I can't see where it's coming from," I said into the darkness. I slipped on a night-robe, lit the lantern and, light in hand, raced from the chamber.

I collided with a groggy Whitney in the hallway, and we clutched each other to steady ourselves.

"That sounded closer than usual." Concern reflected in her eyes as she glanced at the front window at the end of the corridor.

We darted for the staircase as Pippa raced from her chamber, and together we descended to the main floor.

"It sounds like it's coming from the direction of Secessionville," someone said from the parlor.

I shone the lantern into the parlor, where the soldiers who could pull themselves into a sitting position had their eyes on the horizon. Their expressions were anxious.

Mammy and Big John stood in the open front door. I hurried past them and stepped out onto the veranda as Jones and Jimmy raced around the house.

"Do you think they've attacked Secessionville?" I asked Jones, joining him and Jimmy as Tillie and Pete arrived with their son. The boy clutched his mother's hand, whimpering, his eyes wide with fear.

"That would be my guess. Looks like they intend to attack Charleston by land."

"But the marshes would make such an attack difficult and prolonged," I said.

"Whatever is happening, it appears the war is on our doorstep." Jones turned, his shaggy gray brows lowered with concern. "It's best we prepare for any blue coats that creep over the horizon."

"What are we to do now, Missus Willow?" Tillie said.

I shifted from Jones to address the folks gathering in the yard, fear in their faces. "We do as Jones said. If Union soldiers come here, they will imprison or kill the men inside without hesitation. Stay alert, and if you see any movement coming from the tree lines and marshes, you're to inform us at once."

"Yessum," a chorus of voices replied.

"What about the attic space?" Whitney gripped my arm and said in a low voice. "We can hide the soldiers there."

"It's best the space remains our secret as long as necessary. Besides, the room isn't meant to hold but three or four men. We have eight."

"Then we choose which ones we hide." As she voiced the words that had already played in my mind, I flinched. "What?" She narrowed her eyes. "Why am I always the monster?"

"You aren't," I said. "You say nothing I haven't already considered. It just sounds harsher when spoken."

Her hackles lowered. "War forces one to do the unthinkable."

"If it comes to that, and it may not, we hide the officers."

"To choose what life is more important than the next…" Pippa rubbed the chill from her arms while looking back at the house, where soldiers incapable of joining us pressed anxious faces against the windowpanes. "Are we now to play God? If my husband lay inside, he would not be considered worthy of saving."

"Your husband would be saved before mine," Whitney said, no judgment in her voice, merely awareness. "At least yours is a doctor, and the army needs all the medical help they can get. Knox is a recruit with no army training."

"Let's hope we are spared from making such a grim decision." I touched Pippa's arm.

"You heard Mrs. Armstrong," Jones bellowed. "Regardless of what approaches, we all must eat and prepare for the day at hand. Keep your eyes open."

Quarter folks wandered off with their heads tucked together in conversation.

"Should have run when we had a chance," a quarter woman said to her man, twenty years or so her senior.

"My legs ain't what dey used to be, woman. I reckon I die here. All my people lay in dat dere graveyard anyhow…" Their voices faded as they rounded the corner of the house.

As I walked back inside, I considered their words and the despondency in their souls. Hope and faith in a better tomorrow had been the one thing I had clung to, but for them, did tomorrow hold something more promising?

By midmorning, the battle that had awakened the plantation had settled, and the countryside lay quiet in the aftermath of whatever had taken place.

Days later, Mr. Sterling arrived and informed us that the Union had attacked the village of Secessionville in hopes of capturing Charleston, but the Confederates had been victorious.

"One could assume they will turn their strategies to capturing Charleston from the sea." Mr. Sterling sat next to me on the front veranda.

I leaned in to refill his glass with whiskey. "Is there any news of General Johnston and his men?"

He fumbled with the dusty hat resting on his knee. "General Johnston was wounded in the Battle of Fair Oaks, and General Robert E. Lee was his replacement. Last I heard, Lee's Army of Northern Virginia had moved on to defend Richmond against the Army of the Potomac."

"I never thought I'd see the day when I relied on the newspapers and vague reports from traveling peddlers to track my husband's whereabouts."

"Yes, well, that is the world we live in," he said, glancing to the fields, empty of workers. "Your small number of slaves can't make running this place easy."

"And too many slaves would make me worry about how I could provide for us all."

"Making this place a wayside station can't be easy."

I studied the wagon carrying recovered soldiers down the lane, accompanied by the volunteers sent with horses to retrieve them. "I've wondered if we should continue. Perhaps I acted hastily when making the decision. We need more food and supplies, but the army sends less with each shipment of soldiers."

He drained his glass and stood. "I need to be on my way, but perhaps you should consider writing and requesting more rations. They can't expect you to provide that which you don't have." He pulled his hat down over sparse gray hair.

I rose and walked him to his horse. "As always, I enjoyed your company, and thanks for the information you bring. Your service in keeping folks informed can be devastating in one way, while it keeps our hopes alive in another."

He swung onto his horse. "We all must do what we can."

"Be careful out there." I peered up at him.

He smiled fondly, tipped his hat, and wished me a good day before galloping off after the wagon of soldiers.

CHAPTER
Thirty-Two

THE FABRIC OF MY DRESS CLUNG TO MY FLESH IN THE HEAT OF THE afternoon. Jones and I trudged through the cotton fields, inspecting the crop.

"Our harvest will be significantly lower this year, and we must focus on trading and selling our crops locally." He anchored his hands on his waist, stopping to view the fallow fields on the border of our property.

"Last year was less than profitable. And with the army now providing insufficient rations and medicine, I gave notice that we won't be able to continue our care for the soldiers." I rubbed the ache in the nape of my neck.

"Which puts us in jeopardy of having our livestock and what little we have left seized." He dropped his hands, and we circled back toward the house.

"Jones?" I asked after several minutes had passed.

"What's on your mind?"

"What will you do after the war? That's if it ever ends."

"Don't rightfully know. It all depends on what is left when it's over. And I reckon it also comes down to what you and Mr. Armstrong decide to do. When this is over we will be faced with a new world, despite who wins."

"Indeed. Although I agree with the need for change, I wonder what it will mean for our country. If the Confederates win, I fear the repercussions for the blacks and how much harder their lives will become. If Lincoln wins…"

The sound of an approaching wagon drew our gazes to the

lane. Next to the driver, who appeared to be an older man with hunched shoulders, sat another man. I squinted to get a better view but couldn't make out who approached.

"Shall we go and see who they may be?" I looked up at Jones, who eyed the visitors in his usual dubious manner.

"It doesn't look like soldiers. And, whoever it is, they don't appear to be in a hurry," he said and quickened his pace to the house. I hurried after him.

As we drew near, my heart sped up. A soft cry escaped me. "Bowden…" Yes, it was him. "It's Bowden." My legs found renewed strength, and gathering the sides of my dress, I dashed past Jones in a full sprint.

"Well, I'll be," he said, and it may have been my own happiness tainting my perception, but I believe I detected relief and joy in his voice.

I reached the front yard as the driver pulled the wagon to a halt.

"Lard be praised, et Masa Bowden." Mammy waddled out onto the veranda, accompanied by Whitney and Pippa.

Quarter and house folk entered the front yard to see what all the fuss was about.

"Et's Masa Bowden, all right," Pete said.

A cry of delight erupted.

I hurried to greet Bowden, but as I drew near, I noticed how he slumped forward, cradling his middle as he stepped onto the wagon spokes to climb down.

"Bowden?" I put my hands up to assist him.

"Here, Missus, let me help." Pete raced toward us and offered his assistance.

When Bowden's feet touched the ground, he pushed our hands away and said in a weighted voice, "I'm all right." But he didn't seem all right. He gripped the wagon to steady himself.

"Are you injured?" I asked.

"It's not me I'm worried about." He looked past me to Big

John, who stood waiting for instruction. "Big John, my friend, I need your help…" His words drifted as Whitney walked toward us as if in a trance, with her gaze trained on the bed of the wagon.

"Is that Knox?" Her voice sounded hollow with fear.

"I'm afraid so. He's alive, but I don't know for how much longer. He's in dire need of rest and care."

Whitney let out a soft moan and elbowed past us in her urgency to get to her husband.

"Pete," Bowden said with a grunt, placing a hand to his middle. "You will need two strong men to move the brute."

"Dere ain't none left, Masa. Jus' ol' folk, Parker, and me."

"Mind who you're calling old. We got all the help we need." Jones joined us and strode to the back of the wagon.

Whitney had climbed up into the wagon and moved to cradle her husband's head in her lap. "Knox…it's me. I'm here." Silent tears streamed down her pale cheeks as she stroked his hair. I fought back tears. "Everything will be all right. Big John will see you're cared for. You will be up and tormenting everyone before you know it." Her shoulders shook and I heard faint sobs.

Pete and Jones lifted him from the wagon, and Big John and Parker stepped in to assist.

"Take him to the library. The army has agreed they would improve the mens' rations when possible, but we aren't expecting a new shipment of soldiers until the end of the week," I said as they shuffled past me. I turned to Bowden. "Come, let's get you inside. You look ready to collapse. Pippa, can you help me?"

She swept forward in her usual graceful way, and Bowden set his stubbornness aside and slung an arm around each of our shoulders. My concern mounted as he clenched his jaw to stifle the pain as we moved toward the veranda. Once inside, he dropped his arms and brushed us away as though annoyed at his weakness.

"Thank you, ladies," he said, glancing over my head into the parlor. His brow furrowed, and he shuffled to the threshold. He paused and clutched the frame for balance while eyeing the empty cots inside. "It smells of sickness in here." His voice lacked emotion.

Pippa looked at me and nodded before taking her leave.

I walked to my husband's side. He stood staring blankly into the parlor as though his mind had transported him somewhere else. "Bowden?" I touched his arm, and he jumped. My hand slid to my throat at the haunted look in his eyes.

He swiped a trembling hand over his face and shook his head as if to dislodge whatever had occupied his mind, and turned to me with a tender, fixed smile. "I've longed to see you again," he said softly. "You look more beautiful than I've ever seen you."

I smoothed back the tendrils escaping my combs, all too aware of the dust that coated my dress and face. "I think the war has tainted your memory."

His smile deepened, but I saw the underlying fatigue. "It may have in some ways, but not my love for you." He leaned back against the doorframe and held out a hand. "Does a wife not have any affection for her husband?"

I stepped into his arms and rested my cheek on his shoulder. I wanted to absorb his warmth and love, but fearful of hurting him I placed my hands gently on his lower back.

"I've missed you terribly," he said into my hair, inhaling deeply. "I've missed your smell, the softness of your body, and the warmth of your embrace." His voice fractured with rising passion.

Tears welled in my eyes, and I thanked God for his safe return. I leaned back to look into his face before gazing longingly at his lips. He lowered his head and kissed me, softly at first and then with a fierceness that made my body tremble. Our embrace tightened, and I removed his hat, letting it fall to the floor before tangling my fingers in his hair. I ached to be loved and caressed by him.

Someone cleared their throat, and we broke our embrace. Heat washed over me when I spun to discover Mammy standing with an old blanket draped over her arm, looking at us with a toothy grin. I moved in to Bowden's side, and he clasped my hand.

"We happy to have you home, Masa."

"As I am to be here. Although I wish it was under different circumstances." He glanced down the corridor to the library as Pete and Jones exited the room.

"Yes, and my John will do all he can to help Mister Tucker. Now et bes' we git you upstairs and cleaned up," she said. "Mister Jones, you and Pete, here, help de masa upstairs. Tillie and Missus Hendricks are preparing de water for your bath. We git you cleaned up and tend to whatever is happening dere." She pointed at him, and I looked to his middle, where fresh blood speckled his cream cotton shirt.

"Nothing that won't heal," he said. "It's a heap better than it was."

"Well, et ain't 'bout to. Not wid you and angel gal carrying on lak I saw when I come up. Come now." She wiggled a crooked finger at us. Again heat swept over me, and Peter snickered before Mammy scowled at him. Growing solemn, he dropped his head. She strode forward with purpose. "We will git you bathed and in bed. Big John will see to what ails ya." She glanced at Jones and Pete. "Well, come on now. Don't delay. Git him upstairs."

"Maybe you should return to the field in my place, Henrietta," Bowden said with a chuckle. "You would give the Union a real fight. I reckon we got our own Harriet Tubman right here."

"I never be de Moses 'oman. She got more courage dan a whole army of Confederate or Union soldiers. Yes, sah." Admiration shone on her face.

"Indeed she does." Bowden gazed down at Mammy with an equally admiring expression. "I must say, I've missed your dictatorship."

She grunted and said, "Ef us older folkses ain't 'round to talk sense into you younger folkses, I don't know what dis world would become. Most lakly fall apart."

She gestured at Jones and Pete to take Bowden upstairs. As we followed behind, she continued to ramble. I smiled to myself, wondering as I often did if she nattered constantly because she fancied the sound of her own voice.

My steps felt lighter than they had for some time, and joy sprang in my heart.

Upstairs in our chamber, Jones and Pete sat Bowden in a chair.

Mammy marched to the bed. "Help me git dis blanket spread out. Don't need de masa messing up de bes' linens we got left."

Not wanting the happiness in my soul crushed by her disapproval, I rushed to do her bidding.

"Now you menfolk go and git de tub. Bring et in here. Missus Hendricks and Tillie are heating de water."

Later Pete and Jones returned carrying a copper tub and placed it in the middle of the room. They returned several times with steaming buckets of water.

Bowden sat with his eyes closed and his shoulders slumped forward. I looked back at Mammy, whose gaze also rested on him, concern in her dark eyes, and when she turned back to the task at hand and found me studying her, she quickly replaced her worry with a smile.

"Sure is good to have de masa home," she said. "Evvything be jus' fine now."

I smiled, appreciative of her effort to calm my distress.

"Mister Jones, you and Pete git de masa in de tub. When my John finishes tending to Mister Tucker, he help wid de masa."

When Jones and Pete clutched Bowden's arms to lift him, he pulled from their grip and stood. Unbuttoning his shirt, he guided his scowl from Mammy to me. "I will undress myself and accept help to get into the tub, but I won't have anyone bathing me like I'm an infant."

"Bowden…" I said.

The harshness in his gaze silenced my plea.

"It's best you womenfolk go on now. This is man's business."

"Yes, Masa." Mammy took my arm and led me toward the door as I fought to blink back rising tears.

Outside in the corridor, Mammy closed the door behind us, and we moved a short distance away before I turned to face her. "He is so…cold." I wrapped my arms across my chest and glanced at the closed door.

"De masa in pain, is all," Mammy said. "Why don't you go wash your face and change into your bes' frock." She graced me with a bright smile. "Dis is a blessed day. De masa is home, and et would do him good to see his wife in all her fineness. Tillie and I will fix a meal dat will warm his belly and show him how thankful we are for his safe return."

I left to wash up and returned as Big John climbed the stairs to attend Bowden. Knowing I would only be in the way, I descended the stairs to the main floor to go and check in on Knox.

I found Whitney on her knees by Knox's cot, holding his hand against her forehead, lost in prayer. Tears stained her cheeks and darkened the front of her dress.

My throat thickened.

Sensing my presence, she opened her eyes and looked at me. "Willow…" Grief and worry shattered her voice.

I moved to her side and knelt beside her.

She placed her husband's hand on his chest and turned grief-stricken eyes on me. "What a fool I've been. I have put him through so much, and now God seeks to punish me for my sins."

"No, He doesn't. He understands our human flaws." I gathered her in my arms, and she broke, her fingers gripping the fabric of my dress. I'd never witnessed such vulnerability in her before—not when her father's plantation burned to the ground, nor when Knox went off to war. "He is home now. Big John will see he recovers. What he needs now is your love and support. With you at his side, he will recover."

She pushed back and brushed away her tears. "But he will never hold me again. I'll never feel the comfort of his embrace."

"What do you mean?" I looked from her to the scars on Knox's wan face.

She leaned forward and rolled back the linen to reveal a sight I couldn't have imagined. I covered my mouth with a hand to extinguish a cry. Dear God. His left arm had been severed at the elbow, gnarly red slashes left his torso deformed, but it was the festering wound in the center of his chest that stilled my heart. How was he still alive? "I'm so sorry." My words sounded pathetic in response to the fear and despair she had to be experiencing.

Knox's feverish moans rose and drifted. She covered his torso and pulled to her feet. I stood, and we walked a short distance away and looked back at him.

"I feel helpless." She lifted slender fingers to brush away tears. "What if he dies? What if—"

"Shh." I embraced her. "You mustn't think like that. He is here now, and he will get better. You will see."

She pulled back, and fire sparked in her eyes. "Easy for you to say. Your husband returns on his feet. Mine came back with two feet in the grave."

I cringed. "Whitney, I-I—"

"Save it, Willow. Everything always works out for you." She turned her back to peer out the window at the garden.

"Whitney, please." I touched her elbow. "I know you are hurting and that you don't mean this."

"Oh no?" She spun around, and her lip curled as she delivered words that pierced my soul. "I meant every word. I wish it was Bowden in that bed, not my husband." As she vocalized her pain, she became aware of what she'd said. Regret and horror shadowed her face. "I-I—" She veered by me and raced from the room.

I stood rooted and numb, not sure what to do or think. When my legs finally moved, I walked to Knox's bed and knelt beside him. "You are home now." I swallowed my tears. "Rest and recover. We all need you...she needs you."

"Come, angel gal," Mammy said from the threshold, and I looked at her through eyes blurred by tears. I pushed to my feet and walked to her side. She wrapped a comforting arm around my waist. "Don't fret none 'bout what Missus Tucker said. She hurting, and when folkses are hurting, dey sometimes say awful things dey don't mean."

I lay my head on her shoulder. "I know, but it doesn't mean it hurts any less."

"No, angel gal, I reckon et don't."

In the corridor, I stepped away. "Is Big John still with my husband?"

She nodded.

"I'm going to take a walk." I lowered my head, attempting to hide my sadness.

"All right, angel gal. De masa needs some rest and time to heal."

I smiled at her, grateful for her reassurance. "Thank you."

"What for?" She lifted a brow.

"For always being my comfort."

Tears pooled in her eyes. "You a good woman. And you know I love you lak my own. I do anything to save you from de ugliness of dis world."

"You don't need to worry about saving me. Your love has always steered my feet back on the path where they need to be, and for that, I thank you."

"Bless you, gal." She smiled and cupped my cheek before swerving by me and continuing down the corridor. Her rich voice lifted in song, leaving me encouraged.

Gratitude filled my heart for the woman who had loved and accepted me exactly the way I was, without prejudice or judgment.

∽ CHAPTER ∽
Thirty-Three

WHITNEY AVOIDED ME FOR THE NEXT WEEK, DEVOTING HER days to Knox, sleeping on a pallet next to his cot, and eating her meals in the library.

A small contingent of soldiers arrived and I arranged to have them situated in the parlor, allowing Whitney and Knox privacy.

Bowden's strength increased with each passing day. One afternoon, as he and I entered the house after visiting our son's grave, Mammy came rushing down the corridor. "He awake. Lard be praised. Mister Tucker awake." She thrust her hands at the heavens.

My heart leaped, and I looked up at Bowden as he let out a yelp of glee. "I knew he was too stubborn to leave this world." He charged down the hall and I raced after him, pausing to gather Mammy into my arms and squeeze the breath from her before planting a kiss on her cheek. When I freed her, she stood dazed before a satisfied grin spread over her dear face. "Everything will be fine," I said.

At the library, I grabbed the doorframe to slow my pace. Inside I found Big John assessing Knox while Whitney stood back, allowing him to do his work.

Bowden had positioned himself at the foot of the cot and stood with his hands planted on his hips. "You decided you'd grace us with your presence, did ya?" he said with a broad smile.

Whitney glanced at me before swiftly averting her gaze. I swallowed the nerves congregating in my stomach and walked to my husband's side. We all devoted our attention to Knox, who lay back against the pillows, still appearing ashen and thin.

He attempted to grin but grimaced. "Couldn't leave you to maneuver this life alone," he said before looking at Whitney as she drew closer. "The peace of the grave called, but I heard you nattering 'Don't you dare die on me' and figured I wouldn't find peace if I left." He offered her a tender smile before his attention went to the arm Big John unwrapped, and the little color left in his face evaporated. He gagged and looked away. After he calmed his reaction, he said, "Don't know how good a soldier I will be now. Can't fire a rifle or…" His voice faded, and his jaw trembled. "I'm sorry, wife. I didn't want to return less than I was."

Whitney marched forward and knelt beside him. "I won't hear any such talk. You're the same man that left here. It's just an arm."

He laughed. "It will grow back, ya saying?"

A rosiness touched her cheeks, and she dipped her head. "No, of course not, but I want you to know I see you as no less a man than the one who left. I love you regardless."

Knox's eyes glittered with appreciation for the woman who continued to let her guard down and blossom into the wife he had longed for. My heart swelled with happiness for the love between them.

Bowden settled an arm around my shoulders, pulling me into the warmth of his side, and placed a kiss on the top of my head. "I'd hate to see the bastards that did this to you before you went down," he quipped.

The lightheartedness vanished from Knox's expression, replaced by a firm set to his jaw. "It was him." His nose flinched with disgust and loathing.

Bowden tensed, and his fingers dug into my flesh. I looked from him to Knox. "Who?" I asked.

Knox's eyes flickered as though he and Bowden were exchanging a secret code between them.

"No!" I pulled away and turned to face Bowden, crossing my arms over my chest. "I won't have it. Out with it now. What is it you two know that you're trying to keep from us?"

"I'm with Willow," Whitney said.

Bowden swiped a hand through his hair and gestured for Knox to continue.

"It was Reuben," Knox said.

"Reuben?" Whitney and I gasped in unison.

"The bastard took down Bowden, and when I saw him go down, I charged in and, well, you know the rest of the story. Hell itself flashed in his eyes. He left us for dead."

Bowden turned and paced the floor. "But there was something different about him. When I looked into his eyes, it was as though he didn't recognize me at first, and then, as though suddenly enlightened, he went in for the kill. I saw it in his eyes; he intended to gut me from spine to throat." He paused and turned back to look at Knox. "I'm guessing it is only because of you that I still draw breath." His face softened. "I'm indebted to you, my friend."

Knox snorted. "If I hadn't, I would never have heard the end from these two. How could a man ever find peace again?" The humor was for our sakes. When he looked at his arm again, his face twitched.

"What side did he fight on?" I asked.

"He wore Union garb. But the man has no loyalty to anyone but himself." Bowden caressed my arms. "You needn't worry about him."

"No?" A sour taste coated my tongue. "The graveyard is full of people because I chose to not worry about him for one night."

"That isn't your fault. You can't control the demons that possess that man's soul."

"No, but I do hope that, before this war is over, the entire Union and Confederate armies pummel him into the ground." My hands formed fists.

"You aren't alone in your desire. And may God forgive us all," Bowden said.

"Et's good you awake, Mister Tucker." Big John stood. I had almost forgotten his presence in the room. "Et best ef you take et easy. De wounds on de outside are healing, but de damage inside is what we can't assess." He scooped up his pouch of herbs and medicine.

"We will leave you in the capable hands of your wife." Bowden gently gripped Knox's shoulder, his hand lingering a moment.

Knox lifted his hand and patted Bowden's wrist. "Thank you for bringing me back."

Bowden awarded him a tight smile and inclined his head at Whitney before taking my hand and leading me from the room. He thanked Big John before guiding me out the back door and down the steps.

"Where are we going?" I asked.

"Is it a crime to want my wife all to myself?" His merriment returned as he spun me into his arms. I laughed with delight.

"I know just the spot where we won't be disturbed." His eyes lingered on my mouth before he pulled me across the yard and away from the plantation.

CHAPTER
Thirty-Four

I STOOD IN THE CORRIDOR HOLDING BOWDEN'S SATCHEL WHILE HE SAID his goodbyes to Knox. Whitney's husband would not return to the battlefront for some time, if at all; the extent of his wounds had kept him weak, and he had yet to move from the cot.

Whitney regarded me from her position at Knox's side, and the awkwardness between us had made everyone uneasy. Sometimes I found myself offering excuses for her harshness that day in the library, and in the next breath I stewed with anger.

I walked down the hallway and stepped out onto the veranda, seeking fresh air and distance.

"Masa's horse is ready." Jimmy strode into the front yard leading a chestnut bay, with Jones and his mount following behind.

"Thank you," I said through rising tears.

"Why don't you come down here and tell me what be troubling you besides de masa's leaving," he said.

"It's nothing."

"You can't fool ol' Jimmy. I knowed dat face well. Besides, I bin watching you sulk 'round here for a week or more." He craned his neck to look up at me, and the compassion in his face pulled my feet toward the stairs.

I joined him in the front yard and stood without speaking before he urged, "Come now, out wid et."

"It's Whitney."

"What she done now?"

"She hasn't really done anything." I bowed my head. "Well, nothing I didn't deserve."

"Let me be de judge of dat," he said, his tone defensive.

I told him what Whitney had said in the library the day our husbands had returned home, and he gave me a stern look and shook his head in disapproval. "Dat ain't nothing you deserved. Et ain't your fault Masa didn't suffer de same fate as Mister Tucker. No one wants to see anyone hurt. Dat woman do bes' to quieten her tongue. Can't go through life spewing off evvything dat comes to mind. No matter what pain or fear you be feeling."

I understood Whitney in a way most never would. "I know she didn't mean it, but it hurts nonetheless. She was scared and hurting, but the fact that we haven't talked since burdens my heart and mind."

"Let time take care of dat," he said, and glanced past me. "Here comes de masa. You go on now and enjoy a minute or two 'fore he gone."

Bowden exited the house with Mammy and Pippa close behind. "I packed you some food for your journey. You be sho' to keep your strength up and return to us when dis is all over." Mammy held out a small satchel.

"Much appreciated." He smiled and took the food before placing his hat on his head.

I ascended the steps to stand beside him.

"If by any chance you see my husband, please send him my love." Pippa stood with her hands clasped in front of her.

"I will, but I haven't seen Ben since the start of the war."

"His letters aren't getting through. Pippa has only received one in all this time," I said.

"After lying cooped up in an army medical tent, I see what the doctors and nurses go through. There's not a moment's rest. They are stretched too thin, so I reckon there is little time for him to write."

Tears pooled in Pippa's eyes.

Bowden's expression softened. "War leaves one forever changed. A man witnesses horrors and calamities he can't unsee.

Our womenfolk's letters, the memories of your faces, and the dream of returning home help us endure the dawning of a new day. Don't lose heart. Keep sending your care packages and letters; hopefully, they get through."

Pippa compressed her lips and nodded. "Thank you."

"Now, if you don't mind, I'd like to steal a moment with my wife." He clasped my hand and led me across the veranda and around the corner of the house.

Once out of view of the others, he pulled me into his embrace. "I shall miss you," he said. "I pray each night for this war to be over."

"As we all do. Please be careful." Reuben's attempt to kill Bowden and Knox had filled my days with worry. "Keep your eyes open."

"I will not die at the hands of Reuben McCoy's insanity." He cupped my chin before lowering his head to brush my lips with his. Passion heated his kiss, and he drew me closer.

When we parted, I tilted my head to look into his welling eyes before laying my cheek against his shoulder, and the fabric of his wool shell coat collected my silent tears. He whispered soothing words of love and promises of his return.

I brushed away my tears and stepped out of his embrace. "If you are to catch your train, you need to go."

He took my hand, and we walked back to join the others. Bowden said one final goodbye before descending the steps to where Jimmy stood patiently waiting. I followed behind him to stand at the end of the path. Jones sat on his mount, waiting to accompany Bowden to town.

"Et sho' was good to see you, even ef et was only for a short spell," Jimmy said as Bowden tucked the food Mammy had given him into the saddlebag.

He turned and gently clasped Jimmy's shoulder, smiling fondly. "There's no place like home. And nothing more comforting than to sit awhile in the company of loved ones and old friends."

Jimmy grinned. "No, Masa, dere certainly ain't. You mind you take care of yourself and git back here to Missus Willie and de rest of us."

Bowden inclined his head before swinging up into the saddle. His gaze moved over the house folk standing on the front veranda and the quarter folk who'd come to send him off before focusing on me. No words needed to be said because his eyes spoke of his love. Nudging the horse around, he kicked his heels into the animal's side and galloped down the lane, taking my heart with him.

As he and Jones disappeared out the gates, I failed to fight back the tears before turning and racing into the house. Whitney strode into the foyer, and I veered by her and charged up the stairs, wanting to be alone to wallow in my misery.

CHAPTER
Thirty-Five

September, 1862

A T THE CLANGING OF THE CAST-IRON DINNER BELL AND MAMMY'S bellow, I wiped the sweat from my brow with the back of my wrist and arched my back to alleviate the throbbing ache.

Tillie, Pippa, Whitney, and I, along with the scarce few remaining slaves, had taken to the fields at first light. All morning the merciless scorching sun had beat down on us, and the nausea in my stomach since rising hadn't eased. Fingers pricked and bloody, feeling wearier than I did most days, I welcomed the sound of the bell. I strode to the wagon, removed the cotton sack from around my neck, and placed it in the wagon bed.

"Hell itself blazes down on us." Whitney hoisted her overflowing sack into the wagon.

I reeled as lightheadedness washed over me.

"You all right?" Whitney asked. "You aren't coming down with that bout of influenza those soldier boys brought here, are ya?"

"I'll be fine. It's this sun."

Her brow puckered beneath her floppy straw bonnet. "If you say so."

It'd taken another week or more after Bowden had left, but eventually Whitney had come and offered an apology, which I'd welcomed. I hadn't wanted to be at odds with her any more than she had with me.

She clambered into the driver's seat.

"Up you go, Tillie. I'll sit in the back." I held out a hand and eyed her expanding middle. The babe would come around Christmas.

She hesitated and looked to the house. "You can't be seen showing favor to de slaves. I git in de back lak a slave suppose to." She walked to the back and climbed into the wagon bed.

Too exhausted to fuss with her, I waited for Pippa to board before settling myself beside her. We sat in silence on the way back to the house, but the churning in my stomach never ceased.

As we neared the house, Whitney snorted and said, "Well, will you look there."

I peered in the direction she'd nodded toward and saw an officer sitting in a rocker on the back veranda, reading the newspaper and sipping on what appeared to be lemonade.

"We work the fields while they eat our food and kick their feet up and enjoy the fruits of our labor."

Tillie chuckled from her position in the back of the wagon. "Many times, we say dat 'bout white folkses."

Whitney scowled back at her. Pippa and I laughed when Tillie jutted her chin and grinned back.

"She has a point," I said.

We left the wagon in the work yard and joined the silver-haired officer on the veranda. I caught a glimpse of the bold newspaper heading before he lowered it: *Resounding Victory for the South in the Second Manassas.*

"Afternoon, Mrs. Armstrong." He stood and glanced at Whitney, who marched to the door without so much as a "How do you do." He turned an admiring look on Pippa and inclined his head. "Ma'am."

"Afternoon, Captain," Pippa said.

"It's a hot one out there."

"Like you would know," Whitney said under her breath before waltzing inside and slamming the door.

"What did she say?" He cupped his ear. The captain's saggy jowls and droopy lids reminded me of an old coon dog.

"She said, 'afternoon,'" Pippa said in a loud voice before gracing him with a pleasant smile.

He snorted and shook his head. "Her face didn't say that, and neither did that door." He tucked the paper under his arm and strode to the door. "After you, ladies." He opened the door and stood back.

"If you will excuse us, we need to wash up and will join you in the dining room," I said.

He nodded and strode down the hallway and disappeared into the dining room.

Freshened up and changed, we womenfolk joined Knox and the soldiers fit to join us for the afternoon meal. While the table guests chattered, I found myself moving the food around my plate with my fork.

Sailor entered the room carrying a white Ironstone China pitcher. Mammy had insisted that, with us in the fields, she needed his help with the soldiers. "He ain't a babe no more. And I ain't getting any younger," she'd said. I hadn't liked it at all, but short of hands I was left with no choice.

He walked around the table, carefully filling the glasses, and each time he managed to finish without spilling a drop, he looked my way and beamed with pride. I praised him with a small nod.

"Lincoln be damned." A soldier slammed his fist on the table, causing us all to jump. Sailor drenched the white linen tablecloth and the man. The soldier jumped to his feet and backhanded him so hard it sent him reeling backward. Sailor dropped the pitcher, and it shattered.

"Private Daniels!" I scraped back my chair and leaped to my feet.

Sailor cradled his cheek and began to cry. I rushed to his side. He gazed up at me with fear and disappointment radiating from his eyes. "I'm awful sorry, Missus, I didn't mean to."

"Of course you didn't." I glanced back at the soldiers regarding us with perplexity. "Are you all right?"

He bobbed his head, but I felt his body tremble under the hand I'd placed on his shoulder.

"You go on outside and find Jimmy. Don't come back in here until I come and find you," I whispered.

"Yessum." He turned and fled the room.

I looked at Mammy, who had rushed in to find out what had happened. She stood wide-eyed and uncertain what to do. "Henrietta, please bring more water," I said.

After she left, I swung back to regard my observers. "Gentlemen." I gestured at the table. "Please, eat."

I returned to my seat, and those who had stood seated themselves. My jaw twitched as I lifted my fork and looked at the private who had struck the boy. "Private Daniels." I waited until I had summoned his attention and said in an even tone, "You will never treat my servants that way again, or I'll send you back to the army as you are."

"If I had my guess, I'd think you were a damn nigger-lover." He leveled dark eyes on me before swiping a hand through the air. "Ain't been here but a few days, but I can see this ain't no ordinary plantation, the way you interact with your slaves."

"Let me tell you something, sir," I bit out. He stiffened. "If it wasn't for those slaves, you wouldn't be on your way to recovery. If it wasn't for those slaves, this plantation wouldn't still be standing. If it wasn't for those slaves, our crop wouldn't have been planted or gathered to fill your ungrateful belly."

A balding soldier of twenty-five or so with his arm in a sling, sitting to the captain's right, leaned forward. "Ma'am, Private Daniels didn't mean to disrespect you in your home or to disregard the service you provide the army."

The private's face reddened, and his jaw clenched. His anger was minimal compared to mine.

"Apologize to the lady, or see yourself removed," Knox said.

The captain cupped his ear. "What he say?"

Pippa patted his arm and leaned in to speak in his ear.

Private Daniels stood, threw his napkin on the table, mumbled an apology, and hobbled from the room.

"I'm right sorry for his behavior, ma'am," the soldier said. "Ever since Lincoln invoked the Second Confiscation and Militia Act, allowing niggers to fight alongside white men, he has been sourer than ever at the blacks. Can't say I ain't heated by Lincoln's actions, either. I hope he and every last yellow-bellied Northerner lie in the gutters at the end of this war. The way I look at it, the South would be better off without them."

Whitney's eyes flashed. "How do you reckon that? The South depends on the North for their factories as much as the North depends on the South for our cotton."

"If you don't recall, ma'am, the depreciation of Confederate currency is another reason for the South's disregard of the North. Even street merchants are refusing to take our money. My wife entered a shop in Virginia where the shopkeeper rejected her money like it was dirty. Said it was worthless. The North seeks to cut us off at the knees; pardon me if I don't like it much."

"We, too, have encountered problems with the currency. Just the other day, a traveling salesman refused to sell me sugar and flour," Pippa said.

"Major General Loring issued a general order stating that the money from the Confederate Government is secure and should be received for public transactions." Whitney cut her food into precise pieces. "Perhaps if women had a say in political matters, we wouldn't find ourselves at war in the first place."

I tensed as the soldier narrowed his eyes at the insert of her political views, and the soldier sitting next to him regarded her with the same disapproval. "Political matters are best left to men," he said.

"Is that so?" She stretched to her full height.

Knox patted her hand where it lay on the table next to her plate, looking nervous.

"Yes," the soldier asserted. "Can you imagine what would happen to this country if women's input was valued? And God help us if some fool granted them the chance to vote." His chuckle reverberated throughout the dining room.

"There are plenty of women who've made profound progress in this country," I said. "And doing so while having to hide behind their husbands. Not out of cowardice, I assure you, but because they were considered inadequate in all matters. In fact, they are born with gifted minds and possess more courage and brilliance than some men. It's their decisions and actions behind closed doors that advanced their husbands to power."

Throats cleared, and the men adjusted themselves in their seats.

I smiled, and before taking a bite of food, said, "I've had all I can handle on matters of politics and war for the day. Let us talk about other matters, shall we?" I placed the food in my mouth, only to have my stomach revolt. I grabbed my napkin, angled my body away, and deposited the bite into the linen.

"Are you well, ma'am?" The soldier who had rebuked Private Daniels looked at me with concern.

"I fear I may have caught the sickness you all brought with you. I've been feeling under the weather for the past few…for a while…" I stopped as a thought occurred. *No, it's impossible.* I lifted my glass and took a rather long swig. "If you will please excuse me." I laid my napkin beside my plate, and as I stood, the men at the table followed suit. "Gentlemen, it's been a pleasure. I offer my apologies for the disruption. I think I will retire to my chamber." I turned and dashed from the room.

"Willow?" Pippa said behind me as I reached the upstairs landing. I turned to observe her following after me.

"What is it?" I continued on down the corridor to my chamber. Head spinning, I dashed to the basin on the stand by the window and vomited. After expelling the bile from my empty stomach, I used a folded cloth lying by the basin to pat my mouth. Worry plagued my mind. I rested my hands on the stand and squeezed my eyes shut. The influenza strain brought by the soldiers had lasted two to three days, but the ailment tormenting me had taken hold before they'd arrived at Livingston and still lingered.

"It appears God has chosen to bless you," Pippa said behind me, and I turned to face her and rested my hips against the stand.

"What do you mean?" I knew exactly what she referred to, but fear heightened my denial.

She smiled warmly at me. "I've seen my share of women blessed with the gift of life."

"No, you're mistaken." I shook my head and walked quickly to the bed. "We are in the middle of a war. We have no time f-for…" I couldn't say the word.

"A baby," she said tenderly.

"Impossible." I paced in front of the bed before nausea roiled again, and I was forced to sit down. I recalled the lovemaking in the meadow. "No." Misery and fear rushed over me. "It can't be. It's the soldiers. They brought this illness to us." My words lacked conviction. Pippa lowered herself down on the bed beside me. "But I can't be with child." As hard as I tried to deny that I could possibly be pregnant, I knew the truth. What had Bowden and I been thinking? To bring a child into the world in the middle of a war…why, it was downright foolish and irresponsible of us. I broke into a fit of tears.

Pippa gathered me into an embrace. "Hush now, dear one. You mustn't cry. Everything will work out, and when Bowden returns he will be delighted to hear the news."

"But this war could last for years," I said between sobs.

"And if it does, his homecoming will be that much sweeter."

I hiccupped and sat up, taking the handkerchief she offered me and blowing my nose. "Thank you. I don't know how I will do this."

"Your child will be one good thing that will come out of this war." She brushed stray hairs from my eyes and tucked them behind my ear.

"B-but what if I go through this all again, only for the child to…"

"Die?" she said before standing and moving to turn down the linens. "You mustn't let such fear rob you of the joy for the life that grows inside of you. Each day, when you rise, give thanks for another day and your child, and let the Almighty take care of the rest."

"That's what I'm afraid of," I said bluntly. "Death follows me."

"And that belief will ensure it does." She pulled back the covers. "Come, let me remove your shoes. You should rest for a while and see the child gets the best of care."

"All right, but only because I feel I will collapse if I return to the field. Don't get to thinking that I will lie in bed and be coddled; I have a plantation to run." I climbed beneath the linens after I allowed her to remove my shoes.

"Very well; but for today, you rest." She smiled down at me, and I absorbed the warmth in her face.

As she turned to walk away, I grabbed her hand. "Pippa?"

"Yes."

"Thank you."

"Of course."

"I'm glad I inserted myself into Ben's and your affairs," I said with a smirk.

She chuckled softly.

I smiled at her. "Left to him, he may have missed the treasure that gleamed before his own eyes."

The melody of her laughter renewed my spirit. She patted my shoulder and walked from the room.

CHAPTER
Thirty-Six

THE NORTH AND SOUTH FACED THE BLOODIEST ONE-DAY BATTLE since the war's commencement with the battle at Sharpsburg. Publications declared the casualties to be astronomical, and General Lee had been forced to give up his plan to invade Maryland and had retreated back to Virginia.

At Livingston, our patients had recovered and departed, and although I welcomed the quiet of the house, waiting for Jones's return from Charleston with news of my husband had strained my sanity. I sat in the parlor with Pippa, knitting wool socks for the army, and every few rows, I had to remove stitches.

"I hope the soldier who gets these has enormous feet." I held up my work for her inspection.

She laughed.

"Lard sakes, gal, he won't only need big feet but misshapen ones as well," Mammy declared as she marched into the parlor with a plate of sliced apples. "You haven't eaten a bite all day. You got to keep dat babe healthy and fed." She had doted on me since I had told her the news.

I reflected back on the day, and her happiness, and my dismay.

"Oh, Mammy, how can it be so?" I'd thrown myself at her.

"What ya think gonna happen when Masa show up here after being gone so long?" Mammy had stroked my back. "He need himself some loving, and when mens need some loving, dat when babies happen."

"I'm well aware of how babies come about." I'd pushed away and scowled at her with misery and uncontainable fear.

"Ya hear me?" Mammy plucked me back to the present. "Eat." She gestured at the apples.

I laid the knitting aside and took a slice. "I'd rather have a slab of cake."

"Ain't got no flour. I asked Mister Jones to fetch some when he went into town. Mrs. Smith was clean out de last time he asked."

Later, when dusk stretched over the plantation, the sound of a horse approaching lured me to the window.

"Is it Jones?" Pippa asked.

"I can't tell." I pressed my face closer to the window. "No, it looks like Mr. Barlow." I turned and frowned at her. "I wonder what he wants?"

"Let's go find out." Pippa tossed her knitting aside and headed for the door.

We walked out onto the front veranda as he dismounted and handed his reins to Pete.

"Mr. Barlow, good evening," I said.

"Willow, Pippa." He removed his hat and climbed the steps.

"What brings you to Livingston?" I asked.

"I'm returning from patrolling, and I was wondering if you heard the news."

"To what news are you referring? I've about had my fill of news."

"Shall we sit?" He gestured at the rockers. "I'm weary from the day."

"Of course," I said as Mammy stepped out onto the veranda. "Henrietta, do you mind bringing Mr. Barlow something to drink?"

"Yes, Missus." Mammy curtsied and returned inside.

Once we had seated ourselves, I said to him, "It must be important for you to stop in on your way home."

Mr. Barlow brushed the dust from his trousers. "It's news that will send a ripple through the South. Caused quite a stir with Mr. Carlton and the others."

"Oh?" Pippa sent me a nervous glance. "Do not keep us waiting."

"Very well. Lincoln has issued a preliminary Emancipation Proclamation, declaring his intention to free all slaves in new territory seized by the Union Army. Says that states engaged in the rebellion against the Union have until January, when all slaves in Confederate states will be forever freed."

"And what of all the enslaved in the United States?" I said.

"Thank you, Henrietta," he said as Mammy returned with whiskey. After a long, thoughtful swig, he continued. "I suppose they will remain slaves."

"So this proclamation has nothing to do with freeing slaves because it's constitutionally wrong; it's simply a political and military tactic to try and force the South's hand." I shook my head in disbelief. "When will this ever end? If we are to see equity for the blacks, I'm not sure it will be at Abraham Lincoln's hand. He claims slavery is morally wrong but then says the blacks shouldn't vote, hold office, serve on a jury, or marry a white. Therefore, to him, the blacks are less than the whites and not equal members of society. So let's say he comes through with his plan for emancipation; what then? The blacks will still find themselves handcuffed by the Constitution."

"Willow is right," Pippa said. "Lincoln's attempt to dangle the chance of emancipation appears to be nothing more than a military strategy."

"I suppose we'll have to wait and see. But, in the end, if he does come through, then perhaps this war would've been for something. It's days like today when I would like to sit down with your father and discuss the matter." I glimpsed yearning on his face before he shook his head as though to dislodge memories. He pushed to his feet. "Isabella and Callie will be waiting for me."

"Tell my friend I miss her and for her to try to visit soon," Pippa said as he descended the stairs.

"I will." He mounted his horse and rode out.

We turned to go back inside when a rustling at the corner of the house caught my attention. "Parker, is that you?" I called.

There was a curse, followed by the swaying of shrubs before he stepped into sight.

"What are you doing?" I narrowed my eyes, but as I said the words I understood. "Were you eavesdropping?"

He crept closer. "Yessum. I couldn't help but overhear what Mister Barlow said 'bout President Lincoln."

I looked from him to Pippa and touched her arm. "I will join you shortly."

She nodded at me before smiling at Parker as he came to stand at the bottom of the steps. "Evening, Parker."

"Evenin', Missus Hendricks." He bowed his head.

She turned and walked inside.

Parker's eyes flitted about as he stood waiting for my lecture, I suspected. "What is it you want to know?" I asked.

His eyes widened, but he took an eager step forward. "Is et true dat Lincoln wants to free us?"

"That's what Mr. Barlow said."

Hope gleamed in his eyes. "Ef he does, dat means I'd be free and I could marry Kimie."

"On the contrary." I lowered myself down onto the top step. "Come and sit." I patted the place next to me, and after he seated himself, I stared at the fields. "I wish it were as simple as that."

"Free is free, ain't et?"

"It should be, but I fear free comes with conditions. It doesn't exonerate you from being black."

"De Lard a cruel god," he said despondently. "He never gave de black men a fighting chance in dis life. De white man gits richer while de black man dies toiling on deir lands or chained to de whipping post." He looked up at the heavens. "Maybe He, too, is a white man. Reckon He hates de black man too." His jaw clenched, and tears of frustration welled before he leaped to his feet and hobbled down the steps. At the bottom, he turned back and looked up at me, his eyes flashing. "I be damned ef I'm gwine to live de rest of my life wid my neck under de white man's foot. I will marry Kimie, and we will have a piece of land of our own. I ain't 'bout to die a slave lak my pappy." He limped to the corner of the house and disappeared.

My shoulders slumped and I leaned forward, resting my elbows on my knees. I considered Parker and his love for Kimie, and how I'd feel if Bowden and I had faced the same trials. My thoughts turned to Mary Grace and Magnus, and the hardships they would face as an interracial couple.

I looked down at my expanding stomach. I wanted my child to grow up in a world where hate and division didn't label us, but we had to change to do so. But how did one change a generational mindset that extended to every corner of the world?

CHAPTER Thirty-Seven

March, 1863

AT THE BEGINNING OF THE NEW YEAR, LINCOLN ISSUED THE Emancipation Proclamation, ordering black soldiers' enlistment. I altered my apprehensions about the president and conceded that perhaps he could be an ally for the blacks, but I retained some reservations in the matter.

"Damn leg keeps me prisoner." Parker knocked at his leg with his walking stick.

In the field a short distance from the outbuildings and house, we worked the earth to plant vegetable seeds within the coming month.

"Ef I could git myself to Beaufort and enlist wid de Union, dey wouldn't take me anyhow 'cause of dis busted leg. Ain't worth much to dem, I reckon."

I paused to rest a spell as the ache in my lower back that had troubled me all morning intensified. "Do you think racial segregation doesn't follow the army?"

Tillie looked up from working the ground and adjusted her infant son strapped to her back as he began to fuss. "Sally Mae from over at de Hamilton plantation says de black folkses who enlist are given positions as cooks, teamsters, and laborers. Dey don't git to fight alongside de whites. De way I look at et, et ain't no different dan being on a plantation." The baby's wails heightened.

"'Cept dey git paid," Parker said.

"Why don't you find some shade and feed him?" I said to Tillie as she removed the babe and tried to soothe him.

"He ain't gwine to settle till I do." She strode from the field.

"Do you reckon what Tillie said be true?" Parker stared after her.

"Ruby says Saul receives significantly less pay than the white soldiers. He is a strong, healthy man, and he has been assigned the task of teamster. So what do you think?" I struck the ground with the hoe in hopes of finishing the task at hand, but a sudden pain in my abdomen stilled my movement and I winced.

Parker dropped his hoe and shuffled to my side. "You all right, Missus?"

I bent forward and rested my palms on my knees. "I-I think it's time."

"Time for what?" Parker regarded me with confusion.

"The baby."

His eyes widened, and he started yelling and carrying on. "Lard Jesus, I ain't fixing to deliver no baby. I don't know de first thing 'bout et."

I squeezed his arm, and he let out a yelp. "Trust me, I am not giving birth in this field," I said through gritted teeth. "Help me to the house."

"Yessum. Big John take care of dis." He nodded and wrapped an arm around my waist.

We made it across the field and to the smokehouse before another contraction hit. "Wait. Hold on." I stopped and clenched my jaw at the pain.

"Willow, you all right?" Whitney strolled through the yard, carrying buckets of water from the river.

"De baby is coming," Parker shouted back at her.

She dropped the pails and raced to my side.

"No, no." I shooed her away as fear of losing the child took precedence. "Run ahead, tell Big John." She raced off.

The contractions were coming too fast. Something was wrong.

Panic thrummed, and I looked to the heavens. "Please help me. Keep my child safe."

"Missus." Pete's voice. "Missus Tucker sent me." He halted in front of me, and without hesitation hoisted me into his arms.

I wrapped my arms around his neck and broke into hysterics. "I can't lose this child. I can't!"

"Evvything be all right, Missus. I git you up to de big house, and my pappy will take care of evvything." His confidence in Big John's abilities did nothing to still the panic charging through me. Ben had been competent, and still my son had died.

Parker hobbled along beside us.

"Angel gal!" I heard Mammy call, and looked up to discover Big John and her racing toward us as fast as her legs could carry her. Big John reached us first.

"Put me down," I said. Pete obliged and placed my feet on the ground.

"How fast de pains coming?" Big John asked.

"I don't know. Fast." I clutched his arm.

Mammy caught up and stood catching her breath. Sweat glistened on her brow, and worry shone in her eyes, but I assumed, upon noticing my own panic, she shuffled it away. "Don't you worry none. We have ourselves a healthy babe born dis day." She cupped my cheek. "Parker, you go on to de field. Dat earth ain't gwine to work etself. Besides, dis here is 'oman's work."

Big John gestured at Pete. "Hurry, son, git her up to her chamber."

"No, I can walk." I brushed him away.

"Dis ain't no time for your stubbornness," Mammy said with a scowl.

"I will make it," I grunted. I walked past them and headed for the house, but at the back veranda another contraction hit and almost buckled my knees. I halted and grabbed the stair railing, biting down hard to control the pain. My mind raced with the information I had gathered from the book *The Origin of Birth* by Frederick Hollick. After my son's death, I had decided that if I were to find myself with child again, I would become as knowledgeable as I could about reproduction and birth. After the pain subsided, I straightened and eyed the stairs with dread.

On one of the whitewashed rockers, a soldier blinded on the battlefield tipped his head to hear better. "That you, Mrs. Armstrong?" he asked.

"It is." I had taken a liking to the young soldier, who happened to be our only patient at the time.

"I hear your time has come. My wife gave birth only days after this war started. I suppose my boy would be two or more by now. I've never seen him. Guess I never will," he said with a laugh devoid of any bitterness, instead resolved to the loss of his sight. "I suppose this here situation has taught me to not take for granted the blessings one has in life."

"Are you a Christian man, Private?" I asked.

"No; all I cared about was serving my country, but my pa was. He used to say, 'Son, if we can see the love in the smallest things, there is no room for fear.' When I first lost my sight, I was angry. Downright mad at God. Felt like He had cheated me or did me a disservice, but maybe this was His way of making me appreciate the life I took for granted."

Tears tightened my throat.

"I am no good in the service of the army. Soon I will go home, and when I do, I'll embrace my son and wife and give thanks that I returned to them when so many won't. I'll find another way to be of service to my country."

Admiration for the man swelled in my chest, and his courage and outlook on life filled me with hope and determination. I would birth my child, and all would be well. "Thank you, Private."

"For what?"

"For inspiring me to face what comes."

"You're welcome, ma'am. I don't know what I said, but I'm mighty grateful it helped." He smiled the most peaceful smile.

"Come, Missus, let's git you inside." Mammy wrapped an arm around my waist.

I allowed her to help me up the stairs and to my chamber. She helped me disrobe and slip into a nightgown before another contraction hit, and I rested my forehead on her shoulder and grunted through the pain.

"God have mercy!" I moaned into her shoulder as she rubbed my back and hips.

Later I lay in bed while Big John examined me.

"Et comes quick, Missus. You have dis babe soon. Real soon." He dropped the sheet and smiled at me over my bent knees.

"How soon?"

"Can't be sho', but soon. De babe reveals ets head."

Mammy stood at my side, holding my hand, and I clutched it tighter.

An hour later, Whitney studied me from a nearby armchair where she had sat chewing her nails about clean off. "If you ask me, giving birth is a ghastly predicament. After listening to you wail like your insides are about to erupt, I wonder why women let men near them at all. And some go on to birth a tribe of children."

Mammy chuckled and said, "Ain't nothing evvy woman don't think 'fore dey give birth."

As Big John had predicted, my daughter entered the world in perfect health within two hours and lay cleaned, swaddled, and asleep in my arms. Whitney had feigned a headache and left the room before the babe's birth; the ashen look on her face revealed she had been about to faint and prove the fearless Whitney Tucker was indeed fallible.

Tears of gratitude trickled down my cheeks as I regarded my daughter's dark hair and long lashes. Her fingers clutched one of my own, and my heart felt like it would burst with love. "She is perfect," I said.

"Dat she is, angel gal. Dat she is. She luks jus' lak you when you were born."

"Really?" I looked up at her with awe.

"Yessum. She sho' does—a perfect angel. I recall laying you in your cradle after your mama drifted off to sleep and staring down at you. I thought de Lard had blessed Masa Charles and Missus Olivia wid a gift dat would bring dem closer. At de time, I didn't knowed? you belonged to Masa Ben. But et didn't matter none, 'cause you brought de missus and de masa a heap of love. Evvything changed after you were born. Made de missus start to feel somepin' for Masa Charles, I suppose." Tears pooled in her eyes as she relived a memory.

Over the years she had continued to tell me stories of my mother, and I never grew tired of hearing them. She never seemed bored of sharing. Mammy honored her by keeping Mother alive in her memories.

I thought of my mother, imagining her holding me in her arms after giving birth and the love that had swelled in her heart for me. At that moment, I felt a deep sense of connection with her.

"What you fixing to call de babe?" Mammy touched the apple of my daughter's cheek.

"Olivia Henrietta, after the two women who mothered me." I looked up at her and smiled.

Mammy beamed, and her bosom rose and fell. "Dat a right fine name, angel gal. A right fine name."

CHAPTER
Thirty-Eight

THE SUN POURED THROUGH THE NURSERY WINDOW AND ENVELOPED my sleeping daughter with its warmth. I stood by her bassinet and admired how the sun's kiss dampened the dark curls capping her head. Long lashes rested against the rosy apples of her cheeks, and her chest rose and fell with soft breaths. My heart swelled with pride and love for the little being that had blessed my life.

The floorboards squeaked behind me, and I glanced up as Mammy walked into the nursery. "She sho' is a purty chile." She smiled down at the babe.

I ran a finger over the flesh of the baby's arm. "I thought after I lost my son that I'd never love another like I do her."

"Dere ain't no greater gift dan de one of being a mother. Though sometimes et bring you a heap o' worry, et still a gift nonedeless."

"I hope I can be half the mother you were to Mary Grace and me."

"You well be...but you be better. I knowed et. You ain't skeered of nothing. You raise Miss Olivia de same. Your mama was a fighter, and so is you. I reckon et in de babe's blood to make a difference in dis world."

"But Mama didn't raise me." I looked at her. "You did. So I reckon I got some of that fight from you."

Her eyes dampened, and profound sorrow tugged at her features as she continued to regard my daughter. "Dat may be somewhat true, but I spent most of my life being skeered. Mary Grace wants to be anything but lak me. I didn't mean to, but my fears harmed dat gal. Made her want to git far away from me. 'Cause when dis war be over, she leaving South Carolina and heading across the ocean wid my grandbabies." Her shoulders slumped. "Don't know when I see her again. But a mama can only protect her chillum for so long 'fore she got to let dem fly. Den, sometimes, all you left wid is regret. I should have done better. Been better. De chile was free, but I kept her lak a caged bird."

I touched her arm. "You only sought to protect her."

She turned from the bassinet and held my gaze. "I knowed dat to be true, and all a mama can do is do de bes' she know how. And, when you see you did wrong, try and make et right. I can't go back and change my mistakes, but I am telling you dis babe is meant to fly. Don't let your fears of losing folkses cause you to make de same mistakes I did."

I wrapped an arm around her shoulders and led her toward the door. "With your wisdom, I hope I can be that source of comfort and assurance for Olivia. The way I look at it, we women and mothers need to stick together."

"We sho' do," she said. "Dis here war got me believing de menfolk may not have et all figured out lak dey want us to think dey do."

I chuckled lightly as we stepped into the corridor. "We are together on that thinking. Why just the other day—"

"Missus Willow!" Tillie barreled up the stairs in a panic.

"Shh, you luking to wake de babe," Mammy said, looking back at the nursery as the baby let out a cry. "And, gal, since when did you find your voice?"

"Sorry." Tillie's voice dropped to the murmur we were accustomed to hearing from her. "Mister Carlton and his men are here. Dey bring news. You bes' come talk to him."

The baby's wails erupted.

"Don't you worry 'bout de babe, I got her," Mammy said, already marching back to the nursery.

I followed after Tillie. "What did they say?"

"Heard dem talking amongst demselves. Said somepin' 'bout Union soldiers attacking along de Combahee River. Said dey torched plantations, mills, and cotton, evvything."

"Combahee River? That is some distance from here."

"I don't rightfully know, Missus. Mister Carlton told me to git on in here and fetch you," she said as we reached the foyer. "I fixing to make myself scarce. I don't lak dat man much." She curtsied before hurrying down the corridor to the back door.

I strode outside. "Mr. Carlton, is it true?"

Theodore removed his hat. "Reckon so, ma'am. Folks said that a black woman guided Union soldiers to plantations and helped hundreds of slaves escape on gunboats. And that isn't the worst of it. Union troops torched plantations, warehouses, cotton, and mills and took out a pontoon bridge. Shot it to bits, from what I heard."

"When did this occur?"

"A week or so back. I came here as soon as I heard. It isn't safe for you womenfolk out here all alone without a man to protect you. I thought the boys and I could offer you extra protection. We'd be willing to add your plantation to the top of our priority list—come by more often so you aren't left defenseless."

I contemplated his priority list and what hapless souls had been added to it. My stomach clenched at the thought of how he had misused his position since the onset of the war.

I peered past him to the men and boys he had brought with him. "Mr. Barlow doesn't join you today?"

His upper lip curled with disgust. "I won't have no nigger-lover riding with me, not after this attack. He can sit at home with his nigger wife. This is white man's business, and the way I look at it he's nigger at the core."

My heart sped up as concern for the Barlows took precedence.

"Well, what do you say? Do you want the boys and I to stop in more often? Although I'd have to come up with a price." The hungry look in his eyes sent shivers through me.

My back stiffened, and I said, firmly, "That will be quite all right. I appreciate your consideration, but we've managed so far."

"What are you fixing to do if them damn Union soldiers show up here? They'd rape a pretty woman like you without hesitation."

I crossed my arms over my chest and leveled a stern glare on him. "I'll take my chances."

"Suit yourself." He jerked his horse's reins and spun it around. "Don't say I didn't warn you." He waved a hand in disgust. "Come on, boys."

After they rode off, Whitney wandered out on the veranda as I stood waiting for their dust to settle. "What did Carlton want?"

"To offer his protection in exchange for…well, you know the man and his tendencies."

Whitney gasped before her face read murder. "He has a lot of nerve, showing up here like we are some brothel or something, planted here in the middle of nowhere to serve his needs. We've done just fine taking care of ourselves without his help." She paused, and her brow puckered. "What did he want to protect us from now, besides the obvious threat?"

"It appears a black woman led hundreds of slaves onto ships down by the Combahee River," I said with a smile.

"Tubman?"

"I believe so. That woman never ceases to amaze me."

Whitney's expression was one of awe.

"With the good news comes the bad," I said. "Union soldiers pillaged the area, torching everything in sight."

Whitney spun to gawk down the lane. "But the Combahee River is some distance from here. What makes Carlton think they would come here?"

"I don't know if he does. I do believe, however, that he continues to endeavor to embed fear in the womenfolk left to operate their plantations and farms in hopes of satisfying his perversions."

"Taking advantage of women in a time like this," Whitney

scoffed, and narrowed her eyes. "No woman is safe around the likes of him."

"You can say that again. And to think Josephine is married to the despicable man."

"She would have been better off to run with Jethro."

"Some days, I wonder." I looped arms with her and walked back into the house as Mammy ascended the stairs, carrying my crying daughter.

Whitney pulled away and held out her arms. "Here, let me have a go at her."

"You?" Mammy angled her body away to shield the babe from her. "You gwine to bounce de babe's head clean off wid how you try to soothe her."

"And you don't?" Whitney glowered and removed her from Mammy's arms. "All that fussing won't get you anywhere." Bless Whitney's heart, as dry and lacking in warmth as her words came off, the babe's cries softened, and she stared at her with curiosity. Whitney delivered us a cheeky grin and sauntered off down the corridor.

Mammy gaped after her with her arms crossed over her bosom. "I don't git et. Dat woman ain't got an ounce of baby manners to her, but all de babes lak her."

I laughed and nudged her shoulder with mine. "She did handle Evie's fits splendidly." I cringed at the memory of Mary Grace's daughter's screams. "Let's be thankful my daughter doesn't carry on so. I suppose Whitney has more skill than we give her credit for."

Mammy scowled at me. "I be in the kitchen house if you need me." She whirled, and grumbling under her breath, wandered off outside.

I walked to the door and leaned against the frame to peer across the landscape. My daughter would be raised around strong women who would teach her strength and courage, and for that, gratitude sang in my heart.

⚙ CHAPTER ⚙
Thirty-Nine

Bowden
Gettysburg

A POST CARRIER RODE INTO CAMP BEFORE NIGHTFALL, AND I PUSHED through the men clinging to the hope of news from home. A year had passed since I had returned to Livingston, and each time a carrier came through, I stood waiting for my name to be called, and yet it never had.

Tomorrow General Lee would lead the Army of North Virginia into battle against the Union General George Meade of the Army of the Potomac, and a sense of dread hung over me.

"Armstrong. Bowden Armstrong." The carrier waved an envelope high in the air.

My heart leaped. "Here." I threaded through the men to retrieve the envelope and released the air constricting my lungs as I observed my wife's penmanship.

I strode a short distance away from the gathered men and tore the letter open.

April 12, 1963
My dearest husband,
I bring you delightful news. You are a father. I gave birth to a beautiful daughter last month, and she thrives.

I lowered the letter, dumbfounded, my mind spinning. A daughter. I gulped back the tears gathering in my throat and gawked at the black cook stirring the steaming evening meal in a cast-iron kettle. I walked to a log by the fire and sat down before my legs gave out from under me. *Well, I'll be.* I swiped a hand through my hair. I was a father.

"I'm guessing that letter brings news from home?" The cook nodded at the letter.

"It does. My wife sends word that I'm a father." I noted the date on the stationery. "I suppose she would be three months old now."

"A daughter," he said with a grimace.

"You got children?" I asked.

"I did. I had a daughter, and she was cursed from the day she was born with the face of an angel. She died while giving birth to the master's son's child. To white men, a daughter is a gift; to a slave man, she is a curse."

I bowed my head and quietly said, "If only it wasn't so."

Shuffling ended with a grunt as the cook came over and seated himself on the opposite end of the log. I peered sideways at him. His shoulders hunched with age, he sat regarding the happenings around camp.

"I heard what you said. Am I to believe you're a black sympathizer?" he whispered.

I glanced over my shoulder. "You could say that."

"And you're here, fighting for the South?" He kept his voice low.

"I fight for my home and land." I eyed the group of chained slaves huddling together at the edge of camp. During our march north, General Lee had collected former slaves and free blacks with the intention of selling them.

"That look on your face isn't one of vengefulness, but one of empathy." The cook's observation summoned my attention, and I peered back to observe him studying the slaves. He shifted on the log to face me. "I've seen that look once or twice on other soldiers' faces. You sure you're a Southern boy?"

"You sure you aren't a Union spy? You speak with more refinement than most of these farmers I fight alongside." I looked him square in the eye.

His eyes smiled before he said solemnly, "I'm here with my new master. Folks on the old plantation considered me a kept slave. They were right. Masa Williams taught me to read and write. I ate food from his table. Life was good for the most part. But he had a son, and the man hated me. Said his pa favored me, and I reckon he did." He dropped his head and peered at his hands. "My daughter's mother was from the next plantation, and the young masa visited there often. Took a fancying to my daughter, and I reckon that, and his abhorrence of me, caused him to do what he did."

I wanted to give my condolences for his loss, but such a statement felt insincere amidst the adversity he'd faced. I stifled the guilt for my own sins and the families I'd separated, all in the name of personal gain. "You said you came with your new master," I said.

"That's right; a few years back, Masa Williams died. His son purchased my grandbaby and wife from her master before he sold me off the next day. Guess he wanted me to leave knowing he had taken my daughter and laid claim to my wife and granddaughter."

"There are no words I can say that could express my sorrow for what has been stolen from you." I gulped back simmering emotions.

"The sins of another white man aren't every white man's burdens to carry."

Perhaps it was homesickness that overtook me or the sobering knowledge of the countless lives lost in the war, or maybe apprehension of what tomorrow's battle would bring that caused me to say what I said next. "That is true about my wife, but not me."

He regarded me with a perplexed expression. "What is your story, soldier?"

"Born and raised in Texas. Went to medical school and returned home to run my family's plantation outside of Charleston after my grandpa became ill."

He stiffened. "You're a slave owner?"

"I am."

He wiped his hands on his trousers as fear gripped his face. "I thought you said you were a black man's ally."

"I did. Don't fret none. What you said is safe with me." I lifted my hands in a gesture of peace before lowering them and staring into the fire. "Do you really want to hear my story?"

"If you want to share, I'd be obliged to listen."

"Very well, but I can't promise you're going to like it."

"You are an unusual man, soldier," he said. "You claim to be a slave owner. You fight for the Confederacy. But that look in your eyes when you observed those slaves over there wasn't the look of a slave owner, but a man who questions on what side of this war he stands."

"You read much into a look," I said dryly.

"I've nothing to do but analyze people. Besides, this war proved we are all just men trying to make our way in life. I'll do my best to listen with an open heart."

I swallowed hard and continued to let the flames hold my gaze. "Thank you," I said. "My wife was born into a family of slave owners. But her heart has always been for the good of mankind. She has made it her mission in life to right the wrongs of her family. It took some convincing and some hard lessons before I saw the South's ways through her eyes. I suffered a loss that would take me to my knees…" I stopped as an officer walking by paused to give us a questioning look.

The cook and I stood. I nodded. "Evening, sir."

The officer looked from me to him. "That meal had best be ready at seven, sharp."

The cook inclined his head. "It will be."

I thought of the meatless slop we had eaten night after night and how it left your stomach hollow and aching.

The officer gave me another glance before moving on.

The cook waited until the officer disappeared before he gestured at me. "Tell me of this loss you mentioned."

I told him of Gray, and despite the time that had passed the ache of his loss hadn't diminished.

"You buried him in your family's cemetery," he said with reverence.

"In a different world, I would have freely called him my friend. Instead, I hold the friendship as though it is a filthy secret." Bitterness soured my tongue.

"You best not let anyone hear you talking like that, or they'll shoot you dead on the battlefield the first chance they get."

"Yes, well, he was a great man." I stood. "It was nice to meet you…"

"Name's Teodoro. Folks call me Teo." He extended a hand.

I clasped it. "Bowden Armstrong."

"Stay alive, Mr. Armstrong. We are going to need men like you when this war is over."

I bowed my head in respect before turning and escaping into the shadows of the night.

I wandered through the camp, passing soldiers assembled around open fires. They stared back at me with eyes blank with weariness. The cloud of tomorrow loomed heavy over the men.

At the outer boundary of the camp, I paused to gaze up at the moon as it took guardianship of the night. Although I'd never been a praying man, the war had left me no choice but to hope that a greater being was safeguarding my family and me.

"It's me again. I know you got your hands full, but I sure would like to hold my daughter just one time. Reckon I'm here asking you to watch over me out there tomorrow." I grappled with the fear chasing my thoughts and inclined my head. I kicked at the earth and waited as though I expected an answer. After several moments had passed, I turned and made my way back.

CHAPTER
Forty

Willow

Reports of General Lee's defeat at Gettysburg against the Army of the Potomac had left me shaken and worried about Bowden. After his defeat, he and his army had fled back to Virginia, accompanied by a wagon train of wounded troops that stretched many miles long.

Knox had been stationed as a support troop in Charleston and he'd tried to gain information on my husband, but to no avail.

"I'm going to go mad, waiting for news." I rested my elbows on the pasture fence.

Jimmy lowered the horse's hoof he had been tending to and regarded me. "I know et hard. But try not to think de worst. Masa git word to ya as soon as he can."

"It's impossible not to fret," I said. "What if he is left wounded somewhere and in need of help? Or worse, one of the bodies left in the streets for the citizens to bury."

"You got to have faith he will return. Don't let your mind make you a widow 'fore your time."

"This war has taken so many lives and will leave the landscape of the South forever changed. Families destroyed. Wives without husbands. Children without fathers. Mothers and fathers without sons." I stared down at the piece of straw I separated with my nails. "So much death. I just hope it will be worth the cost."

"War is an ugly matter," he said. "Ain't no good dat can come out of et. 'Cept I guess Lincoln freeing slaves. Never thought I see de day."

"I doubted Lincoln's intentions, and after he instated the proclamation I had hope in the man's ambitions. But I've come to see Lincoln's proclamation as flawed. It says nothing about freeing slaves in states faithful to the Union. It exempts freeing the slaves in the Confederate states already under the Union's authority. Furthermore, freedom is promised if the Union Army is successful. However, after the proclamation, the war has been reborn, and it has become about slavery. My hope is that it has awakened the hearts of our country, and freedom for *all* will be achieved."

A broad smile crossed his weathered face. "Dat would be a day of rejoicing."

"Indeed it would." My chest expanded with optimism before old anxieties reared. "What do you plan to do with your freedom?"

He sauntered to the fence and leaned on the rail, and looked at the main house. "Well, I bin thinking 'bout dat, and I suppose my gal Magnolia may want me to go to New York."

My throat tightened, but I peered straight ahead and said in a quiet voice, "For what it's worth, I'm sorry."

I felt his gaze on me. "No call for sorry. Ain't no crime you committed. When Masa Charles purchased me, I was a dead man walking. Coming here saved me. Having you follow me 'round evvywhere I went wid your constant chatter and questions breathed life back into me. You and de masa gave me de option to leave. Risked prison and discovery wid de way you helped people escape to freedom, but I stayed 'cause my heart right here at Livingston. I miss my gal, and I wish I could see her and her family more, but New York ain't no place for me. I was born and raised in de South— dis my home. Bin thinking, after de war, ef you and Masa still require a blacksmith, carpenter, or ranch hand, I would lak to stay on. Won't need but food and a place to lay my head."

I smiled through my tears and shifted to look into his earnest brown eyes. "I want nothing more than for you to remain at

Livingston, not as a slave but a freed man. We would pay you a decent wage. I have grand plans for this place, and I will need all the love and assistance I can get to see them into fruition."

He shook his head and released a hearty chuckle. "You always dreaming up somepin' in dat head of yours."

"If you do not dream, how can you create a future of your choosing?"

"Ain't all dat thinking exhausting?"

"Sometimes," I said with a laugh.

"I prefer to put dese to work over thinking." He held up his hands before stepping away from the fence to go back to work. He paused and turned around. "De mind will eat away at you ef you let et. Make you conceive de worst outcomes."

"Thank you."

"For what?"

"For always offering sound advice."

He waved a hand, and an endearing smile settled over his face. "Now you go on and check in on de li'l miss. She be what breathes life into your lungs."

CHAPTER
Forty-One

Ruby

AFTER MY HUSBAND ENLISTED IN THE ARMY AND RECEIVED A PITIFUL sum for his service, I had no choice but to inquire about my old job at the newspaper office. During Kipling's absence, he had placed a man in charge who hadn't been keen on women in the workplace, and at first he refused, but persistence from colleagues had secured me the job on a trial basis.

Late one July evening, after everyone had left for the day, I sat at my desk and scripted the article about the Gettysburg battle, set to go out in the newspaper by the end of the week.

Clarence, a black man from Five Points hired by Kipling to clean the office in the evenings, paused in front of my desk.

"Is there something I can do for you?" I looked up from my work.

"I've finished and was going to head out," he said before looking over his shoulder.

I glanced past him at a group of men who'd gathered across the street. They stood with torches in hand and eyes on the newspaper office. My heart thumped faster. I'd been so caught up in writing the article I hadn't noticed them.

He looked back at me. "I think it would be wise if you locked up for the night. It isn't safe for anyone out there with the draft riots going on. They burned a black orphanage and a church, and mobs are lynching black folk around the city."

Replacing my quill, I pushed back my chair, walked to the

door, and locked it before gathering my hat and handbag from the peg. Securing my hat, I darted back to my desk and turned out the lantern.

Clarence hurried around the main office to do the same, enveloping us in darkness. The gas lamps lining the streets gave us a view of the men, and as the office had gone dark the group became agitated. Hands struck at the heavens as one man with his back to us rallied the mob.

"Let me walk you out." Clarence steered me toward the back door, moving with urgency.

My heartbeat echoed in my ears, and I whispered a prayer of protection before cracking the door open. Sticking my head out, I noticed a band of men standing some distance off but not looking in our direction. I jumped at the sound of shattering glass and peered back at Clarence.

"They've broken the front window." The whites of his eyes gleamed in the darkness.

Beyond him was a crimson-and-orange glow as the flames took hold. The mob had set fire to the office.

"We need to go, now." I stepped out into the alley with him on my heels.

He gripped my elbow and hurried me past the group, who'd ceased their conversation at the ruckus taking place on the front street.

Clarence gripped my elbow tighter, and I raced to keep up. "It isn't safe for anyone to be out here. And you have a long journey ahead. Let's hail you a buggy and see you safely home."

I wanted nothing more than to return to the safety of my home and the comfort of my daughter.

We hurried on, putting distance between the newspaper office and us before stopping to look back. My stomach plummeted as raging flames rose high above the surrounding buildings, taking with them all Kipling's work for the abolitionist movement.

"Come. There's nothing we could've done," Clarence said.

"The men were coming in one way or another. At least we escaped with our lives, and let us make sure it stays that way."

Heart heavy, I followed after him. We wove between buildings toward the main street. He ducked his head out to ensure the street was safe before stepping out to hail a carriage.

After he had seen me securely seated inside, he smiled. "You get yourself home safely, Mrs. Sparrow. I'll see you soon."

I nodded, but a movement in the shadows seized my attention and my heart stopped. Clarence peered behind him, and before we could act, a shot echoed, and he stumbled back.

"Clarence!" I reached for his outstretched hand, but he stumbled again before dropping to his knees. He tore at his chest where darkness splattered his shirt and coat. "No…" I wailed.

"Go," he said in a hoarse whisper.

The driver whipped the reins and the team launched the buggy forward, and I was thrown toward the open door. The men raced toward the carriage, and I clawed at the doorframe, trying to grasp the swinging door. Tears blurring my vision, I sprang for the door and closed it as the pursuers fell away.

Through the back window, I observed the men standing over Clarence. I balled my hand and struck the seat as another gunshot rang out, and I turned away and buried my face in my hands. He had given his life to save me. He had a family—a wife and a young son.

My guilt melded with heartache as the carriage raced down the street that would take me away from the city. I stared in horror at the bodies of black men, women, children, and the occasional white sprawled in the streets. "Everyone has gone mad," I said into the darkness of the buggy.

As the lights and chaos of the city faded, I sat perched on the edge of the seat, scanning the roadside, half expecting an attack.

Later, in front of my home, I paid the driver and exited the carriage. I stood on the street until the carriage was out of sight before climbing the steps and walking inside.

Aisling, our housekeeper and nursemaid, descended the stairs. "Evening, Mrs. Sparrow. I was starting to worry about you."

"I'm sorry," I removed my bonnet and shawl. "I didn't intend to stay so long, but you know how I get when I have an article to finish."

She offered me a soft smile before it dissolved. "You look exhausted."

"It's been an extra eventful day. Is Mercy asleep?"

"The lass insisted she would wait up for you. She misses you, and with Mr. Sparrow away I thought it wouldn't hurt this one time. But tiredness got the best of her, and I carried her up to bed just before you walked in."

"People in the city have gone mad. They are killing people in the street. Mostly black."

She gasped and looked to the window.

"There hasn't been any trouble here this evening, has there?" I asked.

"It's been quiet. You don't think they would come here, do you?"

"Let's hope the distance will keep them away." I walked to the parlor and sat down in my husband's favorite armchair. Although its upholstery was tattered and faded, sitting in it gave me solace in his absence.

"Let me help you with your shoes." Aisling dropped to her knees before me and started undoing the laces. "Then I will fix you something to eat."

I allowed her to remove my shoes. "I'm not hungry." Clarence weighed heavily on my mind, and I forced back tears I thought I'd exhausted on the journey from the city. "I think I'll turn in for the night." I stood, and she rose. I touched her arm and smiled. "Thank you, Aisling. I don't know what I would do without you."

"We'll get through this, and soon Mr. Sparrow will return, and everything will be good again."

I laughed. "I admire your optimism."

She blushed and ducked her head.

"Good night," I said and walked toward the corridor.

"Night, Mrs. Sparrow."

I lay in bed, gazing out the window at the evening sky and thinking of Papa. Years had passed since I'd seen him. No news had come of how he and my friends at Livingston were doing. Willow's letters had stopped coming, and I wondered if she'd received any of mine.

Despite my concerns over the divide between the North and South, the terrors occurring in the city and the sight of Clarence's body sprawled in the street held my mind hostage. I decided I'd pay his wife a visit the following day and inform her of the sacrifice he'd made. But how do you tell a wife and mother that her husband had died saving you so you could come home to your daughter? Dread churned my gut at the backlash I might face.

✑ CHAPTER *Forty-Two*

Willow

J OSEPHINE LOOKED UP FROM THE CHESS GAME WE PLAYED AND PAUSED to observe my daughter. "She is growing fast."

The babe crawled quickly across the floor and attempted to pull herself up with the assistance of a table, but failed and landed on her buttocks. Instead of crying, she looked back at us and smiled. She was a delightful baby, so full of life and far too much energy.

Sailor strode into the room and set his sights on Olivia right away. "Evening, Missus Willow and Missus Josephine." He paused to bow before turning back to eye the baby. He'd taken a liking to her, often seeking out ways to play with her, but recently I'd scarcely seen the boy.

"I sent for you a while ago. Mrs. Carlton has come to visit. A rare treat these days." I stood. "What has you occupied lately? I haven't seen much of you at all."

"No, Missus." He reluctantly turned his gaze to Josephine and I. "Big John has been teaching me about medicines and herbs. I think that, when I'm grown, maybe I could go to medical school." He beamed with optimism.

I smiled at his ambitions and hoped that such a far-fetched dream would be possible for him one day.

"Speaking of growing." I regarded Josephine before walking to Sailor and draping an arm around his shoulders. "Do you see the size of this boy?"

He grinned up at me before straining to stand taller and looking back at his mother.

Tears glistened in Josephine's eyes as she stood with her hands clasped in front of her. "Indeed I do. He'll be a young man before you know it. I believe he'd make a splendid doctor, too."

Sailor squared his shoulders. "Thank you kindly, Missus Josephine."

"Mind you don't grow up too fast, young Sailor," she said.

"No, ma'am," he said, then glanced up at me. "Do you mind if I sit with Miss Olivia for a moment?"

I smiled and gave his shoulders a squeeze. "Go ahead." I released him.

"Can you imagine our Sailor going to Harvard Medical School?" Her face soft with love and affection, Josephine turned back to our game.

Sailor strode to Olivia and knelt beside her. She swatted her hands with delight and babbled at him as though she had something important that needed describing. He reached out a finger and stroked her arm as if she were a forbidden gem.

"Yes, I can. Black people are rising up all over this country despite the oppression they've faced. If Sailor wishes to go to medical school when he is of age, I will see he goes."

"I wish I could help pay for the expenses, but Theodore keeps a tight hold on our finances. All monies I would inherit from my family were bequeathed to my husband when I breathed, 'I do.' If only I could divorce him like the South did the North." Her mouth pinched as she regarded me over the board. "My cousin says I shouldn't be complaining because at least I have a husband when she and many other girls fear there will be no men left to marry."

"Surely having no husband would be better than being married to the one you've endured." I relocated my bishop. "Check."

She moved a pawn to protect her king. "The laws for women must change." Her rook clanged as she set it down hard.

"As must the ones for your son," I said.

Her hand froze in mid motion, and her gaze held mine. "It has taken some time, and a son, for me to see that perhaps we are wrong in our actions toward the blacks."

"The world is changing, Josephine. If we are to evolve, the South must too, or we will be left in the dust of progress." I studied the board and smiled inwardly as my strategy took form.

"But if the South wins, it will be the North that must change." She carelessly made her next move and stepped into my trap.

"I fear we may be on the losing end of this war."

She stiffened. "You mustn't speak so. Should I question your loyalty to the South?"

"Of course not. My heart is with the South. But it's our unethical behaviors, our actions, and the South's generational legacy that I hold in disregard. We must do better as a society." Passion kindled in my chest as I thought of a better tomorrow. "And" —I studied my next impactful move— "as for the war, the Northerners outnumber our troops. We can have all the weapons in the world, but able bodies are growing scarcer by the day."

"And if the South doesn't—"

"Checkmate." I moved my queen and put in place the final gambit to corner her king.

"Yes, well…wait a minute! You little sneak." She leaned back in her chair, staring at the board in disbelief. "You used all your boring talk of war and politics to ambush me. Your chess skills make me wonder how you'd fare as a general with the Confederacy. Perhaps we wouldn't be on the losing end of this war."

I smiled, thinking fondly of the times I'd played chess with my father as a young girl. "I was taught by the best," I said. "There wasn't a game my father couldn't win."

"He taught you well, my friend. It has been a nice visit," she said with a laugh and stood. "We will have to do it again soon. But I need to get back before my husband returns."

She said her goodbyes to Sailor and bent to stroke my daughter's cheek before I walked her to her carriage.

CHAPTER
Forty-Three

Amelie
May, 1864

THE TORRENTIAL DOWNPOUR PLASTERED MY UNIFORM TO MY BODY like a second skin as our army of 120,000 or more marched on toward Atlanta. Zeke and I were serving under General William T. Sherman after President Lincoln had appointed General Ulysses S. Grant commander of all Union armies and assigned General Sherman commander in the west.

The storm made the conditions treacherous and challenging as we pushed up the serpentine path. We slipped and skidded, trying to gain traction. I lost my footing, and my rifle struck me hard in the jaw. Teetering on the edge of the cliff, I saw my life flash before me, but before I could plummet to my death on the riverbed below, a hand gripped my collar and reeled me back.

Heart thrashing in my throat, I peered into Zeke's panic-filled eyes.

"You won't die today, soldier," he yelled over the storm's howl.

"I need to rest," I said through chattering teeth. Legs burning from the climb, my feet soaked and rubbed raw from my boots, I was miserable and dispirited.

"The captain said we will set up camp in the valley." He pushed me onward.

"I don't know if I'll make—"

A pack horse in front of us lost its footing and skidded back toward us, and I leaped to the side, plowing into Zeke to get out of the way of a thousand pounds of horseflesh. The soldier behind me wasn't so lucky; he and the animal tumbled over the precipice. I cringed at the sound of the impact below and bit down on my lip to stifle my cry.

A brief second of acknowledgment passed between the soldiers who had witnessed the accident but others pushed forward, unaware of the life lost.

Unable to hold back mounting emotions, I gasped, releasing the sob caught in my throat.

"Don't look," Zeke said. "There is nothing we can do. Keep going." He gripped my shoulder and forced me up the path.

Numbness gripped my body and spirit as my thoughts remained with the soldier. Left to the elements and animals, would there be anything left of him to identify or bury? Would his family be added to the infinite list of those who would grieve the lack of closure? Whose loved one became merely another war casualty?

Some hours later, the rain clouds parted, and sunshine blanketed the valley below. Relief rippled through the men, and we made our descent.

While others set up camp, General Sherman ordered foragers sent out.

"You two." An officer pointed at Zeke and me. "You will accompany these men to gather food and supplies. You're to return before nightfall."

Dread settled on my shoulders like a great weight. Although I'd participated in various raids, the duty of plundering and looting had become as hard as the clamor and violence of the battlefield. Some soldiers showed no mercy, and the fear and weeping of the families left in our wake didn't sit well with me. But war was war, right? Or at least that was what I told myself to calm my guilt over our actions.

"We have our orders." Private Cane, a distinguished-looking man with fine features, had been put in charge of the foraging party.

We mounted the horses provided and rode out ahead of the supply wagon to scour the countryside. After we had ridden three or four miles, we crested a hill and saw a farm below.

A soldier let out a yelp of glee. "Well, lookie there, boys. It looks like we won't be eating hardtack tonight. They got themselves a fattened cow." He licked his lips in anticipation.

I glanced in the direction he pointed to the lone cow grazing in a pasture. I had to admit the thought of devouring a hunk of meat made my mouth water.

A dark-haired soldier with a gnarly scar that ran from jaw to eyelid, causing the lid to droop, grinned and said, "Maybe we will enjoy the warmth of a pretty young filly."

"You know the general's orders. The citizens are not to be harmed," Zeke said firmly.

"You heard the man. We are here for food and supplies and to instill a little fear if need be." Private Cane heeled his mount, and we followed after him.

We charged down the hill and across the field to the two-storey yellow farmhouse before reining in.

A young boy stepped onto the porch with a rifle aimed at us. "We ain't got nothing you looking for," he said, striving for a voice of authority much too old for his tender years. "So I suggest you ride on out of here."

"Is that so?" Private Cane said with a smirk. "We will see for ourselves. I suggest you lower that gun."

"I can't do that." The boy's expression held the fierceness of a grown man bent on protecting what was his, but the slight trembling of his hand revealed his fear.

A shot rang out, and the boy let out a wail and dropped the gun.

"Johnny!" a woman screamed and raced from the house as the boy staggered back in shock.

"I just grazed him, ma'am. He will be fine. I'm Private Cane, and we come on request of General Sherman to collect supplies for our men."

She quailed as though from the name of the general commanding us. "We don't have anything left to give. The Union has taken all we have." She was petite, with honey-colored hair. She cradled the boy close to her side.

The scar-faced soldier who had made the lewd comment on the hill leaned forward in his saddle. He eyed the woman like a rabid dog homing in on the hunt. But a flash of movement shifted my attention to a young girl of fifteen or so in a blue frock who was racing across the backyard in the direction of the barn. My heart thumped faster, and I looked at the other soldiers, but it appeared no one had noticed the girl.

"We will check for ourselves," Private Cane said and waved a hand in the air. "Boys, dismount and search the barn and house."

Before swinging my leg over to dismount, I saw terror wash over the woman's face. Her eyes flitted to her right, but she kept her head positioned straight ahead, too scared to look in the direction of the barn.

"You." The private nudged his head at Zeke. "Get that cow and tie it to the back of the wagon." He spun to face the soldier I'd developed a grave dislike for, then looked at me. "You two check the barn."

We all disbanded.

The soldier assigned with me grumbled under his breath. "Probably wants the woman all to himself."

Dread teemed in my gut as I shifted from him and darted toward the barn with him close behind. I hadn't seen the girl disappear inside, but I hoped for her sake she'd bypassed the barn and vanished into the tree line at the edge of the property.

The door screeched as we pulled it open, and the soldier shouldered by me and strode inside. I followed and moved about the barn, looking for grain and hidden supplies while keeping an eye open for the girl.

"She was right. There ain't a thing left in here," the soldier said.

"A small helping of grain is all I've found," I called back before proceeding to another stall. Glimpsing blue fabric peeking out from beneath a pile of freshly scattered straw, I halted. All hopes that the girl had disappeared into the woods vanished.

I glanced at the soldier as he walked my way, pausing to peer into every nook and cranny. I bent and scooped up an armful of straw. "I know you're there. But stay silent," I said in a low voice. "I'll lead him away." I tossed the straw over the visible fabric of the girl's dress.

"Did you say something?"

I jumped back and cracked heads with the soldier, who'd come up behind me. He cursed and stumbled back. "You staggering fool. Is it the first day on your feet?"

"Sorry." I held up the almost empty sack of grain. "I said, I found this."

"And that's all?"

"Yes." I swallowed hard as he eyed me with suspicion.

A nerve-racking minute passed before he turned on his heel and headed for the door. "Let's go, then."

I dashed after him, relieved that the girl would not suffer at his hands. Images of my own childhood always induced fear during raids of plantations and farms, but to my relief, I hadn't witnessed the raping of women and girls.

As we rounded the corner of the house, Private Cane walked out onto the porch. My heart stopped as I looked to the disarrayed hair of the woman who hovered in the shadows of the doorway. The young boy sat with his knees pulled up to his chest on the porch. The private patted the boy on the head as one would an old dog on his way by, and the child recoiled from his touch.

"May you burn in hell, you filthy Yankee." The boy's eyes flashed with anger.

I held my breath at his outburst.

Private Cane chuckled and squatted before the boy.

The woman hurried from the house. "Please, my son didn't mean any harm. H-he is disturbed, is all." I noted her red face, the missing buttons on her dress, and a cold knot lodged in my gut.

The private gripped a handful of the boy's hair and yanked his head back. "You got some fight in you, boy. I hear the Confederates allow boys of all ages to join their cause. Why aren't you out there killing yourself some 'filthy Yankees'?"

"'Cause I need to take care of my mama and—" Panic replaced the rage in his eyes. The color ebbed from his mother's face.

"And who?" The private tugged the boy's hair harder.

"My sister. But she died, the same as my pa." Tears flowed freely from the boy's eyes as despair overwhelmed him.

"Ain't much here but a few chickens and a cow." A soldier held up two squawking hens by the legs.

"All right." The private released the boy with a taunting jab. "Saddle up, and we will move on to the next."

"Please, at least leave the hens," the woman said. "How do you expect us to feed ourselves? That's the last we have."

"Let the Confederates worry about that," a soldier spat. "Let it be known General Sherman leaves a crater in his wake. No animals, supplies, or crops are safe."

I looked to the mother as I swung myself up onto my horse. She gathered her son from the ground and held him in a protective embrace. She regarded us with hollow eyes and an expression of complete devastation.

Tears welled in my eyes, and I kicked my heels into my horse's flanks and hurried after the others.

∾ CHAPTER ∾
Forty-Four

Reuben
September, 1864

I HAD FLED THE ARMY OF THE POTOMAC SOON AFTER LINCOLN released General McClellan from power, and joined up with General Grant and Sherman's army under a new alias. Under General Sherman's command, we had marched on to Atlanta and captured the city. The Confederate coward, General Hood, had evacuated, but he'd detonated the munitions train, entrenchments, and rail installments, and set fire to military supplies before his departure.

The trust General Sherman's men had in him didn't extend to me. The man preached destructive war and how he would rain down fire and brimstone, but he lacked the ruthlessness of a man like myself. In his position, I would have pulverized Atlanta's citizens. He merely aspired to crush the South's spirit. He'd struck at the heart of the Confederacy in hopes of collapsing their war efforts. He ordered the citizens' eviction and their transportation to the south of the city. When we'd captured Atlanta I'd savored the vision of them fleeing in terror, but his approach had hardly satisfied.

I hammered on the door of a mansion. "Out with you. General's orders." I heard scurrying inside before an elderly black woman opened the door. "The family is coming," she said as I elbowed past her and strode inside.

A middle-aged man and woman dashed across the landing

above before hurrying down the grand spiraling staircase with suitcases in their hands. The woman paused at the bottom and leaned in to whisper in the slave's ear.

I seized her arm and thrust her toward the door. "I said out."

The man yelped and raced after his wife as I sent her and the suitcase she had been carrying tumbling down the front steps.

I craned my neck to look at the slave. "You too. Are there any more of you?"

"No, sah. Et jus' me now." Defiance shone in her eyes as she marched past me with her shoulders back and head held high.

I wanted to snuff the spirit right out of her and envisioned hurling her to the stone below, where her masa gathered his weeping wife, but the arrival of a recruit dispelled the notion.

"Missus Sarah, you all right?" the slave said as she scurried to join the couple.

The woman grasped the slave like one would a mother. I gritted my teeth as Willow Armstrong's face flashed in my mind's eye—another white woman coddled all her life by her mammy. Our army had traveled into the heart of the South, advancing me, a wanted man, closer to ending Willow once and for all.

"Check the house. Make sure that is the last of them," I said to the recruit. He dashed up the front steps and into the house.

The man helped his wife and the slave into the back of a Union transport wagon.

Two soldiers exited the mansion next door and shared a few words before the broader of the pair strode down the steps and disappeared. The other paused, and I examined his side profile and scowled. The recruit looked familiar, but I couldn't put a name to him. He descended the stairs and looked up and down the street. Recognition struck. *Amelie?* My eyes narrowed. Yes, indeed. It was her, all right.

She turned and started walking away as the soldier I'd sent inside the house returned.

"That was the last of them, sir."

"Very well." I strode down the stairs and turned in the direction Amelie had gone.

I quickened my pace to close the distance between us. I would see the traitor dead before hour's end. She turned and ducked between two homes, and I darted after her.

"Amelie!" My voice echoed off the buildings.

She halted, and my heart sang. Cautiously she turned, her flesh ashen, and pure, undeniable fear gleamed in her eyes. "Oliver…"

Before she could reach for her weapon, I pulled my pistol and aimed it at her chest. I strode forward, stopping when I stood within a foot of her. She was quite lovely, even in a man's clothing. "The name's Captain Smith."

"Oliver, Silas, Reuben, Smith. Does it really matter?" she said dryly.

"Come now, my darling. Are you saying that you haven't missed me after all these years?"

"A snake like you is impossible to forget." Her lip curled with disgust.

The feeling was mutual. I would quite enjoy ending her life. I took another step forward, and she backed up.

"Stay back." She fumbled for her sword, and it caught.

I lunged at her, and we toppled backward. The uniform couldn't conceal the softness of her body, and a vision of her naked beneath me rose, but I shoved it away.

Her eyes widened with fear, and she clawed at me. "Get off of me."

"Gladly, once I split you arse to throat." I removed my blade and held it to her throat. "And I'll relish every moment."

Her fighting ceased, and she lay limp and unmoving, like the endless dead we had rolled into shallow graves. Damn her!

She sought to remove the fun from the kill. "Do you think you can rob me of this moment?" I seethed, hauling her up by the throat. I pinned her dangling body against the exterior wall of a home. "I won't let you. I've dreamt of this moment for far too long." She scratched at my fingers, fighting for air. "That's right, fight for your life." Calmness washed over me as her eyes bulged and her flesh turned a magnificent shade of purple.

Then a shot rang out, and pain ripped through my chest.

No, no, no...

∾ CHAPTER ∾
Forty-Five

Amelie

I SCRATCHED AT HIS HANDS, FIGHTING FOR AIR, AND THE PRESSURE IN my head threatened to explode.

"That's right, fight for your life." Reuben's face was filled with rapture.

Tears slid down my cheeks from the force of his grasp, and I envisioned Zeke's face as my vision blurred. Our talks of settling down on a ranch somewhere in the west would never happen. History would write about a woman, a Union soldier, who'd lost her life in Atlanta. The truth of my death and the monster who'd taken my life would never be recorded.

A gunshot cracked, and the grip on my neck slackened. I dropped to the ground, landing in a gasping, heaving heap as air raced into my lungs. A grunt made me look up to discover Zeke holding a pistol on Reuben, who stood with blood gurgling from his mouth, looking astonished. He gaped at the hole in the middle of his chest before stumbling forward. I scrambled to get out of the way as he plummeted to the ground.

Zeke hauled me up. "You all right?"

"Yes," I said between gasps. "Is he...dead?"

He rolled Reuben over with the toe of his boot, and I peered into his lifeless eyes. "It appears that way."

I clutched his arm. "No, check his pulse. He has infinite lives."

He squatted and placed his ear to Reuben's chest before straightening. "He's dead."

I covered my mouth to stifle a whimper, relieved but still disbelieving.

He stood and steered me back the way I'd come. "Now, let's get out of here before someone pins his death on us."

As we raced toward the chaos happening on the main street, I envisioned Reuben rolling over after we left him and gasping as life returned to his body. "You're sure he's dead, right?" I whispered as we turned onto the boardwalk and slowed our pace.

"As dead as dead can be," he said through clenched teeth, keeping his gaze straight ahead.

"Soldiers." An officer gestured at us.

"Yes, officer," Zeke said as we halted before him.

"I'm assigning you both to drive this wagon of citizens to the south of the city." He nodded at an overflowing wagon of weeping women and children and solemn-faced men.

"Straightaway, Lieutenant," Zeke said.

We clambered into the front, and he took the reins and steered the team into the flow of wagons heading out of the city.

If Reuben's body was ever discovered, we never heard of it in the weeks that followed.

General Sherman ordered the destruction of warehouses, factories, railroad connections, and private homes. He decreed the city's systematic end, leaving nothing for the Confederates to recoup after our departure. But the Confederates had fled south ahead of our army, leaving destruction in their path, endeavoring to block our advance. They destroyed bridges, hacked down trees, and burned supplies. General Sherman dispatched his own turbulence by pillaging farms and estates, stealing and slaughtering livestock as we advanced toward Savannah. We captured the city in December, and General Sherman delivered Savannah as a Christmas gift to President Lincoln.

∽ CHAPTER ∽
Forty-Six

Willow

"HE DID IT." WHITNEY CHARGED INTO THE HOUSE, WAVING a report. "The United States Congress has approved the 13th Amendment to the Constitution. Slavery is abolished," she announced triumphantly.

"Give it here, let me see," I said. She handed me the paper, and I quickly scanned it, noting the date. "That was weeks ago by this account."

"What you carrying on 'bout now, Missus Tucker?"

Whitney and I pulled our heads apart as Mammy descended the stairs to the foyer.

"Lincoln did it." I darted forward and squeezed her in a massive hug. "Slavery is abolished."

"Sweet Jesus!" Her body trembled. "You sho'?"

I pulled back and held out the report. "It says it right here." Tears gathered in my eyes as I regarded her. "The day we have all longed for is finally here."

"But are ya really sho'? Dat report ain't no trickery, is et?" She looked doubtful.

"No trickery," I said with a tender smile.

Tears streamed down her cheeks. "I got to tell Big John." She turned to dash for the back door but halted as Big John strode toward us. She clapped her hands and flung them to the heavens. "You free!"

His eyes widened, and he looked beyond her to me. "Et true?"

I grinned and nodded. "Whitney just brought the news."

"No more hiding from your masa. You a free man, John. A free man!" Mammy walked into his arms and laid her cheek against his chest, sobbing.

I stepped closer to Whitney, also a mess of tears, and encircled her waist with an arm.

"De Lard finally heard our prayers." Mammy lifted her head and caressed Big John's cheek. He nodded through tears and dipped his head to kiss her. My heart felt like it would burst with joy at the exchange.

"We must tell the others," I said. "But I would like to inform Jimmy myself."

"I will gather the others in the backyard. You go ahead and tell James, but make it swift."

"I will," I said over my shoulder before exiting out the front.

I walked to the forge and found Jimmy hammering at a piece of red-hot metal.

"Hello, Missus Willie. What brings ya down here today?" His smile had a way of hugging my soul. He stepped away from his work and strode toward me.

My tears came in floods, and the smile on his face vanished. "What de matter? Is et de masa?"

I shook my head. "No. It's something splendid."

He stood in confusion, and for the first time, without fear of who was watching, I embraced the man who had been a father to me. "You are free." My words were but a whisper. "Lincoln has succeeded."

He pushed back and looked hard into my eyes. "You say free?"

I nodded through my tears. "You're as free as any white man." I gripped his forearms and laughed. "It is a blessed day!"

He stepped back and paced the floor, and I observed the slight trembling of his hand as he wiped it over his face and pulled down. "I free." He cast another look at me before he sank to his knees and swayed back and forth, moaning and sobbing gently. When he pulled to his feet, he craned back his neck and peered at the rafters with widespread arms. "Nellie, I free. I ain't a slave no more!" he cried.

After a moment, his expression taut and drawn, he plodded back to his work and raised the hammer with quivering hands. "A man longs all his life to be free, and now dat et here, I don't know what to feel." He struck the metal and missed his mark.

I strode to his side and removed the hammer from his hand, and clasped his hand in mine. "Come. No work today." He allowed me to lead him from the forge and out into the work yard.

"Is et true, Missus Willow?" Tillie raced toward me.

I clasped her hands and smiled. "It is."

She squealed and crushed me in an embrace. "My chillum be free!"

"Yes, indeed."

"I was afraid et all jus' a dream." Her face alight with wonder, she released me. "What are we to do now, Missus?"

"You can start by dropping the formalities. I am no longer your master, and gladly so. Perhaps you would consider my friendship?" Hope buoyed my heart.

Tillie grinned and nodded. "I'd lak dat."

"Good." I patted her arm before moving up to the veranda to address the folks. "The day many have only dreamed of is upon us. A day that requires celebration."

Pete stood with his arm draped over Tillie's shoulder, and he looked at her with a wide grin and drew her closer. She leaned her head into the curve of his neck, a breathtaking smile of liberation and hope creasing her face.

Passion elevated my voice as I looked over the teary-eyed and gleeful faces of the scarce few who remained. "Today we celebrate, and tomorrow we discuss what we will each do next."

Parker jabbed his walking cane at the sky and threw back his head to howl in jubilation. "Dey tried, but dey couldn't hold us down. From de dust dey sought to return us to, we rise!"

CHAPTER
Forty-Seven

MY DAUGHTER GAZED AT THE YELLOW DAFFODIL SHE ROTATED between her small fingers as we returned inside from the gardens. I marveled at the angelic child as she tottered down the corridor, her hand in mine. She was petite, with fetching blue eyes and dark ringlets that hung to her shoulders. She bore the eyes of her father, and her only resemblance to me was her hair. Where I had spent my life being a truth-seeker and fighting for what I thought was right, in her mere two years, she had already gravitated to nature and nurturing animals, discovering contentment in solitude.

I paused outside the library crammed with the latest batch of patients, and she halted and stretched her neck out to look past me into the room.

"Well, hello there, little miss." A soldier with a bandage wrapped around his head and covering one eye sat on his cot, propped against pillows.

Olivia smiled and tucked herself into the protection of my side. I capped her head with my hand and pulled her closer before shifting my attention to the young man who had been a pleasure since his arrival. He had the spirit that would see him recovered and swiftly returned to the front lines. "How do you fare today?" I strode into the room.

"I'll be as good as new before you know it." He rewarded me with a lopsided grin.

"Not if he doesn't rest." Whitney entered behind me with fresh bandages and a bucket of steaming water. "Up all night reading whatever he can get you to sneak him from the shelves and keeping the lantern burning well into the night."

I drew closer to his bed and nudged my head at Whitney. "A word of advice. Don't get on that one's bad side."

"Don't think I can't hear you," she tossed over her shoulder.

I grinned at the soldier, and he smiled back before holding out a hand to Olivia.

She smiled at him but pointed at the crimson staining his bandage. "Hurt," she said.

"Yes, little miss. But I'll be all right. Your mama is taking good care of me."

My daughter had aroused delight but also melancholy in the soldiers who had come to Livingston to recover. For a few precious moments she helped them forget about the war, but the magic of her innocence was fleeting as the men pined for their families.

"For you." Olivia held out the treasure in her hand.

The soldier accepted the flower, and tears pooled in his eyes. "Thank you, little miss." He looked up at me. "Your daughter makes one dream a future is possible after the darkness of this war is a distant memory. Perhaps all we've fought for isn't in vain. It's been so long, you come to forget what you're fighting for."

Olivia jumped at the sound of the back door flying open and slamming against the wall.

"The Yankees are coming!" Pete's voice reverberated throughout the main floor.

A murmur rippled through the library, and the face of the soldier before me blanched. I swept my daughter up in my arms and bolted for the corridor.

Pete hunched forward at the back door, resting his hands on his knees while trying to catch his breath. He straightened as I rushed toward him. "M-mister Jones spotted Union soldiers spying on us from de tree line. Told me to warn you," he panted.

"God in heaven!" I looked back to the library. Union soldiers showing up would mean death for the Confederates we harbored, and God only knew what they would do to us. Fighting panic, I looked at a wild-eyed Mammy as she hurried toward us. "Take Olivia up to the nursery and stay with her."

"Yes, Missus Willow." She held out her arms, and Olivia willingly went to her. "Come, angel gal, let's go play."

She smiled and patted Mammy's weathered cheek with affection before pointing at herself. "Mammy play with Olivia."

Mammy pulled the child's forehead to her lips and kissed her, then spun and hurried for the staircase.

"Come, Pete, we need to get these soldiers hidden." I raced back to the library to discover Whitney hoisting a soldier whose leg had been blown off at the knee.

The recruit to whom Olivia had gifted the flower stood on the other side of Whitney, with the soldier's arm draped around his neck. I glanced at the other four soldiers; one lay unmoving with his eyes closed, unchanged since his arrival, while the others lay helpless on their cots, gawking at me with alarm.

"We have a place to hide you from the soldiers," I said. "You will need to use what strength you have to aid us."

Big John raced into the room with Jimmy right behind him. "Ef we move him, he dies for sho'." Big John pointed at the soldier who clung between worlds.

"It's a chance we must take or risk them all," I said. "I will go and meet whatever is headed this way." I turned to Pete. "You come with me." I raced from the room and headed for the closet under the staircase.

"Help me with this," I said. The door of shelving swung wide with one push, exposing the stairs leading to the attic. "We need to arm ourselves." I bounded up the stairs and returned with Bowden's holster and two rifles, leaving the closet as Whitney and the soldier arrived with the first recruit, who appeared to have lost consciousness.

"Well, I'll be…" The soldier craned his neck to peer up the

hidden staircase before considering me with wondering eyes. "You are quite the woman, Mrs. Armstrong."

"There is no time for pleasantries," Whitney grumbled, shifting under the burden of the soldier they supported.

I handed Pete a rifle and the holster containing two pistols. "See that Jones gets that." I gestured at the rifle. "Can I count on you and Tillie to arm yourselves?"

His face showed determination. "Never worked a pistol 'fore, but we do our part."

My heart heaved with gratitude.

"What in tarnation are you doing?"

I spun to eye the soldier draped between Jimmy and Big John.

"Have you lost your damn mind, woman? Giving a nigger a gun." He glowered at me.

I gritted my teeth. "I suggest you hold your tongue, unless you want me to leave you for the Union soldiers' target practice."

He recoiled, and his gray eyes flared, but he pressed his lips together.

"I didn't think so," I said and looked at Jimmy. "Get him upstairs before I throw him out."

They staggered past me, and I swung back to Pete and touched his arm. "Hurry. Go."

He rushed toward the back door and I returned to the library, grateful the shipment of soldiers had not been large enough to require the parlor too. "Good," I said when I discovered Pippa scurrying around, scooping up uniforms and belongings. "We can't hide the cots, but at least if we act as though we have no men in our care at the moment, perhaps we stand a chance." My heart pounded faster as I loaded the rifle and strode out the front door.

A lone soldier charged toward the house on a chestnut bay, and confusion pulled at me. Pete had said there were more. But, as I thought that, I saw the others cresting the hill in full pursuit.

The terror I had envisioned for many days and nights was upon us. Adrenaline pumped through me as I prepared to preserve

Livingston, those we harbored, and all the folks who remained. My determination was accompanied by sheer fear.

Movement at the corner of the house caught my attention, and I saw Jones give me a nod before returning his concentration to the advancing riders. I drew on the strength he had given me over the years and studied the soldier who drew ever closer.

I hoisted the rifle and pointed it at his chest. "Halt, right there," I said with as much sternness as I could summon.

The soldier's eyes flashed with contempt and an unsettling thirst. "You can't hold off an army."

"Hardly an army," I said, taking in the five soldiers who reined their mounts to a trot as they reached the front yard. "Keep your hands where I can see them."

He smirked, and I cocked the rifle; his disdain evaporated. "Up with your hands, now," I said. "Or I'll drop you before your friends take their next breath."

"Today, you die," the soldier sneered, but he elevated his hands.

"Perhaps today the one who will die is you."

"We will see about that."

CHAPTER
Forty Eight

Amelie
minutes before

OUR ARMY LEFT SAVANNAH AND ADVANCED TOWARD CHARLESTON, pillaging and burning everything in our path. General Sherman had split the army into two wings. Zeke and I moved toward Charleston with the right wing and the Fifteenth and Seventeenth Corps while the left wing marched toward Augusta.

Zeke and I had been sent out with a party of foragers to gather supplies, and from our horses we observed the plantation below. A recruit by the name of Thompson, a young man with bright blue eyes, handed Zeke the field glasses. "Looks like there ain't but a few blacks, children, and womenfolk."

Zeke took a look for himself. "It appears so." He lowered the field glasses. "We collect what supplies we can and leave the plantation standing."

Thompson nodded his agreement, but another soldier named Conner snorted and said, "Let the Southerner sympathizers burn with all they own."

I hadn't seen the man before, but it was easy to go unrecognized in an army our size, which explained how Reuben McCoy had been able to live amongst us and I had never detected him.

Zeke narrowed his eyes. "I mean it, Conner. No harm comes to them."

He returned Zeke's glare. "You don't hold a higher rank than any of the rest of us."

"But the lieutenant put him in charge," I said. "Do you wish to be reported for insubordination?"

He sneered, and without another word he heeled his horse and raced toward the plantation.

"That son-of-a…" Zeke charged off after him, and the rest of us followed.

At the front yard's boundary, Zeke raised a hand to signal us, and we reined our mounts to a trot. My gaze went to the front veranda of the mansion, where a brunette woman stood with a rifle trained on Conner, who sat ramrod straight in his saddle with his hands elevated. We proceeded with caution.

"Good day, gentlemen," the woman said as we pulled up alongside Connor.

An armed, gruff-looking fellow of fifty or so positioned himself at the corner of the house. To the right, a black man and woman with pistols in hand stepped out.

"It appears you were expecting us," Zeke said as he observed the revolutionary gathering of blacks and whites intending to safeguard a Southern plantation. The abnormality of the scenario registered on the soldiers' faces.

I regarded the woman, from her worn brown boots to the green gingham frock bleached by the sun. Skin, perhaps once fair and protected, was now brown from days in the fields. The woman broadened her stance, and her piercing green eyes roved over us with grit and keen intellect. "As one would expect with General Sherman wreaking havoc across the Carolinas."

"We come for provisions," Zeke said.

"What more do you expect the war can squeeze from us?" she said dryly. "Furthermore, what you come seeking, the Confederates have already confiscated. We can barely feed ourselves."

"Yet you're fortified with weapons that could assist the Confederate army." Zeke studied the woman with curiosity.

She bristled. "I seek to preserve my lands and the folks of this estate."

Conner laughed and said to the soldier on his right, "The woman is a damn fool. She's spent far too long lazing around in that fine house with slaves doting on her." He returned his attention to the veranda. "Southerners don't know what it's like to put in a hard day's work. You and all the damn fool-hearted niggers in the South can't stop the whipping the Union is unleashing on your asses. Generals Sherman and Grant will see the South continues to feel the brunt of this war."

"Enough, Conner," Zeke said through gritted teeth.

Conner muttered but quelled further remarks.

The woman, however, centered her attention on him. "That may be so, but the North will not prevail without grave losses of their own." Weariness touched her face, but she swiftly concealed it.

Zeke looked at the blacks that entered the yard, armed with pitchforks and hatchets. "Have you not heard that Lincoln abolished slavery?" He directed his question at the woman while gesturing at a black man with a walking cane.

"Yes, we heard." She elevated her chin. "These women and men are free to leave if and when they choose to do so."

The door behind the woman opened, and a middle-aged woman with silvery blond hair stepped out. She strode to the younger woman's side and clasped her hands in front of herself.

"Ma'am." Zeke tipped his hat. "As I was telling, Miss…"

"Armstrong. Willow Armstrong," the brunette said, squaring her shoulders.

Zeke and I both tensed. *Willow? The dreadfully annoying Tucker woman's friend?*

"Well, Miss Armstrong, we must gather supplies for our men. If you and your friends would be so kind as to lower your weapons, we can avoid any bloodshed."

"I told you we don't have anything," she said firmly.

"In better times, it appears you were a woman of wealth. If

not food, I'm sure we can find jewels and silver." Conner craned his neck to inspect the mansion, which had seen better days.

"Our valuables are long gone," Willow said.

"We will see for ourselves." Conner moved to dismount, and Willow fired a shot at the ground in front of him, startling his horse. It reared back, and I looked on with amusement as he clawed at his horse's mane to keep from being dumped.

We reached for our weapons, but the chill in Willow's voice stopped us. "You will remain where you are, soldier. The rest of you remove your hands from your weapons. Or the first one to draw will bite the dust this day."

I questioned the woman's sanity in taking on trained soldiers.

"All right." Zeke's commanding tone gathered everyone's attention. "Everyone remain calm." He narrowed his eyes on Willow. "As I stated, ma'am, we aren't seeking to do you harm—"

"And leaving us to starve isn't causing us harm?" Her eyes flashed. "My husband fights to defend our home and country, and we here at Livingston do our part to ensure he has something to come home to."

"If we return empty-handed, I assure you we will be sent back with more men," Zeke said.

Willow's gaze flitted aside, and concern tugged at her brow.

The door opened once again, drawing everyone's attention. *Tucker?* I tensed.

She leveled a callous look at us as she strode to Willow's side and said something out of the corner of her mouth. Willow's rigid posture eased.

"Very well." She held Zeke's gaze. "Your men are welcome to check the grounds."

"And the house," Zeke said.

Her jaw clenched, and she hesitated before inclining her head. "As you say." She lowered the rifle and moved to the side.

Zeke ordered the men to dismount and spread out before

assigning me to investigate the house. I ascended the front steps, attempting to shield my face from Tucker.

Inside, I paused in the foyer to marvel at the grand staircase and the mansion's artistry before walking to a room that appeared to be a parlor, which had been cleared of most furnishings and replaced with empty, neatly prepared cots. I frowned and peered back at Willow as she and the other women gathered behind me. "What is the meaning of this?" I gestured a gloved hand at the room.

Willow strode to my side and peered into the parlor. "We have converted the home to a wayside station."

"A Confederate hospital?" I braced and scanned what I could see of the main floor.

"And others," the woman said nonchalantly.

"Zeke!" I placed my hand on my pistol. "You better come in here."

Boots echoed on the veranda, and I glanced at the door as he strode inside. "What is it, soldier?"

"This place is a wayside station for Confederates."

He tensed at the news. "You failed to inform us, Mrs. Armstrong." His hand rested on his weapon, and he took a swift scope of the place before proceeding. "Where are the patients?"

"We are between shipments." Tucker's curt reply had Zeke eyeing her.

"Are we now?" Zeke's unsmiling disposition and stature could be intimidating, but not in the presence of Tucker. The woman feared little.

Her brow furrowed as she stared at him. "You seem familiar."

"Perhaps we've met in passing," Zeke said dismissively before proceeding down the corridor to halt outside another room. "It looks like you haven't had time to clean the linens."

"No, the men left this morning." Her gait graceful and one of poise, Willow moved to stand beside him.

"How convenient." He peered down at her. "Yet we met no one along the road."

She shrugged. "I know not where the soldiers go once they leave here. We tend to their wounds, and that is all."

Sensing eyes on me, I directed my gaze to where Tucker stood observing me before shifting my attention back to Zeke. My heart struck harder. Had she recognized me?

"Check the upstairs," he said before turning and proceeding with his search of the home.

Upstairs I passed from one room to another, finding no one; I collected trinkets of value—jewels, a candelabra, a silver brush, and a handheld looking glass—and shoved them into a satchel. Such novelties had long lost their appeal to me, but I'd draw suspicion if I came out of the house with nothing. I was walking down the hall when the sharp bite of Tucker's tongue halted my footsteps.

"I thought after Five Points we'd become friends of sorts."

I pivoted to see her standing at the top landing with her arms crossed, her expression capable of sending the faint of heart scurrying. "How wrong I was." She advanced. "I knew there was something familiar about you and that soldier. I must say, I do prefer you as the uppity Madame Laclaire to a thieving Union soldier."

"Friends?" I said with a curt laugh before sweeping low in a bow. "We meet again, Tucker."

"Under dire circumstances again." She stopped in front of me and eyed the satchel in my hand. "Only this time, you are the enemy."

"I am not your enemy."

"No?" She arched a perfectly shaped brow. "You show up here with Union soldiers, looking to rob us and leave us to starve." She flung a hand at the boarded windows at the front of the house.

"How was I to know this was the home of the famous Willow Armstrong?"

"You can drop the disguise." Whitney fixed her jaw.

Annoyance rose in me. "It's war, Tucker." I swept a hand at the grandeur of the home. "Or have you been so sheltered in the riches of your friend and the comfort of her mansion that you've failed to recognize we are at war?"

She dropped her arms, and her face reddened. "Don't patronize me. I am well aware of the affairs of this country. My husband lost an arm in this war and almost died. And you can thank your past lover for that."

Her statement snatched my breath, and I placed a hand on the wall to steady myself. "Reuben?"

"The one and only." Her voice rang cold. "He enlisted in the Union Army of the Potomac under Major General George B. McClellan—under an alias, one can only assume. He clashed with Willow's husband on the battlefield and would've left him for dead, but my husband intervened. There's no telling where the bastard is now." Her defenses slipped, and fear radiated in her eyes. The same fear I had witnessed at the cafe in New York when I had broached the subject of Willow, and Reuben's intent. Despite personal traits that left one mystified and unsure of her goals, Tucker was fiercely loyal to her loved ones.

"H-he's dead."

"Dead? How do you know?" Her voice squeaked.

"He obtained the identity of a Captain Smith and joined General Sherman's army. A while back he came out of nowhere and attacked me, bent on killing me. If Zeke hadn't spotted me dangling in Reuben's grip, I wouldn't be standing here now."

"Maybe that is for the—"

"The better." I finished her thought. "Perhaps, but maybe it's better Zeke and I showed up here than another party of foragers, or Reuben himself."

"He already did that." Her expression was haunted. "We heeded your warning, but despite the Armstrongs' efforts, Reuben and a gang of Northern militia showed up here." She gestured at the front of the home, the boarded-up windows, and the telltale signs of a fire that had scorched the wallpaper, ceiling, and floorboards. "Willow and her husband were in Charleston. They came in the early hours of the morning, taking everyone by surprise. The slaves of this plantation took up arms to defend the place and sacrificed their lives in the end. Willow has carried the cross of guilt and self-blame every day since. And as you might expect, Reuben slipped into the dark, never to be seen again until the battlefield. I swear that man is the Devil in the flesh. He has countless lives."

"Well, not this time," I said.

She gazed at me in puzzlement.

"He's dead. Zeke blew a hole in his chest." A cold knot lodged in my stomach each time I recalled the day in the alley. "He will no longer wreak havoc on anyone, and thankfully so."

Tucker took a moment to find her voice. "Are you sure...he is dead?" She looked at me with a mixture of hope and disbelief.

"For weeks I could hardly believe it myself, but I've verified the fact that Reuben McCoy is no longer of this world."

She swallowed hard before nodding.

I stepped past her, opened another door, and started at the stout black woman sitting in the middle of the floor with a dark-haired child. The child glanced up from playing with her doll and turned intense blue eyes on me. "Mammy." Panic filled her voice, and she scrambled onto the woman's lap.

I strode into the chamber that appeared to be the child's nursery and looked around. I smiled at the child as she regarded me from the curve of her mammy's neck before squatting to gather the discarded doll. "What a pretty doll," I said as a childhood memory surfaced of me standing on the boardwalk admiring a beautiful doll with blond ringlets and a pale pink-silk dress through a store window. Until my mother had pulled me away and shoved me onward.

I shook my head to dislodge the memory and offered the doll to the child, which she accepted hesitantly. The black woman regarded me like a mother bear, ready to reveal her fangs to defend the cub in her embrace.

I stood and walked from the room with the hovering Tucker

on my heels. She closed the door and turned to me. "Are you satisfied with your search?" The defensiveness returned to her posture.

I strode past her without answering and descended the staircase as Conner walked into the house. He ignored me and gawked at the parlor and the cots before striding down the corridor to inspect the main floor for himself. "What is all this?" he said to Zeke as he and Willow walked from a room at the back of the home.

"It's of no concern of yours."

"Isn't it?" He glanced back into the room as I passed them. "That looks like blood on those linens."

Annoyance filled Zeke's voice. "The home doubles as a wayside hospital for Confederates. Mrs. Armstrong claims the patients left this morning, and we've checked the place and see no reason to believe otherwise. Isn't that true, soldier?" He looked at me.

"It's all clear upstairs." I feigned a grin and held up the satchel of treasures. "Found some loot to disperse amongst the boys."

Greed lit in Conner's eyes as he observed the bag. "We've gathered the horses and what rations we could find in the smokehouse and kitchen house."

"Good; let's be on our way." Zeke marched toward the front door.

I eyed Willow and noted the relief that enveloped her face, but when she caught me watching her she smoothed it away.

Conner shouldered past me and strode after Zeke, but stopped when there was a noise overhead. He cocked his head. Behind me, Willow gasped, and I saw Tucker's hand stiffen where it rested on the banister.

Zeke, catching the sound, froze and swung back as Conner moved to the door under the stairs. The floorboard squeaked behind me, and before I could respond, someone gripped me around the throat.

"Stay where you are!" Willow's panicked breathing tickled my ear.

Zeke and Conner reached for their weapons. Zeke seized

Tucker in one swift movement and yanked her back. "Hold it right there, Mrs. Armstrong," he said.

"Take your men and leave."

"Am I to believe you deceived me?" Zeke crept forward with his weapon aimed and shielded by a seething Tucker, who tried desperately to heel him in the shins, but he avoided her assaults. "Still yourself, woman, or suffer the butt of my pistol."

Conner kept his gun pointed at Willow while opening the door under the stairs.

"Please," Willow said, her voice desperate as she clutched me tighter.

Conner disappeared inside the space under the staircase, followed by grunts and a ruckus, then a loud squeak. "Well, I'll be damned," Conner's voice drifted out. "You best come see this."

Willow's body trembled next to mine as Zeke strode forward with a wide-eyed Tucker. But as he drew closer, a shot resounded, and he jumped back. Bullets from more gunfire ricocheted within the space.

The back door banged open, followed by soldiers bolting through the front door with their weapons drawn. A man's voice erupted next to me: "Lower your weapons, now." I heard the cocking of a revolver. Out of the corner of my eye, I glimpsed the gun a soldier positioned at Willow's temple. *No, no, no!* my brain screamed. It wasn't supposed to happen like this.

I gasped as Willow's arm loosened around my throat, and I stepped from her grip. "Cease fire!" I held up my hands, one in either direction of the corridor, as the gruff-looking fellow from earlier fell into position behind the soldiers standing in the foyer, his gun drawn. I looked to the back door, where the black man and woman who had greeted us on our arrival stood with their weapons pointed.

The gunfire from inside the space under the stairs stopped. Zeke tossed Tucker to the side and ducked inside the opening. Voices resounded overhead, and all eyes turned to the open door.

"Please, they only sought to defend themselves," Willow said.

"Well, they shouldn't have opened fire." The soldier holding her captive shoved her forward.

My brow furrowed as I regarded Willow, who looked at me with teary eyes. I craned my neck to examine Tucker as she gathered herself from the floor where she'd landed after Zeke had discarded her. My legs rigid, I advanced cautiously to the door through which Zeke had disappeared. Inside I discovered a false wall with shelving that groaned and swayed on its hinges, and beyond, a staircase leading into an attic space. "Is everything all right up there?" I called up.

There was the crack of a gunshot, followed by another before Zeke's voice called, "Enough, you imbecile. They are prisoners of war."

A commotion took place, and Conner tumbled backward down the stairs. I jumped out of the way as he crumpled to the floor in front of me. He stared dumbfounded up at Zeke, towering on the landing above.

"I am in charge, soldier, and you will abide by my commands. The general will hear of your disobedience."

Conner pulled to his feet and retrieved his weapon.

"Get out of my sight." The lethal bite in Zeke's tone kept Conner from responding, and he elbowed past me and limped into the corridor.

I looked back at Zeke, already knowing the answer. "The soldiers are up there, aren't they?"

He nodded grimly. My stomach dropped, and I pressed my lips together and backed into the corridor.

Zeke ordered Tucker, Willow, and the others outside. Defeat shone on their faces. Giving up the fight, they allowed us to remove the soldiers from the attic.

While Zeke took care of matters inside, I hustled the women onto the front veranda.

"You too." A soldier assigned to assist me gesticulated with his weapon to the gruff-looking man Willow had called Jones. "And you." He gripped the black man's shoulder and pushed him out the door along with the woman clutching his arm, her eyes flitting to the scene unfolding.

"Tillie, come, it's all right." Willow kept her gaze pinned on the soldier and me while motioning the black woman forward.

My weapon trained on the group, I looked past them as another recruit steered the remaining blacks collected from the plantation into the front yard, noting the young man with a walking stick I had seen earlier and the two older men attempting to console weeping children.

"My babies," a woman's panicky voice cried.

"Mama," a small, terrified voice called.

I returned my attention to the group huddled on the veranda and studied the black woman who peered over her shoulder at the children. "Those children yours?" I said.

She gaped at me with tear-filled eyes. "Yes, sah."

"Go to them."

She nodded and darted past me and down the stairs.

"Please, Amelie," Tucker said through clenched teeth.

I tensed at her mention of my name.

"Amelie?" Willow studied me as though peeling back the layers of my disguise before her brow softened. "As in Madame Laclaire?"

"Silence." I cast a look to the soldier to my right. He had his neck craned, peering back inside the house, appearing not to have heard. "Soldier," I said with authority, and he returned his attention to the matter at hand. "Upstairs there's a child and her mammy. Go get them and bring them here."

Willow flinched and moved to step forward. "Remain where you are." I butted her with my gun.

The soldier dashed back inside the house.

"What are you doing?" Tucker's face reddened.

"Trying to save you fools from yourselves. No more need die

today." I pointed at the body of a Confederate soldier lying on the veranda.

"Are you to tell me, if we hadn't hidden them, your gun-happy friend wouldn't have murdered them in their cots?" Tucker sneered.

I ignored her and waited until the nursemaid waddled onto the veranda with the child.

"Mama?" The sobbing child held out her arms upon seeing Willow.

Willow glanced at me, and I nodded. The nursemaid deposited the child in her mother's eager arms.

Zeke and a recruit carried a second body from inside and laid it on the veranda. "That is the last of them." Zeke straightened and eyed the injured Confederates in the back of the supply wagon. "You two, go and collect the weapons deposited in the corridor and remove the grain and supplies from that room in the attic." The recruits dashed back inside.

"How are we to protect ourselves if you leave us without weapons? And without grain, how will we feed our animals?" Willow coddled her daughter and regarded Zeke with fury blazing in her green eyes.

"After today, you won't have any left to concern yourself with." He delivered an austere look at her before turning as the soldiers returned with sacks of grain, flour, and sugar slung over their shoulders; one carried a crate of preserved goods. "Get it in the wagon, and gather the chickens and goats."

"You sign our death warrant," Tucker spewed. "We'll have nothing left."

He ignored her and descended the steps. I turned to follow him, but Tucker gripped my arm.

"You have to help us," she said. "Leave us something."

"What makes you think that I should help you again?" I said in a low tone. "I have been beaten down and stomped on by my share of Confederates over these past years. Which is more than enough reason for me not to want to help another Southerner."

Her hardened expression softened. "Because you aren't a monster."

"No?" I recalled the congressman I'd murdered and the young women from poor families I'd gathered from the streets to fill my establishment.

"No, you're not," she said with conviction, but her brow knitted with perplexity. "But I see you may believe differently."

I swallowed back the emotions thickening my throat and shook my arm free. "You know nothing about me." I turned and marched down the steps. I wouldn't allow Tucker to get into my head.

I paced the yard for a moment before my gaze rested on the blacks clustered in the yard. My attention settled on an older black man before my heart jumped. He seemed to tower to the heavens, and he was as dark as the night sky. Despite his age he stood with shoulders squared, peering straight ahead; he had a proud, bold spirit. Did my eyes play tricks on me? I blinked and took a closer look.

"Big John?" I gulped and crept forward.

It was him. My pulse raced. After all these years... Tears threatened.

"All right, everyone, mount up." Zeke slung himself up onto his horse.

"I need a moment," I said over my shoulder.

"What is it, recruit?" Zeke said.

"I need to speak with this man."

"What for?"

"Just a moment," I said, ignoring his question.

"Then make it quick."

I strode forward and gripped Big John's arm. He turned his gaze on me, but he moved without resistance as I steered him toward the corner of the house.

"Don't you touch him."

I cast a glance at the fleshy black woman as she hurried to the veranda railing.

"Stay where you are," a soldier ordered her from the yard.

Tears glistened in her eyes as she halted and stifled her protest. "Don't worry, ma'am," I said. "I seek to talk to him, that's all."

"Make it quick." Zeke's voice carried.

I waved a hand in acknowledgment.

Once I had guided Big John out of earshot and away from the others' view, I freed his arm. Taking a few paces forward to put some distance between us, I turned back to look at him. "I never thought I'd see you again." I spoke in my normal female voice.

His brow furrowed, and he peered at me with keen, dark eyes.

"You don't recognize me," I said with a nervous laugh. "Of course you don't." I removed my cap, revealing my shorn red hair.

"You a woman," he said, his expression sharp and assessing.

The tightness in my chest increased. "The last time we met, I wasn't…well, let's just say I…" I couldn't speak the words. I didn't want him to remember me naked and squatting to gather my dress from the jail floor before being thrown into the street.

But as I hesitated, his breathing caught, and his frown deepened. "I only seed hair dat color once 'fore." His jaw quivered. "Dat you, Miss Amelie?"

My tears came in floods, snatching my words and leaving me shaking before him. "It…it is."

"Olorun be praised." He tilted his face to the sky and extended his arms in exaltation. Tears glistened in his eyes when he looked at me. "I never stop thinking of you, gal." He bowed his head. "Never let go of de guilt of de sacrifice you were willing to make to set me free dat night in de jail." He shuffled his feet, appearing uncomfortable.

"Let's not talk of that," I stepped forward and clasped his hands in mine. "Please, for my sake."

He tilted his head and eyed me, his expression tender. "All right, as you say, Miss Amelie."

"How did you end up here?"

"I found my boy. He lives here at Livingston. Got himself a woman and two chillum."

I squeezed his hands with enthusiasm and smiled up at him. "That is splendid news. I can't express how happy that makes me."

He grinned. "And dat ain't de most of et. My Rita, she here too."

My eyes widened. "I...I don't know what to say."

"I free, and I found my family," he said, but with grave sadness.

I frowned. "Why do I sense you aren't happy?"

"Oh, I happy 'nuf. A man always gwine to miss his home country, but my life is here wid de family I made in dis country. What 'bout you? Why you join de Union?"

I shrugged and released his hands. "I suppose I wanted a fresh start...and to balance the wrongs I've done in my life. My life has never held any purpose."

"You sought to find purpose in de war?"

"I suppose I did, but it only weighed on my soul even more—"

"Recruit?" a husky voice said from behind Big John.

My heart thumped at the interruption, and I craned my neck to discover Zeke standing behind Big John.

He strode forward. "What is the meaning of this?" He looked from Big John to my exposed hair.

"This is Big John." I had told him of my time with Big John, and at the revelation of his name, Zeke's naturally stony gaze slipped, and he took a step back before regaining his composure.

"Amelie has said much about you." Zeke thrust out his hand, and Big John eyed it hesitantly. I thought he was uncertain about the display of friendliness between a previous slave and a white man, but Big John's response left me gaping at him.

"Miss Amelie a good woman. Am I to believe you have taken a laking to her?" He narrowed his eyes at Zeke as though peering into his soul and analyzing his intentions.

I gasped at Big John's inquiry.

"If you're asking if I love Amelie, then the answer is yes." At Zeke's reply my throat tightened, and I glanced at him to notice his rigid countenance had never faltered. He'd never proclaimed the words aloud to me, but I'd known he cared.

Big John's imposing gaze rested on Zeke for an awkward moment too long before a wide smile erupted, and he excepted his hand and shook it with passion. "Maybe you a man worthy of a woman lak her." He nudged his head at me, and as his choice of words registered I broke into tears—the ugly, forlorn weeping where one heaves and grunts like a dying animal, but where the restoring purification of your soul ensues.

"We need to go before one of the others come looking." Zeke glanced at me, and I saw the warmth in his brown eyes.

I wiped my tears and replaced my hat, pulling it down low to shadow my face.

"You take care of yourself, Miss Amelie," Big John said with a smile that waltzed on my soul.

I stepped forward and hugged him, not caring if he responded, but to my delight and surprise, he patted my back as I imagined a father would embrace a child. The solace of his caress filled my heart.

"Maybe ef you are in dese parts again when de war is over, you stop by here," he said when we parted.

"If Mrs. Armstrong would allow me on her property after this, I would. But I doubt she would be so cordial, and I can't say I'd blame her."

Zeke and I returned to the front yard and mounted our horses. As we turned our mounts, I glanced at Big John as he joined the others in the yard before looking to the group on the veranda. Tucker eyed me with animosity, and when I locked gazes with her she shook her head and turned away. I swallowed hard and steered my horse down the lane, Zeke and I taking positions on the flanks.

I cast a sideways glance at him and contemplated what the future held after the war ended before my thoughts turned to Big

John. He had found a happy outcome, but I wondered if such a fantasy would ever be mine. I considered Tucker and Willow and what had transpired. Would they ever concede I was following orders and grant me forgiveness? I doubted Tucker would, as I'd never deemed her the merciful sort, and I assumed once she felt wronged by someone it would be next to impossible to change her mind.

The image of the Confederate soldiers' lifeless bodies sprang to mind. "How did you miss the opening under the stairs?" I asked Zeke.

"I didn't." He kept his eyes on the Confederates bouncing and swaying in the back of the wagon ahead of us. "I figured something was amiss, with the brazen Mrs. Armstrong daring enough to take on a group of Union soldiers," he said in admiration.

"But her passion for defending her home and land is something we have witnessed often during our foraging expeditions."

"True, but did you notice how Tucker whispered something to her when she stepped out onto the gallery?"

"I did."

"I was astonished to discover the place was a wayside station, but upon seeing the dirtied sheets I presumed the injured most likely were still at the plantation. I checked the closet and noticed a slight draft under the false door, but hoping to avoid bloodshed I turned a blind eye. But Conner's intruding and defying my direct orders...well, you know the outcome." He grimaced.

"An eventful excursion, to say the least," I said, dreading hitting the next plantation, and the next, until we had accumulated enough supplies to rejoin our unit.

CHAPTER
Forty-Nine

Willow

FEAR HAD RIPPLED THROUGH SOUTH CAROLINA IN ANTICIPATION OF General Sherman and his army's daunting approach. Charleston's mayor surrendered to the Union Brigadier General Alexander Schimmelfennig, and days later, the news reached us. Several weeks passed before reports arrived that Sherman's army had bypassed Charleston and plundered Columbia. Reports alleged his army had been wholly responsible for torching the city, but additional accounts contradicted the claims.

In April, General Robert E. Lee surrendered to Union General Ulysses Grant in Virginia, indicating the commencement of the war's conclusion. Soon after came the astonishing news concerning the assassination of President Lincoln at the Ford's Theater. While others celebrated his death, Livingston's folks were disheartened, as I assumed was the case in most parts of the country.

Whitney had returned home with Knox, and Pippa and I waited on news of our husbands. We had begun planting the spring crop, and Jones projected a less than profitable year.

One afternoon after we had finished working the fields, Jones followed me across the work yard to the back veranda. "The fields are too vast to plant with so few hands," he said after I had climbed the steps.

Sweaty and exhausted from the day's work, I shifted to face him. A bond had kindled between us since the start of the war, and I'd relied heavily on him, seeking his opinion as one would a confidant. "The same issue we've had every year since our situation changed. When my husband and uncle return, we will either hire men or have to reconsider the future livelihood of Livingston."

He rested his foot on the bottom stair and removed his hat to regarded me grimly. "And if they don't?"

Tears welled at the possibility. I had to contemplate the subject, whether I liked it or not. "I will figure it out."

"Marriage is an option you must consider."

I braced as he said the words. Although the thought had invaded my mind in nights past, I'd shuffled it away.

"You have the little miss to consider."

"I'm aware," I said with a heavy heart. "When the dust of this war finally settles, and it doesn't appear peace has been established between the Union and Confederates yet, I'll evaluate our assets and properties abroad and take account of our financials as a whole."

"You hold wisdom far beyond most men. I believe you will find a way. I just worry you may choose the road less journeyed to avoid marrying."

"Perhaps in years past I may have, but if our speculation is true…" I shivered at the daunting thought of my husband never returning. "I have to think of my daughter, and I don't wish for her to grow up without a father."

"Very well." He replaced his sweat-stained hat and turned to leave.

"Jones."

He swung back and eyed me with a somber expression.

"Thank you for being more than a hired hand all these years. Your support has kept me sane."

He bowed in acknowledgment before turning and striding off.

Inside, I climbed the servant staircase to my chamber and paused outside Pippa's door when I noticed her sitting at her vanity, weeping. Concern pulled me forward. "Pippa," I said in a quiet voice. "What is it?"

She glanced at me, her eyes red-rimmed and puffy, her clothing and face dirtied from the field. "It's been a year and a half since I've heard from him."

I went to her side. My own despondency grew at the sight of her sorrow. "I miss him too."

"I know you do, my darling." She took my hands in hers and grappled with concealing her anguish. "Why don't you go freshen up. I will be all right. I had a moment of melancholy, is all." A loving smile graced her pretty face, burned by the sun.

"Are you sure? I could sit with you for a while," I said.

She stood and gave me a quick hug before pulling back to look me in the eyes. "You're a darling daughter." She cupped my chin before letting her hand drop. "You've been so gracious to me, and supported the love between your father and me. You've accepted me as a stepmother when you didn't have to."

I lowered my gaze. "That is where you are wrong. I needed you." I choked back the emotions clotting my throat before lifting my eyes. "Ben and I both did."

Tears dampened her blue eyes, and she gently nodded. "Bless you and that heart of yours."

I embraced her, and she patted my back. "Now, you go ahead and clean yourself up. I heard a certain someone questioning Henrietta on when you would be returning to the house." She gave me an extra squeeze before stepping back.

I left her to wash up and changed into a blue frock before returning to the main floor. I followed the nostalgic words of Mammy's singing to the parlor. My daughter sat on the settee, prattling and playing with a miniature rocking horse Jimmy had carved. I paused on the threshold to admire the beauty of the child and her serene nature. She looked up, and a smile broadened her face before she scrambled off the settee to come and wrap her arms around my legs.

"Mama," she said with delight, the words muffled in the fabric of my dress.

I capped her head with a hand. "Hello, my darling."

Mammy's singing had stopped, and she turned to eye me. "She bin asking for you. She had her eye on de field all day."

"Would you like to go sit by the pond?" I asked Olivia after she let go and stood peering up at me. Each time she eyed me with the jewel-toned eyes of her father, yearning swelled in my heart for his return.

She enthusiastically bobbed her head.

"Would you like Mammy to join us?"

"Yes!" she squealed happily and spun to race to Mammy's side.

"Got no time for dillydallying," Mammy said while allowing Olivia to clasp her hand and guide her toward the corridor. I smiled with amusement as Mammy feigned her protest. I knew as well as she did that she'd become hopelessly enchanted by my daughter. "I got de evening meal to prepare after I git dis parlor finished."

"Nonsense," I said with a wave of my hand and turned to walk to the peg holding our bonnets. "Besides," I said over my shoulder, "you will be disappointed if you don't join us."

Moments later, Mammy and I spread a blanket on the ground before settling under the shady canopy of the ancient oak tree. Olivia strode to the edge of the pond and stood sucking her thumb and watching a pair of swans. The melancholy of Jones's and my earlier conversation rested heavy on my shoulders, and I studied my daughter. What if she never got to meet her father? I had been about her age, or not much older, when my mother had died. I didn't want that for her.

"What is et, angel gal?"

"I worry about Olivia. I don't want her to grow up without Bowden. It breaks my heart that he may never meet her."

Mammy patted my hand where it lay on the blanket between us. "He come home, gal. He come home."

"But you can't be certain. I've tried to keep the faith alive, but it's been so long since I've received word from him. Men who served under General Lee have returned home in time for the planting season, yet there is no sign of him. And Ben..." My voice broke.

"Don't despair. De Lard will return dem both to loving arms." She reiterated the belief she had reassured me with since the onset of the war. "You see...when my man was taken from me, my heart broke, and I believed I'd never see him again, but de Lard, he saw fit to return him to me. Ef a slave can overcome all obstacles to return to his wife's side, den Masa Bowden and Masa Ben can too. You will see."

I looked at her, but she kept her gaze pinned on Olivia. "Mary Grace and Magnus hope to leave for England by the end of summer."

"Et be good for her, I reckon," she said with a hint of sadness. "I come to accept she got her own life to live. Magnus takes good care of her and de chillum." She tensed as Olivia stepped closer to the edge of the pond. "Come on now, chile. Come away from de edge 'fore you fall in."

Olivia walked over to us and paused, pointing behind us. "Horses."

I craned my neck to look around the tree.

"She right." Mammy squinted at the lane.

I pulled to my feet. "I will go see what they want."

I left my daughter in Mammy's care and strode across the grass to the front yard to await the visitors' arrival. As they drew closer, my breath caught, but before I could think, the door to the house was flung open.

"Ben!"

I swung to watch Pippa hurry down the front steps, her face alight with unmasked glee. I turned my attention back to the riders and gasped in delight as I recognized the faces of my husband and my father.

"They have returned." A flash of pink fabric flew by me as Pippa raced for the lane.

Ben reined in his horse, dismounted, and closed the distance between them. He chuckled as Pippa leaped into his arms, and he swung her high in the air.

Overcome with happiness and shock at their arrival, I stood rooted.

"What? No greetings for a weary soldier?" Bowden halted his mount before me, a grin on his face.

I broke into tears as he swung his leg over and dismounted. I rushed forward and crushed him in an embrace. "I can't believe you're home. I feared—"

"Do you think I'd allow another man to steal my wife?" he said merrily. He pushed back and cupped my face in his hands before kissing me with a passion that left me breathless and smiling like a blushing bride.

I smoothed back my hair. "I dreamed of the day you would return home. However, in my vision, I was wearing beautiful silks."

He threw back his head and laughed.

Ben, holding the reins of his horse, his other arm wrapped around Pippa's shoulders, walked toward us. I broke from the trance of my husband's presence and went to greet my father.

"Welcome home." I embraced him.

His arms encircled me, and he held me tight as though not wanting to let me go. After he had I studied his face, seeing the fatigue and age that revealed the hardship he had endured.

"Mama," a small voice said.

I turned as Mammy and Olivia strolled toward us. I held out my arms, and my daughter raced to me, and I gathered her up.

"Et good to see ya, Masas," Mammy said.

"And you, Miss Rita," Ben and Bowden said in unison, but their gazes had fixed on Olivia.

Bowden strode forward, tears dampening his eyes as he glanced from me to our daughter. "Hello, little one."

She peeked at him from the protective curve of my neck. "Hello," she said softly.

"Is she a timid child?" Bowden asked, concerned.

"No, she is an observer," I said. "Olivia, this is your father."
I bent forward to offer her to him, and he cast a nervous glance
at me.

"Are you sure? I don't want to frighten her."

"It's all right." I placed her in his arms, and his jaw quivered
with emotion.

Olivia secured an arm around his neck before pushing back
to give him a closer inspection. Tears pooled in my eyes as I beheld my daughter in her father's arms. She lifted small fingers to
touch the days-old scruff shadowing his face before a soft smile
touched her face.

"When Bowden came to find me, he told me you'd given me a
granddaughter," Ben said with pride as he observed the exchange.

"She has been the light to us all in your absence." My heart
swelled with love and contentment.

He smiled down at me.

"Come, let us all go inside." Bowden waved to me. I went to
him, and he swaddled my shoulders with an arm, and we walked
toward the veranda.

"I fix you all somepin' to eat. Pete," Mammy said as he
rounded the corner of the house, "you go dig up dat bottle of
brandy Missus Willow had you bury for dis day."

"Yes, Miss Rita," he said and cast a grin at Bowden and Ben.
"Welcome home, Masas."

The men exchanged greetings. "It's good to see you, Pete,"
Bowden said. "I wasn't sure who'd still be here upon my return."

"Ain't but James, Parker, my chillum, Tillie, Miss Rita, and
Big John."

"Children?"

Pete squared his shoulders, his grin growing. "Tillie had another babe while you be gone."

Bowden thrust out a hand. "Congratulations are in order."

"And to you." He accepted Bowden's hand and nodded his

head at Olivia before glancing at the front steps as Mammy turned to scowl at him. "Bes' git gwine 'fore Miss Rita start shouting."

Bowden chuckled, and clapped a hand on Pete's shoulder. "You collect that bottle and gather the others. We've much to discuss."

"Yes, Masa," he said before darting off.

Hope buoyed within me, and the future didn't appear so dim as we ascended the steps and wandered into the house to celebrate the men's return.

❦ CHAPTER ❦
Fifty

Summer of 1867

SOME SOUTHERNERS ADHERED NOSTALGICALLY TO THE OLD SOUTH, while others moved forward with the Reconstruction. From the ashes and destruction of war, our nation sprang, and I held to the belief that we possessed the faculties to forge a better country. In a world of my design, hate wouldn't drive politicians', men's, and women's actions, nor would we label another because we lacked the intellect or willingness to accept and comprehend each other. As a whole, humankind had to evolve. The importance of restoring our homeland with devotion and unity while forging a great country for the future's children rested on men's and women's shoulders.

As Bowden and I strolled the grounds, I looked over the property. The slave quarters had been demolished, and to the north sat our new home. We had signed the deeds giving Pete and Tillie, and Mammy and Big John each a section of land and helped them build homesteads. The same offer was extended to Jimmy, and although he claimed his right to the ground he had forgone building a homestead and resided in a small cabin constructed next to Jones's. Jones had agreed to stay on as foreman. Men and women, whites and blacks, worked our land for equal wages, a decision that stirred riots from time to time. Parker had accepted his plot of ground, but had left with Kimie to pursue a life in the north.

I reflected on the suffering of the oppressed at my family's hands. History would document my ancestors and Bowden and I as slave titleholders, and the chronicles would be accurate. Despite my family's transgressions, my love for the estate remained. It was my home, and the place I'd raise my children and tell them of the lives that had passed through Livingston. I would educate my children so they didn't replicate our country's sordid past, and to be better than their father and I had been. To conduct their lives without fear of diversity, so often converted to deep-seated hate and ingrained into our society. Although no one held all the solutions, our Creator had given the human race the ability to open our hearts and minds to learn from each other.

I dragged my thoughts from the past and the future and stopped walking. "Mary Grace writes from England. She says she misses everyone, but she's happy. The children are thriving."

"I'm pleased to hear that. So much has changed." He too halted and turned to me. "There is something I've meant to mention to you."

"Oh, what is that?" The concerned look in his eyes gave me pause. "Go on, what is troubling you?"

"You've read whisperings of the Ku Klux Klan?"

I resumed walking. "Hasn't everyone? What about them?"

"I was approached by some Confederate veterans—Theodore Carlton, amongst others—in Charleston the other day. Carlton led them in trying to recruit me."

"You can't be serious."

"Afraid so."

"What did you say?"

"That I do not wish to relive another war, and I will do my part to see that the South doesn't undergo such devastation again. Also that I believe we must all move toward progress, and maybe devoting our ambitions to the unity of all Americans."

I understood the sense of freedom that had given him as I, too, had felt liberated when I'd voiced a similar belief to the women at a social gathering soon after the war. Beside herself with outrage, Lucille had declared I'd dishonored the South and the Confederates who had lost their lives in the war. She had claimed she'd never speak to me again. If I'd known that was all it would've taken to rid myself of the likes of her, perhaps I'd have done so sooner.

"How did they receive your opinion?" I asked.

"Their scowls and whisperings to one another revealed their displeasure. To my surprise, Sterling and another man aligned with me." He gave me a sideways glance, and hope gleamed in his eyes. "We may be few, those that yearn for a unified America, but I believe others will stand with us. After today we will show our desire for progress." He gestured at the former main house. "The new school will no longer be a secret."

We had Ruby to thank for securing the teachers who would educate the children. Former slaves, the husband-and-wife team had met and united over their passion for educating the blacks. Despite the animosity directed toward the blacks in the South, they'd agreed to move to Livingston and reside at the small boarding house we had built next to the main house. Tillie had jumped at the opportunity to assist the teachers and planned to continue her studies under their tutelage.

As we rounded the main house, I looked to the sign staked by the front stairs that read: *Livingston School for Blacks, in honor of Gray and all those once enslaved here.*

"I know my desire to open a school was a risk, but it is one I was willing to take," I said.

"This will bring more hardships to our family."

"I want our daughter to grow up knowing her family may have owned slaves, but her grandparents and parents before her sought to right the wrongs of her predecessors." I looked to where Olivia sauntered along beside Jimmy as he led a horse from the stables.

"Good day." He grinned as he walked past us on the way to the pasture. "Miss Olive and me 'bout done. I take her home when we finished."

"Jimmy said I could come to the stables tomorrow and help him with the foal." She cast a worshiping smile up at him, and I recalled with fondness how I'd chased along beside him as a young girl.

I saw merriment in Jimmy's eyes as they proceeded toward the pasture.

Bowden stood admiring them. "Never seems to mind her shadowing him."

"He informed me when I warned her about pestering him one day that she 'wasn't causing no harm.' Grinned at me and said, 'She ain't as chatty as her mama was.' One can only assume he welcomes her presence more than he did mine."

"Do I discern dismay?" he said with amusement.

I feigned a pout. "Perhaps a little."

He laughed.

"With his desire to stay here, I'm hoping he'll teach our children the invaluable lessons he taught me."

Bowden placed a hand on my swollen stomach. "I concur, and I hope he schools our son on all there is to know about horses."

I placed my hand over his and looked at my stomach. "You're so sure this babe is a boy. But what if it is not?"

He gathered me into his arms. "It will be," he said with a grin before lowering his lips to meet mine.

COMING 2022

ABOUT
the *Author*

Naomi is a bestselling and award-winning author living in Northern Alberta. She loves to travel and her suitcase is always on standby awaiting her next adventure. Naomi's affinity for the Deep South and its history was cultivated during her childhood living in a Tennessee plantation house with six sisters. Her fascination with history and the resiliency of the human spirit to overcome obstacles are major inspirations for her writing and she is passionately devoted to creativity. In addition to writing fiction, her interests include interior design, cooking new recipes, and hosting dinner parties. Naomi is married to her high school sweetheart and she has two teenage children and a dog named Egypt.

Sign up for my newsletter: authornaomifinley.com/contact

Made in United States
North Haven, CT
29 December 2021